Make America Beautiful Again

A NOVEL

To Bob —

Bo B.

BO BANCROFT

Editor, Creative Director: Wayne South Smith
    www.waynesouthsmith.com

Cover Artist: Kevin Gosselin
    www.kgosselinart.com

Interior Designer: Jera Publishing
    www.self-pub.net

ISBN: 978-1-7375464-0-5

Library of Congress Control Number: 2021913827

Published by Homer Grub Publishing LLC

1.

*N*ot that he was a bad dad, he just knew his limitations and one more day visiting Disney World would not end happily ever after. Chuck had just ridden Dumbo for the third time, and standing in another long line listening to "It's A Small World" was too much for his fragile sanity. His legs ached from dutifully hiking endless miles on hot Florida asphalt, and all he wanted was a comfy chair and a cold beer. From experience, he knew an outburst wouldn't end well—the kids would cry, and Debbie would then lecture him on being a shitty ogre of an insensitive dad.

Before the cursed song made its fifth rotation on the sound loop, Chuck received a well-deserved break—a youngster directly in front of them threw up on his dad's new Air Jordans. As the parents argued over whose brilliant idea it had been to give a 6-year-old a 16-ounce blueberry Slurpee before riding the Teacups, Debbie gagged, threw her hands over her mouth, and sprinted from the line. Chuck was not about to miss his opportunity.

"Let's go, kids. We should probably check on Mom."

Chuck Jr. and Connie plodded along after their father. He could tell his kids were spent from another breakneck day but were doing a good job of wearing a happy face around their mother. Secretly, he was impressed with their stamina—not bad for a seven- and a nine-year-old.

They found Debbie sitting on a shaded bench outside the Taffy and Fudge Emporium. Chuck knew vomit was her kryptonite and she just needed some time to regroup before her cold, steely soul would return.

Keeping a safe distance from his wife, he calmly instructed their kids, "Why don't you go keep your mom company on the bench?"

The kids took position next to their mother and began to fish around in her fanny back for their parents' cell phones since being at Disney World wasn't enough of a distraction.

Chuck turned his back on his family to watch the excited tourists scamper hither and yon. The sweet aroma from the Taffy and Fudge Emporium drifted out where it mixed with the offensive odors of the sweating masses. It reminded him of the average male teenager who thought a heavy dose of body spray was a reasonable substitute for a shower. The sights and smells made his head pound. He would not survive another day of this.

Chuck rarely felt moments of inspiration, but the sudden wave made him feel completely alone. He glanced back at his family on the bench as the plan bounced around in his head. It was a damn good option and just might work. But now was not the time to spring it. Better to wait until she's tired and her defenses are weak.

Just before bedtime with the kids rapt in front of the TV, Chuck approached Debbie as she admired herself in the cramped hotel bathroom mirror while methodically brushing her teeth. Despite Debbie's guaranteed cold shoulder treatment, he thought it was a reasonable compromise.

"What do mean you're not going tomorrow? It's our last day at Disney World!" she said, toothpaste drool oozing out of the corners of her mouth.

He braced himself for battle. "Hear me out, honey. We've got at least a 16-hour drive back to Indy, and if we leave first thing Sunday, we won't get home until after midnight. The kids will be zombies at school, and you know how hectic work is after vacation. Neither one of us can afford a bad day at work."

"But Chuck, I don't want to drive all night."

"You won't have to. You and the kids have a big Saturday at the park while I rest at the hotel. Right after the fireworks, we'll head out, and I'll do all the driving. You'll be beat and sleep most of the way. We'll avoid all the traffic on 75 and get home Sunday afternoon. Hell, you remember how Atlanta was a nightmare. It'll be the middle of the night, and we'll fly through."

"I think it's crazy and the kids will be disappointed. They'll think you don't want to spend time with them."

Chuck thought, the kids are a blast, you're the pain in the rear. He shut it out of his mind and responded, "They barely even knew I was there today. Besides, you're the Disney freak, not me. Trust me, come Sunday evening you'll thank me."

"I doubt that. You tell the kids. I'm getting ready for bed." The clock began ticking on the cold shoulder.

Now he was feeling rather smug as it was 4:00 a.m. on a starlit Sunday morning, and he'd already cleared the gauntlet of downtown Atlanta. He was making incredible time. The only deviation was an unplanned pee break just north of Valdosta, GA, the consequence of three afternoon poolside beers and the necessary rebound coffee. At this rate, he'd be home in time to unpack and park his butt in the Barcalounger before the Colts/Broncos kickoff. Chuck Jr. softly breathed beside him with occasional interruptions by Debbie's snoring in the backseat where she slept with Connie. He glanced in the rearview mirror and cracked a thin smile at the sight of Debbie's gaping mouth flashing in and out of the darkened shadows.

With only two sets of taillights in front of him, he reset the cruise control and shifted in the minivan's bucket seat, trying to find a more comfortable position. He stretched out his right leg, propped his left elbow on the door frame, and draped his right wrist over the steering wheel. The only thing missing was music, but there was no way he'd risk waking Debbie.

A flash off in the distance caught his attention. At first, he thought the sudden burst well above ground level might be a light from a landing plane, but this was a more like a camera flash. As he puzzled, he heard a muffled *boom* and it dawned on him—fireworks. But who shoots off fireworks at 4:00 in the morning?

The second flash and boom were nearly simultaneous and came from the other side of the freeway. Before he could flinch, his side window spider-webbed and a searing pain ripped through his left arm just below the shoulder. He cried out in pain, removing his hand from the wheel to clutch his wounded arm, and the minivan erupted to life.

"Dad, what's wrong?" Chuck Jr. squealed.

"What are you doing, Chuck?" an angry Debbie yelled from the back. "Pay attention, dammit! We're about to crash!"

The rudderless minivan was headed toward the concrete median wall, and Chuck looked up in time to see it looming only feet away.

"Aaaaaahhhhhh!!" the family screamed in unison.

He grabbed the steering wheel. His now bloody hand made a solid grip nearly impossible as he jerked the wheel to the right just before the front bumper grazed the median. The minivan began to violently shake back and forth from the overcorrection. Chuck prepared for the van to flip.

Clearly wide-awake, Debbie began to freak out. "Are you trying to kill us? Stop the van! Stop the van!"

Luckily for Chuck—though it's hard to imagine a henpecked man with a hysterical wife and a bloody, wounded arm would consider himself lucky—the van didn't flip, and the empty freeway gave him plenty of room to glide across the six lanes to the shoulder.

Before Chuck shifted to park, the doors flung open and the recently slumbering family scrambled to the safety of solid ground. Chuck remained in the driver's seat, staring straight ahead, stunned at the recent turn of events. The pain in his left arm beginning to throb.

Debbie's head poked in through the open passenger door, the interior dome light making her contorted face look even more menacing. "What did you do? I told you driving all night's a bad idea!"

Chuck gritted his teeth in pain and anger. "I didn't do anything! I was just driving along minding my own business." He twisted in his chair, showing off his blood-soaked arm. "Look! I think someone shot me!"

Debbie leaned in to study his arm, her expression barely changed. "You've never been shot. How would you know what it feels like?"

As she rubbed her index finger over the wound, Chuck recoiled in pain. "Ow! What'd you do that for?"

"It feels like something's stuck in your arm, but it doesn't look too bad. I think it's only a flesh wound, you big baby." She wiped her bloody finger on the right sleeve of his tropical Tommy Bahama vacation shirt.

"Don't do that! I love this shirt!" he whined.

"I don't. Besides, it's already ruined."

Chuck sat back in his seat and returned his gaze to the dark, empty highway. A passing semi rocked the minivan, and even the gentle movement sent a new round of pain up through his shoulder into his neck. He controlled his temper, giving Debbie a hard stare. "That's all you can say? Someone just about killed me and you call it a flesh wound? Can you show me some compassion just once?"

Chuck's scowl was a poor imitation of Debbie's perfected death stare. She pulled her cell phone out of the fanny pack still clipped on her waist and mockingly held it to her ear. "Hello? 911? My husband just about obliterated his family on the freeway and now complains about a boo-boo. What should I do?" Keeping her glare on Chuck, she motioned up the road. "The sign says there's a hospital off this exit. If your legs still move, get out of the way, and I'll drive you there."

2.

The cell phone shocked Seamus from a deep sleep. He sat up completely disoriented, the pitch-dark room threw off his brain's ability to figure out where he was. Stunned, he groggily tried to focus on something, anything, to jog his memory. His gut told him it wasn't his old bedroom back in Lansing, but that didn't help him remember whose bed he was sleeping in.

He groped around the nightstand in search of the noise. The clock announced it was 5:05 a.m. It came to him—the ringtone was for work. He was in Atlanta. He coughed the sleepy gravel out of his throat as he lifted the phone. "O'Reilly here."

"Inspector? Sterling speaking, sorry to call so early."

O'Reilly's feet immediately hit the floor upon hearing the director's voice. "Morning, sir. Something big must be going on if you're calling." He hoped his bluntness didn't come off as disrespectful.

"Yes, and we're pulling together the team ASAP. There's been a terrorist attack here in Georgia."

"What?" The disbelief was clear in his voice. As a researcher for the Georgia Bureau of Investigation's Antiterrorism Team, Seamus, nor anyone else for that matter, had detected any imminent threat to the state. His mind raced with possibilities as he sprang out of bed only to stumble in the darkness, nearly falling flat on his face. Still gripping his cell phone, he reached to turn on the bedside lamp but knocked it off the table onto the bed. At last, he corralled the lamp and light filled his apartment's bedroom. Being able to see his surroundings had a calming effect. He took a deep breath and fetched his pants off the floor.

Sterling paused a beat to piece together what he knew so far. "Details are sketchy, but a little after 4:00 a.m. this morning, there were multiple explosions in every portion of the state. They were coordinated within several minutes of each other and appear to be centered around the interstate system."

Great, just what Atlanta needs, major interstate disruption. He wasn't living here when the section of I-85 collapsed but heard the cases of road rage went through the roof during the two months it was shut down. O'Reilly took another deep breath and tried to sound intelligent. "What were the targets? Bridges? Overpasses?"

"We're still getting info, but right now it appears the actual infrastructure was not targeted. All reports have been roadside bombs at or near billboard locations. It appears some have been heavily damaged."

O'Reilly stopped struggling with his hastily pulled up pants. "Billboards? Seriously? Terrorists are now targeting billboards?"

"It's damn serious!" Sterling burst. "We don't know the extent or the actual targets. We have one known casualty, but who knows how many more may be injured. We also don't know if there are more bombs out there. I've already talked to the governor, and he's declared a state of emergency. Good thing it's Sunday, so it won't be as hard to keep people off the streets."

"Sorry for my tone, sir. I'll get to the office right away."

"We need you in the field first. How quickly can you get to Kennestone Hospital?"

"I'm almost dressed and should be able to get there in less than an hour."

"Good. The one known casualty is at Kennestone getting treated as we speak. He's also the only current witness we have. I need you to get over there and interview him."

Seamus tried to ignore the bulging knot in his stomach. "Sir, you do realize I'm not really a field inspector. I have some experience from my Michigan State Police days, but my interview skill is limited."

"Inspector, this is an emergency, and all of us need to step up. Now get on it. Time's a wasting!"

Seamus sat back down on the edge of the bed wondering what he had just gotten himself into. He joined law enforcement completely by accident; his favorite professor at Western Michigan knew a young Black man from Detroit, with a history degree and no family connections, didn't have many job prospects even if the country wasn't mired in a recession. He made a couple of calls on Seamus's behalf, and within three weeks of graduating, Seamus was sitting in a cubicle at MSP headquarters doing research. He never really felt like a cop, just a guy who looked up details on scumbags, murderers, and embezzlers.

His only field experience came when an enterprising consulting company suggested that all employees were to be cross-trained. He was issued and learned how to use a firearm. Then, he was teamed with various street-smart agents who could grill a perp but wrote reports in crayon. He picked up basic interview tips, but unfortunately, none of Seamus's research or writing ability was transferred to his erstwhile partners as they suddenly disappeared to the break room when it came time to document the details.

One of the appealing aspects of the GBI Antiterrorism gig was the return to pure research. Sure, the badge and Ford Interceptor were perks—his dad was particularly impressed with the car—but nothing compared to safely being out of harm's way behind a computer or in the bureau's library digging through old cases.

Until today. Now he was thrust into the field, completely alone and unprepared to face terrorists in Georgia.

3.

*C*lad in his white, bulldog-adorned summer shorty pajamas, the cold marble floor on Governor Skip Murray's pudgy bare feet invigorated his body as he nervously circled the massive kitchen island. By his count, in the 20 minutes since receiving the shocking 4:50 a.m. wake-up call from his GBI Director, he'd slowly shuffled around the island 25 times.

As if terrorists attacking his state wasn't bad enough, he desperately needed a cup of coffee, and the Governor's Mansion still used an old-time percolator. Who knows how to work one of those damn things? It would be a good hour before the domestic help showed up, and he'd die before then. How he longed for his trusty little machine back at the farm. What he'd give to pop one of those magical little plastic cups in the holder and get a steaming cup in less than a minute. And it was the fall when they had the pumpkin spice flavor! The entire situation was intolerable. Pacing was his only option as he pondered his predicament.

Pete Sterling had been his friend since college, and tapping him as GBI Director was one of Skip's better appointments. Both were North Georgia boys, having grown up within 25 miles of each other, but they didn't become friends until their junior year at UGA. After graduation, Pete did a stint with the Sheriff's department, then went back to UGA for his law degree and quickly became the county DA. With the legal chops and enough managerial skill not to screw things up, he won the backing of most in the law enforcement community and was embraced as a solid choice to lead the GBI.

Sterling's early morning phone call was the last thing Murray expected on what had been planned as a lazy Sunday. His immediate reaction was concern over possible lives lost, and he was proud of himself for the brief display of sincere compassion. Once he found out the initial reports were suggesting minimal damage and casualties, he began to view the attack as any good politician would—an excellent chance to boost his reelection chances. Granted he was only ten months into a four-year term, but he viewed proper positioning for the next election as his most important day-to-day task. Skip Murray understood being governor was the apex of his career, and he was not about to squander an opportunity.

He won the tightest governor's election in Georgia's history and knew the state's changing demographics made his term tenuous at best. Once in office, he decided to tone down the rhetoric, even proposing policies that would have been considered heresy two short years ago. It had not gone well. Rabid purists were incensed, his detractors skeptical, and those in his party who understood what was at stake were few and terrified to speak.

Now his state had experienced a terrorist attack which, if played properly, could be the seminal point of his legacy. If he projected strength and leadership, he could unify the state and squash the competitors already lining up to challenge him. This could be his moment to shine.

Which was one of the reasons why he was pacing the kitchen island in the Governor's Mansion. After speaking with Pete, he began to work the phone contacting the key allies needed for the crisis. The pacing helped him focus and burn off the anxiety building from his fruitless efforts.

His first call had been to the president. Skip helped him campaign in Georgia and was rewarded with the "special" number to call if he needed anything. He didn't even get a live person, just a computerized voice mail message where he attempted not to sound too panicked. Within five minutes, he received a return call from a monotone female aide asking for details so she could prep the president.

"Are you serious? Woman, this is a national emergency. Please wake him up immediately. We're under attack. Every minute counts."

"I appreciate your concern, Governor, but right now it doesn't sound like a national emergency to me. You've had some explosions, no reports of fatalities, no building collapses, structural damage, or other apparent criminal activity. Use your resources to find out more details, and I'll make sure the president calls after he's had his breakfast. It will only be another hour or so."

The line was dead before he could further plead his case.

His second call was to his Homeland Security contact. With a coastal boundary, the Port of Savannah, and Hartsfield-Jackson Atlanta International Airport, Georgia was considered high risk that merited a direct line. Again, he was greeted by an aide of some sort, no one of real authority. At least this guy pretended to be concerned but also lost interest when told of minimal bloodshed. He assured Governor Murray he'd get the information to his boss ASAP. Fortunately for both of them, he was in Florida scheduled to play golf with the president that very morning. Stifling his exasperation, the governor provided his contact information and a further plea for urgency.

His next call was to General Harper of the Georgia National Guard. General Harper was a typical political appointee with enough related experience to look good in a press release but without the ability to manage a fruit stand. He had strong support from the political base in South Georgia, so he became one of the token appointees for big donors. While impressive in dress uniform, with a striking, authoritative camera presence, he was cursed with a gerbil-like intelligence and the voice to match. Aides always represented the general during press conferences and senate committee testimony. Hearing his voice further amplified Skip's anxiety sweats.

"Good God, Governor, that's shocking. What can we do to help?" Harper's voice hit another octave with the question, a clear sign he asked only out of obligation.

"General, I was hoping you had some ideas. Don't you guys train for just this type of situation? Don't you have a plan for terrorists' attacks?"

Attempting to sound confident, which is impossible for pet rodents, the general tried to reassure the governor. "Of course we do, but since I'm relatively new to the post, I don't know the procedures off the top of my head."

Unbelievable. Skip was grateful for Pete's earlier guidance. "GBI Director Sterling suggested we should mobilize your troops as fast as possible to seal off every interstate entrance to Georgia. He'll coordinate with local law enforcement jurisdictions to block off entrance ramps in the state and try to get people already on the highways to exit. With it being early on Sunday, we have a good chance to shut everything down within several hours. Got it?"

"Yes, sir! My only concern is manpower. Sealing off all the roads into Georgia is quite a task."

"Manpower? Not all the roads, just the interstates, the main highways…the ones with the blue signs! You should be able to do that with a battalion or two!"

"Roger that, Governor. Blue signs. We'll get on it right away."

"Good, and keep your phone handy as I'll be requesting regular troops from the president once we have a chance to talk. Between

Benning, Stewart, and Gordon, we'll have plenty of reinforcements to secure each corner of the state."

"Reinforcements would be great, Governor." The relief in Harper's voice almost made him sound normal.

"One more thing I need from you, General," Skip said, suddenly feeling confident enough to share his own idea. "Get the Air Guard up in helicopters to fly along the interstates and relay traffic information back to the ground team. Can you do that?"

"Yes, sir. We're on it. Do we have a name for this mission?"

"Damn it all, Hank! Call it whatever the hell you want to call it. Just get on it!"

The general's ineptitude magnified the importance of getting the Feds involved, even at the risk of usurping leadership, yet his attempts of reaching anyone of importance had failed. He had no choice but to call an inside man.

James "Bubba" Baker had represented Middle Georgia in the US Congress for years. His district number had changed whenever he felt redistricting would improve his majority. His success at gerrymandering was admirable: 14 years in Congress, and he consistently was reelected with over 60% of the vote. At first, he hid his true self, but as the years passed and his district boundaries became even more convoluted, he became less guarded about sharing his own warped opinions. The governor truly respected Baker's aides as they were prompt and creative when clarifying his most outrageous statements.

Of course, the new president loved him. Whenever he visited the state, he'd hold a rally in Bubba's district. He was a frequent golfing partner of the president, and even Skip shuddered when thinking of their bourbon-induced, post-round trash talk. Realizing he had the president's ear, colleagues were quick to give him plum committee assignments. Bubba had been an early supporter of the governor's campaign, but the infatuation was short lived since

Bubba was the leader of the rabid contingency who looked upon Skip's first 10 months with scorn.

Defeated and resigned, the governor called Bubba for help. His prompt answer and confident drawl was the first sign Bubba was a step ahead.

"Damn, Skipper, are the Muslims attacking us?"

The governor hated being called Skipper. His political life would have been so much easier if his family had given him a normal name like George. At least he didn't call him Skippy.

"You know what's going on?"

"Yeah, the president's office gave me a call and filled me in. Why do you think the Muslims are bombing Georgia?"

Amazing and disturbing. "Hold on, Bubba. Don't jump to conclusions. We only have sketchy information so far, limited info on targets and damage. We have no idea who's doing this."

"If it ain't the Muslims, then it must be some of Jones's Black Panther friends. He still can't believe he lost the governorship to you. No luck in court either, so it was time to pull out the big guns. Those commies love to blow shit up."

"Stop it, Bubba. If terrorists are really attacking us, we need to circle *all* the wagons to protect the state. Figuring out who did it and getting retribution will have to wait."

"I swear, you took that oath and turned into a pansy. Just think about dropping a hint to the press about Jones, would you?"

"Bubba…" The governor took a deep breath to regroup. "I called because I need your help. Sometime this morning I'll need to address the citizens, and I want to say I've spoken with the president and he's agreed to help us out. Will you get him to call me as soon as possible?"

The governor could visualize Bubba's doofus grin, the grin knowing the political favor pendulum had just swung in his direction. "Absolutely, Skipper. Anything for the great state of Georgia."

The call with Congressman Baker kicked his anxiety sweats to a new level. Skip's temples glistened with perspiration, and the shorty pajama top stuck to his back and chest. He set the phone down on the island and stared blankly at the stainless-steel refrigerator, his vision of heroically leading Georgia through the crisis and skating to a second term was as hazy as the distorted reflection looking back at him.

His phone began to bark with, finally, someone calling him back! The caller ID gave him hope. "Jose, thank God it's you."

"I called as soon as I received your message, Governor. Sorry it took so long."

Jose Perez was an appointment many criticized as a token diversity attempt. No doubt, he checked multiple boxes necessary for a politician trying to broaden his base—immigrant parents, military veteran, and opposing party member, but Skip had known Jose since his state representative days and trusted him implicitly. Other staff members were quick to calculate the political angle of every decision in terms of pundit reaction. Jose was different; he'd consider the human impact first, then assess the politics and the necessary positioning.

"That's okay, I'm dying here and relieved to hear your voice," Skip sighed. His nerves calmed, the governor took a seat at the kitchen table and filled in Jose on the morning's activity.

"Like you, I'm not thrilled with having to bring Bubba in, but it was the right thing to do," Jose counseled. "But you can't stay holed up in the mansion waiting for those guys to call back. The people don't want their leader hiding during crisis. You need to either go to the office or get over to GBI headquarters. I'd suggest the GBI. Has more of a frontline feel."

"You're right. I'll go stir crazy waiting it out here. Plus, it'll be ten times worse once Hannah wakes up and hears the news. This might just push her over the edge. I've been tiptoeing around the house, not wanting to risk having to tell her."

"Don't worry about it. I'll come over as quick as I can with a security team to make her feel safe. I just need you to be ready when I get there. I'll have your ride to GBI all set up," Jose said.

"Thanks, Jose. Maybe we have a shot of salvaging something out of this after all."

Skip hung up the phone and silently cursed at the cold, metal percolator. Terrorists, incompetence, Bubba Baker, and no coffee. Maybe being governor wasn't such a great idea.

4.

espite tossing and turning most of the night, Scott bound out of bed at the previously unthinkable hour of 5:15 a.m. Three years ago, he never would have imagined getting up so early to attend a Citrus Crunch fitness class. Of course, back then he also didn't know his wife was banging his Urologist, Dr. Novak. Throwing sweats over his underwear and ratty t-shirt, Scott hit brew on the coffee pot, snapped the leash on his excited mutt, and headed out to the complex's green space for Sparky's morning nature break.

His then-wife knew Dr. Novak from her mixed doubles ALTA team and said he was a great doctor. Her effusive recommendation should have been the first clue, one of many, he missed or simply decided to ignore. And he was a great guy, even worked Scott into one of the coveted Vasectomy slots the day before March Madness tip-off where he had the perfect excuse to sit around watching basketball for 12 straight hours. Little did he know that while cradling his nut sack on a bag of frozen peas, his wife was doing the wild thing with Novak in the backseat of a Cadillac Escalade in the Bitsy Grant Tennis Center parking lot.

After the separation, Scott left the suburbs of Atlanta and moved into Brookhaven Vista. It was an easy choice. He grew up in the area. His sister Pam, brother-in-law Roger, and their brood still lived in their parents' old family home by Central City Golf Club. Even though Dr. Novak had money out the wazoo, Tricia came at him hard during the divorce, citing a whole litany of supposed marital sins. In defending her actions, Tricia actually tried to use Scott's cluelessness of the affair as an example of his inability to be "close" and to "nurture" the relationship; his distance had "created a wall denying her the intimacy" she craved. Fortunately, Dr. Novak's receptionist harbored a long-denied crush on the Urologist and came to Scott's defense with salacious details of the intimacy Tricia craved with the good doctor. Scott just wanted the dog and to be as far away from her drama as possible. The divorce was straightforward for Georgia. He happily gave her the house and some cash before scampering back to his old neighborhood with Sparky.

He loved Sparky, and the scruffy little guy became his muse. With no backyard, Scott was forced to walk Sparky for his daily constitutions, and it became quite clear that while the dog had endless energy, Scott got gassed just strolling around the 'village green.' He also confirmed the long held belief that dogs are chick magnets. The complex was crawling with divorcees, and 90% greeted Sparky with such enthusiasm that Scott found himself wishing to trade places for a quick belly rub. He had very little interest in pursuing a new relationship, but his inability to make even idle chitchat during these encounters confirmed he'd lost his confidence. Getting in shape seemed like a logical place to start.

Selecting Citrus Crunch as his workout method was made merely out of convenience. Brookhaven Vista had everything he needed as it was designed as a pop-up residential community where three to five stories of apartments were built on top of retail. The goal was to instantly create perfect "town centers" complete with bars, restaurants, markets, and, of course, Citrus Crunch, all amongst immaculate landscaping with chill music piped through speakers hidden in the bushes. Everything was planned, and now these complexes were sprouting up from the inner city to the exurbs. The workout studio was a mere two-minute walk past the running shoe store, a woman's clothing shop specializing in free market wool parkas, a nail salon, and a candle shop.

After a quick lap on the village green, Scott tossed the dog's blue poop bag in the trash and took Sparky back up the elevator to their one-bedroom, loft-style apartment. Loft-style meant the developer didn't want to waste money on carpet, hardwood floors, or drywall. The liberal use of concrete reminded Scott of communist block housing, only with granite counter tops, washer and dryer connections, and improved curb appeal. He poured his first cup of coffee and flipped on the TV for the morning news.

The local Atlanta morning shows amazed him. Who could actually show up to work so early and be that damned perky? And maintain that level for three hours? These people couldn't possibly be human, and usually after 15 minutes, they'd wear him out and he'd get dressed for class. Not today. The perkiness had been replaced with a stoic frenzy usually seen only when a snowstorm hits town. Terrorists had attacked Georgia.

Scott was mesmerized by what he was seeing on the TV news. His Grandpa Worthington started Veteran Outdoor Advertising in the '50s right when it was clear the Eisenhower Interstate System would crisscross Georgia with four-lane highways. Most of the land deals back then were easy and cheap. Owners were predominately dirt-poor farmers who were ecstatic to get a yearly check by renting out a small parcel of their acreage. He used his WWII veteran status as a sales tool and to secure start up loans.

Daddy took over in the late '60s and realized I-75 and I-95 would carry a constant stream of Yankees through the state on their way to frolic in the Florida sun. Gas stations as well as nut and peach stands sprouted like dandelions, and Daddy became a pro at selling the Burma Shave-style sequence billboard ads to lure unsuspecting tourists to the next exit. He liked to say that Stuckey's Pecan Logs were responsible for all three of his kids' educations.

The business had changed over the years. Cars with better gas mileage reduced the number of stops; GPS let travelers search while driving; digital billboards were more eye-catching and allowed for multiple advertisers; more restrictive environmental rules regulated tree removal; and mom and pop locations had been replaced with franchises that negotiated as one. The fun and creativity had been sucked out of a business that already suffered from low public opinion. Now most of the advertising was for injury attorneys, repent-to-Jesus warnings, or trucker/titty rest stops. Scott would not be sharing an amusing anecdote on how "We Bare All" sent his daughters to college.

Not that money was a concern for Scott. In fact, it wasn't. His father and grandfather had built a very profitable business and were wise investors. Possibly due to the family money, or his own personal dislike of billboards, Scott possessed no burning ambition to carry the torch as the family business titan. He lived a modest life and saw no benefit in the extra work and pressure that came from being in charge. Conversely, his brother-in-law had no lack of ambition and actually seemed to enjoy the profession. His willingness to let Roger run the family company never settled well with his ex-wife.

His vibrating cell phone pulled him out of the TV news stupor. He didn't need to check the caller ID.

"Morning Roger, I've been watching the news for the last hour or so."

"Can you believe this? What crazy SOB would want to destroy my business? Who'd you piss off?!"

Scott didn't muffle his sigh. "It's our business, not yours. And you're the pro at pissing people off. Didn't you get a threat after stealing the Hartsfield-Jackson contract?"

"I didn't steal it, we won it. But yeah, the Galiones weren't too happy about it."

"Relax Roger, it wasn't some vendetta against Veteran. TV says McArthur, Consolidated, every outdoor company was hit. Sounds to me it's some wacko environmental people."

"Damn treehuggers. We shouldn't have pushed for that tree clearing bill last year," Roger fumed. "I've already heard from the GBI, and they want to talk to us at 9:30, asked us to come to the headquarters. I'll pick you up at 8:30."

"I'm not going, Roger. You're the president, I'm just the operations guy. Besides, I don't really care. I've been thinking this is an omen for me to get out and do something else."

"Oh, you're going. You just said it's our business, not mine."

Scott sensed Roger was proud at deftly turning the tables on him.

"Be out front at 8:30."

"I'll go, but I'll meet you there." Scott hung up before Roger could protest. Best to limit their interaction.

5.

egally speeding, particularly before dawn with no traffic, was a perk Seamus secretly loved. But this morning was different as he was about to conduct his first solo witness interview in a terrorist attack investigation, and flying along the freeway was the last thing on his mind. Most days he felt ambivalence towards his profession. He loved the nuts and bolts of piecing information into a plausible story but wasn't drawn to law enforcement like most of his peers. He was jumbled with excitement and guilt—excitement over the prospects, but guilt that he was fired up over terrorism.

All along the northern arc of I-285, he craned his neck in every direction peering at the looming, glowing billboards that defied the reported attack. Ramping onto I-75 North, the telltale line of brake lights told a different story. Traffic was moving, so Seamus guessed the slowdown was due to rubbernecking.

After several miles, he saw the first set of emergency vehicle lights off the right shoulder, so he wound his way over from the far-left lane to check it out. Two Cobb County Sheriff's deputies were standing just off the berm, staring down into the drainage ditch parallel to I-75. He stopped well short of them. The flashing blue light embedded in the grill of Seamus's Ford Interceptor caught their attention.

As he approached the men, O'Reilly held his badge out at arm's length. "Inspector O'Reilly, GBI. I'm on my way to interview a victim and wanted to see the damage."

The deputy closest to Seamus spoke first. "Glad you showed up 'cause we have no idea what the hell we're supposed to be doing here. Look at that damn thing."

Seamus peered down into the ditch for his first look at the destruction. It was quite a sight. Amazingly, a lone spotlight survived the fall and shone upward on the pole, now naked of its purpose. What had been a two-sided billboard was now a crumpled mass of steels beams bent and contorted in all directions. The neatness of the debris field caught his eye, not the typical result of an explosion. It appeared to have simply fallen off the pole, gravity driving it nose first into the ground.

He directed his flashlight at the twisted metal to get a better look. Two billboard message panels had popped off the frame and were now laying on the ground next to the heap. A faint smile touched the corners of his mouth at the sight of a familiar billboard, a not too subtle suggestion that bald men needed hair to be surrounded by a bevy of babes in bikinis.

What guys would do for women, Seamus mused to himself. Glad I'm past that.

He turned to the deputies. "Mind if I take a closer look?"

"Help yourself."

Seamus slid down the gravel embankment, hopped over the ditch and cozied up to the sound barrier. He couldn't see the base of the billboard pole as it lay outside the freeway's sound barrier. His eyes traveled up to where the platform had been and marveled how the fallen billboard had just missed crashing onto the wall.

He made his way back to the two cops still on the interstate shoulder and stomped the dust off his shoes. He pointed back to twisted pile. "Check it out. That thing toppled in the only spot where it wouldn't cause collateral damage. It didn't hit the sound barrier or the interstate, even missed the power lines. Whoever did this either got lucky or knew what they were doing."

"I hadn't really noticed, and I don't really care" the talkative deputy said. "So, what do you think we should do?"

Seamus began his retreat to the car. "It's being viewed as a terrorist attack, so treat it like a crime scene. That's about the best I can suggest."

The second deputy finally spoke up. "A terrorist attack? Whoever did this is a hero. Damn ugly distractions, if you ask me. Hey, where you headed?"

"Kennestone Hospital to interview a victim."

"Best to get off at the next exit and head up 41. North of here, there's a whole bunch of these blown up and traffic's barely moving."

Seamus took the deputy's advice and drove along the shoulder to the next exit. Once on surface streets, it was a quick 20 minutes to Kennestone Hospital. He checked his watch, almost exactly an hour, just what he promised the director.

He was stunned to see three news trucks already setting up outside the emergency room entrance. Fortunately for Seamus, they were too busy staking out their positions to notice the obvious cop car parked in the no loading zone. He inconspicuously strolled past the excited reporters jockeying for the best video angle of the hospital.

As he approached the entrance, he studied his reflection in the glass door. He was proud of his physique but not like the strutting workout peacocks at the gym. Over six feet tall, he'd maintained his college soccer playing weight though gravity and inactivity had slightly shifted his body shape. The towering afro was long gone, replaced with a clean, close-cropped look.

Once through the automatic doors, he was struck by how calm and serene it was in the emergency area compared to the yelling of the competing news teams. After an introduction, a nurse led him to the central treatment area where he introduced himself to the attending doctor. The doc gave him the patient's name, a quick recap of the injury, and the metal fragment she extracted. The patient and his family were camped out in a room up the hall.

A visibly bored City of Kennesaw police officer was sitting at the door, supposedly acting as a protector. The cop checked his badge and nodded at the door.

The victim sure didn't look like a victim, sitting all alert on the examining table while a woman stood brooding in the corner and two young children sat glued to smart phones. The gauze wrap around his left forearm was the only sign of injury.

"Mr. Givens, good morning. I'm inspector Seamus O'Reilly of the Georgia Bureau of Investigation."

"You've got to be kidding me," the brooding woman in the corner erupted. "Seamus O'Reilly? You're no more Irish than I'm the Queen of Sheba."

Standard reaction of O'Reilly's life. Most people were incredulous, but she seemed to take it personally.

"Relax, Debbie," the man mumbled with calm resignation.

"Relax? You just about killed our whole family! If we left Disney World this morning like I wanted to, none of this would have happened!"

Seamus immediately felt a bond with the poor guy. He moved 800 miles to get away from Peggy, yet here she was in the body of another woman.

"Ma'am, clearly you were in the vehicle with him when this happened. Did you see anything?"

"No, I was asleep. Next thing I know, Chuck's screaming like a baby and we're headed to a concrete wall." The scowl never left her face.

"Okay. If you didn't see anything, then why don't you and the kids go grab some coffee or a bite to eat? Give me some time here with your husband?"

Her eyes and face remained hard, but her body language softened a bit, the idea of distance and air seemed to be appealing. "Kids, let's give these men some time." Never looking up from the smart phones, the kids got up and trailed behind their mother.

Chuck looked at Seamus with relief. "Thanks. The wife gets pretty emotional."

"Been there," Seamus said sympathetically.

Chuck recounted the whole story about leaving Disney World at night, even the poolside beers, to try and beat the traffic to make it home in time for the Colts game. The men engaged in a brief, friendly Colts/Lions rivalry trash talk before Chuck got to the incident.

"I saw one flash off in the distance and was trying to figure out what it was when another big flash and bang happened on my left. My side window shattered and something hit me in the arm. I thought I'd been shot."

Seamus held out the small piece of shrapnel the doc had given him. "It looks like you were hit with a chunk of the billboard pole."

The victim immediately perked up. "That's so cool! Think I can have it as a souvenir?"

"Sorry, its evidence." Seamus quickly put it in his pocket. "How are you feeling?"

"I'm fine. Doc said it wasn't too deep. I've just got some stitches and a good story."

"Did you notice anything else on the drive? Anything in South Georgia along the way?"

"Nothing. It was great driving. Put the cruise control on 80 and didn't need to touch the brakes for a couple of hours. When do you think I can get out of here? Would like to get back on the road."

Seamus almost didn't have the heart to tell the poor guy, knowing he'd likely get shit about it for the rest of his life. He opened his mouth to break the news when the patient room door burst open.

The wife returned with fire in her eyes. "The news just said they've closed all of the interstates in Georgia! Some safety precaution about maybe there being more bombs. Nice going genius! Now, we're stuck here!"

"It wasn't my fault Debbie…I was just trying to get us home!"

"We could've had another day in Florida instead we're in Nowheresville, Georgia. I swear, a turnip has more sense than you!"

Seamus saw complete defeat overtake the victim. He excused himself to avoid the carnage. At the door he looked back and met eyes with the patient, his hopeless expression saying he wished the bomb had just taken him out altogether.

6.

Maggie got out of her car and adjusted her polyester powder blue waitress dress into place. She crossed the parking lot watching Duke's Fine Foods slowly come to life. Duke Evans sat perched on his trusty stool by the cash register, readying the books for another day as smoke from the exhaust fans signaled the kitchen staff had fired up the grills.

Maggie absolutely loved the place, and the place loved her. The casual, friendly atmosphere was perfect, and most of the diners appreciated how she followed her sharp wit and sassy tongue with just the right amount of comforting compassion. Even Duke said she was one of the best waitresses they had in their 40-plus year history. Her skill was no accident, aside from a four-year window in the professional world, she'd been waitressing since high school everywhere from Denny's to Chez Philippe. Duke's stood out as her favorite.

Duke's was one of the last surviving meat and threes in town, most having succumbed to the epicurean tastes of a more urbane, younger Atlanta population. The kitchen was run by cooks, not chefs, who served gravy, not sauces, and the only thought of presentation was to make sure they ladled the meat before the sides. Of course, some concessions had been made. Okra and collards remained staples, but now the menu had sunchoke, kale, and even a light batter option for frying. The result was a comfortable meal of decent food and prompt service, all at a price where leaving a generous tip to your waitress—no servers here—was still possible.

Maggie gave her dress one last tug and went through the side employee entrance. The door opened to a short hall that led past the restrooms and relics of an earlier era: a pay phone and a cigarette machine. She hung her windbreaker on a hook and paused, admiring the diner's simple floor plan. The traffic flow was perfect for a waitress, and the seating layout allowed natural partitioning of the diner's diverse customer base. Arch conservatives, LGBQT-righters, rednecks, rappers, frat boys, Goths, platinum Amex-wielding businessmen, quarter-counting day workers, drag queens, and church ladies all ate here, and being a regular was the only designation that mattered to the staff.

If I ever have my own place it will look just like this, Maggie thought.

"Good morning, Maggie."

Maggie looked to her right where Duke was radiating his ever-present warm demeanor. He was perched on his stool with his reading glasses propped up on his forehead. "Morning, Duke. How are you?"

"Not bad. Have you heard the news? Don't think we'll have many customers today," he said calmly.

"I'm afraid you're right. Unbelievable, isn't it? You want me to go ahead and open?"

Duke checked his watch. "Sure. Why not?"

Maggie reached behind Duke and flipped on the bank of lights washing the shadows from the now-bright dining room. She gently touched his shoulder as she passed to the front door, threw open the deadbolt, and pulled the dangling chain on the neon "Open" sign.

"Thanks, Maggie." Duke gave her a reassuring smile.

Duke and the diner were partially responsible for Maggie still living in Atlanta. Over the last ten years, she tried nearly a dozen cities, and probably twice that many waitress jobs, but Atlanta seemed to temporarily satisfy her wanderlust. She was amazed at its beauty. The trees, hills, and remaining old neighborhoods with tree root-cracked sidewalks gave it a certain charm. The city was large but had secret, peaceful oases where one could hide, and it was progressive, yet with enough southern hospitality to soften the rude edges often found in a metropolis. In short, both the city and her people had manners.

What caught Maggie more by surprise was the number of out-door nature options both in town and a short drive away. Despite her sunny, seemingly outgoing disposition, she was more at ease alone in the woods or on the water. The hiking trails in the North Georgia mountains were a never-ending source of adventure where she escaped almost weekly. Contrary to his appearance, Duke Evans was of the same ilk and gave her the flexibility to go clear her mind. The ability to commune with nature was another factor preventing a move.

In many ways, Georgia reminded her of her childhood state without the overbearing focus on national politics. The flora and fauna of Virginia's mountains and coastal areas were so similar, she often expected to wake up to see her mom bustling around the campsite. But years ago, Virginia figured out that billboards detracted from her natural beauty and enacted stringent zoning laws. She never understood why a state as beautiful as Georgia didn't follow suit. Maybe now they'd reconsider.

The few customers were not enough to stop Maggie's mind from wandering. With time on their hands, most of her fellow employees lurked around Duke's small TV, conjuring up wild ideas on the attack. Maggie wasn't about to share her thoughts, so she made herself busy while keeping an eye out on the parking lot in hopes he'd show up soon. When his truck pulled in the lot, she gravitated to greet him at the door.

"Fancy seeing you today, what with it being Sunday and the war on billboards going on."

"Outdoor advertising, Maggie, not billboards." Scott's correction was a standard response in their banter about his job.

"You're so cute. They'll always be billboards to the rest of us." She led him to his booth in the regular section. "Normal breakfast, or are we feeling adventurous today?"

"Actually, a menu might be a good idea.... It is a special day. Think I'll go out on a limb."

Maggie gave him a soft smile while she handed him the menu. "I'll get your coffee."

She wasn't ashamed to admit her fondness for Scott. He started coming to Duke's her second week on the job, and they became friends. Maggie liked his easy smile and his kindness shone through the mask of reserve. She figured out his initial nervousness with her was due to a previous relationship, like an abused puppy skittish around a new human. So, she treated him as such, cautiously building his trust through encouragement, concern over his well-being, and of course, prompt service.

She weaned him off waffles and bacon while complementing his dedication to the new workout regimen. His confidence grew as he got in better shape and began to realize not all women were like his ex. She had accomplished similar results in other jobs, but this transformation was the most rewarding. This guy actually had intelligence and heart, and she found herself looking forward to their easy banter.

She poured his coffee and stood looking down on him in the booth. A good-looking guy, not striking, Scott seemed at ease with himself. "You're not in a panic over this morning?"

"Not at all, Maggie. Despite not sleeping much last night and not getting in my workout today, I feel pretty damn good. I think it's a sign for me to finish the good work you've done with me over the past two years."

"For me, it's a sign that it'll be a slow day. Look at this place. We have more customers when it snows."

"I'll give you an extra tip. How's that sound?"

"What a peach, but it's not necessary." Her voice and eyes softened. "You're responsible for changing your life, but saying I helped your journey is very sweet. Decided?"

"I'm a creature of habit. The usual is just fine, but toss in some sausage as a splurge."

Maggie kept an eye on Scott as he finished off his breakfast of eggs whites, fruit, and wheat toast. The sausage sat untouched. Having the exceptional waitress sixth sense, she knew the exact moment to swoop in with a coffee refresh and to check if he needed anything else.

"You didn't touch the sausage. Have I trained you that well?"

Scott wrapped the sausage up in a napkin. "It's a treat for Sparky, even though it gives him lethal gas. Feel guilty since I had to abandon him this morning."

"Roger give you a mayday call after Billboard Armageddon? Guess you're wanted at the office."

Scott gave out his small, charming chuckle she adored when he was amused. "Billboard Armageddon. I like the ring of that. You should call the newspaper. It would make a great banner headline. No, actually we've been summoned to GBI headquarters. Seems they want to talk to us."

Maggie tried to hide her concern but figured Scott saw the slight crinkle in her brow. "GBI? What on Earth for?"

"I imagine to see if we've run across any threatening crackpots. Maybe they just want our help in figuring out the damage. Could be any number of things."

"Just don't tell them you come here. The place is already packed with threatening crackpots." She set his check on the table and gave him a long, measured look. "You have a good day, and I hope to see you tomorrow at the regular time."

7.

om's eyes fluttered open. He could sense brightness but couldn't see anything clearly. It was like a misty morning where clouds engulf the land. He shook his head to make sure he was awake. He was, and his brain didn't rattle like it did when he was on a drug bender. He narrowed his eyes trying to focus, but the clouds remained.

"Inhale," he told himself. "Your nose will tell you where you are."

The odors told him he wasn't in his beloved mountains, nor could he sense water, fresh or salt, so he wasn't near the lake or ocean. It was a familiar scent but not one he had encountered recently. Tom willed himself to think, trying to visualize what the smell looked like. The first image that came to his mind was Kandahar, but that couldn't be right. He knew he was thousands of miles away, and this was too lush to be Afghanistan. Another deep inhale brought a wave of panic and anxiety—he was back in the goddamned hospital in Kandahar! He was not about to let history repeat itself. He didn't care how bad off he was. There was no way he's leaving his unit this time! He struggled to get out of bed.

Yet, he couldn't move—arm, leg, and body straps bound him to the bed. Tom struggled with all his might, only to have the straps dig deeper into his skin. Escape was hopeless. The burst of adrenaline from thrashing brought everything into focus, and Tom suddenly knew what he felt and saw were not figments of a drug-induced brain. This was real...and it was not promising. He was strapped to a hospital bed with an IV and vitals monitors on his arms and chest. The room was small, maybe 10x10, with a narrow window high on the wall showing only sky. The door was reinforced metal with no knob on the inside. This was no ordinary hospital; it was a prison.

Like most rational human beings, Tom had never been a fan of hospitals. His two-week stay at the Army Field Hospital in Kandahar had sealed his aversion. He knew the people meant well, but he'd rather die out in the field. His chest tightened as panic and claustrophobia began to eat at him. No matter how hard he struggled, the restraints didn't budge. Ready to lose his mind, he knew this time would be for good.

"Hey! What the fuck's going on, get me outta here!" His screams reverberated off the walls of his tiny cell. "Somebody come in here and let me go! If I don't see an ass in here in ten seconds, I'll kill the first motherfucker who comes near me!"

The door burst open as a big guy in camo came trotting in. "Easy there, Warrant Officer. I'm here, settle down, relax, take a couple of breaths."

Tom thought the guy looked like a typical Army field nurse, size to subdue unruly patients being more important than bedside manner. But this guy was not in scrubs and seemed almost as uneasy as Tom with the surroundings. Not being alone helped, but he was still pissed. "Who the hell are you? Take the damn restraints off. I don't care how big you are. I'm going to kick your ass."

The guy gave an evil little grin and leaned in. "My name's Mike, and I'm half tempted to take them off just to see you try. Now shut up. Doc's coming in soon."

As if on cue, the door swung open and in came Dr. Shaw from the Veterans Administration Hospital. "Glad to see you're awake, Tom. We've had you on some pretty heavy sedation. Time to consider weaning you off."

The sight of Dr. Shaw, one of the VA Army shrinks, surprised him but not enough to calm him down. "What the hell's going on, Doc? Why you got me strapped down and locked in? This is bullshit. Get me outta here."

"Sorry, Warrant Officer, that's not going to happen."

The doc gave him one of those shrink looks, a combination of pity and smugness that seemed to say, "I've got my shit together and you don't." Sad thing, Shaw was one of the better ones at the VA. He actually spent time in Afghanistan, even if it was only in Kabul.

Dr. Shaw moved to the bed. "Don't you remember anything? You made quite a scene at the VA. Took five guys to pin you down."

Tom crinkled his brow in thought. He remembered the group session, stopping by the pharmacy for his meds, then heading towards the exit and some guy hanging by the exit, asking if he needed a lift. "No, Doc, I remember leaving, went outside, I could smell it was going to rain."

"And then you snapped. You were definitely a threat, not only to yourself, but to others. We had to bring you here for your own safety." The subtle change in the doc's voice suggested otherwise.

Tom thought hard trying to recall a fight. He couldn't remember a damn thing, but his body told him the doc was lying. "Shaw, you're full of shit. I wasn't in a damn fight, nothing hurts. You're making this up. Now, get these restraints off. The only person I'm a threat to is you, you son of a bitch."

"Not going to happen." Shaw removed a syringe from his lab coat and injected something into the IV port. Tom's brain told him to keep cussing out the doc, but his tongue felt thick, the sun started to set, and the bank of clouds rolled back in.

8.

overnor Murray wrapped a towel around his waist, noticing the ends barely met due to his dad-bod belly still swollen from the previous campaign's endless rounds of barbeques. Holding a firm grip to keep it in place, he realized the guest suite bathroom didn't have his razor, but skipping that hygiene step was a better option than using the master bath and risk waking Hannah. He left his sweat-sodden PJ's on the bathroom floor and crept down the hall towards their bedroom. He slowly twisted the doorknob, poked his head in through the crack, and was relieved to see his wife sleeping in her customary fetal position. Quietly, he shuffled into the master closet and shut the door.

Once dressed, he quickly retraced his steps back to the hallway. With the door safely shut, Skip took a second to catch his breath as he had unconsciously held it during most of his clandestine mission. He strode down the mansion's grand staircase and wound his way back to the kitchen, amazed to find Jose and a security detail already at the table plotting out the day's logistics.

"Jose, thanks a million for getting here so quickly. You, too, gentlemen." The governor nodded at the four state patrol officers.

Jose looked at him quizzically. "Of course, Governor, but what in the world are you wearing?"

Skip adjusted his tie and made sure his suit jacket didn't have a stain or cigar burn hole. "What do you mean? I'm going to work."

Jose left the table and steered the governor back into the hallway away from the troopers. He spoke barely above a whisper. "But, sir, you're not going to the Capitol to meet legislators. This is a terrorist attack. You need to wear something more…workman-like. The people don't want to see you in a tie at a time like this. Think of W and 9/11. Ditch the wingtips, put on some khakis, a casual dress shirt, and a windbreaker. The non-shaven look is good, but wear a ball cap to tame down your hair." Jose was very good at providing advice without judgment in his tone.

"But Jose, I can't go change. There's no way Hannah will sleep through me sneaking around the room again."

Even though Jose stood several inches shorter and was ten years younger, he'd mastered a calm, fatherly tone when addressing the governor. "I understand your worry, but in this instance, you should be more concerned about your constituents' emotions and fears than your wife's."

The governor couldn't hide his disappointment that Jose was right. Without saying a word, he turned on his heel and slunk back up the grand staircase. He approached the bedroom and craned his neck. The TV was on, she was awake, he was in deep trouble. Skip said a quick prayer and opened the bedroom door.

Hannah was sitting up in bed with the sheets tucked under her chin, her naturally fair complexion even paler, a look of despaired shock on her face as she stared blankly at the TV. Without moving her gaze, she addressed him in a voice eerily calm and flat. "I knew something like this would happen. Why didn't you tell me?"

Skip walked over and sat on the edge of the bed. "I didn't want to upset you, honey, but trust me, everything will be okay. It's not as bad as the TV people are making it out to be."

His wife refused to avert her eyes from a reporter chasing down a police officer in Kennestone Hospital's parking lot. When they switched back to the anchor, Hannah broke her trance and turned to Skip in her goofy cat glasses that some enterprising optometrist convinced her were now stylish. "They'll be coming after you next. The family too. We've got to get out of here."

Skip cradled her cheek in his hand, her face being the only skin poking out from the protective cocoon. "You and the kids are safe. Jose's here, and he brought an extra security detail to protect you."

Tears welled in her eyes. "But you have to go, don't you?"

"Yes," Skip said tenderly. "I have to go to GBI headquarters, and I'm sure nothing bad will happen there. But we'll get you and the kids to the farm as soon as possible, and I'll join you when I can. We're always happiest at the farm."

"Yes, we should all be at Daddy's farm instead of here. It's too dangerous here."

Skip felt a slight easing of tenseness in her face. "Are you okay?"

She slowly turned her attention back to the TV. "For now. I'm sure I'll be a hot mess once this sinks in."

Skip smiled. Despite the suitcase of neuroses she toted, Hannah was incredibly self-aware and honest. It was one of the many things he loved about her. If not for Jose's reminder that his constituents were more important, Skip might have stuck around to comfort his wife. Instead, he quickly changed and hustled out of the bedroom ready to report for duty.

Jose nodded approval as the governor trotted back down the stairs. "Much better, sir. A trooper's out back in the Suburban. You ready to go?"

After successfully dealing with his wife, Jose's approval further bolstered the governor's newfound confidence. "Let's do this."

As the two men headed down the hall to the back door, Jose handed the governor a small stack of index cards. "It's almost 7:30, so I expect the president will be calling you soon. I've written down some notes. It's not a script, just some suggestions on what to say to the president. He'll likely be…well, you know how he can be, so just remember we only want him to say the state has his full support."

"Thanks, Jose. I really appreciate you being in my camp."

The two men shook hands at the door.

"Good luck, Governor. I'm here if you need me."

Safely nestled in the black Suburban's back seat, he began shuffling through Jose's index cards. Skip was quite adept at memorizing and delivering lines. Knowing when to pause and change inflection where needed was a skill he learned taking drama classes at UGA. If he hadn't been mercilessly teased by his fraternity brothers, Skip probably would have gotten into acting instead of politics.

As Jose predicted, Skip's cell phone rang before they made it out of the neighborhood. He quickly adjusted the index cards on his lap, gave himself a quick pep talk, and answered the phone.

"Governor, please hold for the president," announced the monotone female from his initial call.

After a brief second, a very familiar voice came on the line. "Skippy, it's your president."

The cursed nickname was a curveball he hadn't expected. He tentatively responded, "Thank you for calling, Mr. President. I know you're a busy man."

"Not too busy for you, Governor. So, what's this I hear about Black Panther Muslims starting a war in your fair state?"

Skip cringed. Clearly, the president spoke with the congressman. No wonder these guys liked each other. He scanned his lap for the right card. "Mr. President, that is a possibility, sir, but we still don't know who did the bombings or their intentions. We only know the state has experienced a series of explosions that require immediate attention from both the state and federal level." The governor mentally thanked Jose for correctly assuming the president would quickly blame one of the many groups he constantly villainized.

"Guess it could have been those green people, the global warming crybabies," the president piled on. "We'll check 'em all out. So, what can I do for you?"

"Well, Mr. President…"

The governor looked for the cards labeled "requests."

"…we need your help in a couple of areas. If you could authorize the military to be activated from Fort Benning, Stewart, and Gordon, we'd like to coordinate the troops with our local guard to seal off and inspect the highway system. We need to make sure the roads are safe."

"That's easy. I'll make the call right away. What else?"

"Excellent, thank you. Please have your base commanders coordinate with General Harper. He's the head of the Georgia National Guard. Next, we need both Homeland Security and the FBI involved. Our law enforcement is good, but this is a little out of their league. We need your help in trying to catch the perpetrators." Skip nailed that card too, even impressed himself with how official he sounded.

"I'll call Homeland first. Not a big fan of the FBI, so I want them to know they're second string."

The governor wasn't surprised the president wanted to squeeze the FBI after the pressure they'd been piling on him. He figured Pete knew the Atlanta FBI Field Office Chief, and they would call him once Skip got to GBI headquarters.

"Lastly, sir, the media is all over this, stirring up everyone's imagination. We've already received panic calls from many Georgians. We want to issue a press release as soon as possible to try to calm folks down." He paused for effect. "In that release, I want to say that you and I have talked, and tell the citizens the president has promised full resources. Are you okay with that?"

The president's voice became excited. "I'll do you one better than that. I have a commitment this morning with some very important people. Once I'm done, I'll hop on Air Force One and come to Georgia. Should be able to get there by mid-afternoon. How's that sound?"

Skip panicked and quickly shuffled through his script. On the last card Jose had written in large black letters, "Don't let him come to Georgia!" Completely flummoxed, Skip flipped over the card hoping Jose had crafted a response—nothing.

"Uh, er, that's a very generous offer Mr. President, but I think…"

"Tiffany, darling, you still on the line?"

Without delay the monotone returned. "Yes, Mr. President."

"Work out the details with the governor and Secret Service. I'd like to be there before dinner. Have a press conference or speech lined up for me. We can do it on the airport tarmac if need be."

The governor absently suggested, "The GBI Command Center might be better, Mr. President. It would look better on TV."

"Damn, I'm liking how you're thinking, Skippy. Tiffany, make it happen. I gotta go. Tee time's waiting."

The governor couldn't tell if the line was dead or not. He waited a beat. "You still there, ma'am?"

"Give me an hour to work things out, Governor. I'll call you back." The line went dead.

Skip sank down in the Suburban's back seat, wondering how he'd make it through the day.

9.

Seamus peeked through the vertical blinds inside the emergency room entrance watching the TV crews circle his car. The sun had risen, unveiling a glorious fall Sunday morning, and he longed to feel its warmth after spending the last hour under the hospital's depressing fluorescent lights. He knew he had to get back to headquarters but had no earthly idea how to avoid the cameras and shouted questions. Just the thought of being interviewed by excited news sharks raised the hair on his arms.

He saw a security guard making his way through the parking lot toward the commotion. One of the TV reporters also saw his approach and mistook him for the car's driver. To his surprise, the reporter broke into a high-heeled jog in his direction with her cameraman close on her tail. Not wanting to miss a scoop, the remaining pack promptly joined the pursuit. The startled security guard saw the approaching herd, spun, and made a hasty retreat. Seeing his opening, Seamus made a mad dash to his car.

Seamus was impressed with the high-heeled reporter's agility and stamina. Once she realized the true prey, she made a valiant effort by chasing the Ford clear through the parking lot to the exit leaving the gasping cameraman in her dust. He chuckled to himself and turned left toward the interstate.

Once on I-75, he merged to the far-left lane as squad cars were shepherding the remaining traffic slowly towards the exit ramps. In a couple of hours, they might actually clear the roads. Seamus saw several helicopters flying from the general direction of nearby Dobbins Air Reserve Base and guessed they were ordered to make an aerial survey. Strange though, in those first miles on the interstate, he noticed only two beheaded billboards. The first decapitated billboard must have been the one that injured the poor guy back at the hospital.

At this point of his life, Seamus O'Reilly should have been immune from the likes of the victim's wife. His entire adult life, people had reacted with astonishment and derision about his being a Black man with such an Irish name. As a kid, it wasn't bad. Stereotypes and ethnic identity carried very little weight on the elementary school playground. He was a fun kid who made friends easily and an excellent athlete without the ultra-competitiveness that turns some into overbearing jerks. Most of his friends were jealous of his name since they were saddled with boring, traditional names. They loved saying Seamus and gave him cool nicknames like Shamu and Moose.

With age, he quickly realized adults were a different story. For some unexplained reason, many adults lost their childhood enthusiasm and acceptance only to replace those with apathy and judgment. He was certain many of the kids he played tag with on the playground had grown up to be just like the victim's wife from Indiana.

Seamus was extremely proud of his Haitian-Irish-American heritage. His was a true American story, the kind of story often cited as an example of why the country was so great. His grandparents came to America as infants, their parents determined to give their children a life of opportunity. His grandfather's side left Ireland shortly after the World War I armistice, right as the Irish War for Independence began. His grandmother's side escaped Haiti several years before WWI when Haitian President/Dictator Sam ordered the massacre of his political opponents.

Both families settled in Detroit and became upstanding, working class citizens. His namesake grandfather was mechanically gifted and started a long career with The Ford Motor Company in the '30s. When World War II broke out, his skills were so valued the War Department agreed he'd be of more service to his country making B-24 Liberators at Ford's Willow Run plant. One of his grandfather's favorite claims during retirement was the real-life Rosie the Riveter worked his line.

His grandmother was intelligent, patient, and compassionate. Had it been a different era, she likely would have become a doctor. Instead she gravitated toward a profession deemed more suitable for a woman—a Black woman at that—nursing. She served her country during WWII by promptly volunteering for the Army Nurses Corps. Despite the shortage of nurses, the army was not about to send a Black, female nurse to care for predominately white soldiers in Europe or Asia-Pacific. Instead, the small corps of Black nurses were shipped to Arizona to tend over German POWs housed at Camp Florence.

His grandparents' improbable love story began shortly after the war. Like so many immigrants in the north, the Catholic Church brought them together, and their common life experiences created an inseparable bond. Even though Michigan overturned their miscegenation law in the late 1800s, the era still made interracial marriages complicated and often dangerous. But their belief in each other was stronger than social norms, and they enjoyed more than 40 years together.

Seamus marveled at the determination, resiliency, and undying Catholic faith of his grandparents. He was damn proud to be an O'Reilly no matter what anyone else thought or said. He only wished his own faith had remained strong.

So lost climbing his family tree, it took a moment for Seamus to realize he was off the interstate approaching another collection of TV news trucks camped outside the entrance to GBI headquarters. Prohibited from entering the property, this gaggle sat patiently waiting to be summoned for any formal announcement the authorities might make. With the cameras turned off, the reporters mingled with each other catching up like alums at a reunion. He passed through without a ruckus.

Seamus took the stairs to the second floor where the Antiterrorism Team had a section in the GBI employee cube farm. He went to his work station along the outer windows, purposely avoiding the supervisors' offices located in the center of the building. Some of his team were already clustered by the window, theorizing about the bombings. He liked his coworkers. For the most part, they were friendly and professional, yet Seamus was the research guy, so he didn't carry the same status as the other agents. He compared it to the four years he spent as the backup goalie on Western Michigan's soccer team; he was on the team but not on *the* team.

He gravitated to the group. "Morning, guys. Pretty wild day, huh?"

"Sure didn't see this coming. By the way, O'Reilly, the director dropped by saying he wanted to see you as soon as you got in."

"Thanks, Walt," Seamus answered gamely, not showing his concern of being summoned to the director's office. He hovered around his teammates an extra second until it was clear they weren't going to offer him encouragement or question his morning activities.

He headed back up the hall, quietly coaching himself on what he'd say to the director about the interview. He rarely interacted with the man as his boss was the Antiterrorism Team's intermediary with the higher-ups. But Bill Carraway had finally succumbed to his wife's pleading and was off on a Caribbean cruise, leaving direct communication the only option.

He entered the director's outer office where his assistant was already busy typing away. "Go right in, O'Reilly," she said without diverting her attention from her computer.

He paused in the director's doorway. "Sir, you wanted to see me?"

"Oh, yes, come in O'Reilly." The morning's stress was embedded on Sterling's face.

Since it was his first visit to the director's corner office, Seamus didn't know the protocol, so he took several steps and stood waiting for further instruction. The wood paneling, books and trophies, pictures of a beautiful family, and framed certificates of appreciation gave it a feel of a movie set rather than an office where actual work was done. It even smelled cleaner than the rest of the building. After an awkward pause and no invitation to take a seat, Seamus got to the point.

"Unfortunately, the eye-witness didn't have any useful information. I have his statement, but I don't think it'll help much."

Sterling leaned back in his chair. "Not a big surprise. I've heard he'll be okay."

"Hospital already discharged him. I have his contact information in case we have any more questions."

"Just write it up. The case file's already been started in the system."

"Yes, sir. Thank you." Seamus turned to leave.

"Just a second, Agent. I've got something else for you."

"Sir?" Seamus paused at the door.

Sterling held out a file. "The other agents on your team said this is right up your alley. Two groups claimed responsibility for today's attack. One is called Green War and the other Make America Beautiful Again. We have the Cybersecurity Team working it, but I'd like another set of eyes."

Seamus's heart swelled at the acknowledgement from his team as he took the folder. "Will do, sir. The team's right. This is my specialty."

"Very good. Also, in the file is a complete list of all outdoor advertising companies in the state. Start looking into their history, see if anything jumps out. I've pulled together everyone for a meeting at 9:15 in the Savannah Conference Room. Bring what you find to the meeting."

"Yes, sir." Seamus left his office and returned to his cubicle with a spring in his step.

10.

The high-speed police escort up I-75 was a blast. Chuck had never driven so fast for so long; it was quite a rush. He locked his hands on the steering wheel and thought about writing Chrysler a glowing letter on how his trusty Voyager handled like a dream, even when they topped 100 mph.

Most of Chuck's smugness had returned, and he was now a huge fan of the Georgia Bureau of Investigation. He couldn't remember the last time a guy had done him such a solid. One day he'd figure out how to thank him.

About ten minutes after the agent's quick exit, he came back in the room to say he'd arranged for them to continue their trip. Chuck got dressed and was quickly discharged, and then the family was led through the bowels of the hospital to the loading dock where their minivan was flanked by three State Highway patrol cars.

Once on the Interstate, two patrol cars plowed the way, and the third stayed on his rear. The kids gawked, pointed, and laughed as they sped past the lines of traffic trying to exit the now closed highway—they weren't this excited during the entire time at Disney World! The only family member in the car not having fun was

Debbie. After one attempt to get Chuck to slow down, which was quickly vetoed by the rest of the family, she barely said a peep. He didn't know what was better, Debbie's silent stewing or rocketing up the interstate.

Chuck tightened his grip on the wheel and began fantasizing about taking a racing class at the Indy 500 track once they got home. If it was this fun driving 100 in a minivan with a duct taped window, think what it would be like in a race car on the two-mile oval! For the first time on their trip, he was happy. Debbie wasn't giving him a hard time, the kids were having fun, and even his freshly injured arm didn't hurt. He relished the thought that after all of his wife's planning, nagging, and hustling the family from ride to ride, the police escort would be the most memorable part of the trip.

At the border, the state troopers peeled off to the shoulder, and the kids gave them an enthusiastic wave as the Hoosiers entered Tennessee. With the time they made up, the unplanned detour only cost them a couple of hours. At this rate he'd probably catch the second half.

11.

"**M**oon, wait up!"

Barry Whitley stopped trotting along the path, gasping for air. He put his thumb and index finger in his mouth and belted a loud whistle to slow down the rambunctious black Labrador, but her joy was so complete that Barry couldn't find it within himself to inflict further obedience.

It was a crisp morning, and they made good time covering the circuitous two miles to the Ocmulgee River. Like all Labs, Moonshadow loved a good swim and crashed recklessly ahead of Barry knowing what awaited her at the end of the trail. Moon had been trained by Deer Bend Plantation as a hunting dog until she failed the field test. Loud noises spooked her, and she preferred chasing a tennis ball or getting her belly rubbed over fetching a felled duck. She loved life and didn't do well with death. Even roadkill armadillo spooked her.

Barry heard the telltale splash that Moon made it to the river. He emerged from the woods to see the dog swimming in circles while lapping up the cool water, tail flicking back and forth, tossing small beads of water in her wake. He stepped up on the large flat rock on the river's edge, the signal the game was about to begin.

The dog made a bee line for the shore, scampered up the bank onto the rock, and waited until she was right next to Barry before commencing a vigorous nose to tail shake. "You're getting me soaked, girl!" he admonished, more amused than annoyed.

He slowly put his hand in his pocket, the dog transfixed with his every movement, and pulled out the prize—a yellow tennis ball. Moon voiced her opinion with enthusiastic barks. Barry lobbed the ball into the middle of the river and Moon dove off the rock in hot pursuit.

There were few things that Barry loved more than hiking the woods back in his old stomping grounds by the Ocmulgee River. Barry spent the first 12 years of his life here, not a great span considering he was pushing 60, yet those years left an indelible impression that this was home. He felt the land was his even though he didn't own one clump of its dirt. That longing for home was why he came back, and if he wasn't in such a perilous situation, he'd be as happy as that last glorious year in Vegas.

Moon bounded back on the rock and set the ball at Barry's feet, tail batting the air in anticipation. He picked up the sodden ball and gave it a hearty heave. He was grateful Moon would chase the ball until his arm ached. He was in no hurry to get back and face what lay in store at the compound.

Barry and Bubba swam this very spot in the river as boys, even sitting on this same rock to dry out before heading their separate ways home, Bubba to the big house and Barry to his family's ramshackle tenant farm. The Bakers had owned tens of thousands of acres for generations, bequeathing the land to the next in line, evolving the method of land maintenance to currently accepted norms of human exploitation: slavery to share cropping to tenant farming. The Bakers had made a fortune off the grueling labor of others and saw nothing wrong with that. In fact, they were convinced it was their birthright. Barry's dad was one of the few white tenant farmers, renting a shack and small plot from the Bakers several miles southeast of the compound that Barry now called home.

One of the many great things about being a kid is the ignorance of social standing and importance of fun. In those early years, Barry and Bubba were inseparable, except during harvest time when Barry had to work the fields while Bubba couldn't comprehend why his friend couldn't play. They romped these same woods with the exuberance exhibited by Moon on this fine fall morning. If they weren't building a new fort, catching frogs, climbing trees, hunting, or fishing, they'd play Cowboys and Indians or Rebels and Yankees. By 6th grade, things started to change as Bubba began to take on the attitude of his old man and didn't want to hang out with Barry at school. The adventures continued, but now Bubba wanted to play Patroller and Runaway Slave with Barry always being the slave. Not that Barry minded because Bubba was such a lousy tracker that the game usually ended with the slave capturing the patroller.

"I'm getting tired, girl," Barry told the relentless Lab as she dropped the ball at his feet for the umpteenth time. "Two more tosses, then let's head back."

Moon barked in agreement or with impatience. Barry couldn't tell.

His idyllic youth ended when Barry's dad was found dead in his okra field. Heart attack, undoubtedly, though no autopsy was done since they didn't even have enough money for a proper burial. Without an able-bodied man to farm the valuable land, old man Baker had no intention to accommodate what he believed to be squatting freeloaders and quickly evicted Barry, his mom, and baby sister. Fortunately for the family, his mom's sister was married to an Air Force mechanic stationed at Kirkland Air Force Base, so they packed up and moved to Albuquerque. When they left Georgia, Bubba was nowhere to be found.

Despite the traumatic circumstances, Barry thrived in the west and quickly made new friends. He had the rare combination of intelligence, street sense, and affability that others found unassumingly appealing. What his family lacked in resources, he made up for with the same dogged work ethic his father had displayed. He didn't miss Georgia but did carry a resentment from his experience, mostly the low opinion of wealthy landowners.

Unable to afford college, Barry was determined to never again live in poverty. The Southwest was in a boom phase with people flocking to the desert heat, vowing never again to endure a Chicago winter. They needed homes, and the majority of the land was owned by a select few. Thinking of the Bakers, Barry knew he could tap into the egos, motivations, and greed of large property owners, so he decided that selling off their land was a logical career choice. He was awarded his real estate license before he could legally drink.

Barry was a natural. Depending on the client, he could be the suave man about town or the good old boy from Georgia. He specialized in large property deals, acting as the developers' intermediary with commissions varying on who owned the land. He'd take all he could from family trusts and usually cut deals with ranchers, unless they were flaming assholes. He earned his stripes in Albuquerque then shifted his operation to Phoenix before winding up in Vegas. Known for hiking the prospective property with rifle in arm for "critters," he cut a dashingly rugged figure that rich guys ate up. They never suspected Barry was gouging them at a good 10% above market price. He made a killing by the time he was 40.

Barry's arm was numb, but Moon showed no signs of letting up. Ignoring her pleading bark, he crammed the wet ball in his back pocket and looked at the dripping wet Labrador for guidance. "What do you think, Moon? Short way or long way back?"

Moon cocked her head, then, acting like she knew what the human asked, headed south along the riverbank.

"I'm with you, girl. Let's take the long way."

Barry followed Moon down the trail. The path paralleled the river, heading toward the property's southern border which abutted the Middle Georgia Wildlife Management Area. After several hundred yards, the trail cut back east through a grove of towering pines and live oak trees where the increased shade thinned out the undergrowth along the path. As they made their way back in the direction of the compound, Barry's mood sank, and his daily self-chastising began. Just like his dad, he was now under the thumb of the Bakers.

It had been over 40 years since he'd seen Bubba before their chance meeting in Utah five years ago. Barry was only in Utah out of desperation. His heart had recently been broken, and joining old rancher friends protesting federal grazing rights seemed like a good diversion. He knew Bubba was in politics but didn't expect him to be part of a delegation of sympathetic US Congressmen who came to visit the ranchers. After posing for the press, Bubba pulled Barry aside to say he needed help with a new, top secret project.

The Bakers had stopped farming years ago and replaced the old big house with a famous hunting lodge called Deer Bend Plantation. Recently, a select group of "like-minded men," personally hand-picked by Bubba, had formed a silent, ambiguous-sounding land preservation partnership and purchased 1,000 acres of the Baker's property wedged between County Road 5 and the river. Their goal was to create a liberty-loving militia determined to protect and preserve America from devious outside influences. The consortium needed a property manager, and Bubba thought Barry was ideal. He knew the land and the people, plus he had a commanding presence for cameras. The group would pay him handsomely too.

Barry gave Bubba a good hard look. Thinking about the hurt of a 12-year-old boy, he clenched his fist prepared to knock the congressman on his ass. He was not a believer in fate or any of the predestined bullshit, but maybe, just maybe, there was a reason he was at a confusing crossroad in his life. He did love Georgia, and this just might be his chance to get a measure of revenge on the Bakers, or at least finagle money out of them. With nothing else to do, Barry agreed to go home.

The first couple of years were a blast. Barry could care less about Bubba's movement and spent most of those early days exploring all his old haunts, blazing new trails and swimming naked in the river. Once Moonshadow failed her field test, he had a constant companion. The consortium invested untraceable money and transformed an old ranch house into a comfortable, remote militia compound headquarters. As the sole permanent resident, Barry's only official jobs were to manage the property and build the American Liberation Militia's website. His unofficial job skimming Bubba's investments was much more personally rewarding.

But those good old days were long gone. As the ALM's virtual presence grew, so did recruitment. Bubba had befriended a weekend Deer Bend Plantation tracker, an ex-Marine and current high school social studies teacher, and hired him to lead the volunteer corps. The teacher then brought in two brainless psychopaths, JR and Mike, to act as his resident military planners, which was a joke since neither could pack their own lunch box. Once a month, the so-called Volunteer Corps would show up for weekend training maneuvers; basically, a bunch of white dudes looking to escape the wife and kids would shoot their rifles in the woods, drink a couple of cases of Bud Light, and carp about how fucked up everything was.

As if having these two boneheads living next door wasn't bad enough, the most recent compound addition included a fortified hospital-prison with residents supervised by a twisted, visiting VA quack. For the second time in his life, Barry's peaceful existence in Georgia had been hijacked by the heartless Baker clan. Only this time, he was trapped and faced the prospects of some serious jail time, if he was lucky.

He stood at the edge of the woods staring down at the compound, Moon panting next to him. Mike was off to the side of the field below, rifle in hand, acting as if the disheveled, drug-addled man curled in a fetal position on the grass was Saddam Hussein. Doc Shaw was there too, his mind spinning evilly.

Shaw finally noticed Barry, said something to Mike, and then headed off in his direction. Barry told Moon to heel, and the two walked down the slope to meet the doc.

"Is that the prize patient, the bomb guy you've been bragging about?" Barry asked as Shaw approached.

The question hit a nerve. "Of course not. Patient Alpha is resting right now," Shaw answered testily. "That is Patient Omega, and today's his last chance to make the cut."

The doc's comment twisted a knife in Barry's gut. "When will you know?"

"I'm headed back to Atlanta this evening and will return tomorrow morning. If we don't see improvement by then, we'll know."

He looked over at the poor man tightly cradling his knees to his chest, his fate clear in Barry's mind. This would make five bodies buried down the trail Moon refused to take, and Barry had no intention of becoming the sixth.

He snapped his fingers at Moon and dejectedly headed to his house. "Just keep me posted, Doc."

12.

*S*cott stood and stretched with his back arched and palm-up arms reaching to the heavens. He froze in place, soaking in the warm sun on his face. He admired the grace of a red-tailed hawk soaring high above the field adjacent to the half-full GBI parking lot. He purposely parked in the back row next to the field—his excuse was to get some exercise, but truth be told, he just wanted some separation from Roger.

If he could pat his own back, he would as there was no sign of Roger's car in the GBI parking lot visitor's section, and he couldn't remember the last time he arrived at a meeting before his punctually-anal brother-in-law. He found Roger's obsessiveness with time ironic since most other detail didn't really matter to him.

As he made his way toward the building, Scott was reassured to see other members of Georgia's outdoor advertising community congregating near the GBI headquarters' front steps. He and Roger had not been singled out. Despite being cutthroat competitors, they enjoyed a collegial relationship, a solidarity built on the general public's dislike of their business. With sullied reputations, they formed a unified front when needed.

Even from a distance, it was easy to spot the bright reddish-orange hair of Rusty McArthur. Like Scott, Rusty was a third generation member of the family business. Unlike Scott, he actually seemed to enjoy it. His dad, Mac, passed most control of McArthur Outdoor to Rusty but still came to work most every day out of habit or a desire just to get out of the house. Mac and Scott's dad had been quite a pair back in the day, fighting tooth and nail against each other at work while being drunken, carousing partners in crime at night.

Standing with Rusty were two slickly dressed, finely-coifed young executives from Consolidated whose names escaped Scott's memory. As the unimaginative moniker suggested, Consolidated was the national company that gobbled up assets once respectable media companies decided outdoor advertising was no longer a fit for their portfolio. Most of Consolidated's management were young suits looking to pad their resumes with leadership positions before moving to the next, more reputable job. These two were no different. With an over-inflated opinion of their intelligence and the self-importance of financial planners, these two didn't plan on being in Georgia long.

Studying the three men, it dawned on Scott he was terribly underdressed compared to his peers. Fortunately, he really didn't care.

"Morning, guys," Scott announced. "Crazy way to start a Sunday." As Scott greeted the men, he noticed Roger's Beemer zip into view.

The youngest of the young Consolidate executives clearly hit Starbucks on the way over, his words spilled out in a jumbled blur. "Unbelievable. Can't imagine it's something against us, nothing's happened in any other Consolidated states. I called the CEO right away, he said it's only Georgia. You guys have anyone with a vendetta against you, or are we dealing with terrorists that don't know what to blow up?"

Scott wondered if the guy's liberally applied hair product would suddenly ignite if he got his head close to an open flame. And who wears a sport coat pocket square when meeting the GBI on Sunday morning? He ignored him and turned to Rusty. "Morning, Rusty. Sure thought your old man would be here. Bet he's pretty pissed off."

Rusty was in his trusty southern frat uniform of khakis and a navy blazer over a blue oxford button down. He spoke while looking over Scott's shoulder as Roger pulled into a slot up front. "He's mad as hell. Down at the hunting lodge though and couldn't be here."

Scott knew the "hunting lodge" all too well as his dad had used that alibi for years when he and Mac were out trolling for women. He could picture Mac holed up with a Pink Pony dancer in the secret Buckhead condo, ranting like Foghorn Leghorn about how the country's going to hell while Dakota feigned sleep as she thought about what color she should do her nails for tonight's shift.

"Too bad. Think he would have enjoyed coming to meet with the GBI guys...wanting to do his civic duty and all."

Rusty simply shook his head, his eyes pleading for Roger to hurry up and get out of his car. Scott understood Rusty's affinity for Roger since they were the only ones who truly understood and cared about the outdoor business in Georgia.

"You're late," Scott sarcastically yelled out to Roger as he got out of his Beemer and slipped on a blazer. "I've been waiting here for a good 15 minutes."

"Glad to see you dressed for the occasion. You could have at least ironed your golf shirt," Roger fired back before bypassing Scott to greet the others, beginning the round of handshakes. "Morning, boys."

Scott looked at the blazer clad group and shrugged.

Scott didn't mind Roger's dig; he was the first to admit his ambivalence toward fashion. To him, clothes were a necessity but not important enough to get all worked up about. Fashion was the one area where his ex-wife added value to his previous life. Appalled at his inability to tell the difference between navy blue and black, she took it upon herself to buy his clothes and lay out the next day's outfit as if he was still in grade school. Scott took no offense because he didn't care and it seemed to make her happy. After the divorce, he reverted to his disregard of style.

The coffee-jazzed executive quickly spoke up. "Roger, what's this is all about? Admit I'm glad you guys are here. I've never been called in like this. Do you think they suspect us or we're in danger?"

Whenever Mac was absent, Roger became the de facto leader of the outdoor cabal.

"Relax there, Evan. I'm sure they're just looking for our help. We just need to be careful about what we commit to. You boys head on in, give me a quick minute here with Rusty."

Scott had to hand it to Roger. He had an uncanny ability to mask his own concerns and forge ahead with confidence and good old boy camaraderie. Roger thrived in these situations while Scott found it all quite tiresome. He was glad Mac was preoccupied with a nubile young professional; Roger was the man for today's emergency.

Scott led the other ad men into GBI headquarters while Roger and Rusty held a brief powwow.

13.

*P*am held the two long-sleeved athletic shirts, wondering which might look better with her navy yoga pants. The green was out. She'd already worn it once this week and, in her neighborhood, it was a serious faux pas to be seen wearing the same outfit twice in one week, even for workouts. She tossed it on the bed and pulled the pink top over her sports bra. Pam never pranced around in just a sports bra.

Roger was highly upset over the terrorist attack on their business. After he left in an agitated huff to meet her brother at GBI Headquarters, Pam decided she and the kids could skip church. Teenagers being teenagers, the morning news was met with grunts as they both stumbled back to bed. She figured they wouldn't emerge until noon at the earliest.

Pam went down the curving front staircase, her hand gently sliding along the mahogany railing. She paused in front of the foyer mirror for a final inspection, inching in close to inspect her makeup one last time. Most women in her social status had jumped on the Botox train, but Pam was proud of her wrinkles, believing they were more like life's merit badges than a sign of age. Besides, her mom always said a woman can age gracefully as long as she never left the house without lipstick. Pam dug through the top drawer of the hutch under the mirror, selected the perfect shade to match her pink top, and made two quick, experienced swipes on her lips.

Pam knew it was wise to follow mom's advice and was grateful to have come from a good stock of female Worthington genes. Despite the financial success of the Worthington men, the women were the steady rocks that kept the family from ruin. As a child, she just thought Nana was a bossy woman, ordering Grampy around then ganging up with Mom against Dad once he inherited VOA. But with age, Pam learned the truth. Her Grampy was basically a drunk and her father a serial philanderer, both known to disappear "on business" for days on end. If not for Nana and her mother, and Pam for that matter, VOA would not be in business today.

The thought of Grampy and her father was disconcerting. Why did the Worthington men insist on disappearing without telling their family? The clickety-clack of dog nails on hardwood floors from the upstairs hallway brought her back to the moment.

"Blitzen? Want to go for a walk?" Pam called out. Her adorable mutt raced down the stairs, leapt from the lower landing, and came to a skidding halt at the door. "Quite an entrance. Guess that's a yes!" Pam gave her a pat on the head.

They headed out the front door, past the pansies and mums the landscapers planted last week, and down the long driveway to the street. It was a glorious morning, so she paused for a moment, gazing at the blue sky, allowing the sun to warm her face. Checking her sports watch, it was just after 9:00 in the morning. Plenty of time for a long walk to solve her conundrum. She tapped "start workout" and headed up the street towards the Central City Golf Club.

Pam was not upset about what the morning's attack meant to VOA's business. The company was on solid ground and would be just fine. VOA faced bigger turmoil back when a green 25-year-old

Pam was thrust into running the company shortly after her father's death while her mother fought cancer. VOA not only survived under her leadership, it thrived, and it will do so through this crisis too.

But she never felt the same enthusiasm for Veteran like the older Worthington women— running the company was not an acceptable long-term arrangement for her. Knowing full well her brothers weren't capable, she decided to find and marry a suitable replacement. She met Roger at a charity function and immediately saw his potential. Wary of her grandfather and father's histories, she paid close attention to his behavior at the gala, seeing only one, maybe two glasses of wine and eyes that wandered to find the next business titan instead of evening gown cleavage.

She was coy during the courtship to test his character and perseverance. Much to her relief, she discovered he was basically personable, honest, and dull. He couldn't handle his liquor, didn't view sex as a conquest, didn't change his mood if the Dawgs lost on Saturday, and remained friendly and polite to strangers and dogs. He was, in fact, an exceedingly average guy solely interested in becoming a respected businessman with a fat bank account. While not the pick of the litter, Pam knew he would be a responsible steward of the family business, giving her more time and energy to focus on the family.

And the family, specifically her brothers, required her attention. Basically, Scott and Tom were good guys with honest intentions wrapped around idiosyncrasies. Dig a little deeper and discover both are classic male knuckleheads, possessing tons of potential but capable of simple oversights and colossal poor decision-making. She tried to stay out of their lives but found herself drawn back in despite her best efforts.

Her older brother Scott turned out to be the most stable of the two. Not overly athletic, he was the introverted member of the family. Smart and inquisitive, he preferred details, technology, and mechanics over social interaction and dialog. While pleasant to be around, he often seemed to be lost in his own mind which sometimes led to being taken advantage of. His ex-wife Tricia ranked as prime example.

But Scott was doing much better now. With his girls in college and his move away from suburbia isolation, he became more social and got in shape. The life change had done him wonders. He was still the same old Scott but now acted like a more responsible, reliable adult, which Pam desperately needed as little brother Tom had gone completely off the rails.

She turned onto Club Drive to begin the two-and-a-half-mile loop around the country club grounds. Off in the distance were the club's tennis courts, already packed with players enjoying the cooler morning temperature. For a brief moment, Pam thought she saw a teenaged Tom laughing as he smashed forehands at his overmatched older brother. Outwardly, Tom was the complete opposite of Scott: outgoing, loud, athletic, boisterous, and simply fun to be around, yet he was cursed with his grandfather's addiction gene.

He made it only one semester at college since smoking weed and drinking beer with his buddies wasn't deemed an official major. Not mature enough to work at VOA, Tom decided to follow in his grandfather's footsteps and join the Army. It was a perfect fit; he received the discipline he desperately needed while the Army got a gung-ho, skilled recruit.

Tom sailed through basic training at the top of his recruit class and was immediately deployed. Highly skilled with weapons, the Army wanted him to join the sniper corps. Sitting in a deer stand, picking off a buck for venison was something he could do, whereas hiding among rocks, taking out another human being just didn't seem right. In an effort not to disappoint his superiors, he volunteered for the most dangerous and least desirable assignment: Explosives Ordnance Disposal, the bomb squad.

Whenever on leave, he looked hale, healthy, and happy, his posture and physique that of a professional soldier. But after 15 years, he suddenly came home. He refused to share details, but the telltale signs of PTSD were evident…and the substance abuse returned. He'd show glimmers of his old self, and sometimes it would last for a good three months, but he was a broken man not overly interested in seeking help.

Pam did what she could. Being on or near water and away from crowds seemed to bring him the most peace. So, they moved Tom to the family pontoon houseboat up on the lake and brought him to town three days a week for treatment at the VA hospital.

Dark days would often envelop Tom, but he was not a threat to others, only himself. Pam could manage the mild episodes when he'd sequester himself on the boat and usually emerge within a week, looking haggard and emaciated. The severe episodes were a different story. Three to four times a year, he'd simply disappear. The shortest was for ten days and the longest nearly five weeks.

She sensed movement up the street and quickly caught a glimpse of Marcia Tippins out for her own morning walk. Pam found her insufferable and was in no mood to be interrogated about this morning's bombings or hear the exploits of the supposedly perfect Tippins family. Besides, she had too much on her mind already.

She stopped staring at the tennis courts and picked up her pace. Tom was missing again, and she had to find him fast. Though she was positive he had nothing to do with the bombings, she had a hunch the authorities would zero in on the fact a Worthington was an explosives expert. And they couldn't find him first. A confrontation would not end well.

14.

S eamus grabbed his papers from the laser printer and hustled to the conference room where his pulse increased as he scanned the attendees. Standing room only, the space was packed with GBI, Governor Murray, and other seemingly important people he didn't know by name.

At the head of conference table sat Director Sterling with the governor to his right, and Seamus assumed the man in uniform to his left was General Harper of the Georgia National Guard. The carriage of the other men at the table suggested they held some official capacity either in law enforcement or politics. He began to have second thoughts as the assembled team suggested political theater would overshadow real investigation. Seamus gravitated to the far side where his team stood against the wall.

This was the first time Seamus had seen Governor Murray in person. The open UGA windbreaker exposed a solid belly straining the buttons of his dress shirt, and the GBI ball cap looked like it had just been retrieved from the supply closet. The governor fiddled with a manila file on the table while nodding and mumbling "Good morning" to attendees as they arrived. He thought the governor looked to be the most nervous man in the room, which was quite a feat considering how tense Seamus was.

Director Sterling kicked the meeting off promptly at 9:15 a.m. by quickly rattling off the name and responsibility of the VIPs at the table. Seamus was right, the FBI, Homeland Security, State Police, the Transportation Department, and mayor's office were all represented. Once finished, he looked at the governor and gave a slight nod.

"Thank you, Director."

The governor cleared his throat, his voice not as rehearsed as the times Seamus had seen him on TV.

"State agencies have prepared for terrorism hoping to never face the test. It is our job to gain control of the situation, protect the citizens, and track down the sick bastards that did this. The state of Georgia is relying on you men to lead this effort."

Sterling took the cue. "Then let's get to it. Here's what we know so far. Approximately one hundred explosive devices detonated between 4:00 and 4:15 a.m. on billboards along Interstates 75, 85, 95, 16, and 20. At this point, no other targets are known or identified, and only one minor injury confirmed. Within the last several hours, two groups have claimed responsibility, Green War and Make America Beautiful Again. Local law enforcement, the Georgia National Guard, and US Army troops have been mobilized to clear the interstates and secure critical state infrastructure locations. Per Governor Murray, Georgians are requested to stay home. All activities are postponed until we give the all-clear sign. Those are the highlights, gentlemen." Sterling sat back and took a big gulp of water.

The assembled men exchanged glances, stalling for someone to speak first.

Governor Murray broke the silence. "Can it really be as simple as crazed eco-terrorists blowing up some billboards? Don't get me wrong, but that seems more manageable than the..." He hesitated, looking for the right word. "...alternative."

The man introduced as FBI spoke up first. "The concept of eco-terrorism would not cause the same type of public panic, which, as you correctly noted, would be more manageable. However, if Green War is behind this, we should be extremely diligent as they've been known to target pipelines, nuclear facilities, and shipping lanes, all three of which are prevalent in Georgia. Four years ago, they sank two Japanese whaling boats in the China Sea. Bombing billboards is within their capabilities, but the randomness is of question."

The governor pressed on. "What about the second group? Aren't they the ones with the crying Indian?"

The agent grimaced. "No, sir. You're thinking of Keep America Beautiful who ran the famous anti-pollution ad with the Indigenous person."

The governor's flushed cheeks were impossible for the room to ignore.

"This group is Make America Beautiful Again," the agent continued, "and they're not on anyone's radar and very well could be pranksters or crackpots trying to take advantage of the situation. We doubt it's a credible group with the resources necessary to pull this off."

"From the Federal Administration perspective, terrorism is terrorism," the guy from Homeland Security piped in. "We must keep the country secure, and all groups and motives are open as possible suspects until we know for sure what we're dealing with."

The governor looked at the man distrustfully. "I spoke with the president this morning and understand his concerns. He will be visiting Georgia later today to publicly offer his support."

The men all exchanged glances, the Homeland Security guy visibly excited over the thought of a potential brownnose opportunity. Seamus hoped to avoid the president as he had no enthusiasm for politics in general.

Sterling wasn't about to let the conversation go down a rabbit hole. "Eco-terrorism is our best lead but not the only route we're going to investigate. Our top priority is to make sure this isn't some diversionary tactic, and we need all Georgia and Federal resources focused on potential secondary targets. And I mean everything from bridges to water supply and places of worship. General Harper, this is your job. Coordinate with the military and report back to us."

Seamus was taken aback by the general's expression. He looked more like a squirrel straddling the double yellow line than a military man.

The director went on. "From the FBI, we need your experts to help us inspect the bombing locations and your lab to identify the bomb materials to see if that leads us anywhere. We need this quickly. Right now that's the best lead we can get."

Seamus watched the FBI guy nod in agreement.

"Before we break, we have executives from the billboard companies waiting outside to meet with us. For all we know, this may be nothing more than a disgruntled employee or some kind of weird industry war. Let's get them in here to see if they can be any help."

As an assistant scurried out of the conference room, someone on the Antiterrorism Team cracked in a hushed tone, "Pissed-off employee? I thought our jobs sucked. Who knew billboards could be so brutal?"

Seamus wistfully chuckled, longing to one day be included on all the inside jokes.

Seamus carefully watched the billboard executives enter the conference room single file. Four looked like they belonged, dressed in casual professional attire wearing seasonal blazers. The fifth man was out of place, wearing jeans, running shoes, and a rumbled Polo shirt. He either got dressed in a hurry, wasn't fashion conscious, or just didn't care. Seamus immediately felt kinship with the guy who was the outcast of the group just like he was the only person of color in the room.

Seamus glanced at the brief bios he printed out minutes before the meeting and tried to match the men to a name. He assumed the two older blazer clad men were the sons or grandsons of the Veteran and McArthur founders. The youngest two had to be the Consolidated guys, they sucked up to each hand they shook, not necessary behavior from an established Atlanta business. Seamus had the sensation someone was looking at him. He glanced up and locked eyes with the rumpled man who gave him a friendly smile and nodded in greeting. Instinctively, Seamus returned the nod.

The governor immediately rose and went over to one of the Old Atlanta guys and shook his hand in more of a politician-to-donor manner than long-time friends. The executives watched the exchange and made no attempt to interrupt. This guy was the obvious leader of the group. Seamus was surprised to hear the man was not a Worthington or McArthur but Roger Fischer. He discretely opened his folder again to check his bio.

The men were directed to the remaining open conference table seats with Fischer sitting next to the governor. Director Sterling wasted no time on introductions and dove right into an abbreviated version of the details shared earlier with the agency officials. Seamus watched the ad men as Sterling talked. All eyes were following the director's every word with the exception of the rumpled guy, who was scanning the other attendees looking for reaction. Again, his eyes met Seamus. He gave the same smile and nod.

Sterling got to the point. "This morning, two different eco-terrorist groups claimed responsibility for the attacks. We are taking these seriously, but the investigative team must pursue all possibilities, including personal grudges against your companies and potential disgruntled employees."

The comment created a murmur amongst the ad executives.

"Excuse me, Director. Scott Worthington speaking. How were these claims made? Email, phone call, note?"

A GBI agent on the opposite wall spoke up. Seamus recognized him from the Cybersecurity Division.

"One was on Facebook, and the other, Twitter. Neither came from an official site, not that these organizations have sites. They used spoofing tools to mask their identity, and we're currently in the process of tracking the source. These are hard to track down, but we feel we have better than a 50% chance."

"Thank you, Agent." Sterling nodded approval.

Either due to the shock of realizing the rumpled man was actually a Worthington or just plain absentmindedness, Seamus quickly spoke up. "Mr. Worthington, why the interest? Does it matter?"

"Probably not. Just wondering if it was local. Can the claim be pinpointed to Georgia? It just seems so random. Why here instead of, say, South Carolina? Makes no sense, but I agree it's logical to look at the industry and employees first."

"Glad to hear you understand the situation," said Sterling, "because we need your help and resources with the investigation. We request access to management, employee, and office communication. We respect privacy rights but need to find out if any previous threats were made, even if benign. Time is critical. That's why we're asking for your approval now rather than having to track down a judge for a subpoena."

The Consolidated guys began to voice tepid objections about needing corporate approval, but Fischer abruptly cut them off. "Director, we're at your disposal. Let us know what you need, and you've got it. What else do you want from us?"

The governor nodded at Fischer appreciatively.

"Thank you, Roger," Sterling replied. "We also need your help in damage and risk assessment. Law enforcement and military resources will secure each location for evidence collection. What we need from you is a complete inventory of all billboard locations, how many of your total were destroyed, and construction specs for our crime technicians. Of greater importance, we need your expertise in the structural integrity of the damaged billboards and inspection of those left untouched."

Rusty McArthur was the first to react. "Director, we can supply a complete inventory of locations and construction specs, but if you're asking us to go out and inspect every billboard in the state, that poses a problem."

"That's exactly what we're requesting."

Rusty continued. "Well, sir, the sheer number would require an immense amount of time and manpower. To do what you ask would take hours, even days of overtime, and cost us a great deal of money. Our budget is pretty tight."

Roger was about to speak when the governor cut in. "We understand the measures we're asking of you. In such an emergency, we may be able to find state dollars or work with your insurance companies on some type of compensation plan."

Roger was visibly relieved. "Thank you, Governor. Rusty's understandably nervous. The damage done will definitely hurt our business, and adding extra labor on top of that puts us in a tough spot. We're more than happy to help, but it will be a strain on all of us."

Scott spoke up again. "Roger and Rusty might be concerned about money but not me. Inspecting poles that were blown up is easy and no problem, but there's no way I'm sending an employee up a pole to see if there's a bomb or not. It's a dangerous enough job maintaining them. Checking for bombs is not in the job description."

The other executives quickly realized safety was a much better argument and unanimously jumped on Scott's rationale; safety of employees sounded a lot better than being cheap.

Seamus stood watching the discussion that broke out. Having made his point, Scott sat back and resumed his careful observation of the group and their comments. Seamus couldn't help but like the guy. He was logical, thoughtful, and, at least based by his dress, a man who didn't posture to power and authority figures. Again, Seamus and Worthington's eyes met, and again, he smiled and nodded.

Not shifting his gaze, Seamus unconsciously spoke again. "Helicopters." The room became quiet as Seamus captured their attention. The director gave him a quizzical look.

Seamus went on. "On the drive over, I saw we have helicopters in the air. Let's use them to verify if more billboards have bombs. Once every location is determined to be safe, these guys can proceed."

Scott nodded his approval. "That makes sense. You'd be able to get close enough to see if a pole's been tampered with and cover ground a lot faster. By the time you're done, we can have our resources together and an inspection plan in place. Probably best if we pool our resources and divide up the state, so we're not all trying to cover the same ground."

Governor Murray brightened at the idea. "General, what do you think?"

Seamus was shocked a grown man, who looked so fine in uniform, could be cursed with such a high-pitched, squeaky voice.

"Absolutely. Simple change of orders. We just need to know what to look for." The general nervously looked around the room for validation.

Scott continued to concentrate his attention on Seamus. "Give me an hour, and I can have a map of all the billboards in the state along with common construction schematics and what you should look for to tell if it's been tampered with."

One of the Consolidated guys piped in. "We should be able to do the same."

"Not necessary," Scott countered. "Our maps include all of your, Rusty's, and the independents' billboards. Important to track the competition."

Stunned at the local yokel sophistication, the Consolidated guy sank back in his chair.

The meeting adjourned with the governor, Roger, Rusty, and Director Sterling leaving the conference room while the remaining men were left to figure out the logistics. Seamus was pleased when he was appointed as Scott's primary contact for all data coming out of Veteran. His preference had been to go directly to their office, but email would have to suffice as Seamus was needed at headquarters to further investigate the billboard companies, as well as for a review of Green War and Make America Beautiful Again. He met Scott at the door with his business card in hand.

"Mr. Worthington, we didn't officially meet. Inspector Seamus O'Reilly." He stuck out his hand.

"Good morning. Please call me Scott," he said as he accepted the handshake. "Great name. May I call you Seamus, or do you prefer Inspector?"

Up close Seamus noticed he had a calm face with age wrinkles amassed around his eyes and mouth, his tousled hair was grayer and thinner than it appeared at a distance. He was in good shape but carried some excess skin around his neck, suggesting he had not always been on the slender side. Some would say he fell in the disheveled category, but Seamus thought he was simply ambivalent of others' opinion. He guessed they were about the same age.

"Inspector or Seamus, whatever suits you." He tried to mask his surprise over Scott's casualness.

"I'd prefer to call you Seamus. It's just more fun to say. My name is rather boring, don't you think?"

Seamus handed him his card. "Here's my cell phone and email address. Once you get the documents, give me a call and I'll lead you through our secure site to download the information."

"Any particular format? Believe it or not, some of the engineering schematics for billboards are complicated. DITA is our standard, but I can merge over to PDF or JPEG, if need be."

"Good question, Mr. Worthington. That's a little out of my league. I'll make sure to have IT support with me when it comes time to download."

"It's Scott, Seamus. I'm not my dad. With the road closures, it may take a while to get to the office, but once there, it won't take me long."

"We need this ASAP. I'll arrange an escort to get you through the roadblocks. I'd also like to meet with you later today to pick your brain on the dynamics of the industry and get your take on things," Seamus said with growing confidence.

"Seamus, I'm more than happy to help, but I have a feeling you guys will have your hands full with other stuff. Every day I have breakfast at Duke's Fine Food. Meet me there at 7:30 tomorrow if you still think my opinion would help."

"Okay. Sounds reasonable."

The men shook hands again, and Seamus turned back toward the conference room before having second thoughts.

"Mr. Worthington, er, Scott? I actually have a couple of more questions."

"Fire away."

"Roger's your brother-in-law, yet he runs the company instead of you. What's up with that?"

"I'm just not cut out for managing or leading people. My sister got that trait from dad, but I didn't. Hell, I couldn't even manage my own marriage. I like to think of myself as a friendly introvert, good with people but better working alone with detail, logistics, planning, that sort of stuff. I spoke today because of the topic. Roger was out of his comfort zone and knew better than to make any suggestions. That man couldn't change a tire, but I guarantee you he's smooth talking the governor out of something as we speak." Scott lifted his palms. "Just look at me. Does this look like a leader?"

Seamus gave a half-shrug. "I think you sell yourself short, but I understand where you're coming from. Do you mind taking orders from Roger? Do you like the situation?"

"Roger's not bad. He leaves me alone and respects what I do. Besides, my paycheck's bigger and he can't fire me. In all honesty, what I don't like is the business. Sure wish granddad had started a hardware store or dry cleaner instead of billboards. Damn eyesores, if you ask me. Bet most of Georgia agrees and will pool defense money whenever you catch the culprit."

Seamus watched Scott walk out to the parking lot with his head spinning in thought. He found Scott relatable. Seamus's mom had called him a friendly introvert too. But what was this about hating the business and catching the culprit, singular? What does this guy know?

15.

"This is bullshit!" he yelled as he grabbed a dirty t-shirt off the floor and threw it at his TV.

JR stomped about his glorified sharecropper's shack, ranting above the TV blaring more updates on the bombings.

"Goddammit, here we sit on our asses, not doing a damn thing, while pansy-assed eco-freaks show they got the balls to fight. Blowing up billboards makes no sense when the real war is returning rights to white men." He was so mad he could spit, which he did in his trusty spit cup.

His militia's inaction was a somewhat legitimate reason for JR to be angry, not that he was lacking for an excuse to be pissed. His daddy bragged that when JR was born and the doc slapped his behind, baby Jerry Ray took a swipe back at the doc. The few surviving baby pictures showed a scrawny little towhead with crinkled brow and menacing stare.

It wasn't easy for JR growing up poor in middle Georgia. It didn't help that his dad was a racist with incredibly poor work habits and lackluster skills as a criminal. Eddie Ray bounced around the Georgia prison system with such regularity he deserved to earn membership reward points. Whenever he was home, he'd drill his son on the superiority of white men and how they were the real victims of today's society. It never dawned on JR that his dad's trouble might be traced to the fact he only had a second-grade education, was lazier than an opossum, and was more interested in spending money than making it. Eddie Ray was not the best role model, but his son idolized him.

JR was only ten when Eddie Ray's Aryan rants at Jackson State Prison finally got him knifed. Though a sorry excuse for a dad, Eddie Ray's death left no male figure in his life until his sophomore year in high school when Andy Nelson came to teach at Upchurch County High School. Now, just the thought of him boiled his blood.

"Fucking Nelson! You're the reason I'm stuck here with a bunch of pansy asses. Some damn militia this is," JR muttered under his breath while cracking open his last Bud Light. Who cares if it's only 11:00 in the morning? JR needed a beer.

JR never liked school. To be popular you needed to have at least one redeeming trait: a winning personality, book smarts, athleticism, or a really cool skill. The cards were stacked against him. A known sourpuss, JR's personality would never win anyone over. He had neither the intelligence nor discipline to excel with books. And despite being somewhat agile, his short stature and slight build eliminated his chances on the sporting field. This left him with trying to develop one really cool skill.

It was only natural for JR to gravitate towards fighting. What other options were there for an angry young man with limited intelligence? He quickly learned that his best skill was his ability to take a ruthless beating and still get up. His pugnaciousness could not be matched, but his size only intimidated grade schoolers. Never one to back down, he quickly developed the nickname Scrap for his scrappy, relentless pursuit despite incredibly poor odds. It was easy to doubt his common sense, but no one could say he wasn't tough.

Then Andy Nelson, a Marine veteran and alumnus of Upchurch County High School, returned to teach Social Studies and started a JROTC program. JR was among the first to sign up and liked the JROTC about as much as he liked anything. The drilling and marching were boring, but the uniform was cool and he actually made a couple of new friends. More importantly, in Mr. Nelson he found an adult, male figure he respected and trusted…or so he thought.

During his senior year with the encouragement of Mr. Nelson, JR announced to his mom that on his 18th birthday he planned on enlisting in the US Army. Momma was proud but mostly relieved since she had yet to tell JR she was moving to Alabama with a siding salesman she met in Macon as soon as the last stanza of "Pomp and Circumstance" ended.

JR tilted his head back to suck the last remaining drops out of the Bud Light bottle and tossed it across the room in the general vicinity of the trash can. It bounced and skidded across the well-worn wooden floors and spun two rotations under the kitchen table. On TV, the governor was droning on about it being some isolated incident when he announced the president was coming to Georgia to offer his support.

"Fuck! Not you too!" Like many in the movement, he was convinced the president understood what was at stake for guys like JR. "Don't you be getting worked up over the eco-freaks. They ain't the enemy!"

He resisted the urge to kick the TV to shreds. He needed another beer and some space away from this shithole. He grabbed his truck keys, stuck a handgun in his pocket, and stormed out the door.

Just as he was getting in his truck, a voice called out, "Hey, JR, where you going?" It was Mike, standing across the small field with a M4 cradled in his right arm.

"None of your damn business. Just away from here," JR shouted back.

"You're on duty at two. Better be back to relieve me."

"Yeah, yeah, I'll relieve you one of these days, you dumbass lughead," JR mumbled under his breath. He fired up his truck and took off in search of beer.

The drive to Stonewall's took 25 minutes, a route JR made so often he could do it blindfolded, which, in reality, he'd done many a time after the 140-pound man pounded ten beers in his favorite bar. About the only advantage of his current situation was the county sheriff was afraid of the congressman and the American Liberation Militia.

Stonewall's was an institution in Upchurch County, a hardscrabble bar serving real ice-cold beer and none of that microbrewery crap. The outside wasn't much to look at, the inside only marginally better due to the low lighting. The U-shaped bar was to the right of the front door and, even at 11:30 on a Sunday morning, three guys were already camped on stools. The bar itself was actually quite beautiful. Dark well-polished wood with rounded trimming, comfortable for leaning against, and brass piping about six inches off the floor for foot-propping.

But the focal point was the bust of Stonewall. Centered on the wall behind the bar, splitting the liquor bottle shelving in two and above the old-time cash register, was an elaborate alcove where a marble Stonewall Jackson gazed over his admiring flock. The lighting for the bust was perfect, not too bright to reflect off the marble and not so dim where his strong features would get lost in the shadows. It was quite a work of art.

Not wanting to socialize, or see more damn TV coverage of the bombings, JR grabbed a stool at a high-top with his back to the bar. A beer magically appeared on the table.

"Here you go, JR. Don't think I've seen you on Sunday morning before."

"Thanks Ed," JR mumbled. The old, goateed man simply nodded and returned to the bar.

With his back to the other patrons, JR scanned the bar in hopes the comforting surroundings would improve his mood. Stonewall's was decorated in a low budget style with flags being the primary wall covering. Stars and Bars of various sizes outnumbered the one American flag even though the American flag did occupy the most prominent location on the wall directly opposite the entrance. Posters and signs were tacked up haphazardly: babes on Harley's, babes washing pickup trucks, a smoking guns Yosemite Sam with the caption "Don't Tread on Me," and neon signs of every Anheuser-Busch beer product. Despite it carrying memories of Mr. Nelson's second colossal con on JR, he still thought it was the best bar he'd ever been in.

JR took a healthy gulp of beer and continued to stew. He'd kind of forgiven Mr. Nelson for the first con—his brief, disastrous military career. Even JR admitted his post high school job prospects in Upchurch County were bleak and the military was worth a shot. But he was past forgiving the man for the second con—how he manipulated JR into joining the ALM, pretending like they were friends or something, united in a common fight. JR thought of the conversation they had at this exact high-top after his army discharge.

Mr. Nelson gave him a knowing nod. "Been there, buddy. I love my country, but my idea of America just seemed to clash with the brass. Hell, I don't even know if some of the guys in my unit were actually dudes, and I was supposed to give my life for them! No thanks, enough of that shit for me."

JR was relieved that Mr. Nelson understood. "You got that right. I expected Black guys. We got enough of them round here that I could deal with that. But toss in all the women, the Mexicans, and the gays…hell, we even had Muslims! It was just too much."

JR gave a nod to the Stars and Bars. "If we'd have won, things would've been different."

Mr. Nelson lifted his beer. "Amen, JR."

They clinked longnecks and both took a manly gulp.

Mr. Nelson leaned in and lowered his voice. "JR, I have an opportunity for you. I can line you up with a job, and then on weekends, you help us train recruits for the war we all know is coming next. Our war to return some sense to this great country."

JR had only been home for a week spending most of his time at Stonewall's milking his military service for free beer and not really thinking about what he was going to do next. "I sure could use a job," he admitted.

"Well, it's yours if you want it."

In the three years since that fateful meeting at Stonewall's, JR had been a faithful lieutenant of the American Liberation Militia while doing odd jobs at Deer Bend Plantation, the fancy hunting lodge across the street owned by a bigwig US congressman. The mission had so much potential but turned out to be a frustrating waste of time.

It was the complete inaction that drove him crazy. At least in the Army they did stuff. Aside from occasional target practice, drilling, and the rare killing, here they basically sat on their butts and talked big. Even worse, when they actually did do something, they acted more like hippy liberals by staging wimpy protests at the state capitol and in Stone Mountain Park. Charlottesville was the closest they came to delivering on their training, but then rank amateurs messed up their momentum.

A fresh beer arrived without the asking. "You look like you've got a lot on your mind today, JR." This time Ed didn't immediately retreat back behind the bar.

JR took his eyes off the babes using power tools poster on the far wall and looked at the crusty old proprietor. "I can't believe eco-freaks have more gumption than we do. I'm just damn tired of cooling off and waiting for the right opportunity. It's getting too much for me to take."

The wizened old man nodded in understanding. "Maybe you're thinking about this wrong. This could be just the diversion you need. Strike while the focus is on something else."

JR knew he should listen. The man had seen it all. "But Ed, I don't get to call the shots. Hell, if I did, shit would've been done years ago."

"I don't doubt that JR, but you're thinking big picture. I'm not talking about the mission, I'm talking about you." With that, the old man returned to the bar.

JR sat peeling the beer bottle label, trying to figure out what the old man meant. It took a moment then his words sank in. JR chugged the beer, put a ten spot on the table, and left without a word.

The afternoon brightness blinded JR. He paused for a moment for his eyes to adjust. The old man was right. Time to think about yourself, don't rely on others to make you feel better. JR just needed to figure out who, or what, would feel his wrath.

His direction determined, he hopped in the truck to report for guard duty.

16.

The loud pounding on the door was followed by a muffled, "Mr. Worthington! We'd like to ask you a couple of questions!"

Scott left his office to check on the disturbance and was shocked to see a TV reporter standing outside the Veteran Outdoor lobby's glass door with a cameraman capturing her furious raps. He quickly sought shelter in the office bathroom to figure out what he should do.

It was a little past 1:30 on Sunday afternoon, and he'd finished reviewing the files via video conference with GBI Inspector Seamus O'Reilly a good 30 minutes ago. He chastised himself for lollygagging around the office instead of leaving before the nosy reporter showed up. He studied himself in the bathroom mirror hoping she'd lose interest, but her persistent knocking made it clear the reporter had settled in for the long haul, determined to wait him out.

He knew he couldn't hide in the bathroom forever and briefly wished he had an iota of Roger's glibness. Scott had delayed long enough—he ran his fingers through his hair, splashed cold water on his face, and steadied himself for the pending inquisition.

The reporter was on him before he locked up the building. "Sir, sir! Jessica Richards, Action 10 News. Can we get a statement from you?"

Scott tried his hardest to look solemn for the reporter, but words escaped him. He lowered his head and hurried toward his truck.

The reporter scurried after him, quite nimble in her heels. "Sir, how does it feel to have your company be the victim of such a horrific act?"

The inanity of the question stopped Scott in his tracks. He spun to find the reporter at arm's length with the sweating, panting cameraman twisting the camera's focus as he straggled behind. Scott wanted desperately to say something witty or profound, but his mouth just hung open.

The reporter thrust the microphone to within an inch of his face. "Sir, any comment for our viewers?"

"We have no comment at this time," Scott stammered before turning and escaping to the safety of his truck.

He drove a block making certain the enterprising reporter was not hot on his tail before summoning his truck's GPS system. "What the fastest way to Brookhaven Vista?" Scott asked. Georgia recently enacted hands-free mobile legislation—for communication devices, that is, while the Carry Everywhere Law meant a Georgian could still clutch a handgun while driving—so having a vehicle voice system was a must.

Scott debated returning Pam's earlier voice mails but instead spent most of the drive home fantasizing about how life might be like without the anchor of VOA around his neck. He didn't know if he was up for such a radical change. Forging uncharted territory was not a very Scott-like behavior, yet getting a divorce turned out to be one of the best things he'd done. Maybe leaving VOA would be a good thing...but then again, maybe not.

Sparky lost his mind when Scott entered the apartment. The dog sure knew how to make him feel loved and appreciated. His whining and barking intensified once he caught a whiff of the aged-to-doggie-perfection sausage Scott still had from Duke's earlier in the morning. Scott decided calling his sister could wait because Sparky needed a walk and he could use a pint.

Dunleavy's was a great Irish bar on the ground floor. The inside looked like it had been shipped over directly from Killybegs, and outside was a large, dog-friendly patio. Two women from his building were camped out on the patio enjoying margaritas in the sunshine. Scott never understood why you'd go to an Irish bar for margaritas when two authentic Mexican joints were in the complex. Today it didn't matter. He was glad to see the girls.

Emily, who lived across the hall, stood as she saw Scott and Sparky approaching, "Scott, you poor thing! We just saw you on TV! Come join us! We have an extra seat!" Emily spoke like she texted, every sentence required an exclamation point.

Scott never partook in the sexual shenanigans often found in upscale apartment living, opting instead to take on a more fatherly/ big brother role. He was sought out for occasional career or relationship advice, both of which he was totally unsuited to provide since he failed at marriage and enjoyed the complete job security of a family run business. The relationship sagas Emily shared only steeled his resolve to avoid complex affairs and filled him with pity for her suitors.

"Good afternoon, ladies." He tried to sound solemn. "Thanks for the offer. I'd love some company."

With Emily was Whitney, and once through the patio gate, Sparky was beside himself trying to decide which of the avowed dog lovers he should pounce on first.

"Are you okay? What a horrible day." As her voice quavered, Scott couldn't tell if Emily was full of pity, fear, or margaritas.

Derek interrupted before Scott could answer. "Hey, Scott, you want something?"

Derek and Johnny ranked nearly as high as Maggie when it came to taking care of customers. Derek could wait more tables than any two of his coworkers, and Johnny was an amazing barkeep.

"Hey Derek, I'll have a Guinness. How about some fish and chips too? And tell Johnny not to worry about the pour. Today, speed is more important than perfection."

"You got it," Derek replied as he was already halfway through the door.

Whitney reached over and touched Scott's arm. "Comfort food. You must really be upset."

"Frazzled more than anything. Been too busy with the GBI today for everything to really sink in."

"The GBI!" Emily jumped in. "You had to meet the GBI?!"

"And the governor, FBI, and some people from Homeland Security." Scott paused for effect. "They pulled everyone in on this."

The two women began talking excitedly at the same time, and Scott only heard a word or two from each, enough to see how anxious they were. Derek broke the chattering as he returned with Scott's beer, a bowl of water for Sparky, and a couple of milk bones. Of course, the Guinness was beautiful; as two-time reigning champion of the Atlanta Perfect Pint competition, Johnny knew what he was doing.

"That was fast. Thanks, Derek."

"Johnny and I grabbed someone else's order. No way he wasn't going to do you right. Your food should be out soon."

Scott lifted his beer in a toast. "To Veteran Outdoor Advertising."

Whitney leaned in. "What did the GBI say? Do you really think it's Muslim terrorists or some Antifa group?"

"You've been watching too much TV." Scott gave her the half-disapproving paternal look he learned from raising his own daughters and then savored another sip. "Ladies, you really have nothing to worry about. Real terrorists want to do physical harm.

They wouldn't do a hundred little bombs on inanimate objects. They'd do a couple of big bombs where people are hanging out." Scott knew better but couldn't resist. "They'd pick someplace like here where folks are having a good time and not suspecting anything."

The women gasped and began nervously looking around at the other patrons. Emily regrouped and pinched Scott's arm. "Sometimes, you can be such a jerk! That wasn't funny!"

"You're right ladies. Sorry about that. Listen, I imagine it's all over the news, but two different eco-terrorist groups have claimed responsibility. Since only billboards were blown up, the GBI thinks that's the most likely explanation. They're looking at them along with other environmental groups or employees that might hate outdoor advertising. I agree with them. That makes the most sense."

Emily gave a sigh of relief. "Environmentalist or disgruntled employees? I guess I can see that! Do you really think an employee hates you or Veteran that much?!"

Scott looked at the women and suddenly felt tired of keeping the façade. While they might be gossips about neighborly indiscretions, they had been true friends that held his personal confessions in confidence. It was time to come clean.

"To tell you the truth, I hate Veteran that much, and I've been thinking this might be my chance to do something different," Scott admitted, then noticing their expressions, he hurriedly continued. "Of course, I didn't do it! You know me, I'm too much of a chicken to do anything crazy. Hell, being sensible is about my only redeeming quality. It's just...well, personally I've discovered how exciting and fulfilling a new start can be, and I see this as an opportunity to do the same with my professional life. Understand?"

With impeccable timing, Derek bound out the door with Scott's fish and chips. The interruption provided just enough time for Scott's comments to sink in.

Without her normal exuberance, Emily spoke with an uncharacteristic calm. "That's great, Scott. The circumstances are weird, but I'm glad for you. You do seem a little different today, I mean that in a good way."

His history with Emily was the longest and most complex. He was grateful she was somewhat encouraging. Whitney mumbled in agreement.

"Thanks, Emily. That means a lot. So, enough with the gloom and doom. Any good dirt from the weekend?"

The women were grateful the subject changed and went off on the previous evening's adventures. Scott enjoyed his meal and second Guinness as Emily and Whitney one-upped each other on who was drunker while dissing on a new tenant each thought was a floozy. He was content sitting in the sun, sharing their company and contemplating a third beer, but he couldn't ignore his sister any longer. After a round of hugs and Sparky adoration, Scott retreated to his apartment to call Pam.

"Afternoon, Sis."

"It's about time, Scotty. Roger's been home for hours. I expected you to call earlier."

"Sorry, Sis, thought he would have told you I had to go to the office for the GBI. It took me longer than expected. What's going on?"

"It's Tom. I'm really worried about him. He's on the run again."

"Figured as much. Since when?"

"It's only been a little more than two weeks, but this is different. Then with the explosions today, Roger assured me you two didn't mention him to the GBI."

"It won't take them long to figure out his army past. We both know he didn't have anything to do with it, so there's nothing to worry about." Scott tried his best to be reassuring.

"How can you be so sure? He's so unpredictable."

Scott thought he detected a hint of accusation in his sister's voice. "That's why it's not him. Whoever did this had to plan it out weeks, months in advance. Tom isn't capable of that. Don't you still have to coordinate all of his appointments?"

"You're right, but I still worry what he might do if confronted by police. That's why we have to find him first. The big problem is I'm at a dead end. Things just aren't adding up."

"In what way?"

Scott not only loved his sister but admired and respected her. She possessed the best qualities of her brothers without the excess baggage they both carried. Pam was the most talented sibling and excelled at everything she did, as she demonstrated during her brief stint at Veteran, but wielding power or authority never interested her. Compassion drove her, which was why she was so determined to be the family guardian and why her spare hours were spent working the trenches of low-visibility charities rather than accepting the countless invites to chair highfalutin society galas like the other Central City Golf Club women. Very little shine but tons of polish, Pam was a solid citizen and person. He was damn proud of her.

And he knew when to trust her instincts. Roger often bragged about her woman's intuition, but Scott knew it was more than that. She had a visceral sense of people, more so with her brothers, where she often knew what they were thinking and feeling before they did.

"This week I just felt something wasn't right, so I decided to start looking for him earlier than usual. He showed up at the VA for his therapy session with Dr. Shaw and the group meeting, but once he left, he just disappeared. I went to all his favorite homeless vet camps in town, ran into a bunch of the regulars, but no one had seen him for a while."

"Even the Mayor of Clairmont?" Scott asked, referring to the encampment at the underpass on South Peachtree Creek next to the VA hospital.

"The Mayor of Clairmont was having a rough day when I saw him Wednesday. Two new squatters at the camp and neither vets. So, I went back yesterday. He was the most lucid I'd seen in quite some time and positive Tom hadn't been around."

"Guess he went to the mountains then." Scott was trying to be reassuring but knew Pam was a step ahead.

"That's what I thought or hoped. Yesterday I went up to the marina to check the boat. No one had seen him since he went to town and all of his gear was still on the boat. His sleeping bag, hammock, weed, everything. Scott, he can live off the land for weeks, but he's never gone up to the mountains empty handed! You know how paranoid he is of snakes? Even his hunting knife was still in the drawer!"

"You're right, Sis. Something's wrong. You want me to make another round at the camps this afternoon?"

"You can if you'd like. I'm thinking about contacting Andrea, see if she can help out."

"Andrea? We haven't talked to her in forever. Is she even in the states?"

"Scotty, maybe you haven't talked to her, but I have. We had lunch last month when she had a layover at Hartsfield. She's stationed at Fort Bragg in North Carolina, promoted to lieutenant colonel."

Scott was honestly surprised. "I'll be. I had no idea you two were so close."

"She loves our brother, and I love her for being his one remaining loyal, Army friend. You know she checks in on him more than you do. Sorry, I know that didn't sound right."

"That's okay, I know what you mean. I'm just poorly suited for that kind of stuff."

"You make up for it in other ways. Anyway, she's had a standing offer to come help if we need her, says she built up time for leave just in case."

Scott knew his sister was right. "With all the other stuff going on, it's probably a pretty good idea. Let me know what she says."

Pam gave the deep little chuckle that Scott loved so much. He could sense her smile over the phone. "She says she'll be here tomorrow afternoon. We're meeting at the Starbuck's near our house at one. Can you join us?"

"You little imp! Why didn't you just tell me you had it all arranged?" Scott retorted with more amusement than anger.

"I wanted you to feel like you contributed. Be there tomorrow?"

17.

Maggie was expending more energy tossing and turning in bed than an average morning shift at Duke's. Even cuddling her only childhood keepsake, a well-loved koala stuffed animal named Zippy, didn't provide comfort. She wanted to blame her secondhand mattress but knew it wasn't the guilty party for her lack of sleep. Even a king mattress in a fancy hotel wouldn't stop the thoughts from dancing in her head.

She enjoyed mostly a stress-free life—moderate expectations and modest living removed most complications. Then yesterday set her on edge. Not the bombings as she knew the explosions weren't a threat. No, it was Scott's near giddiness to meet with the GBI and her realization how much she truly cared for him. Life's so much easier when you're flying solo.

Maggie snatched her wind-up alarm clock off the night stand and held it close to her face, straining to see the time. Best she could tell it was 2:30 a.m. She'd functioned on less sleep before, so she might as well start her day a couple of hours earlier instead of flopping in bed and getting more worked up. Maggie got up, tossed a robe over her tattered University of Memphis t-shirt, and left her cramped bedroom to brew a pot of coffee.

Her feet felt the warped wooden floors as she blindly shuffled down the dark short hallway past the tiny, powder blue tiled bathroom to the kitchen doorway. Just walking in the house, she felt its personality. The slightly musty scent found in older homes saying it had experienced the many joys and sorrows of life. The rented Scottdale bungalow had its own soul, and it was a calming, gentle spirit. Maggie flipped the light switch and admired the kitchen, her favorite of the five small rooms. Still trapped in the '60s, the counters were Formica with the original appliances some would consider an ugly mustard yellow. Maggie didn't care. She loved them even though they weren't Energy Star compliant.

She rented the house from Bob Hopper, who grew up in the small house with his mom and sister. The neighborhood of rickety wooden homes, at least those still surviving gentrification, had been built by the now closed Scottdale textile mill where Hop's mom had worked. Maggie told him she loved the house's character and not to worry about fixing up anything as long as he didn't mind if she painted some walls and turned the detached garage into a workshop. Hop was touched by her enthusiasm and knew his mom would want this woman to be the house's caretaker.

She added two extra scoops of coffee grounds to compensate for getting up so early, poured in the water, and hit brew. As the coffee maker began its gurgle, she felt fleeting envy for those Keurig machines that cranked out a fast cup of coffee. The selfish thought quickly passed. Not having Energy Star appliances was bad enough. No way she could be responsible for adding more of those damn little dispenser cups to the Earth's plastic waste crisis.

She stretched her arms over her head while arching her back, slowly working the kinks out of her body in hopes that might help her relax. Her mom taught her techniques to compartmentalize her worries in grade school shortly after her dad abandoned the family. The irony wasn't lost on Maggie that the main periods of her life when she needed mom's coping skills were her college and professional years, the two experiences her mom never had but urged her daughter to try.

Maggie liked college and would have liked it more if Mom didn't die during her undergrad years. A serious student, she didn't have time or money for the hijinks many in her program felt were a college requirement. Her professors were so impressed they urged her to stick around for a graduate degree. With her mom gone and not knowing what she wanted to do with her life, she readily agreed. Despite her studies and TA responsibilities, she continued to waitress.

After graduation she dove into the real world. It did not turn out as planned. In her zeal to complete grad school and "grow up," she grossly misjudged the realities of adulthood. Out on her own, the demands, responsibilities, and expectations found in the real world gnawed at her soul. She fumed over workplace inequities, couldn't fathom the general public's abuse of Mother Nature, got downright angry over self-righteous religious posturing, and despised the social status hierarchies. No matter how hard she tried, Maggie knew she didn't fit in. After carefully developing a plan, she left her previous life behind and became a gypsy waitress looking to create her own little world.

The beeping coffee pot snapped Maggie out of her prolonged stretch. She grabbed a Duke's Fine Foods souvenir coffee mug out of the cabinet, poured herself what was likely the first of many cups, and took a seat at the funky art deco kitchen table she found at a local flea market.

Maggie took a sip of coffee, the vinyl seat squeaked under her as she slouched down in thought. The ticking second hand of the sunflower wall clock was the only sound in the room.

This is unacceptable, she thought. I need to be busy, or this will be a long night.

She got up, found her thermos in the small pantry, and filled it with the freshly brewed coffee. She grabbed her workshop key off the hook and went out the backdoor, still in her robe and bare feet. The backyard was not much larger than a basketball court and, like the front, dominated by a towering oak tree. The early fall green acorns made the short, barefooted walk to the garage a test of her pain tolerance.

Standing in her garage shop, Maggie studied her immaculate workbench. She wanted to do something whimsical since her last project involved delicate, detailed work which left her physically and mentally exhausted. The workbench sat perfectly clean, awaiting her next burst of creative energy. With furrowed brow, she stood thinking. The energy was there, but unfortunately her creativity was tapped out. Turning from the workbench, she opened the supply shelves on the opposite wall to see if her odd assortment of scavenged materials might provide inspiration. She began to wonder if she was too distracted to distract herself...is that even possible?

Knowing she had to do something, Maggie rummaged around until she found supplies from two years ago. Her neighbors still kid her about her wind chime phase, though they all proudly display them on their front porches and back patios. It's funny how something as simple as a handmade gift can bring people together. When she first moved in, everyone was friendly but somewhat aloof. They'd wave when she drove up the street, but that was about it. Once she began passing out her wind chimes, the waves became actual conversations. Connection, even over something as tacky as a scrap metal wind chime, is a base emotion everyone seeks and too often lacks.

Perched on a stool with her soldering gun and various odds and ends, Maggie got to work. As hoped, she got lost in the details, so engrossed she didn't realize the sky was lightening in the east and it was time for her to go to work. She stretched, closed her eyes, and took a quick mental checkup. At last, her mind was clear.

She maintained that sought after tranquility until about 7:00 in the morning. It quickly dissipated right when Scott took his seat at Duke's and told her a guy from the GBI was meeting him there for breakfast in about 30 minutes. Maggie could not hide her concern.

"Really? I thought you talked with them yesterday. Why does he want to talk again?"

Scott gave her a reassuring look. "I'm sure by now he knows all about Tom, probably also knows that few people hate Veteran more than me. Doubt it's anything more than that."

"I hope you're right."

"Relax, Mags. Trust me. Besides, I think you'll like him. He's a good-looking Black guy with a killer name...Seamus O'Reilly. I watched him closely yesterday. He seems to be sensible, a thinking man."

"I'm reserving judgment. I'll get your coffee and hold your order 'til he gets here."

Scott smiled warmly and touched her left hand. "You're the best, Maggie."

At least business today had picked up at Duke's. Waiting on the customers might help her from worrying about Scott talking with the GBI.

18.

om's eyes darted around the room while his brain computed with a clarity he hadn't felt in years. He immediately recognized the knob-less steel door and slightly squirmed his body to confirm he was still strapped to a prison hospital bed. He craned his neck and spotted changing leaves through the small window, glistening in the morning light. Strangely, the sense of panic had subsided, and he wasn't the least bit angry. He should be royally pissed, but he only felt, well, best guess is serene. How could that be?

Drugs, no other explanation. Tom took pride in being a jack of all trades but did consider himself to be an expert in certain areas—backwoods survival, deep water navigation, explosive devices, and mind-altering drugs. What began as a recreational pursuit graduated to a coping mechanism and eventually to doctors' prescriptions. No doubt about it, docs always had the best shit.

The problem about docs and meds was that they'd give you too much of what you didn't want, not enough of what you liked, chastise you if you didn't follow the dosage, and generally didn't consider how they'd interact. Take morphine. They juiced him up in Kandahar, and the initial euphoria was a pleasant mind erase. But after several days, he couldn't remember his sister's name, and his bowels felt like rocks. Their solution was to add a stool softener while they kept the morphine drip flowing. The first dump was almost more painful than the injury.

Tom looked up at the IV bag and wondered what they hell they were giving him. He ran a couple of math exercises through his head. His cognitive thinking was good, so it couldn't be any of the 'ine' drugs. The antidepressants he'd tried in the past usually gave him dry mouth and a low pulse rate. He couldn't check his pulse, but his breathing was steady and his lips were moist. Whatever they were feeding him was damn good…and he wanted more.

The door opened and in came a different guy from yesterday. Also in camo, this one was scrawny with a hyper look in his eye and the quick sudden movements of someone who was paranoid or lacked confidence, probably both.

"Morning Warrant Officer. You seem calm today. Finally chill out?"

"Must admit I feel tip-top this morning. And who are you?"

"Go by JR. I'm Captain of this here unit."

Dr. Shaw entered behind the scrawny guy. "Don't listen to JR. We don't go by rank around here, except for you Warrant Officer. You've earned it."

JR gave Dr. Shaw a quick, lethal glare then stepped aside.

"So, Tom, how you feeling? Must admit you look pretty good this morning."

"Gotta tell you, Doc, this is best I've felt in a long time. What's in the bag? Some kind of magic elixir?"

The doc gave a hearty laugh. "Magic elixir. I love it, wonder if they'd let me patent that! I've been studying your charts, pouring through your history of diagnoses, and created, well, I guess you could call it your own signature cocktail."

"Whatever it is, keep it coming. My mood is definitely elevated, and I don't feel any kind of drug hangover. It's calming too. No agitation or anxiety."

"That's great news, and let's hope we're on to something. But we best temper our enthusiasm and let it play out, see how long it lasts and if any side effects pop up. We're treading unknown ground, so it might take several days to make sure you're stable."

"I'm good with that. Anything to make this feeling last. For once, I'll do whatever you say."

"Excellent. I'll check your vitals, then we'll get you out of those restraints and let you go outside with JR to get some fresh air. We're still going to limit your activity and keep you in a secure space until we know for sure how you're reacting, but no harm in letting you move around some."

A broad smile spread across Tom's face. "Whatever you say, Doc."

19.

With binoculars in hand, Governor Murray peaked through the drapes of his bedroom window, slowly panning the masses protesting in front of the Governor's Mansion. The high angle and massive lawn made him think of watching a goal line play from the opposite end zone executive suites. He was amazed that such an angry horde had amassed overnight. They popped up faster than job seekers after a successful election.

The dawn sun finally crept over the tree line, giving Skip a much better view of the protestors. Focusing on the signs, it was clear each group the president insulted during yesterday's press conference had quickly mobilized: Latino rights groups, climate change advocates, Muslim advocacy supporters, and Atheists. He lowered the binoculars, shaking his head over the shitstorm the president left him to face.

It all began going downhill yesterday afternoon once Air Force One landed at Dobbins Air Reserve Base. With the fervor of a teenager after three Mountain Dews, the president had fired off an astounding number of Tweets during the drive to GBI Headquarters. By the time he arrived, the press was in a frenzy of anticipation, and he didn't disappoint. Midway through the president's comments, Governor Murray began to sweat profusely as he struggled to figure out how, or if, he could dig himself out of the hole being dug for him. Fortunately, most press conference cameras focused on one GBI agent's facial contortions and not the pools of sweat engulfing the governor's underarms.

Skip let the drapes fall back into place and turned from the window. Only his half of the bed was rumpled from his attempt at sleep last night. At her psychiatrist's urging, a heavily-sedated Hannah and the kids had spent the night in the relative safety of the basement while his staff planned their transfer to her daddy's farm. He loved his wife dearly and carried a large burden of guilt for her fragile mental well-being. Hannah was basically a farm girl at heart who thrived back in their small hometown away from the public eye. She didn't handle complicated adversity well and slowly slipped into paralyzing nervousness as Skip's political ambitions grew. She was aghast when he actually won the governorship and begged him to let her stay with the kids back at the farm. He should've listened to her and wouldn't push for her return to Atlanta if they make it through this in one piece. He took a deep breath before heading to the closet to change.

A quick learner, Skip wisely selected light gray jeans, a black UGA pullover sweater, and work boots, not his real work boots but his campaign trail pair. Leaving his red, bulldog adorned summer pajamas on the floor—he made a mental note to share his displeasure with the staff that his lucky white PJ's hadn't been cleaned yet—Skip left the bedroom as ready as ever to face the day.

At the top of the staircase, he could hear the mansion was already abuzz with activity. Feigning confidence, he purposely strode down the stairs and was greeted in the foyer by unknown faces from the increased security staff called in once the protesters swelled. After a polite, solemn nod, Skip headed toward the kitchen where his officially assigned security team was mapping out the day's logistics.

"Morning, Governor. We're in here," Jose's familiar voice rang out. Skip spun to his left where Jose and a gaggle of aides were stationed around the large, formal dining room table. Papers were strewn on the table amongst laptops with their cords dangling in all directions, seeking the closest power source. He assumed the collection of young aides at the far end of the table were the so-called social media team poring through the online chatter. The only sound coming from the room was the nervous clatter of keyboard keys.

Skip was clearly surprised to see his staff already hunkered down. "Good morning. Thanks, everyone, for getting here so early."

An aide spoke without looking up from his computer. "No choice, Governor. We've got our hands full today."

The governor did not mask his annoyance. "Really? Try telling me something I don't know. Let me get some coffee then I'll take an update."

Skip continued up the hall and mumbled greetings to the State Troopers poring over maps spread on the kitchen island. At least someone had figured out how to fire up the damned percolator. With a coffee in hand, he returned to the dining room doorway.

"Okay, what's the latest?"

The now contrite aide took his eyes off his computer screen. "Unfortunately, Governor, we're getting it from all sides now. There have been no major developments on the investigation which only gives the protestors and crazy internet bloggers a louder voice. Add in the political angle, and we've got ourselves in quite a pickle."

"We do have some positive news," Jose piped in assuredly.

"I'll take whatever you've got."

"The feedback on your handling of the situation yesterday was very good." As he spoke, Jose grabbed papers from the printer amongst the laptops and cables. "Here, take a look at these reports."

Skip took the reports, grateful that Jose's nature was to constantly look for silver linings rather than exploit fear. "These are a bunch of charts. Jose. What do they mean?"

"We've been tracking mentions of Georgia in the press and on social media." Jose moved in next to Skip and pointed at the first graph. "Sir, the national TV and print press is having a field day with the president's comments and the protests outside the mansion. These diverging lines show how the press's focus shifted from the terrorist attack to the president's comments and protests."

The governor's brow furrowed. "Okay, so why is this good?"

"I'm getting there, sir. The second graph shows the same trend on social media. As soon as the press conference ended, the terrorist attack became secondary."

Skip tried to hand the papers back to Jose. "This is all very interesting, but I don't see why this makes a difference. The president has always diverted attention away from the real problem. It's his go-to strategy."

Jose gave Skip his patented paternal look. "I know that, sir, but just bear with me. The team did some great work overnight that you'll want to see. Go to the next page."

Skip dutifully did as he was told.

"We tracked mentions of you throughout the day then charted them here. During the day, you tracked positive, but after the press conference, the rating of how you were handling the crisis moved to 'very favorable.' Check out that graph line from 6 p.m. and all through the night. The opinion of you skyrocketed in both the press and social media!"

The mention of "very favorable" and "skyrocketed" lifted Skip's spirits. "That is good news. Must admit I'm sort of surprised after the way I stammered after the press conference."

Jose accepted the report back from the governor. "It could have gone either way, but I'm glad your approval rating is up. You did great yesterday, even with the stammer you remained poised and on message. I got calls from two of the crustier local reporters, one your nemesis, who both sang your praises."

Those watching the governor could sense his posture improving. "Really?! Well, maybe we do have a chance to salvage this after all."

Jose gave Skip a steady look. "You'll need to keep your A-game going today, sir. The president isn't going to back down or be quiet. We've already heard Congressman Baker will be a guest on *Badger and Buds* this morning. I'm sure he'll drive the president's story and take some good shots at you."

"That asshole will waste no time trying to throw me under the bus," the governor fumed. Skip didn't care about the profanity. It wasn't the worst thing his staff had heard him utter about the congressman.

"Which is why we need to act now, change the game, take preemptive action."

The governor felt a tinge of optimism. "What do you have in mind, Jose?"

"We need good press optics and continued leadership for your constituents. You can't stay holed up in the mansion, and you going to GBI Headquarters without a comment to the press is unacceptable."

Jose paused for effect, his staff all ears as they knew what was coming next. "I've prepared a statement for you. It's short, basically saying we need to let professional law enforcement do their job and not rush to unsubstantiated conclusions. I want you to walk out the front door, go through the gate to the protesters, shake some hands, and then give the statement once the press circles you."

The entire room heard Hannah Murray gasp. Unbeknownst to the group, she left the safety of her underground warren and was huddled in the hallway listening to Jose's plan. She skittered into view.

"He can't do that! You see the crowd. It's way too dangerous!"

"Give me a minute with my wife, boys."

His staff knew the drill and returned to their computers, pretending to work.

The governor walked over to his wife, taking her cold, nervous hand in his. She trembled like a rabbit in an open field.

His voice was soft and warm. "It's okay, darling. I haven't agreed to it and won't do anything without security saying it's completely safe."

"I have a bad feeling about this. You need to go to the farm with us," she pleaded.

Skip gently wrapped his arm around her shoulder. "I will, dear, but just not yet." He gently steered her back to the basement door and used the most reliable strategy to redirect Hannah. "Why don't you go back to the basement? I'm sure the kids need you."

"Okay, you're right. They need me." At the door to the basement, she gave him a desperate hug and whispered in his ear, "Promise me you won't do anything foolish."

"You have my word. We'll be okay, I promise." Skip watched her until he was certain she wasn't going to return, then he closed the door and went back to the dining room.

In his brief absence, Jose had summoned the security team from the kitchen. Skip directed his question to the Georgia State Patrol team lead. "Sergeant, is it safe for me to go meet the crowd?"

The beefy trooper spoke in his sweet, south-Georgia drawl. "Governor, we've been monitoring the crowd all night, and it's probably the least armed group of Georgians ever assembled. I'd say more folks are carrying at a church revival than outside your gate right now. We'll still send a couple of troopers with you to be sure."

Skip didn't need additional encouragement. "Okay then, let's do this. Do you have the statement, Jose?"

"Yes, but there's a little more to the plan. You'll finish the statement by saying you're headed to GBI Headquarters where you can remain close to the investigation. The last step is a visual for the press. While you're out making the statement, we'll have security pull the vehicles up to the end of the driveway. Once you're done, you walk through the protesters and straight to the waiting SUVs. The cameras will catch you wading through the crowd, shaking more hands, then climbing in the truck before driving away. Guarantee you every news organization will run that clip."

Skip liked the idea but thought of Hannah. "Won't that be more dangerous? I just promised the wife I wouldn't do anything foolish."

Jose shook his head. "Security assures me they've got you covered. It's important to do this. It demonstrates courage and leadership, and I guarantee it will go a long way in neutralizing Congressman Bubba's TV performance."

A noticeable smile crossed Skip's face. "Sounds like a damn good plan. Take the offensive against that suck-up. Give me the statement. I'll need about ten minutes to memorize it, and then we'll be good to go. Anything else?"

It was Jose's turn to smile. "Yeah. Try not to sweat when you're addressing the press."

20.

*S*eamus wiped his sweaty palms on his slacks, trying to muster the courage to go ask the director's permission to meet Scott Worthington for breakfast. He didn't have much time but was finding it difficult to leave the safety of his cube. His trepidation was made worse by what the director might say about Seamus's embarrassing performance during the president's press conference. Not much he can do about that now, but at least the report he submitted late last night was rock solid.

Most of the files from Veteran, McArthur, and Consolidated contained the typical employee beefs, occasional irate customer, and petty internal politics. One farmer in South Georgia had threatened to blow up a Consolidated billboard on his property but quickly became contrite once they offered to increase his yearly land lease price. There was no mention or receipt of anything from Green War or Make America Beautiful Again.

One theme caught his attention and was cited by other individuals and even appeared within the man's own correspondence: Scott Worthington hated his company. Clearly, he was good at his job and knew the business inside and out, but his contempt for what they did was undeniable. Once Seamus received an abbreviated Army file on Warrant Officer Tom Worthington, demolitions expert, he began to think the brothers were in cahoots.

"O'Reilly? You out there?" The unmistakable voice, decibels louder than a normal human, boomed across the cube farm.

Seamus stood up, surprised not only at the number of other heads popping up so early in the morning but to see Bill Carraway standing outside his office.

Carraway waved his arm like a third base coach signaling a runner to score. "Get on in here!"

He locked his computer and hustled to his boss's office.

"Come on in, O'Reilly, and take a seat. I believe you know FBI Agent Wynn."

Seamus didn't know the man but did recognize him from yesterday's meeting with the director.

"Good to see you again, sir," he said as he shook the FBI agent's hand. Turning to his boss, Seamus couldn't hide his surprise. "What are you doing here, Bill? Thought you were someplace in the Caribbean with Evelyn?"

"Thank God for the bombing!" Bill boomed, then realized his error. "Sorry, know that didn't sound right, but it gave me an excuse to get off that damn boat. You ever been on a cruise? Worse than hell, if you ask me, stuck with a bunch of strangers with hardly any room to move. And all they do is eat! Felt like a damn calf in a cage. They should call it a Veal Cruise instead. Of course, Evelyn loved it. She's probably working her fourth crepe as we speak. No, after I got word, I jumped ship in St. John's and got back as quick as I could."

"Cruises suck," Agent Wynn chuckled in agreement. "Went on one once myself. Never again."

Seamus warily took the chair. "What's up? You need me to bring you up to speed?"

"No, I'm good. Been reading the reports, and Agent Wynn's been filling in the gaps. Gotta say, Seamus, your report in particular is damn good. You dug up some great intel."

"Thank you, sir. It sure helped that Veterans' file security system is virtually nonexistent. It took a while, but their servers were packed with solid data."

"You also wrote up the interactions you had with Scott Worthington," Carraway continued. "What do you think of the guy?"

Seamus gave a brief glance to the FBI agent on his left. "He's worth a look, a longshot at best," he answered. "He appears to have the means and motive but everything else, his personality and history, are inconsistent with the crime. He's probably not worth a lot of dedicated resources, yet I'd keep an eye on him."

Carraway nodded toward Agent Wynn. "The FBI agrees with you."

Agent Wynn jumped in. "I noticed your conversation with him after the meeting yesterday. Looked like you two quickly developed a rapport."

Seamus turned in his chair to get a better look at the agent. Probably in his 50s with eyes that suggested he'd seen a lot and the facial expression of a professional observer. "I found him… intriguing. He suggested we meet for breakfast today if I had any more questions," he replied hopefully.

The FBI agent's smile was warmer than expected. "Perfect, because we'd like for you to stay on him. As you mentioned, we need to use our resources wisely, and assigning an FBI agent might get his defenses up. Better to go local with a guy like Worthington."

The unexpected turn of events was thrilling. "I'm more than willing as long as you understand my field experience is limited," Seamus said to the agent.

"Which makes you even better for a guy like this."

"I agree with the agent," Carraway said. "The family's quite powerful in the state, so we need to proceed with caution. The GBI is less intimidating than the FBI. You did just fine with the victim yesterday, so I have confidence sending you into the field. Go have breakfast with him and keep us posted."

Seamus made a futile attempt to stifle his grin. "Thank you, sir. I must admit I enjoyed getting out yesterday."

"Excellent. Now, get to work!" Carraway exhorted with playful brusqueness.

Seamus half sprinted back to his cube, grabbed his jacket, and made it halfway to the door before realizing he didn't have his car keys or trusty, small spiral-ring notepad. He quickly circled back to his cube for his belongings, then took the stairs two at a time and burst from the building like an athlete running onto the field through pom-pom-waving cheerleaders.

Seamus drummed his fingers on the sides of the steering wheel as he headed north on I-285 toward the I-85 Spaghetti Junction. Though filled with a degree of doubt—more than a degree if he was honest—the prospect of an expanded role in the case was exciting. He knew he was a bit player in the overall scheme which was fine by him.

After traveling south on I-85, he exited Lenox Road and made a left. Within several hundred yards, the street changed names to Cheshire Bridge Road, a long standing norm from the segregation days of Atlanta where whites didn't want to have the same street address as Blacks, so they changed the name at an established separation boundary. Seamus had never driven down Cheshire Bridge and quickly understood how it earned its eclectic reputation; a strip club, a sex toy shop, and a gay bar were intermingled with a gourmet grocery store, a baby furniture store, and several family restaurants. Duke's was well up the street on the left, and he was surprised to see a packed parking lot after driving eerily empty streets on the way over.

He backed his Ford Interceptor into an open slot in the back row. After a deep breath and quick pep talk, he left the safety of his car.

"Good morning. Table for one?" spouted a cheery older man sitting on a stool behind the cash register.

Seamus returned the smile. "Actually, I'm meeting someone here."

"Oh, you must be Scott's friend. He's right over there," the old man said, pointing across the diner to a row of booths along the window.

Seamus followed his point to see Scott Worthington eagerly waving him over. Seamus wound his way through the tables filled with customers ranging from buttoned-down professionals to riff raff. Duke's clearly accepted all.

Scott rose as Seamus approached, his smile melting into his conference room smirk. "Good morning, conquering hero. How's it feel to be an internet sensation?"

Seamus grimaced. His sister was the first to call to tell him his video was trending on social media. Late yesterday afternoon, the president and Governor Murray held a press conference on the steps of the GBI headquarters. As the only law enforcement representative of color present for the event, the media handlers insisted Seamus take a prominent location standing behind the president. At one point during the president's remarks, something about immigrant terrorists, Seamus unconsciously made a face that immediately took the internet by storm.

"You saw that?"

"Of course! Most of America has by now. So, was that your 'holy shit, I can't believe he said that' or 'please, somebody shoot me for having to stand here' expression?"

Seamus gave a little chuckle wishing he liked all suspects as much as this guy. "Probably a little bit both. It was quite a show."

"It was. I never realized Hondurans hated the outdoor advertising industry in Georgia so much."

"He actually blamed the Guatemalans. We even prepped him beforehand. Guess he didn't listen or didn't care. It was a natural reaction. I didn't even realize it."

"Well, I thank you. Your reaction spoke to many of us. Hope your bosses don't give you a hard time."

Scott sounded truly genuine, and Seamus appreciated the concern.

"I expected an earful this morning but nothing yet. Maybe when we solve this, there might be a problem, but right now everyone's too busy to care."

Before Scott could respond, a waitress bearing menus and a pot of coffee appeared at their table. Seamus was immediately taken by how healthy she looked even in her polyester uniform and apron: slender not skinny, well-toned with an agile spring in her step, brunette hair pulled back in a short ponytail, and hazel eyes that twinkled with playfulness.

"Good morning...coffee?" she addressed them both.

"Good morning, Maggie," Scott said. "I'd like you to meet Seamus O'Reilly with the GBI."

Seamus instinctively went to shake her hand even though they were occupied. "A pleasure to meet you, Maggie."

She gave a little half-curtsy instead of taking his hand. "The pleasure is mine, Mr. O'Reilly. It's not often we have internet celebrities visit our humble diner. You're getting a free meal out of your performance. The entire staff thinks you're a rock star."

Seamus quickly glanced around the diner. Sure enough, most of the employees were looking in their direction, and even the cooks were peeking through the server's window. Not accustomed to such attention, Seamus shuffled his silverware and sheepishly mumbled, "As a government employee, I'm not supposed to accept gifts."

Maggie gave a half-laugh while she filled his coffee cup. "Then I guess we'll just have to keep it as our little secret. You need a minute to look at the menu?"

Seamus looked up at Maggie and smiled. "Yes, please."

She took a step away and then turned back to the table. "I'm sorry, but I have to tell you that I love your name. I gotta say, the fact you're a strapping African-American makes it even better."

"Thank you. Technically, I'm not African-American. My family's Haitian-Irish-American."

Maggie gave him a warm look. "You've taken double consciousness to a whole new level. You must have a lot of fortitude."

He watched her walk away, awed at her reference to DuBois until he felt Scott staring at him. "Safe to say she's not your average waitress."

Scott gave him an agreeing nod. "Maggie's amazing. Waitress, friend, psychiatrist, sometimes even clairvoyant, she pulled me out of a pretty dark time a couple of years ago. Why do you think I'm a regular? The food's hit or miss. I'll coach you with your order to be safe."

Seamus took a sip of coffee and chastised himself for his amateurism. He had been trained to be dispassionate with interviewees, using his stature, calm demeanor, and badge to his advantage. Now, for the second day in a row, he cracked open his emotional door and allowed personal opinion to sway his approach. Yesterday he gave a hen-pecked Hoosier a police escort, and today he's gone soft on a suspect just because he likes the guy and is impressed with a waitress. Time to stiffen up.

As Seamus set his cup down, Scott beat him to the punch. "So, I imagine this morning isn't a social breakfast. After digging into my family, I bet you have some interesting theories."

Seamus leaned forward slightly in the booth and looked Scott dead in the eye. "I do. It's well documented that you don't like your job or Veteran, you even admitted as much to me yesterday. In fact, several employees' immediate suspicion was directed at you. Add in the fact your brother is a demolitions expert gives you access to the technical skill the FBI guys are saying was required to build such a contained explosive. I don't buy eco-terrorists. That's just a tactic to create hysteria when this is really just a crime about vengeance."

As if on cue, Maggie reappeared. Seamus was grateful for the interruption. He wanted that to sink in, give Scott a minute to ponder an answer.

"You decided yet?"

"The usual for me, Maggie."

Seamus passed the menu back to Maggie. "I'm good with coffee. I had breakfast earlier."

Maggie gave him a little wink. "Wise choice. Don't know how Scott's lived so long eating at this place."

Scott waited until Maggie was several steps away. This time he leaned in slightly. "Are you saying I'm a suspect?"

Seamus paused and gave Scott a steady, firm look. "More like a person of interest. We're looking at this from every angle and, you must admit, your backstory has caught some attention." Seamus stopped there, closely studying Scott's face for his reaction.

"I can see how that makes sense," Scott began, a tinge of excitement in his voice but no increased tension in his facial muscles. "In a way, I'm kind of flattered, a suspect in a terrorist case! My entire life I've been the good guy, never taking risks or doing anything crazy. Now, I'm a suspect. Gotta admit to a little adrenaline rush."

"Person of interest, not a suspect," Seamus corrected.

"I like being a suspect more. Sounds dangerous. I've never been dangerous."

"What about your brother? Is he dangerous? He certainly has the skill set, and it appears stability has been an issue with him."

For the first time in their two brief meetings, Seamus witnessed a change in Scott's demeanor. His body stiffened and his eyes went cold. Clearly, he hit a soft spot.

"Yes, I admit my brother's a complicated, damaged soul. After our father died, substance abuse was an issue, but the military straightened him out. Unfortunately, he came back with different demons, and civilian life has been a struggle for him. We're trying to help but it's a challenge, and he's a constant worry, especially to my sister."

"I've seen his records, decorated and now being treated for PTSD. I'm sure you can understand our interest." Seamus tried to sound more compassionate. He didn't want Scott to keep his guard too high.

"Like I said, it makes sense, but the only danger he poses is to himself."

"Still, we need to talk to him, and I was hoping you could arrange the meeting. He's not the easiest to find, and his VA address is your sister's house."

Scott gave Seamus a long look, clearly debating what to say next. Only Maggie swooping in with breakfast broke the moment. Scott leaned back half-smiling at the waitress. "Thanks, Maggie. Seamus here thinks I'm a suspect and wants to question Tom too."

"Did you tell him you're a chickenshit?"

"Don't hold back, Maggie. Can't you give me a little manhood dignity?"

Maggie gently touched Scott's left shoulder. "Inspector, I doubt Scott's done anything wrong or daring his entire life. He's a little boring, and maybe too sarcastic, but genuinely, he's a nice guy. There's not many like him left so don't ruin my image by trying to make him a dirtbag. His brother on the other hand…well, good luck finding him." And with that she was off to the next table.

Seamus noticed Scott's reddened face. "Looks like you have a fan. So, what's this about finding your brother?"

Scott didn't look up as he toyed with the egg whites. "Tom has the habit of disappearing. It happened a lot when he was living with Pam, so we moved him up to our family pontoon boat on the lake. Fewer people and the water seemed to calm him, but he still wanders off for weeks at a time, usually up into the mountains or hangs with homeless vets scattered around in the city. You wouldn't believe how many vets are on the streets."

"Way too many," Seamus agreed. "Where's your brother now?"

"Don't read too much into this as I'm sure he has nothing to do with your investigation but…" Scott took his focus off his breakfast and looked straight at Seamus. "…we have no idea. He's been gone for over two weeks. Pam's freaking out because it's different this time. All his mountain gear is still on the boat, and he hasn't shown up at his usual homeless vet camps."

Seamus knew his expression gave away his thoughts.

Scott pounced. "See? You immediately have the wrong idea! Tom's real skittish, and sending the Mounties after him will only drive him deeper." Scott returned his attention to the egg whites, rearranging them on the plate with disinterest.

They sat in silence for a moment. Seamus finally spoke.

"We've got to find him. Will you help?"

Scott pushed his plate away. "If he's in the mountains, you won't find him. Remember the Olympic bomber? He was on the loose for years, and he was a rookie compared to my brother. But I'd start with the boat. Check it out to see if there's something Pam and I missed…hell, I'm sure you want to search it for bomb shit anyway, so be productive and see if you can find anything. I'd also hit the streets and check the homeless camps. They're not the most talkative bunch, so don't expect much." He gave a half shrug and his voice softened. "And talk with Pam. She's had better luck finding him than I have."

"Thanks for the advice. We will want to search his boat. Do I need a warrant, or will you give the official approval?"

"It's fine by me, but better get the okay from Pam. The boat's in her name. I'll text her and let her know you'll be reaching out. Will you do me the favor and let us know if you dig anything up that might help us find him?"

Seamus swung his legs out from under the diner booth and stood next to the table. "Sure, anything we find that I can share, I will." Seamus reached out to shake Scott's hand. "Thanks for your time."

Scott shook his hand and his warm smile returned. "One more favor. Since I'm a suspect and all, don't you want to search my place? I could use the street cred with my neighbors. Most of them think I'm a pansy."

Seamus returned the smile. "Seriously? I admit searching your place was a thought, and I'd be happy to arrange it, if you want."

Scott fished out his key chain, removed his apartment key, and held it out to O'Reilly. "You have my approval, and I assume you know where I live. Take some big guys, make it look ominous. Just do it around 5:00 so my neighbors see you. Maybe even knock across the hall on 408 and ask a young woman named Emily questions about me. She's the building gossip. My status will increase by nightfall."

Seamus couldn't help but laugh. "408, huh? Okay, consider it done. What about your key? Leave it with 408?"

Scott barely contained his excitement. "Brilliant! A perfect plan...I'll owe you one."

Seamus pocketed the key, waved to Maggie, and headed out to his Interceptor. Looking through the window, he saw Maggie seated opposite Scott, a look of concern on her face as he shared the details of their conversation. He was about to drive away when he noticed her reach across the table and take his hand.

21.

Barry wished he was a dog. As his mind raced with the likely outcome of Dr. Shaw's decision on Patient Omega, Moon blissfully rolled on the ground in what was undoubtedly boar scat. Both Barry and Moon were wallowing in shit, only Moon was enjoying every minute of it.

His arm ached from a prolonged session of fetch at the river, and his legs were spent from wandering nearly every trail in the forest. He'd run out of delay tactics and had no choice but to return to the compound for the verdict, a decision which would likely ruin this perfect fall morning.

The view from the edge of the woods was similar to yesterday—guard, patient and Dr. Shaw were in the compound's field. Only today, the twitchy and unpredictably volatile JR was on guard duty, and the patient stood squarely in the middle of the field with his arms stretched out, facing the early morning sun. The man turned in Barry's direction and his hopes for Patient Omega's miraculous recovery were dashed when he realized this was a different man.

"What a magnificent beast!" the man yelled from the field.

123

Barry looked down at the panting, wagging Moon. "Release," Barry commanded, and the Lab took off to greet the wonderfully-smelling stranger. As Moon loped across the field, the man broke into a huge smile and squatted down to dog level. Man and dog were soon rolling in the grass like long lost friends.

He descended the small slope from the woods to meet the gloating Dr. Shaw. "Looks like you've made progress with this one. He the bomb guy?" Barry asked.

"Yes, on both accounts, but again, he's Patient Alpha not 'the bomb guy.' Medically, we've had a breakthrough, and I'm moving him on to phase four later this evening." Shaw turned and looked back at the field, the big greeting now followed by belly rubs and face licks. "Didn't realize he's a dog guy. That could be to our benefit in phase four."

Barry gave Shaw a harsh glare. "Leave Moon out of this." It was hard for Barry to hide his disdain for the doc.

Shaw put on his professional voice. "Phase four is psychological, and knowing the patient is comforted by a dog will help as he experiences fluctuating emotions. Your dog will be just fine."

The two men gave each other a cold stare. Shaw broke the silence.

"I'm also worried about JR. The recent events have put him on edge. I'm afraid he may break soon."

Barry found the comment laughable. What a brilliant psychiatrist you are! He came out of the womb an ignorant lunatic, and you're just noticing now? He regrouped before speaking. "Yes, he does seem to be more wired than normal. Maybe it's time for a quick three-day leave. That usually gets him back on track."

"In my opinion, a three-day leave is insufficient. He possesses too much negative energy which suggests a more drastic adjustment is necessary. Fortunately, a decision has been made on Omega, and carrying out that duty tonight should do the trick."

Barry's heart sank knowing what Shaw meant. He tried not to sound pleading. "Plantation's got a hog hunt tomorrow. Will that do?"

Shaw looked Barry dead in the eye. "No, and I don't care for your tone. You're either committed to the program or you're not. Bubba's coming for the hog hunt. I'd hate to tell him you're being uncooperative."

Barry didn't know what was worse, the doc ordering the execution of an innocent man or the concept of JR needing to kill a human to gain mental equilibrium. He wondered if hell was like this: beautiful scenery populated with diabolical moral depravity. Only his strong survival instincts stopped Barry from ending it all.

"I'm not trying to be uncooperative. I'm just wondering if we might have other options."

"No. Experiments carry a price." Shaw returned his gaze to the man and dog in the field. "Patient Omega's been here for three weeks and has not responded to treatment. I had my doubts about him from the beginning. He was a random selection without the proper screening like Patient Alpha. He will not be missed."

Tell that to his family, Barry thought, but he said, "Whatever you say, Doc." He left Shaw in the field for the sanctuary of his little house. On the front porch he let out a feeble whistle. "C'mon, Moon."

22.

L ieutenant Colonel Andrea Leonard walked the entire length of Concourse A in Hartsfield-Jackson Airport without one person offering a sign of deference or thanking her. It was a lonely feeling to be like the thousands of other invisible passengers changing planes or making Atlanta their final destination. It had been so long since she'd traveled in civvies, she forgot what it was like to be inconspicuous. She was oddly uncomfortable.

She didn't visit Atlanta often, but when she did, it was easy to see why so many people lived here. At one point, she considered requesting a transfer to Fort MacPherson, but then Fort Mac was hit with budget cuts so she kept Fort Bragg as her base of operations. The thought of retiring here was now foremost in her mind. She imagined an African-American woman, who just so happened to be a retired lieutenant colonel, would have a ton of options in a town like Atlanta. Her stroll through the terminal made her reconsider the thought of retiring anytime soon.

At the airport baggage claim, she proceeded to the Marta station and rode the Gold Line to the Brookhaven-Oglethorpe Station. She exited the train carrying only a black backpack and small duffel. Unlike the bustling airport, few cars were on the road as most Atlantans were still heeding the governor's stay at home recommendation after yesterday's terrorist attack. Even with the empty road, Andrea waited patiently for the crosswalk sign to give her the okay to cross the six lanes of Peachtree Road.

She entered the Starbucks and saw Pam at a corner table with a man she didn't recognize. It definitely wasn't Roger, and this man was considerably thinner than the Scott she remembered from years ago. They both rose as she neared, Pam with a big smile and the man now looking more like her brother.

"Andrea!" Pam gave her a big hug. "You have no idea how much better I feel now that you're here."

"I'm glad I could make it. You sounded pretty desperate yesterday." Andrea gave Pam what she hoped was a reassuring squeeze. "Good to see you, Scott. I almost didn't recognize you. You've gotten in shape."

Scott took her hand and smiled. "That's a polite way of saying I'm not as fat as I used to be, and I accept the compliment. Good to see you, Andrea. Thanks for coming." He pointed to the seat opposite his sister. "Can I get you anything?"

"I'm good, thanks for asking." Andrea took a seat opposite Tom's siblings, surprised at their resemblance, noting different features of his in each one of them. Pam was at ease, but Scott appeared a little tense and was nervously staring at her. "You okay, Scott? You're kind of giving me the eye."

"Sorry, Andrea. I've just always seen you in uniform and never really thought about what you looked like. I was expecting a soldier, and well, there's a woman underneath the fatigues."

The women laughed. "Andrea, I believe my brother just said you're hot in his typical smooth man fashion."

Andrea reached across the table and gave Scott's hand a little pat. "Well, it's my turn to accept the compliment."

Scott blushed and gave her a sheepish smile.

Pam leaned in and lowered her voice. "Thanks for coming on such short notice. I'm worried sick. Something just doesn't feel right this time."

Andrea gave Pam a tender look then directed her question to Scott. "And what about you? Does this feel different to you too?"

Scott shifted his eyes between Andrea and his sister. "I learned many years ago to trust my sister's intuition, particularly when it comes to Tom. Disappearing is not out of character for him, and Pam is like a bloodhound. Usually she can find a trail. If she thinks something's wrong, then something's wrong."

Andrea nodded her head, knowing full well what it was like to have that sense, the voice in your head, the welling in your soul, telling you a situation was not right. She never bought in to the whole woman's intuition thing, but she didn't deny it existed. It was one of the reasons she had excelled in the military, though she'd never admit it to any superior officer.

"Okay then, I better get started as soon as possible. I know you've already done it, but I'd like to check his boat and the VA. That was the last place he was seen, right?"

"Yes, he had his standing Monday appointment with Dr. Shaw, his psychiatrist, then went to a group meeting. That was the last time anyone saw him. The group meets again today in about 30 minutes. Maybe one of them will open up to you." Pam pushed a set of car keys across the table. "Here's the keys to Roger's pickup. He hardly ever drives it."

As Andrea pocketed the keys, Scott told her the GBI was probably up searching the boat right now, so she might want to delay the lake visit until tomorrow.

Andrea was visibly peeved. "Civilian law enforcement amazes me, thinking Tom might have anything to do with the bombing. A close look at his military records, and they'd know better."

Scott was puzzled. "What do you mean? They suspect him because of his military experience and knowledge of the family business."

Andrea shook her head. "Yes, your brother was an explosives expert but washed out after his experience because he refused to touch a bomb again. You can't dismantle an IED if you won't touch it. It's all in his file."

Scott's expression made her immediately regret the comment. She knew what was coming.

"Andrea, what about Tom's experience in Afghanistan? He never talks about it with me, seems like if we knew, we could help. Has he ever told you Pam?"

His sister shook her head no.

Andrea studied the pleading expressions on the Worthington siblings' faces. It was all too common for soldiers to hide the truth. Even with the increased public attention, any form of trauma that fell under the category of mental illness, no matter how justified or scientifically proven, carried a measure of shame, of weakness.

"It's not my story to tell," said Andrea, a line she used all too often with veteran families.

Pam leaned over and grabbed Andrea's wrist. "But, he won't tell it. Please? I feel like I've been spinning my wheels with him. We can't keep going on like this."

Lieutenant Colonel Leonard took a deep breath. Tom was more than a soldier in her command; he was one of the best friend's she ever had.

"Okay, but don't be dismissive, thinking it's trivial. Nothing is trivial when it comes to war." She reached down and fetched her water bottle out of her pack, took a big drink, and began.

"It all started with a fucking scorpion of all things, pardon the French. The desert was crawling with them. GIs were constantly getting stung, and it usually was no big thing, just painful and irritating for several days. Tom got bit on his lower right leg, and he must have been allergic or something. Anyway, he waited too long for treatment, and after several days, his leg was big as a balloon and he was running a high fever. The field docs began to run out of ideas, so he was medevacked to Kandahar. It was actually touch and go for a while. They even thought he might lose his leg."

The pain was clear on Pam's face as she anxiously fiddled with the table's sugar caddy. "I had no idea. Poor thing."

Andrea took another drink of water to buy time before sharing with the worst part of the story. "While he was in Kandahar, some young sergeant took the lead of his demolition unit. They were stationed at a forward base with infantry constantly out on patrol looking for insurgents, snipers, and IEDs along the supply lines. One unit found a section of road they thought was mined and did what they were supposed to do, call in the location and move forward.

"Tom's unit, now technically the young sergeant's, were ordered to go check it out. Problem was, the night before, some fool, one of our own guys, had shot down the base's surveillance drone. Tom never would have taken the unit out. He would have waited until the backup drone was in place or would have a cover unit go with them. The sergeant was inexperienced and ready to prove he could lead a unit, so they went."

She saw the expression change on both of their faces. "They were ambushed, all six killed."

Pam's entire body sagged. "Guilt. He blames himself. I'd probably feel the same."

"As would I," Andrea added. "The military is all about responsibility and protecting each other. We're a family who would do anything for each other and often do with our life. You're Tom's blood family. That unit was his family too. He was devastated."

Scott shook his head in disbelief. "A scorpion, a dumbass GI, and an eager sergeant. Unbelievable. What happened to the dumbass? Court martial, I hope."

"He was quietly shipped out and discharged. I was stateside at the time and didn't find out until it was all buried. The military is not big on letting mistakes like that go public."

"I'd like to get my hands on that son of a bitch."

"So would I." Hoping to avoid further questions, Andrea stood up. "I best be going if I want to get to the VA in time."

After hugs with Pam and Scott, she drove Roger's truck to a hotel on the I-85 corridor where Pam had booked her a room. She wanted to look more official for her visit to the VA Medical Center, so she quickly changed into fatigues, pulled her curls into a tight bun, and pinned the silver oak leaf insignia on her collar.

It was a short drive to the VA Medical Center, and the information clerk was prompt and polite in directing her to Dr. Shaw's office. Andrea exited the elevator on the 3rd floor and turned left to the Transition and Care Management Services department. She had no intention of meeting the doctor. Instead, she wandered the main hall as if on recon to identify egress points. The hall was quiet, and she assumed Tom's meeting group was behind one of the closed doors. She checked her watch: 15 minutes before 3:00 when the group ended. Andrea decided to continue down the hall and take the stairs.

Once back on the ground floor, she confirmed the door to the outside was an alarm-armed fire exit. Tom wouldn't have gone out that way. She exited the staircase into a hallway that housed administration and general services offices. Making her way back towards the main entrance, she took another left that led to a visitors' waiting section and eventually the cafeteria. Security at the Medical Center appeared lax, only the ever-present cameras built into the acoustical tile ceiling panels belied the notion. Andrea would need to pull some strings to view the footage. She hoped it wouldn't be necessary.

She made the entire circuit in ten minutes, interacting with others only via eye contact, empathetic head nods, and the occasional verbal greeting. With 20 years of service, she had expected—maybe dreaded was more accurate—to run into at least one familiar face, but she moved through the building virtually unnoticed. Back in the main lobby area, she sat on a bench with a direct view of the elevator bank.

Shortly after 3:00, the elevator doors opened, and a group of male vets exited, exchanging friendly chatter unlike most people who share elevators. She watched them walk across the lobby and figured the odds were 50% the men just came from Tom's group session. She left the bench and followed the men outside, where three peeled off for the parking deck. The other two went around the corner of the building and stopped at the designated smoking section.

She approached just as they lit up. "Hey, guys."

Both men naturally stiffened. You can take a man out the service, but you can't take the service out of the man.

"Afternoon, Colonel," they responded in near unison.

Andrea tried to keep it casual. "I was wondering if you know a friend of mine, Warrant Officer Tom Worthington. Understand he comes here sometimes." Andrea left it at that. No need for more detail.

The younger of the two spoke up. "Sure, we know Tom. He's in our group but hasn't shown up in over a week."

"When did you see him last?"

"Maybe two, three weeks ago. We always come out here for a smoke, and some guy picked him up."

Andrea didn't want to interrogate them, so she bummed a cigarette from the young, chatty one and sat on the bench. They relaxed as she told them how she knew Tom, the units they served, and the shit they'd seen. The vets nodded in agreement, and then shared a bit about where they had been stationed and what they missed, and didn't miss, about being in the service.

After 20 minutes and two cigarettes, Andrea had the information she needed. Tom left the VA Medical Center in a black Chevy Suburban, very clean with tinted windows. Andrea's smoking buddies figured it was an Uber ride since Tom didn't drive in the city and his family had enough money for him to take the fancy option. They didn't see the driver and weren't sure if Tom knew him or her. It could've been a her since neither one got a look. But the older vet did notice the license plate. It was one of those special tags easy to remember—DEER 3.

It had been five years since her last smoke, so she made sure the nicotine rush had subsided before she attempted to stand. She thanked the guys for their help, wished them luck, and went back to her hotel room to track down the Suburban.

23.

"You didn't mention a dog."

"He didn't tell me about a dog," Seamus answered defensively as the three GBI technicians hovered in a semi-circle around him. He faced the apartment door with a dog going ballistic on the other side. "It sure doesn't sound like a big dog. Probably one of those small excitable types."

"The little ones are the most vicious, you know, Napoleon dogs," one of the technicians deadpanned. "My cousin's hand was maimed by an ex-girlfriend's Chihuahua. His thumb still don't work right."

Another technician snorted in amusement.

"Then what do you suggest we do?" Seamus asked the team.

"Shoot it," advised a different voice behind him.

The other technicians began to crack up.

"I'm not going to shoot a dog!" Seamus was getting tired of the wiseass technicians. His field inexperience became clear when they investigated Tom's boat, and the three stooges didn't miss a chance to tease him or point out his mistakes. "C'mon guys, help me out, I've already admitted I'm new to this. What do you normally do in a situation like this?"

"We send the lead agent in first. If you don't get bit, then we go in."

The stifled snickers from the clowns echoed up the hallway.

The hell with it, Seamus decided to take his chances. He used Scott's key and slowly opened the door to a scruffy mutt whose barking face looked to be smiling. "Hello little fella." The dog immediately began to spin in excited circles. He tentatively knelt down to give the pup a friendly pat on the head when the dog promptly flipped on his back, seeking a belly rub. "This is one ferocious animal," he reported sarcastically, "but I think we'll be safe."

The giggling technicians filed in past the kneeling Seamus. "You're one brave agent. Maybe we'll recommend you for valor."

He found rubbing the dog's belly a soothing respite from his tormentors. At least they were good at their job.

Without saying a word, the technicians split up—one to the bedroom, the other began in the main room while the third went straight to the laptop sitting on a clutter free desk.

It's strange rooting through someone's underwear drawer searching for clues. Seamus left Tom's houseboat rather depressed after discovering the man didn't have many belongings, mostly just essentials of a meager existence which provided very little insight. Photos, keepsakes, even cheesy souvenirs weren't displayed, suggesting a man who didn't care about, or was trying to erase, his past. The only links to a real person was an Army photo of six smiling soldiers in the desert found in an overhead cabinet, a bag of weed in the fridge, and four different prescription medications in the ship's head. Studying the labels, Seamus was concerned the guy was on the loose without his meds.

Scott's place was a different story. Though he lived alone, he clearly wasn't lonely. On the end table, his bedroom dresser, and the wall by his kitchen table were framed photos of Scott's daughters at various ages in life. No wife in the pictures, which wasn't a big surprise for a divorced man. Seamus was relieved he and Peggy had remained childless; divorce was hard enough without involving kids.

As he poked through the apartment, Seamus was drawn to Scott's bookshelf. Seamus loved to read and appreciated the fact Scott had real books that showed signs of actual use rather than simply for display. Seamus studied the spines, nodding in approval over the diverse selection of titles. Realizing he was being watched by one of the technicians and the dog, he pulled Doris Kearns Goodwin's *No Ordinary Time* from the shelf and pretended to search behind the books.

What struck Seamus was the apartment was almost too perfect. Everyone has some sort of vice or bad habit, but so far, nothing turned up during the search—no empty liquor bottles, or full ones for that matter, and the browser histories on his TV and computer would've made a Priest proud. There wasn't even a single controversial title to be found in his bookshelf. Seamus was pretty dull himself, but even he had a couple of racy books in his collection.

Seamus stood in the main room studying the tidiness of Scott's apartment and wondered if he'd been set up. Scott had been pretty damn eager for the GBI to search the place, and it almost seemed like he was too innocent. A divorced guy in his 40s should have something to raise an eyebrow. He looked at his watch, 5:15 p.m. The technicians had made it clear he wasn't of much help, so maybe a conversation with 408 was a good use of his time.

A soft voice came from the other side of the door a good minute after his knock. "May I help you?"

Seamus held his badge in front of the peephole. "Seamus O'Reilly with the GBI, ma'am. Do you have a minute?"

He heard the deadbolt slide and the door opened to a blondish woman, maybe in her late 20s or early 30s. He gave her a quick once over, somewhat befuddled over her outfit of yoga pants with a blouse and blazer. She noticed his expression.

"Sorry, I just got home from work and was changing to go to the gym. I saw you guys searching Scott's apartment. Is this about the terrorists?" she asked excitedly.

"Yes, ma'am. We're just investigating every angle, and I was hoping to ask you a couple of questions."

"I've never been interviewed by the police before! Would you care to come in?"

He took a step before remembering protocol. "That wouldn't be proper, ma'am. Here is fine." He glanced over her shoulder at a mirror image of Scott's layout. An item of clothing was tossed on the floor, a coffee mug sat on the counter next to a grocery bag, and a laptop was open on the kitchen table. Unlike Scott's, it looked like a normal apartment.

"I'm not surprised you're here. Scott basically admitted doing it yesterday afternoon!"

Seamus took an involuntary step backwards. "Excuse me? Did you say Scott Worthington confessed to bombing the billboards?"

"Well, not exactly. But he did say he hated his job and was glad it happened, something about it being a sign to do something new with his life."

"So, he didn't actually admit to the bombing, just that he was glad it happened," Seamus corrected, beginning to understand how this woman was considered the building gossip.

The woman's shoulders drooped a bit in contrition. "He never really said he was glad it happened, just that he hated his job." She suddenly perked back up. "But doesn't that show motive, right?!"

Seamus tried to remain professional. "I'm sure he's not the only one who hates his job, ma'am. Aside from what he said, have you noticed any behaviors that might lead you to think he's a suspect? Odd hours, secret visitors, strange behaviors?"

"Not really. Scott's always had weird hours. He travels the state a lot, you know, and, like, is his own boss, so he works when he wants. He never has visitors, except for his sister, and doesn't socialize as much in the building as some people."

"In other words, nothing out the ordinary. What about the last several months?"

"No, he's the same Scott. Kinda quiet, but a real nice guy in a big brother way. I'm glad he's my neighbor, and I don't think he'd do anything wrong."

Seamus nodded. He could sense she was just getting warmed up and would talk through the evening if allowed. He eyed her outfit again. "You mentioned you just got home from work. Wasn't most of the city closed today? Last I heard, the governor only permitted travel for essential workers."

"My office is here in the complex, and I walk to work. It was okay with my boss. You can talk with her if you'd like," she said defensively as she began to inch the door closed.

He pulled a card out of his breast pocket. "That's not necessary. Thank you for your time. Here's my card. Please feel free to contact me if you think of anything else."

"You're welcome...and good luck finding the terrorists. I'm freaking out about it."

Seamus began to walk away before remembering the key. "One last thing. Scott asked that we leave his key with you. I'll put it under your mat when we're finished."

Once the team wrapped up their work, Seamus hid Scott's key then headed back to the Panthersville headquarters, arriving just before 7:00. Overall, it was a good day, and he was privately glad they didn't turn up evidence against the Worthingtons. Though he was supposed to be unbiased, he liked Scott and felt sympathy for Tom. The Worthingtons were in the clear in his book, at least for now.

The Antiterrorism Team's cube area was noticeably quiet. Only a few agents were back from the field, and they were busy at their computers, writing up reports. Seamus settled in at his desk to do the same. As he waited for his computer to boot up, he leafed through the stack of research requests that had been placed in his cubicle while he was out. He'd been so caught up in the events of the day that his real responsibilities completely slipped his mind.

"O'Reilly? You out there? Thought I saw you come in," Carraway's voice boomed across the office.

O'Reilly popped his head up to see his boss standing in the doorway.

He gave him the same wave as he did earlier that morning. "Come in here!"

Seamus traversed the cube farm only to find FBI Agent Wynn camped in the same chair as if he'd spent the entire day in Carraway's office. "Grab a seat, O'Reilly," his boss motioned to the other visitor's chair. He warily looked at the two men and took a seat, and then Carraway nodded at the FBI agent.

"The FBI has determined the source of the explosives used," Agent Wynn began. "By law, each manufacturer of construction plastic explosives must contain a signature component. A fingerprint, you might say, for control and tracking purposes. The billboard explosives match those stolen from a demolition company in Louisiana over a decade ago. The same signature was found in explosives used two years ago to attack our border with Mexico."

Seamus was flabbergasted at the implication. "You mean a Mexican drug lord is behind this after all? I remember that attack, but I don't recall what became of the investigation."

The FBI agent's voice took a more somber tone. "The Guadalupe Cartel took credit for the border bombing, but we've been unable to get the Mexican authorities to cooperate. The tie to Georgia doesn't seem logical, but we know the explosives match the manufacturer's fingerprint. Further, the blasting technique is similar, what's known as a precision bombing that's focused on a specific target with very little collateral damage. This very well may be another diversion tactic on their part. There are certain government officials who will demand immediate action, so we're forced to investigate this thoroughly."

"That's where you come in, O'Reilly," Carraway jumped in. "The FBI's heading down to Louisiana tomorrow to interview the owner of the demolition company where the explosives were originally stolen. They've talked to the guy a bunch of times, but circumstances as they are, need to talk to him again. We'd like for you to go along."

Seamus was momentarily speechless. "Are you sure? Not that I'm not willing, but this is outside of my expertise. Shouldn't you assign one of the other agents? Take Walt. He's really good at interviews."

"I appreciate your honesty, but while you might not be our best investigator, you're our top analyst." Carraway then slid a thick file across his desk to Seamus. "This is the FBI file on the explosives theft. Whoever goes on this trip has to know everything in the file before they head down. You're the only one on the team capable of digesting all this information in such a short window. Study this and be prepared to bring up anything you think was missed. You don't need to lead the interview. An additional perspective is all we're asking of you."

His awkwardness with the Brass aside, he knew they picked the right man. No one with the GBI was more adept at poring through records and transcripts to sort facts from supposition, and then create a plausible explanation and logical plan.

"Thank you, sir. I'll do my best."

"I know you will, O'Reilly. Be at PDK by 11:00 a.m. I'll send you additional details in the morning."

Seamus scooped up the file. "Got it, and thanks again."

Only when he got back to his cube did doubt crawl in, disputing that he had the chops for the assignment. He noticed the research requests and silently swore at himself for not mentioning his ongoing workload with Carraway. Seamus set the Louisiana file aside to tackle his day job.

24.

Maggie shot up in bed and swatted at the old-timey clock whose kitschy appeal didn't make up for its obnoxious alarm. Its ear-shattering clang sounded like an out of tune school bell. She hurriedly got out of bed and pulled on sweats and a hoodie to ward off her bedroom's chill. She always slept better with the windows open but had forgotten to check the weather, not realizing it was going to be such a cold night.

Maggie shuffled down the short hallway and flipped on the kitchen light. The sunflower clock confirmed it was 4:30 a.m. Though a little earlier than normal, she still had to pack. She started the coffee pot then went to the little bathroom for a shower. When she emerged from the bathroom, the rich aroma of coffee permeated the bungalow. With fresh coffee in hand, she retreated to the spare bedroom where she kept her gear.

Usually on Tuesdays she'd work a full day, but Duke Evans sensed she was still discombobulated and gave her the okay to split after the breakfast shift for a brief overnight jaunt in the mountains. Since it was only a one-nighter, she didn't have much to pack in her backpack: tent, sleeping bag, clothing layers for the fluctuating fall temperatures, and food for dinner and breakfast. With the drought ending in September, the ban on open fires had been lifted, so there was no need to bring her camp stove.

Her spare bedroom was more of a large storage closet than an actual room. The only furniture was her reading chair, a pole lamp, and an end table with an autographed photo of Iron Eyes Cody. Several years ago, she discovered he was actually Italian, but she loved the Keep America Beautiful message of anti-pollution and didn't really care if the whole thing was contrived.

Maggie began tossing what she needed on the reading chair. Her mom was the original granola woman, teaching Maggie the joys of the outdoors and how to live off the land. She was an extraordinary woman of simple means and infinite character. She encouraged Maggie in school, nudging her towards math and the natural sciences but never in an overly pushy way. Her #1 goal for her daughter was to be a strong, independent woman, a goal she never got to see fulfilled.

Maggie was devastated when her mom died. For the first time, she was truly alone and lost. She sat in their little ranch home for a week and cried. When she could cry no more, she loaded her mom's kayak on their Subaru and headed for the sea where she spent the entire summer paddling the swamps and Intracoastal Waterway, camping on small, uninhabited islands, and living off fish and roots. She was so intent on channeling her mom that by the end of the summer she was convinced she even looked like her. To this day, spending time alone in the wilderness was Maggie's way of gaining comfort from her mother, a form of extrasensory communication that invigorated her strength.

Maggie leaned her backpack against the chair and began to load her gear. A wave of melancholy overtook her as she realized this was her last trip to the Georgia mountains. At least it wasn't the weekend when there's nothing worse than trying to find solitude with hordes of Atlantans jockeying to find the perfect fall colors. Maggie wasn't going to take any chances. She'd drive a remote forest service road to the Three Forks Trailhead and then hike in to her favorite camping spot.

She hefted her pack, went out the back door from the kitchen, and tossed it in her Pathfinder parked next to the workshop. It was a glorious morning, too perfect to be sitting inside. Maggie headed back inside, poured another cup of coffee, and went through her living room to the front porch. Pulling the hood up over her head, she parked in one of the rocking chairs that faced the neighborhood.

Early morning to Maggie was between 4:00 and 5:00 a.m. This was the best time in Atlanta, guaranteed to be the coolest of the day, which was a big deal during the increasingly long, oppressive summers. As she gently rocked, she welcomed the darkness of her street. The massive oak tree towering over the porch even shaded the streetlights and dwindling moonlight.

Best of all was the near absence of machine noise. The southeasterly wind carried muted highway noise from I-285 two miles away, and a siren off in the distance was likely headed to DeKalb Medical Center. But the only other noises were the cicadas, crickets, and tree frogs. It wasn't the complete natural quiet like the forest or the Intracoastal, but no infernal buzzing of leaf blowers, fools racing motorcycles on Ponce, or trucks driving up the street with another Amazon delivery. She took a deep breath and slowly exhaled.

She rocked, enjoying the moment as the porch slats creaked almost in time with the morning bugs. Maggie knew she'd miss the house and her neighbors, but it was time to move on. She had overstayed her originally planned window by nearly 18 months, a deviation so severe it might jeopardize everything. Nostalgia, sentiment, friendship, or comfort weren't rational reasons to stick around. In fact, her very survival necessitated a change of scenery.

Maggie finished her coffee and went in to get dressed for work. One thing she wouldn't miss was the powder blue, ill-fitting, 100% polyester dress Duke insisted his waitresses wear. Aside from being hideous, the fabric made her break out in rashes and put off a funky smell after a full day of soaking up diner grease vapor. On the plus side, she didn't have to buy or clean her own since Duke used some service that swapped out a week's worth of uniforms every Monday.

Car packed, teeth brushed, and all dressed for work, Maggie sat down at the kitchen table and fired up her laptop to check messages and updates on the bombings. Buried within the standard overnight spam was the one email she hoped to find. While reading it, she gave out a muffled "Yes!" then hit delete.

Next, she opened her news feed for bombing updates and was greeted by a "Breaking News" banner, screaming "FBI Identifies Explosives Origin." Maggie read the details, a smirk rising on the corners of her mouth. She quickly switched over to social media and nearly laughed out loud at the posts and reactions. While she was enjoying her coffee in the peace and solitude of her front porch, the leader of the free world was on a Twitter rant with his followers. He was crowing well before even the most eager rooster was awake.

Maggie closed her laptop. Yes, it's definitely time to move.

25.

overnor Murray sat at the edge of the bed, delaying the inevitable. Believing out of sight, out of mind, Skip stashed his cell phone in the bedside table overnight, knowing it would be constantly buzzing with messages. He cautiously opened the drawer for a quick peek then quickly closed it again. Eventually Skip would have to check the online carnage, but he wasn't quite ready for the shock.

He slept marginally better than the night before, thanks to his family being safely ensconced at the farm and the waning enthusiasm from the protesters outside the gate. He knew the break from both was temporary.

He stumbled over to the window and pulled the curtain aside to assess the crowd. The numbers had thinned considerably, and most were sitting in small clusters. Maybe the little bootlicker at Homeland Security had kept his word, for surely the protesters would be at fever pitch again if the president was aware of the latest development. He stood at the window, rubbing his solid round belly and convinced his lucky white bulldog summer PJ's had done their job. He attributed a good deal of yesterday's misfortune to the housekeeping staff's laziness for not cleaning them promptly.

With a contented sigh, the governor let the curtain fall back into place. Skip left the window and waddled into the bathroom for his morning constitution, his bowels being about the only part of his life he could count on no matter the circumstance. He assumed the throne and began to replay the events of yesterday.

For the most part, Monday had been a damn good day. If not for the last several hours, it may have ranked as one of the top ten of his life. Jose's strategy was inspirational and wildly successful. Hell, even the BBC ran footage of the governor bravely mingling with the horde of angry protestors then boldly marching to the waiting SUV to seek justice. The video clip was nearly superhero-like.

Jose was also spot-on about striking before Bubba hit the morning news show. Of course, he still spouted a wild-eyed "we're under siege from foreigners" rant, which he did most everyday regardless, yet the governor's performance had changed the dynamic. After Bubba spewed his mind, the talking news head of *Badger and Buds* had no choice but to mention the governor's comments—Jose's actually—that justice, not judgment, was law enforcement's priority. Choosing to ignore her question, Bubba retreated back to his tried-and-true speech about what's wrong with America and the countless groups contributing to her downfall. The only variation was now the inclusion of environmentalists to his enemies of the state list. The governor won that round.

As the day wore on, most of the news was mixed. Helicopter reconnaissance of the entire state came back with no outward signs of further bombs, satisfying the billboard companies enough for them to begin their own inspections that afternoon. Sweeps also came up clean at key infrastructure points, power plants, water treatment facilities, the Savannah harbor, Kingsbay Naval Submarine Base, and commercial airports, suggesting further carnage was not suspected. The governor gave the green light for businesses and schools to reopen.

Law authorities zeroed in on three key facts during the day's investigation: billboards were the only targets, the terrorists were selective in their choice of location, and the precision of execution avoided damaging power lines, property, streets, or cars. The explosive experts were impressed with the terrorists' planning, as well as their knowledge of burst pattern and physics to minimize collateral damage. What first appeared to be a hodgepodge target selection process was now considered a tool in profiling potential suspects. Whoever did this really hated billboards.

Armed with the data, the FBI's profilers confirmed the early theory that eco-terrorists or those with a personal vendetta were the most likely perpetrators. They briefly considered morality groups in the vendetta category, since many of the targeted billboards carried advertising of questionable taste for the general public. It didn't take long for the FBI to realize questionable advertising was the nature of the business. Morality groups were stricken from the list.

With most other personal grudges eliminated, the FBI narrowed in on the Worthington family. The grandsons of the founder included the disgruntled second in command at Veteran and a medically-discharged veteran whose expertise just so happened to be explosives.

The governor was not so surprised about the development. As a young man in the Georgia Assembly, he knew, and liked, their father. A genial yet shrewd businessman, he steered Veteran from the humble beginnings of his father to a state-wide powerhouse. It was a well-respected and extremely politically-generous company. To think they could have anything to do with this was almost laughable.

But he had to admit that Roger Fischer was a smarmy pain in the ass who had the potential to drive any peace-loving individual over the edge. Sure, like his father-in-law, he was a good businessman and generous with donations, but he put off an aura that made

Skip want to shower after talking with him. He empathized with the son stuck working under him and had to admit the theory had some credence.

Unfortunately, that trail quickly went nowhere. Authorities searched both of their residences and found not a single microbe of incriminating evidence. It also turned out the vet's medical discharge was from a developed aversion to touching explosives. Poor guy was struggling to survive even with good care from the VA. And the other Veteran off-spring? A law-abiding milquetoast without even a speeding ticket to his name.

The crushing news came shortly after dinner, and the governor immediately understood the ramifications. The FBI placed all of their forensic resources on analyzing the bomb evidence and came to a startling conclusion: the explosives used were likely tied to a previous criminal act done by the notorious Guadalupe Cartel. Drugs. Mexicans.

Not just any Mexicans either, this cartel was the most despised by the president, the ones he always held up as the most threatening bogeymen the country had ever seen. His animosity came from events that occurred two years ago in rural Texas. Several weeks after a flashy press conference unveiling 15 miles of border fencing, the Guadalupes tunneled underground, not to sneak in but to blow the fence up. It was quite a spectacle. Three sections were blown to smithereens, leaving gaps 20 yards wide.

While the president was left ranting and rushing resources to Texas, the Guadalupes smuggled five tons of cocaine into the states through the now understaffed legal points of entry. Blowing up the fence as a diversion was an amazing and audacious ruse. It took the DEA and FBI six months to figure out what the cartel pulled off, but the snookering was never shared with the public.

The Feds determined the Guadalupes' explosives matched those stolen from a company in Louisiana nearly a decade earlier.

Lafitte Demolition and Salvage reported the theft in the weeks following Hurricane Katrina, though no one knew exactly when the crime was committed. Like so many Louisiana businesses, Lafitte's had been heavily damaged with many of their employees displaced by the storm. Once the recovery began, they made the discovery. Obviously, the crime was never solved, but the FBI was convinced the explosives from the Guadalupes' border bombing and the Georgia billboard attack both came from Lafitte.

The Homeland Security guy was so excited he almost wet his pants. He couldn't wait to tell the president and let all hell break loose. Both the FBI and GBI pled relentlessly for him to hold off, or at least to get the president to wait before going public as they needed time to notify authorities the billboard attacks may well be another possible diversion. He agreed, but all in the room knew he'd make the call the minute they left him alone.

Governor Murray had been sitting there so long his legs fell asleep. Time to face the music. He flushed the toilet, washed his hands, and headed to the bedside table to fetch his cell phone. Cringing, he hit the power button, certain his phone was on fire.

26.

arry stood in his doorway watching the daybreak shadows slide across the field the militia boys ceremoniously dubbed the parade ground. He had been awake for several hours expecting the call and was somewhat surprised it hadn't come in the middle of the night.

He was grateful for the extra time as he needed to nail his performance with Bubba. He knew the psycho shit weasel doc was whining to the congressman about his dedication to the cause. Knowing Bubba was going to be at the big house later today, Barry was further motivated in hopes of avoiding a face-to-face meeting. As he worked through his thoughts. Barry became more confident in his strategy to placate Bubba.

He answered his cell before the second ring. "Morning, Bubba." He left the doorway and hurried across the cramped living room, taking a seat in front of the computer at his small desk.

The congressman's voice was both condescending and accusatory. "Hey, Barry, surprised I caught you up so early."

Yes, the weasel ratted Barry out. "You kidding me? After the heads-up from your office last evening, I've been camped out here in front of my computer. The situation is too perfect. Been using some of the aliases I created to support the president's latest Tweet on the Mexicans and am working to update our blog. Need to get something out fast. Strike hard and early to get the most exposure."

"I'm glad to hear that, Barry. Thought you'd be out walking that flunky dog of yours. Good to hear you got your priorities straight."

Barry took a deep breath, ignored the dig, and stuck to his rehearsed lines. "That can wait. Hell, everything can wait!" That was too enthusiastic, he thought to himself. Tone it down some. "I was about to call. Wanted to bounce a couple of things off of you before I get too far ahead of myself."

Bubba took on a completely different tone. "Absolutely. Fire away!"

Barry muffled his triumph. Over the years, he came to understand that the rich and powerful viewed themselves as more intelligent than Joe Paycheck. It didn't matter if a toadstool could outshine them on *Jeopardy*, they believed the larger the investment portfolio, the higher the IQ. It was worse for those who started with family money or just got lucky—yes, dumb luck played a part—as they couldn't comprehend the success of hard work. Instead they floated through life with egotistical entitlement. Barry's experience had taught him how to appeal to their sense of smug self-brilliance to get what he wanted. Right now, he only wanted to survive.

"As you know, this weekend is our monthly ALM training exercise here at the compound. The blog I'm about to post, in essence, is a call to arms. The Minutemen were a militia of Patriots fighting for our nation's liberty. The ALM is the militia protecting America's liberty." He purposely kept his historical references at Bubba's level of comprehension.

Bubba enthused, "Damn, Barry! That's downright poetic. I like it, but don't get the boys too fired up. You know we can't fire the first shot."

"You're right, Bubba, we can't. But we can make ourselves such an inviting target the enemy can't resist. Once they make a mistake, it's open season!"

"What do you have in mind? Don't go too wild. I'm not a fan of getting any of our boys hurt so soon."

"A little late for that, isn't it, Bubba? Doc accused me of being soft, don't want him to get the wrong impression of you too." Barry broke into a sly grin. He'd set up the congressman perfectly. All was working as planned.

"Dammit, Barry, that's a totally different ballgame. Doc's in pursuit of a valuable scientific breakthrough." He paused for second and conceded, "But I get your point. Sacrifices are necessary."

"I'd be surprised if this first step will result in bloodshed. Anyway, my thought was to hold an open ALM enlistment in Atlanta this Saturday. No protests or rallies. We'll show up with the regulars and make it like a damn career day! Do your patriotic duty, stop the radical infestation, help us protect everything we hold dear. No mention of white rights or illegals. We know that's what it's about, and hell, everyone else does too, but we don't publicize that. No, the day is a peaceful gathering to encourage others to join. Done right, we'll come off as the defenders, not the aggressors. What do you think?"

The silence was brief as Bubba thought it through. "You might be on to something. I admit I like that 'defender not aggressor' line. Bet the counterprotestors would go ape shit. Probably good video of decent, calm men signing up to do what's right while the punks yell and scream."

Barry didn't speak. He wanted Bubba to work it out in his head.

"Where would you hold it? Location is important."

"I've been giving that some thought, and your opinion would be great." Barry tried to slip into his subservient mode. "Stone Mountain is out. The press would just lump it as another KKK rally. I thought about Centennial Park, but the press would dig up the Olympic bombing and tie us to that loner crackpot. Piedmont Park is a good option, but I'm leaning towards Liberty Plaza. Being right next to the Capitol might piss off the Governor. You okay with that?"

"Okay, with that?! I think it's fantastic! That boy's turned out to be a major disappointment. He actually wanted to smother the news about the Mexicans, saying the FBI still thinks it was some lame Eco group. Can you believe that? Liberty Plaza, it is! Put some pressure on that yellow-bellied traitor."

"I was hoping you'd feel that way, Bubba. So, you're okay with the plan? You want to check the blog before I post it?"

"I'm sure whatever you write will be fine. You've always been better at the written word than me. Carry on, Commander! Hey, why don't you come to the Plantation this evening for a bourbon?"

"Thanks for the invite, Bubba. Depends on how much I get done today. Lots of planning needed if we're to be ready Saturday. I'll let you know."

Barry sat back in his chair, proud of his handling of Bubba and relieved to have successfully diffused any doubts the doc might have sown. The social invitation was a good sign that he bought himself some time.

He booted up his computer to finish the recruitment day ALM blog post only to come face to face with his screensaver photo of the lovely Francisca. The euphoria from the call with Bubba instantly evaporated. It was his favorite photo of the two of them, taken in front of Caesar's Palace less than a week before she slipped out of Vegas.

Deep down, he knew his relationship with Francisca was doomed from the start, but his inherent naïve optimism prevented him from seeing that basic truth. Aside from their decades of age difference, she was an intelligent, principled woman studying Law at UNLV, determined to return to her hometown of Manaus, Brazil and defend the native farmers' logging rights from the never-ending litigation brought by tree huggers. With such passion and drive, it should have been clear to Barry that his charm and money would be appealing for only so long.

And that window was only about one year. Two days after the photo was taken, Francisca graduated with honors, and three days after that, she sold most of her belongings to a pawn shop off the Strip and bought a one-way ticket to Manaus. Barry was crushed. Her Dear John letter did offer some solace as she professed a true caring for Barry, but her life's destiny lay in the jungles of Brazil, not the deserts of America. He gave fleeting thoughts to giving chase but thought better of it once he discovered Manaus was deep in the rainforest more than 900 miles up the Amazon River.

Barry couldn't help but think how his life might be different if Francisca hadn't left him. He definitely wouldn't have slinked off to Utah with his tail between his legs, licking his wounds. And Utah was where Barry reconnected with Bubba, which ended up with moving back to Georgia and getting knee deep in this shit show.

He clicked his computer's enter key and Francisca's image gave way to the ALM's website. Now was not the time to dream or consider what ifs. He gave his blog another quick spellcheck then hit post.

27.

The beeping of a garbage truck, backing up to the dumpster three floors below, woke Seamus up. He was still in his La-Z-Boy, feet up with the FBI's Lafitte Demolition file splayed on his chest. His throat was scratchy, undoubtedly from snoring, and his mouth was so dry his lips felt stuck to his teeth. At least he caught some sleep.

Seamus pulled the lever to lower the footrest and slowly stood up, spine creaking as he rose. It was light outside, not glaring, so it still must be early. Plenty of time to study the files some more, shower, and grab breakfast before hitting PDK.

For lack of better options, or maybe out of curiosity, he decided to give Duke's a try. After all, it was close to PDK by Atlanta traffic standards. He arrived right as Scott was at the front register paying his bill.

"Morning, Seamus. You here to see me?"

"Hello, Scott. Not here for you. Thought I'd see what the breakfast's like."

Scott pretended disappointment. "Guess the search cleared me. My time being edgy was brief. But thanks to you, I'm the talk of the complex. I'll try to milk that for a while."

"Between your dog and the woman in 408, it was an interesting afternoon."

Scott softly laughed under his breath. "Sorry I forgot to mention Sparky. Unless you're a Dorito, he's pretty harmless. Emily admitted she accidently threw me under the bus. She's a sweet girl but has verbal filter issues."

Scott finished paying for his meal and tossed the loose change into the Muscular Dystrophy container. "Thanks, Duke. Why don't you seat Seamus at my table? The food won't bring him back, but maybe Maggie will."

It finally dawned on Seamus that Scott was wearing a Veteran Outdoor shirt and work boots. "Looks like you're on official business today."

Scott nodded his head. "Once you guys knocked off the aerial inspection, we started to inspect the undamaged locations. I hope to knock off I-85 to South Carolina today. You okay with that, even though I'm a suspect?"

Seamus's broad smile made his eyes squint. "Person of interest, not a suspect. No one's told me otherwise, so I don't see any reason why you can't check your property. Besides, we've gotten pretty sidetracked since yesterday's developments."

"Imagine sidetracked is an understatement. Bet the shit hit the fan with the whole Mexican thing. As if blowing up billboards wasn't weird enough."

"You have no idea." Seamus stopped there despite his impulse to go into greater detail. Maybe it was studying Scott's bookshelf, but he suddenly realized how comfortable he was with this guy. If it wasn't for the investigation, he wouldn't mind grabbing a beer with him.

Scott gave him a guy pat on the upper arm. "I best be going, lots of ground to cover. Good luck, Seamus."

As he headed out the door, Seamus said, "Scott, if it's any consolation, you're still on our list, just at the bottom."

Scott gave him a thumbs-up as he walked across the parking lot.

Seamus followed Duke to a table where a fresh setup and a hot cup of coffee were waiting. He took a sip and looked up to find Maggie had magically appeared. "Welcome back, Inspector Seamus. Glad to see we didn't scare you away."

He gave her a quick once over, not in a lecherous way, just soaking in her friendliness. "Good morning, Maggie. I decided I'd give the food a try today. Recommend anything?"

"Joking aside, the food's pretty good. It depends on what you're in the mood for or if you have any dietary restrictions. Also depends on what you're doing today. Will you be sitting around or active?"

"Wow, I didn't realize there was so much to consider." Seamus swore her eyes sparkled when she smiled.

"Seamus, this is a special place. We're a holistic diner, here to satisfy basic and spiritual needs."

He put down the menu. "You're right. I have a busy day and don't know when I'll eat again. I'll have the western omelet, hash browns, and wheat toast, please. Glass of OJ, too, with ice, if you don't mind."

"A good hearty meal. I'd suggest one change. Go with the cheese grits over hash browns. If you really want hash browns, there's a Waffle House up the street. Ours are a poor imitation."

"Let's do the grits. Thanks, Maggie."

Her gait toward the kitchen resembled a bound, not a glide, amble, or stroll—a springy step more like a running back looking for a hole to cut through than a waitress with order in hand. Her size was average, but she moved like an athlete, probably one of those women who kicked ass at yoga.

The coffee tasted extraordinarily good this morning, and Seamus found himself enjoying the moment. Maggie was back in a flash with his OJ.

He thanked her. "Maggie, don't take this the wrong way, but you seem, I don't know, perky today. There's an extra bounce in your step."

She cocked her hips to the right and put her hand on her waist. "You're an observant man. I am perky today. Once this shift is over, I'm headed up to the mountains for the night. Just a quick trip, I'll be back for tomorrow's lunch."

"That sounds fun. You have cabin or friends up there?"

"Silly, I don't need a cabin. I'll just hike until I find a spot that looks good for the night. Tons of places you can camp. The wilderness is manna for the soul. There's nothing else like it."

"I'm impressed. Not to sound like a dad, but is it safe for you to be out there by yourself?"

"Sweet of you to worry. I'm not alone. There are deer, bears, all sorts of critters that make a nature girl like me feel right at home."

A bell rang from the kitchen.

"I bet that's your breakfast, be right back." With that, she spun and pranced across the diner.

Seamus was truly impressed. Growing up the closest he had come to camping was sleeping in the backyard with his brother, and they only made it until midnight when a screeching alley cat sent them scrambling to the safety of the house. He liked the outdoors, and star gazing was fun, but something about sleeping unprotected with beady eyes and fangs lurking in the shadows unnerved him.

"That was fast," Seamus said as she set breakfast before him.

Maggie gave him a wink. "I asked the cooks to hurry. You're my last customer, and I'm trying to get rid of you. Need anything else?"

"I'm good, thanks."

She smiled and moved on to the next table as Seamus took a bite of his omelet. Either it was really good or he was starved.

He savored every bite as he surveyed the other customers and watched the staff work the room. He spent two summers working in restaurants and admired the efficiency at Duke's. The wait staff, bus boys, cooks, and even Duke moved like a choreographed dance troupe.

And the cheese grits were unbelievable. As a Midwesterner, he had been skeptical of grits at first, only establishing a taste after experimenting with increasing amounts of butter and pepper. These grits needed no such modification.

When Maggie swung back by with a coffee refill, Seamus announced, "You're right about the grits. They were sensational."

"Glad you liked them. Finished?"

"Yes. Thanks, Maggie. I'll take the check whenever you're ready."

Maggie stood studying Seamus. "Can I ask you something?"

"Sure," Seamus said, somewhat puzzled.

"We get a lot of law enforcement in here, and you just don't seem to fit the type." Maggie shifted the tray on her hip. "I don't mean that in a bad way, but most of them, the women too, have, I don't know, a hardness in the face. Not a grumpy look, but you can see the stress in their jaws. They have worry lines around their eyes and mouth. You might look a little tired, but your face is softer, in a good way. Either you're new to the job or a naturally peaceful guy."

Seamus was awed with her perceptiveness. "Now, you're the observant one. You can tell all of that by looking at my face?"

"I've been a waitress for a long time. It's important to size folks up when you're at their mercy for tips. The face tells me a lot about the person, sometimes more than I care to know." She kept her gaze locked on Seamus.

His response was involuntary. "Truth be told, I'm not really a field agent but a researcher. Majored in history and just kind of fell into the profession. I'm working this for a couple of reasons, but mostly because it's a big case and we need everybody."

The twinkle in her eyes returned. "History major and researcher...I like it. It suits you." She pulled his check from her apron pocket. "Please pay Duke up front. I hope you come back when I'm not in such a hurry."

"I'll do that, Maggie. Frankly, I'm in a hurry too. Got a plane to catch."

"Plane?" Maggie's brow furrowed in thought. "Don't tell me they're sending you to Mexico. Thought that was one of those fake internet stories."

"Hard to believe but it's true, though I'm going to Louisiana, not Mexico." He immediately chastised himself for saying too much. He wondered if it was the relaxed atmosphere of Duke's that muddled his mind and not his inexperience.

Seamus noticed her slight change of expression. The face tells a lot about the person. Two can play that game, he thought.

The spunkiness left her voice. "Sounds like you have a big day. Safe travels and don't be a stranger."

28.

The sun was barely up as Andrea drove Roger's pickup across State Route 21 toward Deer Bend Plantation. The military grade satellite reconnaissance photos were on her open computer sitting on the passenger seat, and a GoPro mini video recorder unit was affixed on the dash for later study.

The drive from Atlanta in a pickup truck had been fun. Pickup trucks were foreign to her though she now understood the allure of sitting up high in a vehicle with lots of metal. Of course, it helped that Roger's truck was fully decked out. She drove most of the way with the windows down, enjoying the cool breeze rushing through the truck and to see if any rednecks reacted to the Black, female arm resting on the door frame.

With an officer's rank and years in the service, Andrea had developed a wide network of allies, and it didn't take her long to find those who could help her out. Within an hour of returning to the hotel after her VA visit, she found out the Chevy was registered to a hunting lodge located in central Georgia called Deer Bend Plantation LLC. As her contacts dug for more information, Andrea began an internet search and came up with public records on the LLC's ownership structure, county tax map, and previous sales of property.

Andrea's research painted an unexpected picture. Deer Bend Plantation was the boyhood home of Congressman Jim "Bubba" Baker, a confidante of the president and the powerful Chair of the House Armed Services Committee. She was well aware of the congressman's reputation. Years ago, the congressman and his younger brother transformed the family farm into destination hunting lodge catering to the rich and influential. Bubba's influence drew politicians and businessmen to Deer Bend for deal cutting and king crowning. The list of past visitors told Andrea it was a secure location. It made no sense for Tom to be associated with these guys.

Additional tax records showed acreage to the west of Deer Bend had been sold off by the Bakers to an internationally-registered partnership called American Natural Preservation. The financial trail appeared to be nonexistent with no details on the amount paid, and the Cayman Islands incorporation papers provided no names, companies, or organizations. Somebody wanted to hide something.

While her service connections were unable to identify land ownership, they did link the property to a second-tier Nationalist group calling itself the American Liberation Militia. Definitely a fringe group, the ALM was best known for a well-designed website and blog packed with detailed white power policy statements and the occasional threatening rant. The property the Bakers sold was used as the ALM's weekend training facility.

Studying the reconnaissance photos, Deer Bend Plantation was a massive swath of land bordered by county roads. Red clay vehicle tracks crisscrossed the property, connecting fields and three small ponds. About a mile off the main road stood a large structure surrounded by two smaller buildings and a barn. The ALM property to the west was a wedge-shaped slice, bordering Deer Bend along

County Road 5 on one side and the Ocmulgee River on the other. A short drive up a dirt road from County Road 5 led to a small open field with a cluster of buildings set amongst a heavy forest.

Andrea saw a bridge up ahead and knew the ALM property was just across the Ocmulgee River on the right. She slowed the truck and quickly zipped up the windows. Once on the bridge, she hit record on the GoPro.

The terrain was flat, filled with dense brush, trees, and marshy areas. Private Property-No Trespassing signs were nailed to trees every 20 yards. The signs and barbed wire ranch fence discouraged random foot traffic from entering the property off the road. As she neared County Road 5, the dividing line between ALM and Deer Bend, she spotted a billboard on the northwest corner of the ALM property announcing the Middle Georgia Wildlife Management Area boat ramp four miles down County Road 5.

Straining to look up, she saw the Veteran logo at the base of the board and said out loud, "Excellent."

Passing County Road 5, the Deer Bend property began. The terrain was more rolling while the dense woods continued, with fancier Private Property-No Trespassing signs equally spaced out. Tucked in the woods about 12 feet off the road, she could see a barbed wire ranch fence similar to what protected the ALM property. After a mile, the fence changed from a ranch fence to one typical of a Kentucky horse farm with sturdy stone posts supporting six horizontal slats freshly painted white on either side.

The trees began to thin as she neared the entrance to Deer Bend. Andrea slowed to just above a crawl as she passed the main drive. Two large iron gates greeted visitors. An intercom/card swipe box was on the left, and video cameras were mounted to catch both the front and rear view of any vehicle trying to gain entry. The road leading in was paved and eventually disappeared into woods. She checked the satellite map and saw the road ended at the house.

Andrea gently accelerated and continued down Route 21. The horse farm fencing gave way to the barbed ranch fence after half a mile, and at three miles past County Road 5, the ranch fencing jutted back into the woods, signally the end of Deer Bend's property line. The land then cleared and several small, working poor farms dotted Route 21 until she came to Youngstown Road, which ran parallel to County Road 5 at the far eastern side of Deer Bend Plantation. At the corner, she pulled into a long abandoned, kudzu encased roadside vegetable stand to compare her mental notes with the satellite images on her computer.

Seeing it in person confirmed what she thought last night while studying the maps in her hotel room: accessing Deer Bend would not be easy. The property was huge with the wooded outer perimeter providing a natural barrier. If Andrea ventured south down Youngstown Road, the first house she'd find belonged to Congressman Baker's younger brother Dave, followed by a line of small farms all abutting the east side of Deer Bend. Even at night, she was not about to traverse open farmland and risk an encounter with a shotgun-toting farmer. Route 21 or County Road 5 were the only logical ingress points.

Andrea pulled away from the dilapidated vegetable stand to make a return pass of Deer Bend along Route 21. After seeing the video cameras at the gate, she closely studied the property lines looking for mounted cameras on poles. None were obvious, but that didn't mean they weren't there. She drove slowly until she neared the gated entrance then sped up to appear like normal traffic. Past the gate, she let off the accelerator and resumed an easy 25 mph as she continued to scan the Deer Bend property line. Nothing new jumped out during this second pass.

At County Road 5, she turned left and momentarily stopped to get a better view of the Veteran billboard and the small gravel road that led to storage sheds at its base.

Definitely a possibility, she thought.

County Road 5 wasn't much more than a mixture of asphalt, gravel, and dirt, wide enough for two cars in the unlikely chance someone was headed the opposite direction. The Middle Georgia Wildlife Management Area was a good four miles down the road, and judging from the reconnaissance maps, most visitors entered the Wildlife area from the more accessible opposite end of County Road 5. The remoteness was ideal for penetrating the perimeter, but where to stash her transportation was a problem.

Off the beaten path, Andrea drove just above idle while she canvassed both sides of the road. Ranch fencing hugged both the Deer Bend property on her left and ALM on the right. After about 50 yards, she stopped the truck, glanced around, and decided to get out to take a closer look. She studied the posts, wire, and barbs, and then crossed the street to the ALM side, finding it exactly the same.

She got back in the truck and preceded south. After a half a mile, she came to a drive on the right, the entrance to ALM according to her map. The drive was mostly Georgia red clay, but that's not what captured her attention. Two large iron gates, an intercom/card swipe box, and two mounted video cameras, all strikingly similar to Deer Bend, prevented access to the property. Either a skilled salesman sold a package deal or it really wasn't two separate properties. Not wanting to get captured on video, she didn't pause at the gate.

Further down County Road 5 was a bridge spanning a stream that fed the Ocmulgee. The newer, wider, and substantially built bridge was out of place on the run-down county road. Andrea pulled over to check it out. Peering over the side, the bridge's purpose was evident. It not only spanned the creek but a dirt track that connected the two properties, bending on each side back in the general direction of the main buildings. The track was well worn from frequent use.

Andrea got back in the truck and continued the drive south. In a couple of miles, she was greeted with the brown "Welcome to the Middle Georgia Wildlife Management Area" sign, complete with the requisite bullet holes. She never understood the attraction of sign shooting, a target too large for any self-respecting marksman. She turned right into a parking lot where a park ranger was unloading canoes from a double trailer and carrying them down to the boat ramp. She stopped Roger's pickup truck well short of the ranger and pulled out the satellite map.

Zooming in, the dirt road connecting the ALM buildings to Deer Bend Plantation's main house was plain as day. An eyeball calculation told her it was between two-and-a-half to three miles between sites. She figured ALM was only about a mile from the river, but the forest canopy blocked any view of a potential path or road down to the river. She quickly decided this was the best option: head from the river, recon ALM, then follow the dirt road to Deer Bend. Roundtrip, ten miles tops and easy to do in the middle of night with the proper gear. She stowed her laptop, strung binoculars around her neck, and went to talk with the park ranger.

"Good morning," Andrea announced as she approached the ranger as he unstrapped another canoe from the trailer.

The ranger stopped wrestling the canoe and smiled. "And good morning to you! I was wondering if you were going to get out of your truck."

Andrea returned the smile. "Just checking my maps. I didn't know if I was in the right place or not."

"You a chaperone for the kids? What a perfect day for a field trip." He hoisted a canoe on his shoulders and began the walk down the boat ramp.

Andrea followed behind. "Kids? No, I'm just visiting from Atlanta for a quiet day of birding. I didn't know a pack of monsters would be here too."

The ranger deftly swung the canoe off his shoulders, gently dropped it in the water, and slid the bow up on the riverbank. He straightened and turned to Andrea. "If they're anything like the last group, monsters are what I'd call them too. Guess it's to be expected of middle schoolers." He pulled a bandana from his back pocket to dab a bead of sweat rolling down his cheek. "So, you're a birder. Don't really know if…"

Andrea politely finished his thought. "Don't really fit the profile, do I? I get that a lot. Not many of us Black birders."

The ranger nodded, obviously grateful he hadn't offended her. "You picked a great spot. Over 200 species have been identified here. Must admit I'd like to join you rather than trying to explain the beauty of nature to disinterested kids."

"I bet a couple will be interested. You may be surprised on the impact you make. It was a field trip many years ago where a ranger sparked my interest." Andrea convincingly lied. It was really her dad that got her into birding, but it was a necessary to get the ranger on her side.

"Thanks. I hope that's the case."

Andrea pointed at the canoes. "So, how much is it to rent one of these?"

The ranger's eyebrows arched in surprise. "I'm sorry. These canoes are for the kids. We don't rent canoes to the public."

Andrea's disappointment was sincere. "Oh, that's a shame. I saw you here and thought how perfect it would be to do some river watching. You sure I can't rent or borrow one, just for a couple of hours?"

They could hear the school bus before it pulled into the parking lot, the riotous din of excited tweens escaping through the half-opened windows. The bus made a loop in the parking lot before stopping next to the boat ramp, chaos erupting inside.

The ranger looked at Andrea, complete defeat in his eyes, "Okay, but please take me with you."

Andrea laughed sympathetically. "You still have time. We could make a break for it right now. Your expert knowledge of the river would be a huge plus."

"I would if I could," the ranger sighed. "Take the green one. It's already got a paddle and life jacket in it. Just be back by 2:00."

She resisted the urge to hug the ranger. "This means a lot. Thank you so much."

"Us birders need to stick together. Now hurry up before I change my mind." As if on cue, the bus doors opened and pandemonium erupted.

Andrea scrambled into the canoe and began paddling upstream away from the excitement. The ranger's generosity gave her a good five hours to scout the river. At the first river bend, she looked back and saw two teachers vainly trying to stop a rock fight between a pack of rambunctious boys while the ranger avoided the line of fire and squatted with a couple of inquisitive kids at the river's edge.

Past their view, she began a vigorous paddle. The Route 21 bridge crossing the Ocmulgee was her target. Once there she would leisurely float-paddle back downstream as if she were a legitimate birder. She planned on two hours upstream and three back, plenty of time to get a lay of the land. The current was stronger than she had imagined, and it would be a tough slog to Route 21.

The river truly was beautiful, with long straight stretches broken by wild serpentine turns where she hit all four points of the compass. The forest grew close to the river, creating a tunnel that muted outside noise, only her paddle and the occasional creature breaking the silence. True to the ranger's comment, it was a perfect place for birding. Within the first 20 minutes she saw American Coots, a Belted Kingfisher, a Green Heron, and heard the call of a Whip-poor-will. Andrea reminded herself this wasn't a sightseeing tour. She was on a strict schedule and needed to keep up the pace.

After an hour of paddling, the Private Property-No Trespassing signs reappeared, telling her she'd reached the ALM property line. On the plus side, there didn't appear to barbed wired ranch fencing along the river or any video cameras positioned in trees. Video cameras were a concern though she knew it was a technical and logistical headache—only a Wi-Fi network could capture video on such a large piece of property. That was a problem she'd need to address later. Not breaking her pace, she pressed on, making mental note of the several locations where a path led out of the ALM woods to the river.

She reached the Route 21 bridge before 10 a.m., having not seen a soul since the ranger and the kids. The southeast corner was ALM property, so she went under the bridge and landed the canoe on the northwest corner. After stretching the knots out, she hiked up a narrow path to Route 21. Patches along the shoulder had been worn down from parked cars, probably locals stopping to fish or swim in the river. She liked the spot with its easy access to the river and close proximity to the ALM property.

Andrea returned to the canoe, pulled camo out of her backpack, and made a quick change of clothes before getting back in the canoe. She also got her sidearm just in case. She paddled back under the bridge, now hugging the left side of the river looking for the first path leading onto the ALM property.

As she drifted along, she heard a huge splash ahead, way too big for a fish or bird. Gator, she thought as she unholstered her gun. As ripples spread across the water, she brought the canoe to a halt next to an overhanging tree and grabbed her binoculars.

Another huge splash made Andrea hold her breath. Then she saw it: a black Labrador swimming furiously towards a bobbing yellow tennis ball, lunging to grab it, then spinning back to shore. Unfortunately, the tree blocked her view of the thrower, but fortunately, the Lab remained too damn excited to notice anything else. After what seemed to be a hundred tosses, the dog began to bark furiously at the thrower. Andrea didn't speak Lab, but the message was clear: "What do you mean that's it? Keep throwing. This is a blast! I'm not the least bit tired!"

The barking stopped. She waited several minutes before letting go of the tree to drift downstream, binoculars in hand to look like a birder in case they were just taking a rest. She came to a rock outcropping several feet above the waterline, the wet rocks evidence this was the dog's launching pad. No sign of the dog or thrower.

Andrea sat for a moment. "Oh, what the hell," she muttered as she pulled the canoe into another set of trees and set off up the path, trailing the dog and thrower.

29.

"Where you going, JR?" Mike called out from his post on the opposite side of the parade ground.

JR didn't look up but yelled back, "Checking my work from last night." Then, in a voice not loud enough to carry, he mumbled, "Keep your pants on, you big wuss."

JR took the path behind the so-called barracks and plodded up the trail. Last night's chore improved his mood, but the need to follow up didn't sit well. Guess it was better than standing guard with Mike.

His spirits were lifted enough that he pretended to be back on scout detail in the Army. His rifle cradled in his right arm, he'd take several steps, then stop and hold up his left arm to signal the imaginary corps to follow his lead. Of course, he never led anyone in the Army. The fact that after four years of active duty he never made it past Private was proof enough.

Looking back, he really did enjoy parts of the Army. When in uniform, people treated him with respect and seemed to be genuinely concerned about his welfare. He learned about, and got to use, all sorts of really cool guns and explosives. Some of his fellow

GIs were pretty decent, and they began calling him JR, a much better nickname than Scrap.

Those were the highlights, and nearly everything else only pissed him off. It started in boot camp when he found out his unit included women, Blacks, gays, and even a Muslim. Seriously, this is the Army of the great U.S. of A., not some type of liberal slumber party! What made it worse was he came in nearly dead last on every basic training measurement: obstacle course, stamina, marksmanship, and, not surprisingly, discipline. It was bad enough sharing mess with this ragtag group of so-called Americans, but having his butt kicked in basic training skills by these fruitcakes was downright humiliating. His drill instructor found it all too amusing and often used JR as the example of what not to do.

After boot camp the situation didn't improve. Desperate for new recruits overseas, JR's unit was shipped off to a succession of bases in the most god-awful parts of the world, each nearly identical outposts of sand, rock, and heat. His commanding officers quickly surmised JR's service record of ineptitude was correct and made sure to assign him menial roles, mostly in the motor pool or on KP. The symbolism wasn't lost on JR. He knew in WWII the Army assigned the Black soldiers to kitchen duty, and now here he was, an original white American, considered a second-class citizen. His dad had been right.

JR's military career ended one night out in the desert foothills of Afghanistan. His unit spent two, long grueling weeks out on patrol while JR remained at base camp performing routine maintenance on a fleet of Humvees. With the unit out on mission, pickings were slim for soldiers to perform critical base security duties, such as night sentry. JR finally got the call to guard the base's western perimeter and was determined to demonstrate his mettle.

The heroic romance of sentry patrol wore off in less than an hour. The best thing about standing out in the desert after midnight were the bright stars, not that he was a fan of anthropology or whatever the hell they call looking at stars. Boredom had long set in after walking the same patch of sand for a good four hours, so his mind and eyes began to wander. At first he thought it was just a bright star, but this thing was moving. He stopped in his tracks. Not only was it moving, he could hear a little whir sound coming from its direction. He couldn't believe it. The damn Taliban had a drone and was about to attack! JR raised his rifle.

For the first and only time in his military career, he showed incredible marksmanship. He felt a surge of prideful adrenaline as the drone emitted a flame and then plummeted into a mountainside, bursting into a glorious fireball. It was a thing of beauty.

The sentry unit sergeant ran up to JR as he stood admiring his handiwork. The damn guy lit into him. "What the hell did you just do, you dumb son of a bitch?!"

JR had been expecting a well-deserved congratulation, not attitude from some East LA dude. He got in the Sergeant's face. "While you sat on your ass in that trailer, I was doing my job by saving the unit from a damn Taliban attack!"

"The Taliban doesn't have drones, you moron. That was ours!"

JR didn't even think of that. "Ours? That don't make sense us having drones here. Shouldn't they be looking for the enemy?"

"They are! What the hell do you think I was doing in the trailer! Now, our entire outer perimeter is blind, and we have no surveillance support for our forward troops. You've got to be the most worthless GI in history! Get the hell off my unit. You're dismissed, Private!"

About the only good thing to come of that night, aside from nailing that sucker with one shot, was that within 24 hours he was discharged, and in less than a week, he was sitting on a bar stool at Stonewall's getting free beer.

JR stopped and held up his left hand again. He paused for a moment to make sure the coast was clear then waived on this ghost corps. "Not a big fan of woods," he told his men, "but it's a helluva lot better than sweating your balls off in Afghanistan!"

After a hundred yards, he turned left onto one the main paths leading to the river. The constant stopping for recon added a good ten minutes to the half-mile hike.

"Okay, men, you guard my flank," JR ordered. "I'm going in solo."

He split to the right onto a small trail that only he used. It veered further from the main path and stopped in a small clearing surrounding by three large live oaks. He went over to the freshly filled hole. No critters had been rooting around, so the body was buried deep enough. The sight of the dirt mound brought him back to reality. He spat on the grave for good measure.

The doc had decided JR was best suited for killing the test rejects; something about channeling his inner anger caused by parental abandonment. What a load of psychobabble bullshit. The real reason being doc was too much of a pussy to do it himself, even though technically he offed two of them with his quack drug experiments. JR didn't mind the killing but couldn't understand why he had to bury them too. Seems like Mike could do something. Hell, the big lug could at least dig the hole.

JR was fed up with these fools, field training, and marching, only to go protest at some park. All show and no action. Too many times he'd heard the lame excuse that they had to build a fighting force first, a solid unit able to stand up to the enemy. But a force isn't built by holding weekend keggers in the woods and trying to brainwash drugged out homeless vets. No, only firm action would rally the believers. He spat on the grave again and turned to head back to the compound.

JR stopped in his tracks, his left hand instinctively held up in the halt position. Up ahead on the main trail, he sensed movement that was too big for a boar. It wasn't rooting around like an animal. The motions were slow and methodical, almost like stalking. His eyes narrowed, trying to get a better look. The leaves and underbrush obscured his view, but he definitely saw patches of black mixed in with what sure looked like camo.

"Fuck me," JR mouthed to himself as he nestled the rifle against his shoulder and leveled his aim. "Someone's broken our perimeter." He squeezed the trigger.

"Hold your fire!" a voice yelled from the woods as a black blur shot from the bushes, hightailing it towards the compound. "Dammit, JR! It's me and Moon. You hurt that dog, and you'll be the next one buried out here."

JR watched Barry run up the trail. "Your precious mutt is fine, probably already sitting on the porch. Ain't never seen such a worthless hunting dog. Damn chicken."

The old man was panting from the trot. "I swear you've got no sense. If you weren't such a shitty shot, we wouldn't let you carry that damn thing around."

JR gave him a cold stare. "I wasn't such a shitty shot last night."

"No, no you weren't," Barry's eyes drifted to the ground.

JR was glad to see his comment hit home.

"C'mon, JR, let's walk back together. I want to talk about this weekend."

The old guy waved his hand, and JR led the way.

Barry settled in behind him. "JR, there's been a change in plans for the weekend. We're canceling the monthly maneuvers."

"Don't bother me none. Never thought they were much use anyway." JR kept his pace slower than usual.

"They do serve a purpose, but after speaking with Bubba this morning, we decided to do something different this weekend."

JR excitedly spun to Barry, but the old man's expression dashed his hopes. "Not another protest! I ain't going on any more protests! Damn waste of time. We just stand there looking like fools with queers yelling at us."

"It's not a waste of time, JR. It's a very important part of the strategy. Our job is to instigate the enemy, prod them to take the first step. Once they make a move, our response will not only be justified but cheered. We can't take the first shot. Some fool did that in Charlottesville, and we lost any chance at momentum."

"Whatever. Still a pansy-assed thing to do. No way for a self-respecting fighting man to act."

"Well, we're not calling this weekend a protest. It's a recruitment conference."

JR paused again and looked over his shoulder at the old man.

Barry continued. "Bubba thinks we can use the Mexican's bombing of Georgia as our window of opportunity to get recruits. Anxiety and suspicion are high, perfect for us to get defenders."

JR forged on through the woods fuming. "Bubba's full of shit. His last brilliant idea was bringing in that fake doc and infesting this place with wacked out druggies. No way any of those guys will ever be worth a damn. We'd have better luck going to Morehouse to get soldiers."

The old man let out a hearty laugh. "I'm impressed, JR. Excellent display of irony! We agree on the doc. He's as clueless as they come. But Bubba writes the checks, so let's give this a try. It just might work."

JR didn't know what was so funny or what irons had to do with anything. He tried to tune Barry out as they made their way back to the compound. The old guy sure could talk, going on and on about holding the recruitment at the aptly named Liberty Plaza, having all the weekend warriors standing at attention in full camo, getting together an official looking color guard with American flags flapping in the wind, positioning JR front and center to greet new recruits, all while patriotic songs blared over a sound system. It would be epic! Even if they didn't get many new sign-ups, the visuals would be great for TV. Hell, maybe even

CNN would cover it! JR liked the thought of standing front and center, but the rest was bullshit.

JR and Barry stopped at the edge of the woods with the ALM parade ground opening up in front of them. The wimpy black Lab was paws up on the grass getting his belly rubbed by the doc's prized patient. JR could tell the guy wasn't feeling good today. Lughead Mike was still on guard duty, standing off to the side supposedly keeping an eye on the patient, but JR knew he was probably half asleep. The doc was busy "observing" his patient while occasionally scribbling notes in his journal. JR found himself feeling half bad for this one. He wasn't nearly as worthless, but he'd end up buried in the woods just like the others. The doc was the real moron who threatened the operation.

30.

Congressman James "Bubba" Baker admired himself in front of the master bathroom mirror in his swank, multimillion-dollar Georgetown brownstone. He wore his favorite suit, just a dab of makeup for the TV cameras, the necessary red tie with thin blue strips, and an American flag label pin. Satisfied with the image, he bound down the stairs where his staff was waiting to usher him to the waiting limo.

Bubba had good reason to be walking on air this fine Tuesday morning. Nothing could be better than to follow breakfast with a full slate of network appearances to smugly tell the smarty-pants press he and the president were right and they were wrong. Follow that with a quick trip to the Plantation for quality schmoozing, fine bourbon, and potential female companionship, and it had the makings of a perfect day. Bubba floated into the climate-controlled limo oozing with self-righteousness.

Mexican terrorists attacking his state was a gift too good to be true, so ideal he almost didn't believe it when the Director of Homeland Security called him last evening with the heads up. The president's reserve holding off the announcement until early this morning gave his staff plenty of time to line up the interviews even before his feet left the bed. He'd hit the other networks first then wrap it up with his friends at *Badger and Buds* before heading back to Georgia.

Now in his eighth term, Bubba was riding the crest. With his family name, political capital, gerrymandered district, and massive campaign war chest, he had job security even nepotism couldn't provide. He latched on to the new president knowing full well it would play great back in his district and earn him huge points with a man who treated loyal mouth pieces better than his own children. This devotion landed plum seats on the Appropriations, Armed Services, Energy and Commerce, and Veterans Affairs Committees, each giving him the power to direct funds to key state allies and make the connections he needed to line his own pockets. A side benefit was valuable press face time for the voters back home. Putting on a little makeup and chatting up a reporter was a hell of a lot easier than shaking hands and kissing babies. The press loved his name, soft drawl, downhome humor, and steadfast conviction that the president was always right.

Sure, it was hard work, but most of the heavy lifting was done by his passel of aides, all willing to work interminable hours for the privilege of listing the experience on their resumes. Now his main concerns were figuring out the PACs with the deepest pockets and lowest expectations, meeting lobbyists with the biggest expense accounts, and disguising boondoggles as fact-finding trips. Spouting about troubles, subversives, interlopers, and mooches on TV was a full-time passion; passing meaningful legislation was a waste of time and energy. Letting the idealists worry about that, Bubba had different priorities.

After making the morning TV rounds, he was whisked to Reagan Airport where a shadow PAC-funded private jet—flying commercial was for uncreative losers—waited to take him to

Georgia. On the jet, he changed from his suit to his standard out-doorsman outfit that worked well with constituents and hunting lodge guests. Landing at the county airport, the runway extended for jet traffic courtesy of federal government funding provided by Congressman Baker, Bubba's mood was lifted even further when he saw two Atlanta news trucks parked at the hanger.

He strode off the jet and approached the waiting microphones like a conquering hero. Before launching into his litany, he held up his hands as if to stop the nonexistent applause. Bubba stuck to the same basic script as he had with the national press in DC but tossed a couple of solid hits at the governor for being soft and not willing to stand up for true Georgians. Bubba left the microphone bank after fielding three questions and hopped in the back of a Deer Bend Suburban where Andy Nelson sat at the wheel with a huge smile.

"Truer words were never spoke, Congressman. Great to have you back."

"Thanks, Andy. Good to be back with folks who understand. If the shit that's been going on doesn't wake them up then nothing will. Bunch of naïve fools."

"Amen to that. Sorry you missed the hunt. They won't be back until late afternoon. You still want to go to the big house or to the river?"

"Big house is fine. I'll grab some lunch and take a nap. Been burning both ends. Admit it'll be nice just to kick back for a couple of hours. You been over there lately?"

Andy looked in the rearview mirror at the congressman. "Dropped by after work yesterday. Guess they're making progress with one guy, but one didn't make the cut. JR's as wired as ever. Hope that boy keeps it together."

The congressman shook his head and chuckled. "Fucking JR. That boy's a damn mess. But once this all starts, we'll be glad he's on our side."

Andy nodded his head, and they drove on in a rare silence.

Bubba caught Andy's eyes in the mirror again. "Speaking of work, why aren't you in school today?"

"Called in sick to pick you up. Didn't want the USA's best congressman getting picked up by the regular help. Figured the kids would enjoy a day with a sub. Let them screw off some."

"Must admit I was glad it was you." The congressman stared out the window as they crossed the Ocmulgee on Route 21, a contented look on his face. "Surprised nobody's parked at the bridge today."

"It being a Tuesday, most don't stop by until after work. By supper, I'm sure some boys will show up."

Bubba stared out the window and didn't respond. He never understood the allure of fishing and couldn't imagine how anyone would willingly just sit there watching some floater bob in the Ocmulgee. He didn't begrudge fishermen in general. Hell, he even bought a fancy deep sea fishing yacht as another influence peddling tool. But he never set foot on the boat, leaving others to act as his proxy. No, Bubba held firm in his belief that a gun was the only sensible implement for a sporting man to kill something.

The Suburban slowed and turned into Deer Bend. Andy removed a key card from the visor, held it up to the pad, and the massive steel gates slowly creaked open. Bubba rolled down the window and inhaled the same smells his ancestors had for so many years. Well, almost the same air; the pungent cloud of cow dung no longer hung in the air since they stopped farming. He strained his ears hoping to hear hunters blasting away at boars but only heard the tires on the pavement winding to the big house.

Bubba and his brother Dave had torn down the original family homestead, knowing it wasn't stately enough for the fees they charged their clientele looking to get away for manly time. In its place stood a classic plantation home complete with a wraparound veranda on the ground floor with doors on all sides opening to the porch. The house had eight bedrooms, six guest bedrooms upstairs, each with access to the second-floor porch, and two more bedrooms safely stashed in the basement for the live-in help.

The main floor had a grand hall leading from the front to the back of the house. To the left was the dining room, and to the right was the bar/trophy room decorated with the obligatory kill heads mounted on the wall. Past the staircase was the large den with plenty of seating, 60" flat-screen TV, a smattering of books on a bookshelf, and French doors opening to an equally large screened-in porch that was glassed in during winter months. Bubba loved everything about it.

As Bubba's importance grew so did the popularity of the Plantation. Demand remained high even after repeatedly jacking the rates, which was no surprise since mostly corporations or PACs were paying the tab and price was never an issue. Within the last four years, they added two cabins that straddled the big house, one for more hunters and the other as Bubba's private lair. He realized the allure of the big house and setting one room aside for his whim was costing some serious change. His own cabin kept the revenue stream high and gave him his own space. Bubba could drink and tell stories in the trophy room then escape to his cabin where Andy usually arranged to have a young, lithe visitor waiting. Andy was damn good at finding volunteers.

Andy pulled the Suburban into the horseshoe past the big house, stopping in front of Bubba's cabin where Horace dutifully waited.

The door swung open. "Welcome back, Mr. James. Good to see you again."

Bubba bounced out of the Suburban. "Good to see you too, Horace. How's the family?" This was his standard greeting even though he didn't give a shit, much less remember the names of Horace's brood.

"Just fine, just fine. Thanks for asking. I'll grab your bags. We have lunch ready when you're hungry, or I can get you a beverage to unwind after your trip."

Bubba checked his watch to confirm it was past noon. He tried his damnedest to hold off cocktails in the morning. "Think I'll take that drink first. Have you heard from Shaw today?"

"Yes, sir. He wanted me to give him a ring once you got here. Says he wants to talk to you before going back to Atlanta."

"Go ahead and tell the good doctor I'm back. I'll help myself to that drink."

"Yes, sir. Right away, Mr. James." Horace rustled Bubba's bags from the Suburban and up the steps into the cabin.

Bubba circled the Suburban to the driver's window. "Appreciate the lift, Andy."

"Anything for you, Congressman. You looking for company this evening?"

Bubba's wry grin said it all. "Wouldn't want you to go any trouble but..."

"Consider it done. I'll keep you posted." With that, he zipped up the window and left the horseshoe.

Bubba headed up the steps to the veranda where all the doors and windows stood open, airing out the house after another stifling summer. Fall was his favorite time at Deer Bend: good hunting, not too hot or cold, and perfect for sleeping with the windows open listening to crickets instead of the infernal AC. He went in through the trophy room door and poured himself a generous Maker's Mark, plopping in a whiskey cube fetched from the freezer built into the bar. About the only thing useful to come out of the current bourbon fad was the non-melt ice cube. Everything else, like aged $400 bottles blended with apples—you don't put fruit in bourbon! —were just marketing BS to suck dollars out of unsuspecting 20-something fools. Bubba didn't need that, unless, of course, a generous donor was willing to give him a case of Pappy.

He settled in a rocker on the front porch facing the southwest where any minute he expected to see the dust cloud from Dr. Shaw's Jeep signaling his approach along the back trail connecting the compound to Deer Bend. Their relationship began innocently enough when the congressman's committee was assigned to investigate complaints on the inefficiencies, failings, and potential corruption within the VA Medical System. Bubba took a sip of Maker's and laughed to himself; Congress is the last body any sane, logical individual would assign to such a task, at least when it comes to efficiencies.

Corruption on the other hand was right in their wheelhouse and, being pros at it themselves, it didn't take long for the committee to ferret out the skimming and pilfering. Several splashy headlines later, they were being heralded as saviors of a system the previous administration had turned into shambles. But in reality, it was simply out with the old, in with the new. In cahoots with several other committee members, new, better disguised scams grew like weeds in districts and states represented by the oversight members. Bubba made sure Georgia, and his own portfolio, got their fair share.

It was through this committee work that Bubba met Dr. Shaw at the VA Medical Center in Atlanta. Doc turned out to be an enthusiastic supporter of reform and wasn't shy about ratting out anyone and everyone in order to ingratiate himself with the committee. His eagerness to sacrifice peers resulted in only one defamation lawsuit, quite low by Congressional Oversight Committee standards. Bubba took a quick liking to the doc. His methods were occasionally questionable, but no one could quibble with his conviction.

Bubba still had a hard time figuring out Shaw's medical specialty. Just what the hell is a Psychopharmacologist? Simply putting the words together looked like it meant he was a crazy pharmacist, which in reality was closer to the truth than the stated specialty of a psychiatrist specializing in medications. The doc tried to explain that any psychiatrist could provide therapy and hand out Prozac like Tic Tacs, whereas a Psychopharmacologist used his vast knowledge of medications to tailor a unique program for each patient.

Yeah, yeah, Bubba thought to himself. The doc's just a drug dealer with a medical certificate.

There was no denying Shaw was smart as hell and closely aligned to Bubba's thinking when it came to societal ills in America. During the Oversight Committee work, the two men came to understand each other and often stole off to bemoan the country's direction over a cocktail. It was during one of these sessions that Shaw shared his theory and how it could only be proven with human test subjects. The intentions of eugenics were sound, but the overriding flaw in the movement was thinking that controlled breeding was enough to create a superior human race. Shaw acknowledged breeding was critical, but without behavior modification, humans were susceptible to emotional weakness. He was convinced that intense therapy and proper medication were needed to complement breeding. Bubba said it sounded like chemical brain washing, and the doc didn't argue.

With all the weird shit going on in America, Bubba's interest in Shaw's theory grew. Questions turned into strategy, and before long Bubba had siphoned off federal funds into a fancy sounding veterans rehabilitation grant for Shaw's personal use. With redirected federal funds already supporting his American Natural Preservation project, and the similarities of their missions, Bubba erected a new building on the compound for the doc to use. He tried his best to keep Shaw at arm's length, but the doc's enthusiasm to share every detail made that nearly impossible.

The first death should have been Bubba's sign to sever ties with the project, but against his better judgment, he stuck with the doc. As a master at possible scandal survival, Bubba devised an elaborate screen to pin the entire scheme on his brother Dave, Barry, and the ALM if anything went wrong. His only concern was trying to insulate Andy from any blow back. Not only was Andy a trusted lieutenant, but he was also the supplier of Bubba's evening entertainment. Face it—certain things are sacred.

Bubba spotted the dust well before the doc's Jeep came into view, cresting the small rise southwest of the big house. He downed the last of his Maker's and swirled the whiskey cube counterclockwise in his glass as he debated a quick refill. Bubba tried to gauge the speed of the advancing cloud. Slow and methodical suggested bad news whereas fast meant the doc was in a chipper mood. While the cube still spun in Bubba's empty glass, the Jeep slid to a stop in the horseshoe.

"Congressman, great to see you!"

"Hey, Doc" he replied, not caring to stand to greet his visitor. "Horace said it was important we talk. Take a seat."

Shaw bounced up the veranda's steps and ignored Bubba's invitation, standing directly in front of the congressman, grinning like a fool. "We've had a breakthrough, sir. A patient has responded well to the treatment and is rapidly advancing through the stages!" Shaw began to pace excitedly on the veranda. "We're on the cusp of something big. All indicators suggest we're close to success. I knew this patient was special, and he's proving it!"

"Either sit down or stand still. You're distracting my view."

Bubba only wanted the highlights, and Shaw was wound up in sermon mode. Shaw stopped pacing and leaned against the veranda rail, trying to tame his excitement.

"There, that's better" Bubba said. "Now, tell me what you got but spare me the detailed bullshit."

Bubba could see Shaw's mind trying to form an abbreviated version of the saga he had hoped to share with the congressman.

"Well, Patient Alpha, I'm calling him Alpha now, has moved to phase four. The first man to do so! We've developed the perfect combination of pharmaceuticals for his diagnosis, personality, and dependence. He's entered that critical phase where he understands what we have is what he needs and wants. Now, we begin to condition his behavior. We slowly increase his stability and mood as he adopts our desired attitude. It won't take long for him to realize we can control how he feels, and over time, his new thinking will become rote."

"Sounds like you're trying to train a dog."

Unable to contain his excitement, Shaw began to pace again. "Well, yes, it's the process of classic conditioning. Pavlov's achievements with dogs overshadows the later work Watson did with humans. It's simple patterns of stimulus and response. In our experiment, it's finding the right stimulus, and we've done so with Alpha. That's a huge discovery that allows us to take this to the next level!"

"Glad you're finally making progress, Doc. I admit my patience was beginning to wear. So how long will it take? When will we know if your plan works?"

"That's hard to say. It could be weeks or months. Based on the makeup of this patient, family history, previous drug dependency, higher than average intelligence, and general emotional frailty, I'd estimate we're looking at weeks, maybe even days."

Bubba smiled at Shaw for the first time. "Excellent. Tell me about the patient. Does he bring any value to our overall mission? Frankly, we don't need another dipstick on the team."

Shaw gave Bubba the slightly condescending smug expression many doctors have perfected over the years of treating anxious patients. "That's the best part. Our goal is to build an elite force within the militia to carry out special projects. Not only is he a seasoned, decorated veteran, he's a demolitions expert."

Bubba slapped his knee. "Hot damn! Nice going, Doc!"

"Thank you, sir. But let's not get too far ahead of ourselves. We still have several critical phases before claiming success."

"Understood. At least you've finally made some progress. I was beginning to think you might be a bad investment." Bubba stood, his normal signal the meeting was officially adjourned.

"Congressman, one last thing. I know I've said it before, but I feel it's my obligation to reiterate my concerns about your man running the operation. I question his conviction and if he's up to seeing this through."

"My buddy White-ly? Don't worry about him. He's just fine."

"I believe he pronounces it Wit-ly, sir, and, in my professional opinion, he's not fine."

Bubba stepped up close to Shaw and lowered his voice. "I'm the boss around here, and I'll pronounce his name however I want to, and I happen to like White-ly instead of Wit-ly."

He took another step towards Shaw, almost nose to nose like a baseball manager arguing an umpire over a bad call. Dropping his voice to a whisper, he snarled, "Furthermore, in White-ly's professional opinion, you're a fucking quack. From what I've seen so far, I'm inclined to agree with him. Your little breakthrough just bought you some time. Don't fuck it up or your ass might be the next one buried in the woods. Now get the hell out of here. This meeting's over."

Shaw scrambled off the porch and was pulling on to Route 21 before Bubba refreshed his Maker's.

31.

Seamus waited on the tarmac where the PDK service rep told him to stand, and sure enough, a private jet soon taxied up, parking only 20 yards away. It was almost like waiting for an Uber ride. The door opened, and a staircase folded down.

"You Agent O'Reilly?" a man in uniform called out.

He couldn't exactly hear over the roar of the jet's turbines, but it sure sounded like the man said his name. "Yes!" Seamus nodded and shouted back.

The man gave a hearty wave and yelled, "Well, come on in."

Seamus now knew what it was like to be a rich person. Sure, the cabin was a little claustrophobic for the above average-sized man, but that was a small price to pay. No TSA hassles, crammed terminals, or screaming babies. Just walk across the tarmac and climb on in. It was beyond civilized.

The man in uniform turned out to be a flight attendant. He pointed to a nice cozy oversized chair. "Have a seat and buckle in."

Across the aisle sat a younger man in a nice suit.

"Morning, O'Reilly." He stuck out his hand and flatly said, "I'm FBI Agent Marzano."

"Nice to meet you, Agent." Seamus clasped the extended hand.

"We'll move to the back and talk once this bird's up." He sounded downright grumpy this time. The FBI agent nestled back in his chair and closed his eyes.

Though Seamus wasn't prepared for such a rude greeting, he settled in, marveling at how the seat was more comfortable than his trusty La-Z-Boy. Trying not to appear like a novice, he took a quick inventory of the private jet. Its rich wood trim, plush carpeting, and posh leather chairs reminded him of a flying version of the director's office. Seamus and the FBI agent sat in the two forward chairs, split by a narrow aisle and facing a small galley. The rear of the jet had four more seats, two on each side of the aisle facing each other with a compact table separating each pair. He guessed the aft door must be the head.

Seamus could barely contain his excitement; it was almost like he'd never flown before. After a brief taxi, the pilot mashed the throttle, and the jet hurtled down the runway. Like a kid, he stared out the window watching Atlanta spill out beneath him.

Once the "fasten seat belts" light turned off, the two agents moved to the rear section, sitting to face one another. On the small table between the seats sat a thick file which Seamus assumed was a duplicate of what Carraway provided.

Marzano opened the file. "I understand you went through this already. Thought we'd hit the highlights during the flight to make sure we're on the same page."

Seamus got the sense the agent didn't really care if they were on the same page or not.

"Yes, I've studied the file and am puzzled by a couple of things. You've been on this since the border bombing. What happened to the agent who investigated the original theft?"

"Died on us. Not in the line of duty. A heart attack while cutting the grass. One of the reasons I live in a condo. Too much stress and work with a yard."

"Or you just hire a kid to cut your grass," Seamus grunted.

Two can play the curmudgeonly game, he thought while sorting through the file looking for the lab report. He found the stapled pages and opened it to the third page.

"This is what I don't get," Seamus continued. "Yesterday, FBI Agent Wynn told me the explosives from Georgia, the border, and Lafitte were the same. But the lab could only prove that all three came from the same manufacturer. Seems to me that's a pretty flimsy connection."

"Flimsy's an understatement. Now you see why this whole trip is a complete waste of time. Getting assigned to this case has been a major pain in my ass."

Seamus was secretly relieved the agent's disdain was for the case and not about having some state guy tagging along on his investigation. He poked at a line on the lab report. "I looked into the manufacturer last night. Since they specialize in explosives that can also be used underwater, they're more of a niche player in the market. Even as a niche player, they've made over 25 tons of the product over the last ten years. Why is the FBI so zeroed in on Lafitte?"

Agent Marzano leaned back in his chair. "Who knows? All I know is that we've been trying to track down every pound of the stuff ever made. Companies are supposed to keep detailed records on how much they buy, and where and when they use it. Some are good at it, and some aren't. And that's only US companies. A bunch was sold overseas, and it's been a bear tracking that down. We've been able to account for all but about 4% of everything they've made."

"That's 2,000 pounds of which the Lafitte theft only accounts for 500," Seamus cut in.

"Yeah, but we estimated it only took 50 pounds to blow the border fence. Hell, 50 pounds is a rounding error that can be skimmed anywhere, and no one would know. We're never gonna figure out where the Guadalupes scored the explosives, and even if we did, there's no way we can conclusively tie it to Georgia."

"Then why are we doing this?"

"Simple ass-covering exercise. The higher-ups have been in a wad about the border bombing and are desperate. Georgia's only made it worse."

Seamus understood the frustrations of being stuck on a hopeless case. But the private jet to Louisiana for an interview was an experience he never expected, and he wasn't about to let a disgruntled partner dampen his day. Not wanting to dwell on the topic further, he turned his attention to the file and pulled out a picture of the theft victim.

"Must admit, I like this guy's style. Living in Louisiana and calling his business Lafitte Salvage and Demolition, changing his last name to Long. Bet he's one smooth BS-er. No wonder he gets along so well with the politicians."

"I don't blame him. Think I'd change my last name too if it had been Longerbaum. Imagine he was teased a lot in school."

"And some kids are teased about their names and just suck it up." Seamus opted not to give his name speech to the crabby agent. "No, this guy changed his name to win business. I'm sure the name Long opened doors for him in Baton Rouge. Hard to be ignored in Louisiana with the last name Long."

"What do you mean? What's so special about the name Long?" Marzano asked.

"Does the name Huey Long mean anything to you?"

Recognition poured over the FBI man's face, and he perked up for the first time. "Of course! Defensive Hall of Famer for the Raiders and does NFL TV commentary now. My wife thinks he's hot, even though he's an older guy."

Seamus let out a laugh. "That's Howie Long, not Huey. Huey was known as The Kingfish. He controlled Louisiana politics in the early 20th century. Huey was the governor and a US senator who was actually assassinated while in office. Several Longs came after him. There for a while nothing in Louisiana could happen without a Long involved. Our friend Longerbaum knew what he was doing by taking on the name."

"Makes sense. He's connected all the way up to DC. I'm sure you saw in the file he's won several federal contracts. Hurricane work mostly, but he's also landed a sweet deal on the platform oil spill."

"I saw that. Looks like that work began after Katrina, at least that's when he changed the name to Lafitte Environmental. Personally, I liked Lafitte Salvage better. More appropriate." Seamus smiled as he finished the sentence.

Agent Marzano looked at him leerily. "Okay, trivia man, I'll bite. What's so special about Lafitte."

Seamus was thrilled the guy didn't have any idea. Rarely did he get to show off his history degree. "I'll cut you some slack. Jean Lafitte is a little more obscure even though parks and streets all over the state are named after him. Lafitte was a pirate who sailed the Gulf of Mexico coastlines in the early 19th century. During the war of 1812, he played both sides then placed a bet on the US, so he offered his services to General Jackson in exchange for a pardon. Andrew Jackson wouldn't have won the Battle of New Orleans in 1815 without him, a moot battle since Britain had already signed the Treaty of Ghent admitting they lost. Anyway, winning that fight made Jackson famous and was probably the reason he became president. Without Jackson, the modern Democrat Party may never have formed. Imagine that. There may never have been Democrats if it weren't for a pirate!"

"No surprise there," Marzano deadpanned. "All politicians are crooks, if you ask me."

Seamus nodded. "I agree, but that's beside the point. I'm just saying naming a salvage company after a pirate is brilliant. I look forward to meeting this guy."

"You really geeked out on me there. You should be a teacher."

Seamus agreed. "The thought's crossed my mind, but we've gotten off track. Tell me what you know about Long, not what's in the file, but your take from talking with him."

Marzano shrugged. "You're right about him. He's smooth but not in a smarmy way. Not much else really. I don't expect he'll be much help with your case. Hell, he wasn't any help the last time we talked. Told that to the higher-ups, but they insisted we check him out again."

"Maybe, maybe not. I've made some notes, several details I'm curious about. Making a joint interview with the FBI is new to me. You mind if I ask questions?"

"Knock yourself out. Now, unless you have any more fascinating history lessons for me, I think I'll take a nap before we land."

Not waiting for Seamus to respond, Marzano got up and moved back to his original seat.

Seamus held on to the picture and closed the file. He truly was interested in talking with John Long. Longerbaum grew up in the little community of Saint-Gerne along the Mississippi River. One of the smaller hamlets in Marais Parish, it was on a major bend between Baton Rouge and New Orleans. His father was the head golf pro at the Parish's premiere country club and envisioned his, strong, athletic son as the next Jack Nicklaus. Much to his disappointment, John found the mighty river more entertaining than the championship layout at Egret Marsh County Club.

Described as Huck Finn with ambition, Longerbaum spent most of his youth on the river making a buck anyway he could. By the time he reached high school, his father—having abandoned living vicariously through a tour pro son—convinced several well-heeled club members to invest in a worn-out river towboat, and Longerbaum Salvage was born. To their collective surprise, John spent all his free time from school overhauling the boat, and by his senior year became the go-to guy for the inexperienced barge captains who ran aground navigating the ever-changing river bends south of Baton Rouge. The kid was a natural.

Business was so good that John opted to forego college. Before his 20th birthday, John bought out the country club investors, changed his last name to Long, christened the company Lafitte Salvage, and began to build his empire. Known for his skill at the helm of a towboat, his youthful exposure to the club crowd made him equally adept at navigating boardrooms and the state capital. During these early years, John demonstrated exceptional character which built him a sterling reputation as the most reputable company in a not-so-reputable business. With lucrative contracts pouring in, John expanded his fleet, purchased riverfront acreage further south towards New Orleans, and added demolition to his portfolio.

The next dozen years were extremely good for John, and he was beginning to believe he had the Midas touch. Then Hurricane Katrina hit. Within a four-week period, the flooding nearly ruined his business, his most trusted Lafitte manager suddenly died, and thieves made off with 500 pounds of construction-grade plastic explosives from the company's armory. He was physically and emotionally crushed by the drastic change of circumstance. Through sheer will and very good insurance, John rebounded. Lafitte Environmental was born.

The "fasten seat belts" light came on, and Seamus felt the gradual loss of altitude. He put John Long's photo back and closed the file. No offense to Agent Marzano, but it was quite peaceful being alone in the back of the jet, so he buckled up in the rear seat. Below him, the vast wetlands of southern Louisiana flowed into Lake Pontchartrain just north of New Orleans.

Every History major dreamt of being an author, and Long was the kind of American story Seamus wanted to write about. Not in a preachy, "this is what history teaches us" kind of way some historians employ, but for the pure story of character. The current culture was wrapped up in politics, sports stars, reality TV wannabes, and celebrities, all people undeserving of adulation yet constantly being written about in gushing prose. This guy, John Longerbaum, was the real America. Granted he came from country club stock, but he was responsible for his own success, then lost it all and fought his way back. Seamus really was looking forward to meeting this guy.

FBI Agent Francis from the New Orleans office was waiting on the airport tarmac to drive O'Reilly and Marzano the 35 miles up I-10 to Lafitte Environmental. A native of New Orleans, he was the chatty type and clearly enthusiastic to escort the visitors around his home turf. Seamus couldn't resist asking about Lafitte, which kicked Francis into a long saga about the state's famous pirate. As the story continued, he could sense Marzano's exasperation and periodically glanced over to make sure his temporary partner didn't pull a sidearm from his holster.

Lafitte Environmental was an impressive riverside compound. A small armada of ships and barges were docked in a marina carved off of the river. Immediately inside the gate, elevated offices overlooked the impressive dockside warehouse and cove. The property was clean and professional, not quite what Seamus had envisioned.

Agent Francis was warmly greeted by Long's administrative assistant, who led them into his office to wait while Long wrapped up down on the docks. Francis and Marzano occupied the chairs directly in front of his deck while Seamus surveyed the office. The office was large but not flashy. The massive desk had one open and one closed laptop, several files in a neat pile, and three framed pictures standing on the left-hand corner. Behind the visitor's chairs stood a small conference table with a stack of nautical maps in a neat pile. The wall art was an eclectic mixture of Saints and Braves sports memorabilia, ship paintings, pictures of his family, and children's art. Seamus could see himself in an office like this.

John Long was more handsome than his picture. Average-height, he looked to be quite fit and had the complexion of a man who worked in the elements.

"Terry, so good to see you again!"

Agents Francis and Marzano stood.

Receiving Long's vigorous handshake, Francis said, "Good to see you, John. How you been?"

"Things are great, aside from the weird stuff in Georgia. Agent Marzano, good to see you too. Guess you're back trying to track the Mexican connection."

Marzano accepted Long's handshake. "Yes, sir. Agency's still trying to figure that out."

Long turned to Seamus. "And who are you?"

"Agent Seamus O'Reilly, sir, Georgia Bureau of Investigation."

Seamus noticed the calloused roughness of Long's hand, the strong grip of a man who believed success didn't mean getting soft by avoiding hard work. The weather-produced wrinkles added distinction to what could be described as a boyish face.

"Well, welcome to Louisiana, Agent O'Reilly. Let's take seat here at the table. Don't know if I can provide any more information than when Marzano was here on his last visit, but it's worth a shot."

The four men sat at the table, Long in the chair facing the window that overlooked the docks.

"You gents care for water, coffee, or a Coke?"

The agents declined. Marzano glanced at Seamus and nodded approval to start.

"Mr. Long, I've read your file with great interest," Seamus began. "I admire your perseverance and drive. You've built yourself quite a business."

"Thank you, Agent. We've certainly had our fair share of growing pains," Long said with more modesty than bravado.

"I have to admit I liked the name Lafitte Salvage. It had a more appropriate connotation. Why'd you change it?"

Long leaned forward, elbows on the table. "Didn't have much choice frankly. After Katrina, we had to get out of demolition. The insurance company refused to continue coverage after having 500 pounds of explosives stolen from our supposedly secure facility. We had to change to survive. In our salvage work, we actually did some environmental cleanup, so shifting, or as they like to say nowadays, pivoting our business model made sense."

"And your timing couldn't have been better."

Puzzled, Long looked at him, his tone was noticeably curt. "Katrina was a terrible disaster for all of us who lived through it. Yes, it provided the business opportunity for us to head in a new direction, but it's not something I'd want to live through again."

"My apologies. I didn't mean to suggest I thought you were opportunistic with Katrina. I was thinking more along the lines of the oil platform disaster. I doubt you would have been the government's lead contractor if you hadn't already established Lafitte in the environmental sector."

Long nodded in agreement. "Yes, stated that way, you're correct. Without those two years under our belt, we never would have gotten the contract. But we had been considering the move even before. Katrina was the catalyst."

"Really? Mind if I ask why? Seems like the original business was doing pretty good."

Long looked at the other two agents and then back at Seamus. "Give me a minute."

He stood from the table and crossed the room to shut his office door. "I'm sure you read in the report about the tragic loss of Becca Averett around Katrina. She was the best employee I ever had."

He walked over to the file cabinet next to his desk, rummaged through the top drawer, and pulled out a well-worn file. "Becca was smart as a whip. Engineering, computers, the environment, business, great with employees, she was something else."

He set the file in front of Seamus. "She created this business plan, said it's the right thing to do and money could be made. She was an environmentalist before most people knew it could be a business. After she died, we had the theft and couldn't get insured, so I figured it was a sign. She was talking from the grave, telling me to follow her plan."

Seamus opened the file and scanned through the graphs. "So, she was right?"

Long smiled. "She underestimated the potential revenue, but she was right about everything else. I often wonder what she'd think about us now, what new thing she'd want us to do. Amazing to think Becca's fingerprints are on everything, even after more than ten years."

Seamus closed the file and looked back at Long. "Do you mind going through that with me? Hurricane Katrina, then two weeks later Ms. Averett disappears and is presumed dead, then two weeks after that the theft. I know it's quite a story so just the key parts as you see it." Seamus turned to Marzano. "Do you object, Agent?"

Marzano's disinterest was obvious. "Have at it, O'Reilly. Everything else seems to be a dead end."

Long checked his watch. "If that's what you want, but I've got a hard stop in 30 minutes." He sat back and began. "This whole area was underwater after Katrina. Our larger towboats were okay as we had pulled them upriver, but most of other ships had broken free and were all over the place. My focus was here, trying to secure the assets and getting our towboats down river, so we could help evacuate New Orleans.

"Becca worried about our employees. Back then, we had about 20 full-time employees and up to 50 we used on a temporary basis.

As Agent Marzano here knows, many of those workers were illegals. I guess undocumented is what you're supposed to say now, but our business had tons of manual labor, so we had a regular pool we used when needed. Becca was their champion, spoke Spanish, knew everybody's name, and made me increase their pay. They all loved her. While I was busy here, she went out to try and track everyone down, see if they were okay."

Seamus remembered Agent Marzano's notes on the most recent investigation after the border bombing. The FBI focused on the two full-time Latino employees still working at Lafitte's since Katrina. Both were extremely cooperative, but years had passed and the itinerate life of an undocumented laborer was impossible to track, particularly after an event like Katrina where people simply scatter. With nothing more than names, approximate ages, and general descriptions, the FBI quickly typed up a report and dedicated resources elsewhere.

"She have any luck?" Seamus asked.

Long shook his head. "She found a couple of families, but most were gone, either evacuated or dead. Those folks didn't have the best living conditions to start with, and Katrina pretty much wiped out those living on the edge. It tore poor Becca up. She was nearly out of her mind with worry. Her searching became an obsession."

"Is that what led her out into the bayou where," Seamus paused trying to think how to say it, "where she, uh, disappeared?"

Long gave a little grin. "You can say she was eaten by a gator, I don't mind. In fact, her story is lore around here, turned her into a folk hero."

Seamus reddened even though the others couldn't tell. "Sounds like a gruesome way to go. What was she doing in the bayou? Still looking for people?"

"Hell, no, she was out having fun! I swear she must have been a pioneer in an earlier life. She was most happy when she was doing something outdoors, the ultimate nature girl. Whenever she'd get wound up, she'd head to the woods, bayou, anywhere. She said nature was food for her mind or something like that. So, when the waters began to recede and her searching for the workers became fruitless, she took her kayak out on an adventure."

Seamus sat up straight in his chair, stared at Long, and slowly said, "The wilderness is manna for the soul."

"That's it! That's what she used to say. How'd you know that?"

Seamus's mind began to spin. Surely it was just a coincidence. Maybe it was a well-known saying amongst the granola eaters. Glancing at Marzano, who still sat stone-faced, he collected this thoughts. Turning back to Long, he tried to shove the excitement out of his voice and said, "I've known the type. They ditch technology and just want to live off the land."

"Maybe so, but for Becca it was more spiritual. As I said, she was brilliant. Advanced degree in Computer Engineering, or maybe it was Mechanical. I get all the engineering degrees confused. She revolutionized this place using satellite mapping, computer generated simulations, even figured out how to minimize the use of our explosives. She was a Renaissance woman, if there is such a thing, and the bayou was her spot to unwind."

Seamus took a breath and wrote a couple of notes, more of a stall tactic as he wrapped his mind around the concept churning in his head. "No offense, Mr. Long, but from your description, I find it surprising she'd want to work for a salvage and demo company. Doesn't really sound like a good fit."

Long smiled. "No offense taken, Agent. It was all luck and timing. I was up in Memphis on business, the river had shifted, and back then we did some dredging. I took prospective customers to dinner at the Peabody, and Becca was our waitress. Damn good waitress too. After several drinks, my cohorts began to flirt with her but were no match for her wit. After a couple of laughs, she started talking with us and found out she was about to graduate from Memphis with an advanced degree in engineering and was looking for a job. We were woefully behind in our technology, and I had been contracting out engineering services for years. I offered her a job right then and there."

"Waitress" swam in Seamus's mind. He asked, "You knew nothing about her, yet you offered her a job and she accepted?"

"Becca just had something about her. I could tell right away she could do just about anything she wanted. But no, she didn't accept right there. We met again the next day for a real interview, and I offered her more money than I should have. Turns out she was past ready to leave Memphis and her mom was dead, so she had no other place to go. My offer was first, and the money was damn good."

Seamus looked at his notepad where he had scribbled "environmentalist, Spanish, nature girl, manna, explosives" and now "waitress."

He looked up at Long. "You wouldn't happen to have a picture of her, would you?"

"I might have something in my files." He returned to the same chest-high file cabinet and began to root around. "I've been meaning to purge some of this stuff. I can be a pack rat when it comes to records. Better safe than sorry is my motto. Here you go, her new employee photo's stapled on the inside cover." He handed it to Seamus.

Seamus concentrated on the girl staring back at him. It was hard to tell. Maggie was a woman, and the face looking at him had not gone through the maturation change women often experience in their 20s. Her cheeks were slightly hollow, longer hair, lighter and draping across the temples, but the bone structure was similar. He couldn't tell for certain if they were one and the same, yet the eyes said differently. He'd seen that twinkle before.

He handed the file back to Long. "You clearly were close to her. Ever interested in more than just a business relationship?"

"I'm a happily married man, Agent. Now, I'd be lying if I didn't say I was attracted to her. It's hard to describe." Long's gaze drifted up as if he was looking to find the right words. "The woman wasn't what you'd consider a knockout but just had something about her that made her beautiful and appealing. Anyway, it didn't matter what I thought since it was pretty obvious she looked at me only as her boss. Truth is I was intimidated by Becca. She was way too smart for a guy like me."

Long set the closed file down on the table.

"So, Agent, what's so interesting about a woman who's been dead all these years? Thought you were coming here hoping to find a Mexican connection with old employees?"

Seamus looked at the two equally-puzzled FBI agents and back at Long. "One more question then I'll tell you. What about her past? Where did she grow up? And family? What can you tell me about that?"

"Very little. She grew up in Virginia on the peninsula close to Norfolk. Mom died a couple of years before I hired her. Dad had abandoned them when she was little, and she never checked to see if he was still alive. No brother or sister, no relatives that she ever talked about. No, the woman was alone, which is why I think she accepted the job and became mother hen around here. The Lafitte employees became her family." Long checked his watch. "Now, what's with the questions?"

Seamus leaned back and looked at his audience. "I realize you may feel this is farfetched but hear me out. Unless you have anything new, which you already said you don't, the trail with your employees remains stone cold. Heritage is the only tie, nothing else. But Ms. Averett can be tied to all the pieces. She worked here, spoke Spanish, had personal relationships with Latino employees who disappeared after Katrina, knew about explosives, and was an environmentalist. In my book, too many links exist to be ignored."

"Except for the fact that she's dead," Agent Francis quickly added.

"Is she? Her body was never found. It could have been an elaborate hoax."

"Not finding bodies in the bayou is more common than you would think," Francis continued. "We employ some of the state's best trackers, and often people disappear without a trace. It was different with Ms. Averett. While her body wasn't found, the trackers found clear engagement markings on land, and the lab confirmed the blood, which was copious, was hers. I'm quite certain nothing was left. Sorry, John, didn't mean to be so blunt."

"Thank you, Agent. I know you didn't mean anything."

Seamus paused then added, "I understand your position, and I agree it's not likely, but I do think it's possible."

Long stood up from the conference table. "Believe what you want, Agent, but there's one more thing that ruins your theory. The kayak. She never would leave that behind. It was her late mother's and Becca's most valuable possession. She'd die before parting with that, and that's just what she did. Now if you'll excuse me, I'm expected upriver in 45 minutes."

32.

At Camp Merrill, Scott turned his Veteran Outdoor F-150 4x4 work truck right onto a gravel forest service road that wound up the mountain to Cooper Gap. With a disregard for his own safety, he sped up the treacherous primitive track as it twisted through ravines, crossed streams, and hugged cliffs. Several times the truck slid on the gravel, coming perilously close to the edge, but he was not about to slow down. The sooner he got there, the more time he'd have.

Scott spent the morning inspecting I-85 north of Atlanta. The billboard carnage in this section was limited compared to other more remote sections of I-75, I-20, and I-16. Suburban sprawl had reached the 60 miles to Braselton which left the terrorists few locations void of potential collateral damage. Most of the destruction was focused around Commerce, Georgia where a slew of massive, now bare, towers once tempted drivers into competing outlet malls. Another attack cluster was near the South Carolina border, leaving poor travelers with no earthly idea where to buy fireworks.

Rather than heading directly back to Atlanta, Scott got off near Commerce and cut his way on state routes over to Dahlonega.

After a brief stop at a specialty grocery store catering to tourists, he headed north out of town, slowly rising into the Georgia Mountains. While not a state route, the road was well maintained as it led to Camp Merrill, a small US Army Ranger mountaineering training facility.

At Cooper Gap, the forest service road forked, and he turned left on a different meandering path that hugged the ridgeline. He bounced along with an increased sense of urgency and covered the next six miles in 20 minutes. At the next fork, he veered to the right heading down the north side of a mountain as the road narrowed. A trickling stream emerged on the left that grew in size during his descent, similar to how the mountain rhododendrons increased in density, giving the sensation he was entering nature's womb. Even in October, the green was lush and deep.

The road bottomed where the stream merged with another, forming a much larger mountain creek. Here the Forest Service had widened the road to allow parking spaces for hikers. Scott pulled his F-150 behind one of four parked cars at the trailhead, a small crowd for a beautiful autumn Tuesday. He dropped the rear gate, sat on the edge, and changed from his work to hiking boots. He put the bag of recently purchased supplies in his day pack, flung it over his shoulder, locked up the truck, and hit the trailhead.

Scott began a gradual ascent following the white blazes of the Appalachian Trail as it paralleled one of the creeks, often ducking to avoid the valley canopy. The recent rains softened the trail beneath him while the elevated creek level put off an amplified babble. As the trail rose, the rhododendrons thinned out, providing a more expansive view of the valley below.

After a mile, the trail met a trident. The well-worn trail on the left led most casual day hikers downward to a waterfall. To his right, the maintained Appalachian Trail branched off, taking hearty souls on a much longer journey. Straight ahead, the slightly overgrown, seldom traveled Benton-MacKaye Trail appeared to vanish into parts unknown. Scott followed the Benton-MacKaye.

The narrow trail's ascent continued while the hushed roar of the falls began to fade. Well past the falls' crest, a narrow log bridge crossed the creek leading to a steep upward hike on the opposite side. The first several times he hiked this one-mile section, the 500-foot elevation gain left Scott gasping for air. Not anymore. Thanks to Citrus Crunch, his pace was brisk and strides were strong.

At the top of the mountain, the trail burst into a vast open K-shaped field, a hundred yards wide and probably three-quarters of a mile long. In the autumn, the wheat-like grass grew above his knees. Hikers had trampled down a path through the grass where the Benton-MacKaye dove back into the woods on the far side. The trail line cut the center of the K and was the field's ridge with the long arms of the field gradually falling off on either side. The field baffled Scott. It was like someone had once cleared it for farming, but for some reason, the forest never reclaimed the land.

He followed the trampled trail halfway across then made a sharp right, cutting through the grass heading down the K's main leg. Once he was 50 yards off the trail, he could see her from the back, sitting motionless on blanket next to her tent. He paused for a second, knowing exactly what she looked like from the front: cross-legged, hands resting on her knees, and eyes shut in a Zen-like trance. He began again, slowing his pace to creep through the grass.

"It's about time you got here. I was thinking you weren't coming," she called out, not moving from her lotus position.

Scott shouldn't have been surprised. "How do you do that? I swear you've got eyes in the back of your head."

Maggie stood up and turned to face him. "Either it was you or Sasquatch crashing through the field."

Scott quickened his pace to meet her.

Maggie smiled, wrapping her arms around his neck to give him a passionate kiss. "I'm glad you're not Sasquatch," she whispered in his ear.

They held their embrace a little longer than usual, then they released and stood gazing intently at each other.

Maggie broke the silence. "Thanks for reworking your day. I was really excited when I got your email this morning saying you could make it."

"I sure love this spot, Maggie. Supposed to be a real clear night. Wish I could stay and star gaze with you."

Maggie turned from Scott, staring off down the field admiring the vista beyond. "It's perfect, isn't it? I'm sure going to miss coming here."

Scott's chest and throat tightened. "Guess it is about time."

Maggie turned back and gave his cheek a quick kiss. "What's in your bag of tricks?"

They both flopped on the blanket, and Maggie opened Scott's pack, pulling out a bag of grapes, a block of Manchego cheese, crackers, and bottle of pinot noir. "Look at you going all fancy and romantic. So much for roughing it."

Scott leaned back on the blanket and stretched his legs out in front of him. "I knew this was our last time, so I figured I'd make it special."

Maggie swatted his thigh. She handed him the bottle. "At least make yourself useful and open the wine."

Scott retrieved the corkscrew from his pack's side pocket while Maggie leaned inside the tent and emerged with two metal cups. As he poured the wine, she used her Swiss Army knife to cut open the cheese wrapper and deftly carve off several chunks.

He handed her one of the mugs and raised his in toast. "To us."

Maggie pinged her metal cup to his. "To us."

They sat quietly enjoying the wine and cheese as the grass swayed in the slight breeze. The sun broke from the occasional cloud, cutting the slight chill in the air. Neither minded the lack of conversation; the rare chance of time together was more important than words.

Scott finally broached the subject. "When are you leaving?"

Maggie, ever the waitress, put the cheese and grapes back in the pack as she spoke. "Sunday at the latest. I haven't started packing, but I don't have too much to take with me. Several days should be enough for me to wrap things up. Probably Saturday."

"Saturday? I thought the plan called for later next week?"

Maggie set the pack aside and laid on her back with her head cradled in Scott's lap. She tilted her head back to make eye contact. "This is just a slight adjustment to the plan. There's no way we're changing the end goal. I love you too much. We're in this together."

Scott looked down at her, gently brushing hair off her temple. "I love you too. And it's a good plan, but change isn't as easy for me as it is for you. Tom missing isn't helping my thought process right now either."

"Scott, you should know GBI Seamus went down to Louisiana today. I sense he's smarter than the others. It's better to accelerate the plan no matter what Tom's up to. We don't have much choice."

Scott's brow crinkled. "You're right, accelerate the plan."

Maggie's smile was barely perceptible. "I like Seamus. I find him interesting."

Scott laughed. "I like him too, but I don't think it's a good idea to get too buddy-buddy at this point." He wasn't about to let Maggie change the subject. "Saturday…guess I better break the news to Pam."

"Speaking of Pam, do you think she'd like to have my kayak? I'm not going to need it and would rather give it away to a friend than sell it to a stranger."

They studied each other for a moment.

"Pam would love your kayak."

Maggie's eyes lightened. "Excellent!" She sprang back up facing Scott. "What time do you need to be back in Atlanta?"

"With the hike and drive, I have about another hour before I should leave."

Maggie leaned forward, her mouth inches from Scott's as she whispered, "Now, what do you think we could do to occupy that hour?"

33.

*O*n one of the motel beds, Andrea spread her newly borrowed gear—a service revolver with sound suppression, night vision goggles, a tactical field knife, and a new terrestrial signal scrambler that worked on both cell phone and Wi-Fi systems. She double-checked the scrambler's user guide and tried out the goggles. No instructions were necessary for the gun and knife.

The motel room smelled of cheap air freshener which Andrea admitted was better than the alternative. It didn't really matter. It was 8:00 p.m. after a very long day, and she only needed it for several hours to rest before her mission. A mission that had morphed from recon to rescue.

She parked Roger's pickup truck right in front of the door to her 1960s-style motel room in Forsythe, Georgia during the dwindling light of sundown. The motel was perfect. She didn't need an ID and paid in cash, plus a highway construction crew was using it as their base, so Roger's truck blended in. Granted, his was a lot fancier and the only one with a motorcycle strapped in the bed, but it didn't look too out of place. The construction crew had taken over the abandoned pool area and were too busy drinking beer and laughing to notice her arrival. She slipped into her room unseen.

Andrea flopped down on top of the second bed. No way she was going to touch the sheets in this fleabag. She set the alarm on her mobile phone for midnight in case she actually slept. She took a deep breath and closed her eyes.

Andrea had been shocked when this morning's lark led to Tom. She barely made it in the woods to follow the man and dog when a gunshot rang out. Military grade, not a hunting rifle, it sent her crashing to the ground. She restarted her pursuit with caution, service revolver tightly gripped, well aware she had the advantage of stealth. Ahead she could see a clearing through the woods, so she left the trail and inched her way forward on her elbows and knees, coming to a stop concealed in the underbrush.

Before her lay an open field with six buildings spread out on the perimeter. Directly across from her was a small, brick ranch-styled house with an aluminum-roofed carport. To the left of the house was long building, possibly cinder block, with evenly spaced narrow windows placed well off the ground. To the right of the ranch house were three structures, two small wooden shacks and another long building with a large awning over six picnic tables. In between the wooden shacks ran a gravel road that Andrea assumed led back to the entrance on County Road 5. On the near side of the field, barely 30 feet away from her, was a sixth building, a small cinder block shed without windows.

Andrea recognized Tom immediately, sprawled in the center of the field rubbing the belly of the tail-wagging black Labrador. She didn't need her binoculars to determine he was under duress. Two men—one rather large, the other scrawny—stood on opposite sides of the field with rifles at ready. Under an oak tree near the ranch house were two more men. Andrea guessed the older man in hiking boots was the black Lab's companion. He was attentively listening to the second man, too well dressed to be tramping around in the woods, reading notes from a clipboard. She had seen enough—Tom was being held prisoner.

By the time Andrea inched her way back to the open path, she developed her plan. She went double time to the canoe and took advantage of the downstream flow, making it back to the river landing quickly. The ranger and middle schoolers were nowhere to be found, so she loaded the borrowed canoe onto his truck's boat rack and placed a quick thank you note under his windshield wiper. It was 11:30 a.m., and though it would be a close call, she had enough time.

The next eight hours were a blur of rushed activity. Andrea's first stop was to Fort Benning where a sergeant was a good enough friend to be counted on for a discrete favor. She then sped back to Atlanta for more practical mission transportation. The motorcycle rental shop employee gave Andrea the same quizzical look as the ranger when she told him she was a birder as Black women motorcyclists were another rarity. Her Ohio motorcycle license eliminated some doubt and then her military ID generated instant respect. They tried a couple before she found a bike big enough for two but not obnoxiously loud. She also rented two helmets, a black jumpsuit, and a ramp so she could load the motorcycle in the back of Roger's pickup. Lastly, she swung by her Atlanta hotel to pick up several items before heading south to Forsythe. It had been a breakneck day, and the somewhat lumpy motel bed felt great.

The buzzing cell phone woke Andrea up. Instantly alert, she grabbed it to silence the alarm but saw it was yet another text from Pam pleading for information. She quickly texted back, "Sorry, busy day and I'm beat, will fill you in tomorrow." It was now 11, and she'd gotten a good three-hour nap which was more than enough. Time to roll.

Andrea put on her camo, strapped the knife to her lower left leg, holstered her standard service sidearm, then pulled the black jumpsuit on cover the outfit. After one last final inspection, she loaded the additional gear in her daypack and was ready to go. She paused at the door for one final pep talk.

The racket from the construction crew's happy hour was replaced with the low roar of nearby interstate traffic. Rolling the motorcycle off Roger's pickup made more noise than expected, and she occasionally paused to make sure no one was watching. Fortunately, the beers had done their job since it appeared the crew was more content snoring in their pillows than checking on parking lot activity. She strapped the spare helmet to the back of the seat, threw the daypack over her shoulders and fired up the motorcycle.

Andrea was glad the State Route 21 exit off I-75 was a minor exchange with only one truck stop and a Mini Mart gas station. It was just past midnight, and the light traffic thinned as she went east. Within three miles of the interstate, she had the road to herself. On the bridge over the Ocmulgee River, she cut the headlight and engine, coasting to the side of road where ALM's property began. She hopped off the bike and quickly led it down the embankment toward the river, well out of sight of any passing cars. Crouched under the bridge, she prepared for the hike to the compound.

Security cameras were her biggest concern. She'd taken a huge risk going on the property today, but Andrea spent over 30 minutes lurking in the woods and no one had come after her. That told her they had limited cameras or didn't care to monitor them on an ongoing basis. If they didn't monitor during the day, it was a safe bet they wouldn't at night. Still, she couldn't afford to take that chance. Andrea booted the scrambling device, and it immediately identified three active Wi-Fi networks. Activated to always on, the device's sand timer rotated then confirmed the networks were disabled. She then did the same to take down cellular communication.

Confident the networks were disabled, Andrea took off the jumpsuit and draped it over the bike, putting on black lightweight nylon gloves and a tight knit cap before slipping the night vision goggles on her head. Holding the sound-suppressed pistol in her right hand, she took a deep breath and activated the digital video recording feature on the goggles as she slid them over her eyes. Andrea set off for Tom.

Cutting through the underbrush, she hugged the river until she found one of the trails leading away from the Ocmulgee toward the compound. The goggles gave the impression she was watching a black and white movie, and though she was grateful to see, the lack of peripheral vision made her feel vulnerable. The heat sensing mechanism identified a pack of what she guessed were wild boars in the distance. The boars didn't need goggles and trotted off well before she got near them. As she approached the compound, she veered south until she linked up with the trail from her afternoon discovery. Remembering the location, she proceeded on hands and knees until she was at the same spot where she had watched Tom.

She had seen four potential targets yesterday, two she knew were armed but she had to assume they all were. With Tom likely locked in a cell, she expected only one would be assigned to overnight guard duty. She was fully prepared to take him out.

Prone on the ground, Andrea began to survey the situation. The two small wooden shacks had one human each, and the ranch house held two creatures, probably the man and dog. Tom would not have been left alone in one of the houses, so three targets were accounted for.

Andrea moved her view to the long structure on the left of the field. Her heart sank—six warm figures were spread evenly throughout in what appeared to be separate rooms. She guessed Tom was in the building, but it was impossible to tell which body was his and know the other inhabitants' status. They could be fellow prisoners or a small fighting force. She was mentally prepared to take on a couple, but the odds were not in her favor to take on five. At least not tonight without a proper plan.

For the next hour, she didn't move and alternated focus on each building. At one point, the figure in the ranch house went and used the bathroom. She guessed it was the old guy.

Having waited long enough, Andrea, pistol up, slowly crept from her position and advanced to the back wall of the small building that stood closest to her. She edged around the building. In front of her was the open field, maybe a hundred yards long with the ranch house directly on the far side. The small building was cinder block with the door facing the field. The size and lack of windows led her to believe this must be their armory. She slipped around to the front of the building and leaned in close to the steel door so the video in her goggles could capture its details.

Andrea retreated back to the rear of the structure then half-trotted to her left along the perimeter shadows until she reached the long building. Approximately 50 feet in length and also cinder block, its five narrow windows were evenly spaced a good seven feet off the ground. The goggles identified four people on this side, and each appeared to be lined up proportionally to the windows. She crept up directly under one window and confirmed her suspicion that it couldn't open. She then panned the roofline in search of potential weak spots.

Andrea ventured to the side closest to the armory where the line of sight from the ranch house and shacks was still blocked. The building was about 20 feet wide with two similar windows high off the ground. She peered around the corner. The front door was right in the middle under an awning but in clear view of the ranch house, now only about 50 yards away. She quickly scanned the ranch house and two shacks. The occupants were still asleep.

As with the armory, this also had a reinforced steel door but with one important difference: the door hinges were on the outside.

Typical outside doors open inwards, and the hinges are on the inside of the house to thwart tampering by intruders. Hinges on the outside suggest the builder was more concerned about people breaking out, not in.

Andrea returned the way she came and stood behind the building contemplating her next move. She considered checking the ranch house and shacks but didn't want to risk an enthusiastic Labrador alerting armed men. Instead she retreated back to the trail to watch the compound.

The three hours that ensued passed slowly and uneventfully. The old man got up to pee again, but the others were sound sleepers. Every rescue scenario she ran through her head simply wouldn't work. To break into the long building she'd have to kill or disable the other three men first just to be safe. And what about the six men in the long building? No one had moved, so if one was a guard, he was clearly asleep too. Were they guards or prisoners?

She checked her watch again, almost 5:00 a.m. and only an hour away from sunrise. Andrea inched away from her vantage point until she hit the trail, then backtracked to the hidden motorcycle. Once she pushed it to the far side of the Route 21 bridge, she fired up the engine and headed back to the cheap motel.

34.

"Jesus, O'Reilly, we wanted a new perspective on this case but not some sort of fantasy. You serious about this?"

Seamus stood inside his boss's doorway where FBI Agent Wynn was once again camped out across from Carraway. It wasn't even 6:30, and his Wednesday was off to a rocky start. He tried to not to sound defensive. "Well, sir, I know it might sound remote, but I think it's plausible given the other dead ends."

The FBI agent snorted. "I don't think plausible is the word I'd use. This isn't some movie. Dead people suddenly don't show up as bombers."

Seamus tried to speak, but nothing came out. He mustered his inner courage. "Under the circumstances, it just seemed logical to consider all possibilities. Sometimes, the unlikely turns out to be true."

The FBI agent abruptly stood. "I need a coffee refill." He nodded at Carraway and glared at Seamus before leaving the office.

Carraway left his chair and sat on the desk corner near Seamus. Though not much older, Carraway had the same look Seamus's dad used to give him as a kid, somewhere between anger and disappointment. The silence was unnerving.

"Did I really screw up that bad? I admit the idea was a long shot, but I didn't think it was crazy."

"I take some of the blame, O'Reilly. It wasn't fair of me to throw you to the wolves with so little experience. I thought the trip needed our coverage and was rather harmless. But yeah, think of it from my end. An agent meets some waitress at a diner, and a day later says she might be some not-so-dead ex-employee who's stealing explosives and blowing up billboards. That's not just crazy, that's bat shit crazy."

Seamus's palms began to sweat. This was sounding ominous. Not that this was his dream job, but he'd moved from Michigan to try and start over. Unemployment was not the new beginning he'd envisioned. "I understand," was the only response he could think of.

The tension eased somewhat in Carraway's face. "You're a damn good researcher, O'Reilly. Probably the best we ever had. When the dust settles from this case, your report will be a footnote. Agent Wynn might keep it around for laughs, but it really won't matter."

The laughs comment stung Seamus hard. He'd always been proud of this work, and the Louisiana report was no exception. Guess he really wasn't cut out to be a field agent.

Carraway got off the desk and returned to his seat. "Don't worry about it, O'Reilly. It's just a blip. We still have a case to solve, and I've been told there's a backlog in research requests waiting for you. The team needs you. Go tackle those."

The team. Seamus hadn't even thought about them. Word of this gets out, and he'll remain on the outside looking in. He turned to leave the office. "Yes, sir. And sorry if my work disappointed or embarrassed you. Let me know if there's anything I can do to make up for it."

"Shake it off, O'Reilly. We're okay." Carraway's attention returned to the papers strewn on his desk. Seamus hoped for invisibility as he slunk to the door. His boss's voice stopped him.

"Actually, there is something you can do."

Seamus turned to see Carraway holding a file out in his direction. "A bunch of protestors are threatening to take to the streets of Atlanta this weekend. The Mayor's office is nervous and is holding a strategy meeting at noon today. We need someone there."

Seamus took the file. "I can do that. You sure you want me to?"

"Your job will be to observe and report the details back to me," Carraway smirked. "No opinions, no promises, just note what was said and who said it."

"I can do that. Thanks."

Carraway waved Seamus off. "I know you can."

Seamus returned to his desk, wrestling once again with the mixed emotion that seemed to becoming the norm of his adult life—chagrin with faint hope of redemption. It hadn't always been that way, or maybe he never paid attention to the complexities of life in his youth. His father always preached the importance of experience, only he failed to tell him how much disappointment played a role. His father suffered his fair share of defeat, yet rarely showed the scars. He persevered and rose each day ready to plod on. Now, it was Seamus's turn to do the same.

He logged on to his laptop, pulled up the Louisiana report he filed late last night, and quickly saved it to his personal memory stick. He had to admit the narrative was barely believable, but it made for a damn good story. Combined with the John Long narrative maybe this was the topic he'd finally write about in the book of his dreams. But that would have to wait.

Each research request was in its own manila folder. It was a short form listing the requesting agent, information desired, and project number in the computer database. Seamus would need to log into the system and enter the project number for more specific details. He'd do the necessary research, attach his findings electronically in the system, then fill out his completed report number on the original request form before returning the paper file to the agent. It was a rather convoluted system designed to try and match electronic data files with a physical paper trail.

Seamus began to prioritize the requests based on topic and time required to research. As he read through the pile of requests, it became increasingly clear the terrorism case was going nowhere and the agents were grasping at air. Several requests were so inane it made his Louisiana report look like crack detective work.

Why was he singled out by Carraway? Only one reason seemed logical—the color of his skin. But he counted his boss among the few people in the building who treated him as an equal. He'd even stood up for him publicly numerous times. Was this coming from the top? Maybe it was the FBI. Their biased history was notorious, and he could see them singling Seamus out as a scapegoat to divert attention. He sat back and stared at his computer screen. In this light, Carraway's reprimand made some sense.

The revelation pissed him off. The hell with this job. He stood ready to march right back in to give the men a piece of his mind then thought better of it. Now was not the time to let emotion take control. Better to do your job and figure out how to respond later.

Seamus scrolled through the requests and decided nothing was pressing, mostly just busy work that he found very unmotivating under the current circumstances. He then opened the file Carraway had just given him on the Atlanta protests. The top page listed 15 different organizations with web posts announcing their intention to participate. It was a who's who of mainstream and radical organizations. He immediately decided this file would easily entertain him until the meeting in the Mayor's office.

Many of the groups were very familiar and some were obscure. With no clear plan, he decided to go down the list in alphabetical order. The first organization was a group called the American Liberation Militia, who also just so happened to be the instigators of Saturday's planned main event. Seamus pulled himself back up to the computer and started his research on the ALM.

35.

oo exhausted to stand, Governor Murray pulled the arm-
chair over so he could sit and watch the protestors from his
bedroom window. He didn't have the energy to fetch his
binoculars for a closer look. He already had showered and dressed
in his official crisis attire even though Jose hadn't told him yet if
the plan was to spend another day at GBI headquarters.

Last night, the raucous crowd returned. The police presence
had grown, and temporary fencing had been erected to create a
six-foot buffer zone between the pro-immigration tree huggers
on his right from the pro-president forces to his left. The amassed
crowd was bigger than most of his campaign rallies—not a good
sign. He sat marveling at their stamina. They'd been at it all night.
At least, Hannah was still at the farm since all of this would have
been too much for her.

Skip knew sitting there was just a sorry excuse to avoid starting his day. At some point, he'd have to go downstairs to hear the
latest status and plan out Wednesday's agenda. At first, watching
the protestors was a diversion, but now they heightened his anxiety.
He stood, pulled the curtains shut, and left the bedroom.

Jose Perez and the gaggle of aides were already camped out at the dining room table. Jose met him in the hall. "You look like hell, Governor. Protestors keep you up?"

Skip appreciated his sincere concern. "I only got a couple of hours of sleep. I should have moved to one of the back bedrooms, but I kept thinking they'd eventually quiet down. We have lots of angry people out there. Maybe after coffee I'll shape up." Skip went into the kitchen and filled up one of the large inaugural souvenir coffee mugs.

Returning to the dining room, he took a seat at the head of the table where the first sips of coffee swatted away the top layer of cobwebs from his brain. "Any chance of good news today?" he asked hopefully.

Their elongated pause answered his question. Jose said, "I spoke with Director Sterling, and the trip to Louisiana was a bust. Really no surprise since the FBI's been looking into it for years. Our GBI man came back with a theory which the FBI quickly discounted."

"Great, glad to hear we made such a good impression." Skip's mood darkened. "So, nothing positive?"

Jose shook his head. "Sorry, no further developments on the investigation. The FBI has another lead in Mexico they're tracking down, and they're going over the crime scenes again to see if anything was missed. Lots of chatter on the internet, but nothing of substance, at least yet. It sounds like most of yesterday was a wash."

"At least that explains why the protestors are still there." Skip took a big slug of coffee, slightly scalding his tongue. He didn't care. "Guess the president must really be stoking the fire since there's nothing to stop him."

"He's getting a big assist from Bubba too," Jose added. "He's been on Twitter and has called a press conference down at his farm today."

Skip began to rub his left temple. Maybe he should've stayed in the chair watching the protestors. "When's the press conference?"

"Not until 1:00 p.m. He doesn't want to complete with the morning news, and it gives the reporters plenty of time to wrap up slick packages for the evening cycle. I imagine the Atlanta TV stations and CNN will cover it for sure, but I don't know about other outlets."

"Bubba's trying to kill me. Any ideas?" Skip nearly pleaded. "Should I go out to greet the protestors again?"

Jose shook his head again. "I don't think that's a good idea. We already did that, and the security team thinks this crowd might be teetering towards violence."

"I was watching them this morning, and they do seem pretty wound up," Skip agreed. Needing a moment to think, he went back to the kitchen and topped off his cup with a small splash. He returned to the dining room where Jose watched him closely.

Skip got the cue. "What's on your mind, Jose?"

"Governor, Bubba's press conference is not the biggest problem right now. I think it's best if we leave him alone."

Skip sank back into his chair. "What's my biggest problem? "

"Remember yesterday I told you about the American Liberation Militia sending out a recruitment notice for this Saturday in Liberty Plaza?"

"Bubba's lackeys, even though he denies it. I thought we agreed to squash the permit?"

"We were too late. Bubba lined it up before we even knew about it, and now it's turned into a shitstorm."

Skip idly spun his coffee cup on the table. "How bad a shitstorm?"

"According to the GBI, a big one. All night long, groups have been staging their own protest announcements. Supporters and counter protesters are all coming. Eco and climate groups, immigrant rights, white rights, Antifa, alt-right, you name it. Saturday, Atlanta will be ground zero."

"Damn, this is not good." Skip got up from the table to pace the dining room. "Unbelievable. A perfect storm of whack-jobs.

Any options on trying to stop this craziness from happening? Can I legally declare a public safety threat and ban all protests?"

"Legally? Yes, you can declare an emergency and ban virtually any activity you want," Jose answered, "but I'd advise against it as that would play right into Bubba's hand. I'm sure part of his press conference today will be all about Patriot rights. If you closed down the city, he'd cut you to shreds, saying you're anti-America and anti-Constitution. He'd make you out to be a weak, frightened pansy."

The governor stopped his pacing. "I know, I know. Unfortunately, he's pretty good at it. So, what do we do, Jose?"

"It's not the best option but about the only thing that has a chance to work. Just like the police have done outside, we try to contain the factions."

Skip went over to the dining room window to look at the protesters, his ground-level view obscuring the temporary fencing dividing the groups. His back still turned to his staff, he said, "Containment sounds pretty heavy handed."

"It's done all the time, sir." Jose moved from the table to the window next to Skip, watching the protesters with the governor. "Think of how they handle national political conventions. Designated protest areas are set up for each group with barricades and buffer zones. Combine that with a heavy police presence, maybe even the National Guard, depending on the final attendance projections. Fortunately for us, the protestors have already started making this strategy feasible."

Skip continued to stare out the window. "In what way?"

"Well, the ALM claimed Liberty Plaza, so it's a safe bet the white righters will join them there. The eco groups are planning to mass at Centennial Park, and word has it most of the immigration groups are headed to Woodruff Park. That gives us several blocks of natural separation. Of course, Antifa and those looking for confrontation will be the wild cards. That's where the police presence will be needed to keep an eye on those roaming the streets, trying to stir things up."

The governor turned to Jose. "And that's just what Bubba wants, to stir things up." Aware of the others in the room, Skip decided it would be best not to show his complete trust in Jose's advice. He addressed the only staff aide over 40 years old. "What do you think?"

The aide nodded his head. "A little heavy handed, but it's probably our best option. We'll make it clear they have the right to protest, but we won't tolerate confrontation or any sort of violence. Bubba will still call you out on something, but at least he won't be able use the timid card."

"I think I can partially neutralize Bubba," Jose piped in. "It's all in how we position it to the press. Angle here is the governor is respecting the rights of all Georgia citizens, their right to protest, *and* their right to safety. I like it, it's definitely doable."

Skip looked back out the window, trying to grasp the entirety of the situation. "What about risks? What might bite me if we go this route?"

"A lot can go wrong with this, Governor," Jose said somberly, "but it's the best option. Really the only option."

"Okay," Skip finally said. "Let's do it."

"The mayor's office has a meeting set for late this morning. I'll let them know our plan."

Skip didn't take his eyes off the protestors. "Thanks, Jose."

36.

*P*am rearranged the salt and pepper shakers, syrup bottle, sweetener basket, and jelly packet cradle for the third time.

Not satisfied, she moved the sweetener basket to the front, so the composition went from shortest to tallest. She knew quite well there was no such thing as perfect order, but she was anxious and had to occupy herself as she waited for Andrea. She'd arrived at Duke's early for their 10:30 a.m. brunch meeting since waiting around the house was even more unnerving. The mostly empty diner only heightened her anxiety.

She contemplated a new arrangement when, in her head, she heard her therapist chastising her for messing with the condiments, saying she couldn't control anxiety by trying to keep everything in order. Maybe not, Pam thought, but at least it makes me feel better, which is something you haven't been able to do with these blasted therapy sessions.

"Here's your coffee, ma'am. Just let me know if you need anything else." The unfamiliar waitress set a mug in front of her.

"Thank you. I'll wait until the others arrive."

"Hey, Sis." Scott squeezed in the booth next to Pam and gave her a quick kiss on the cheek. "Hope you weren't waiting long."

"Hi, Scotty. Not too long. Where's Maggie? I thought she'd be working today. I wanted her here for support."

"She'll be here soon. She spent last night in the mountains and is only working a short shift today." With a sly grin he reached over and moved the syrup bottle to the front row.

Pam slapped his hand. "Stop that! It's not funny, I'm a nervous wreck. Something in Andrea's tone suggested she doesn't have good news."

"You said that on your message. What exactly did she say?"

Pam lowered her voice even though the few patrons were at tables far from their booth. "She knows where Tom is, and it's complicated. I asked her if she spoke with him, but she said she couldn't get close to him without being seen. I asked her what the heck that meant, and that's when she said we have to talk. I have a bad feeling about this."

Scott wrapped his right arm around his sister and gave her a hug. "You're usually right about this stuff. It's okay to be nervous."

Maggie entered Duke's still in her hiking gear and went directly to Pam and Scott's booth. "Hi, guys. Am I too late?"

Pam immediately brightened. "No, and I'm glad you're here. Scott is so useless when it comes to conversations like these. Please join us."

Maggie reached over and touched Scott's shoulder. "Give me a minute. I need to change since my shift's starting soon." She headed off toward the restroom with a gym bag over her shoulder.

Pam gave Scott a good long stare. "She's a keeper, Scotty. Tricia only had ulterior motives. She never really loved you. Don't mess this one up."

"I'll try, Sis, but it's really complicated. Maggie's not what you see in here. She, well, let's just say there's a lot to her that can't be explained."

"I know more about her than you think," Pam said in that all-knowing way of a big sister. "Thank goodness, here's Andrea!"

Winding her way through the vacant tables to their booth, Pam could tell Andrea was worn out. Her face was taut, and she braced her hands on the empty chair backs in a fashion that suggested she needed help with balance. It was not the confident stride from Monday.

"Scott, Pam, thanks for coming so quickly." Andrea slid into the booth opposite the Worthington siblings. "It's been quite a couple of days."

"You look exhausted, Andrea," the concern not hidden in Pam's voice.

"That I am. Haven't gotten much sleep since I saw you. Nothing that coffee shouldn't take care of."

"Let me take care of that." Maggie, freshly changed into her Duke's uniform, set three mugs and a coffee pot on the table. "Hi, I'm Maggie, a friend of the family. You must be Andrea."

The women shook hands while Maggie deftly poured out the coffee with her left hand before sitting in the booth next to Andrea.

"I'm not working yet. Thought I'd join you for the update."

Andrea glanced over at Pam who nodded her head. "I asked her to join us. She knows everything about Tom. So, what did you find out?"

Andrea shared the details of her last 42 hours to a spellbound audience. Pam occasionally gasped. Scott looked befuddled, and Maggie fumed. As if addressing troops, she stuck only to what was observed without conjecture, color commentary, opinions, or strategy options. Andrea finished her story and sat back to stunned faces.

"Unbelievable," Scott finally muttered. "I know the area. We lease property from them with a board and a small storage facility underneath."

Pam simply shook her head. "Daddy used to hunt down at Deer Bend all the time. Roger went once, but they didn't invite him back, something about almost shooting a hunting dog. I can't believe this. Are you sure he's being held prisoner?"

Andrea set down her mug. "That's what it looked like. There were well-armed men watching his every move, not that he looked strong enough to overpower anyone or run away. The building he's being kept in is designed like a prison and built with concrete."

Tears welled in Pam's eyes. "We've got to tell someone, report this to the police or something. They can't just hold someone against their will!" She glanced around the diner to make sure heads didn't turn at her outburst.

Andrea reached across the table and held Pam's hand. "I agree, but that's where this gets complicated. We have no probable cause for the police to go searching the compound, and the only evidence we have is from a trespasser who just so happened to disable their security cameras and take video on private property."

"You're right. The police would be a dead end," Maggie added. "What about his doctor at the VA? An off-the-record kind of conversation?"

"I debated that," Andrea said, "but looping the military in, even a doctor, carries other complications. They'd probably say it's a civilian issue, and we'd be right back here."

Pam reached over and moved the syrup bottle back to its proper place in a feeble attempt to control her anxiety. "Well then, let's just go break him out! We can't just let him stay there!"

In a steady voice directly to Pam, Andrea said, "It could be done with a small unit, maybe three or four. Unfortunately, there's a high probability of casualties, not on our side, but there's a good chance someone would be killed. I don't think that's a risk any of us want to take."

Pam was on the verge of tears. "No, you're right. We can't do that.." She suddenly brightened. "Scotty, what about that GBI guy? You said he seemed nice. Maybe he could help?"

Maggie interrupted before he could answer. "Pam, with everything that's going on, I don't think that would be a good idea."

Pam and Maggie stared at each other for a prolonged second.

Pam tried to stifle her sobs. Crying in public was not what Worthington women do. "We have to do something. There's no way he'll make it being a prisoner. We'll lose him for sure this time."

Her voice carried and heads swiveled in their direction. The unfamiliar waitress started moving toward the table, only to stop when she saw Maggie hold up her hand.

"Yes, I don't think he'll make it if he stays there," Andrea whispered.

Maggie's spoke with a hushed firmness. "If rescue's not an option and we can't call the cops, we need to figure out a way to make the cops want to search the grounds. If they have a legitimate reason, no one can stop them. Isn't that right?"

"Sure, I guess so," Andrea answered. "I imagine it would have to be a pretty damn good reason."

Maggie gave a wry smile. "Well, I have an idea that should do the trick."

"No, Maggie!" The alarm in Scott's voice startled Pam and even drew Duke's attention.

Maggie's glanced over at Duke then something out in the parking lot caught her eye. She leaned in to the group. "You need to trust me, Scott. This will work and may solve our other problem too."

"But—"

Andrea cut him off. "What other problem?"

Pam's urgent voice got their attention. "Please stop. Let's hear Maggie's idea."

Maggie looked outside again then stood up from the booth. "We can't discuss it here. Besides, our favorite GBI agent's sitting out in his car watching us. I get off at 2:30. Let's meet at my place at 4:00."

37.

*S*eamus sat in his car and watched the four talk intently in Scott's usual booth. Maggie was next to an African-American woman. One of the heads he saw from the rear definitely belonged to Scott, and he guessed the other was his sister. Their body language and gestures told him the conversation was personal and serious.

Stinging from his encounter with Carraway, Seamus just wanted a quiet lunch before the mayor's meeting and didn't feel very sociable. Deep down, he knew that wasn't true. If he really wanted a quiet lunch, there were hundreds of other restaurants to choose from. No, for some reason he was drawn to Duke's, and watching the four of them talk made him long to be part of their conversation.

Once Maggie stood and left the group, the other three leaned back into more casual postures. Seamus felt it was his cue to enter Duke's.

Maggie was the first to greet him near the door. "Seamus! This is a surprise. Good to see you. You here to eat or for official business?"

Her friendly charm disarmed him. "I, er, just thought I'd grab a quick bite."

"Come join us," Scott called out from his booth. His greeting sounded sincere.

Maggie gently took Seamus by the elbow and directed him around the empty tables to the booth. "I'll be back with menus in a minute."

Seamus stood awkwardly at the end of the table. "Good morning, Scott. Hope I'm not interrupting anything."

"Not at all. We were just talking about Tom. You've spoken to my sister, but allow me to formally introduce Pam."

"Nice to meet you, Pam." Her hand was the softest he'd ever felt. He could tell she had been crying and assumed the news on Tom was not good.

"The pleasure's mine, Agent O'Reilly."

Scott then motioned to the other woman. "And meet Lieutenant Colonel Andrea Leonard. She's a friend of Tom's and has been trying to find him."

Seamus was immediately enamored. Though he did find her very attractive, it was not her looks. There was something different about her mere presence, a comfortable confidence and intelligence that permeated the air. She simply had a positive aura. He suddenly realized he was holding her handshake longer than socially acceptable.

"Pleasure to meet you, Colonel."

"Likewise, and please call me Andrea." Her smile was easy and gentle, her brown eyes exuded warmth. "Care to join us?"

"I'd love to." Seamus's voice cracked slightly as he slid in the booth next to Andrea. "Have you had any luck tracking him down?" He tried not to focus on her lips as she began to speak.

"Unfortunately, no. He went to a group meeting at the VA then simply disappeared. I even pulled rank and had other VA facilities checked. Pam had neighbors look for him at their family cottage down on Skidaway Island, but I'm going down there this afternoon just to see if he's hiding on the grounds somewhere. We're running out of options, so it's time to widen the net."

Seamus sensed a fib in Andrea's story but didn't really care. He was too enchanted with her. He even liked her voice—assured, smooth and consistent. He could picture her in uniform as one of those calm yet passionate leaders. "Anything I can do to help? After all, I am in law enforcement with resources at my disposal."

"You are so sweet!" Pam exclaimed. "Scott told me you were a nice guy, and I'm really touched by your offer. I don't know if we're quite ready for that. What do you think, Andrea?"

Seamus could feel Andrea next to him. His heart and nerves all jumbled as he turned to look at her.

"It's certainly something we should consider," she said. "Let's see if I make any progress at the coast. If that's a dead end then I'll ask for your help."

Seamus fished a card out of his jacket pocket and focused on keeping his hand steady as he passed it to Andrea. "Just let me know. I'd be glad to help."

Maggie snapped him out of his schoolboy trance. "How was your trip, Seamus?"

He had no idea how long Maggie had been standing next to him with menus in hand. "Fine, just fine," he stammered. "Actually, it was so uneventful that they've pulled me from the investigation." It was his turn to lie.

"Really? Well, it's their loss." Maggie tilted her hips and held up the menus. "Is anyone eating, or are you just booth squatting?"

"I need to get to work," Scott said as he slid out of the booth.

Pam was right on his heels. "I need to get going too."

"I'm starved," Seamus admitted. Summoning nerve he hadn't tapped in years, Seamus looked at Andrea. "Buy you breakfast?"

"Thank you, I'd like that."

Pam lingered behind her brother. "Thanks for your help, Andrea. Please let me know if you need anything or if something comes up down on Skidaway."

"I'll call you once I get there."

Maggie handed menus to Andrea and Seamus. "Just let me know when you two kids are ready to order," she said mischievously.

Seamus accepted the menus and handed one to Andrea, turning slightly in the booth to face her.

"Are you a regular here too?" Andrea asked.

"No. Before Monday, I didn't even know this place existed. I haven't lived in Atlanta long and don't get out much."

"Where you'd move from?" Andrea asked.

Seamus was grateful for the small talk; he could handle small talk.

"Michigan. I grew up in Detroit but spent most of my time after school in Lansing."

"You seem like a Midwesterner. I grew up in Cleveland."

"Wow. We only met a few minutes ago, and you already pegged me as a Midwesterner?" Seamus was honestly impressed.

"One of the advantages of being in the Army is you meet people from all over the country. After a while, it's easy to tell different accents and speaking patterns." Andrea's eyes drifted above Seamus as she spoke.

"Y'all decided?" Maggie asked.

Seamus fumbled with the menu having forgotten he was there to eat.

Andrea stretched her lithe arm across Seamus handing the menu back to Maggie. "I'll have the oatmeal please. Can you add a sprinkle of cinnamon and some bananas?"

"Oatmeal?" Seamus arched his eyebrows. "You like oatmeal?"

Andrea gave him an easy smile. "I love oatmeal. I grew up on the stuff."

"Me too," Seamus nodded. "My mom gave it to us all the time. She said it was a good hearty breakfast, but once I got older I realized it was about the only thing we could afford."

"Same here. That's another working class Midwestern thing."

Seamus swam in Andrea's eyes for a moment then turned to Maggie. "I'll have the oatmeal too, but hold the cinnamon and I'll take blueberries, if you can."

Maggie gave him her knowing look as she took his menu. "We can do that for you, Seamus." Her voice was reassuring.

Seamus tried to steady his mind. It had been a long time since he'd been in a situation like this—he'd forgotten what it was like and didn't want to blow it. Better to ask questions, he thought. If he spoke too much, he might say something stupid.

"Lieutenant colonel. That's pretty impressive. Did you always want to be in the Army?"

"I wanted to go to college, and the Army was really the only way I could afford it. I joined JROTC in high school, and one thing led to another. I never thought I'd be in the service this long and never dreamt of achieving this kind of rank."

"Well, you must be good at it. They don't just hand out ranks to anybody." Seamus hoped his comment didn't sound like gratuitous flattery.

"I guess I am," Andrea said modestly. "As a kid, I was very structured. There was quite a bit of...I'll say, uncertainty in my family, so I compensated by trying to control my own little world. Since the Army is built on structure, I fit right it. My parents weren't surprised I joined the Army. My getting a college degree probably surprised them more. I'm the first one in my family to get a college degree," she said with pride.

Seamus perked up. "Me too! I mean the college degree, not the Army." He silently chastised himself for effusively repeating the "me too" comment, but it was hard to think straight. Their parallel backgrounds were hard to ignore.

"Okay, one oatmeal with bananas," Maggie announced as she placed a steaming bowl in front of Andrea, who smiled and nodded. "And one with blueberries. Can I get you two anything else?"

Seamus was grateful for the interruption as he needed to regroup. "I'm fine. Thanks, Maggie."

Andrea and Seamus sat up next to each other with spoons in hand. Not thinking about being a lefty, he conked her elbow as they began to eat. It was the first time they touched since the prolonged handshake.

"Sorry about that," he said shyly. "I should have thought about that. Do you want me to move?"

"That's okay. We'll make it work," Andrea said. She tucked her right arm in a little, and they scooted fractionally away from each other.

Seamus's mind raced as they ate in silence. She was okay with him sitting next to her rather than moving to the opposite side, so maybe he has a shot after all. He slyly inched a bit over in the booth to make up the lost ground from the elbow clank. He was close enough where he could almost feel her which only jumbled his entire body, making the thick oatmeal difficult to swallow. A clump dribbled off his chin, and he caught it with his free hand before it hit his lap.

"Nice reflexes," Andrea said playfully as she plucked a couple of extra napkins out of the silver holder. "Here you go. I won't tell your mom about your lapse of manners."

Seamus normally would have been humiliated, but their hands touched during the napkin exchange. He was hopelessly ill-equipped for the moment. "She's seen worse," he mumbled.

"You missed a spot."

Seamus froze as Andrea reached up with her napkin and gently dapped a chunk of oatmeal off his chin. Once again, his eyes were drawn to her lips as she puckered them slightly in concentration.

He squeaked out a sheepish, "thanks," thinking his head would burst. He fought to control himself or the next incident might involve Andrea using the Heimlich to dislodge a blueberry from his throat. Seamus focused on his oatmeal with added resolve.

They finished eating at about the same time.

"That was a good call, Andrea. Thanks for the trip down memory lane," Seamus said, relieved he'd avoided any additional embarrassing dining mishaps.

"Not as good as my mom's, but it will do," Andrea agreed.

The efficient Maggie was on them like a hawk. "Glad you liked it." She scooped up the dirty dishes, stacking them on her tray. She gave them an impish smile. "I promise not to interrupt you two again."

Seamus looked at his watch and immediately wished he hadn't. "Unfortunately, I have to leave. I need to be downtown in 20 minutes."

Maggie's eyes twinkled. "That's too bad. You two look awful cozy there."

"Uh," Seamus stumbled over his tongue, "yes, it was nice meeting Andrea. I'll take the check please."

Maggie ripped their check off her pad and handed it to Seamus. "Well, I hope you have a good day. Thanks for coming in." Maggie hefted the tray and left them alone again.

Seamus stood. "Sorry I have to leave. I really enjoyed your company." He took $20 out of his wallet and put it on table with the check.

Andrea scooted across the bench closer to where he stood. "You like being a GBI agent?"

The question took Seamus by surprise, not the parting exchange he'd been running through his mind. He hesitated before answering.

"I'm not really a GBI agent," he admitted. "I head research for the Antiterrorism Team. I only got involved this week because of the scope. Most of the time I'm in the office on the computer, working with other agencies."

"You're more of the brains rather than the brawn then."

Seamus tried not to react to what felt like a slight. "Well, I think I have plenty of brawn. I just prefer to use my brain," he said with a touch of bravado.

She reached out, gently resting three fingers on his left kneecap. "Some women find brains sexier."

"I, er, thanks, I guess," Seamus fumbled, his embarrassment obvious. Desperate to keep his composure he quickly added, "Will you call me if you find anything out about Tom?"

"What if I don't find him?" she asked coyly.

Finding courage he didn't know existed, Seamus blurted, "I'd still like to hear from you." He quickly retreated out of Duke's before he could hear her answer.

38.

Bubba sat on the veranda wondering where the hell Horace was. He'd finished lunch a good ten minutes ago, and that slacker still hadn't come out to clean up his plate. He made a mental note to talk to his brother about the Plantation's domestic help. Might be time to upgrade. Tired of looking at dirty dishes, he moved over to his favorite rocker to run through the short speech he'd written for the press conference.

One of the great things about visiting the Plantation—and there was a long list of great things—was that Bubba could shake all the toady, overcautious aides that followed his every move back in DC. He'd received several panic-stricken messages from those aides once they heard his plan to hold a 1:00 p.m. press conference. When it was clear he was determined to proceed, the aides' approach shifted to not-so-subtle coaching of his message. Tough shit, kids. On the Plantation, Bubba does what he damn well pleases.

Bubba slowly rocked while taking in the Plantation's view. He did his best thinking in a rocking chair, and today he was feeling extremely content. The last 24 hours had been just about perfect—quality TV face time, a grateful president, fine bourbon, holding court for rich and powerful men, and a young, nubile woman in his cabin. About the only thing missing was the smell of gunpowder and a successful hunt. He had second thoughts about heading back to DC this afternoon, but it was necessary if he wanted to continue this lifestyle.

He heard car tires coming from the entrance up the driveway. A sparkling clean Deer Bend black Suburban pulled into view and drove around the circle stopping with the passenger side in front of the veranda's steps. The driver hopped out and came around the truck.

"Afternoon, Congressman!"

"Andy, thanks for taking another day off. Appreciate your help." Bubba continued to rock. "Come on up here and join me."

Andy took the steps in two long strides and sat in the rocker next to Bubba.

"How's it looking out front?" Bubba asked.

"Looking really good. They set the canopy up in the field just inside the gate. There're at least eight TV trucks parked on 21, and most of the cameras are set up, waiting for you to show up. I'm not a pro at this like you are, but it looks like a good turnout for a Wednesday."

"That is a good turnout. Anyone we recognize?"

"Sorry, Congressman, I can't help you much on that. Don't pay too much attention to TV unless you're on."

"And what about Dave?"

"He's got his truck parked in the drive to make sure no one tries coming up to the big house. He's staying in the truck. Don't need to worry about him saying anything."

"Good," Bubba nodded. "I love my brother to death, but the boy can be dumb as a post in front of a camera."

"When do you want to head down?"

"Let's enjoy the moment for a while. Besides, I find it's better to make the press wait and squirm a little bit. Get them a little anxious, but don't wait too long to get them angry."

Andy nodded at the congressman and commenced his own rocking.

The men rocked in silence until Bubba heard the rattling of dishes behind him. He didn't turn to speak. "Thought you up and died on me Horace. Those things have been sitting there forever. I need my bags in the car. We'll be leaving in a couple of minutes."

"Yes, sir, Mr. James," came the reply.

Bubba and Andy watched as the old Black man left the veranda to fetch Bubba's bags from the cabin. He emerged a minute later with the two travel bags and loaded them into the back of the Suburban. His gait was slow and purposeful as he climbed the steps.

"Have a safe trip, Mr. James. See you next time."

"Thanks, Horace. See you next time." He rolled his eyes at Andy then tapped his wristwatch. "Let's go do this."

The two men climbed into the Suburban. Bubba took the front passenger seat, so the press wouldn't think he was getting chauffeured. As they left the driveway circle, Bubba finally told Andy what was really on his mind.

"You outdid yourself last night Andy. That girl was incredible. I swear she could work for Cirque du Soleil. And smart as a whip too."

Andy smiled. "Glad to hear that, Congressman. I thought you'd like her. You're right, she's a star student and has political aspirations."

"Really?" Bubba instantly thought of the butt-ugly pages on his current staff. "Maybe I could help her out. Think she'd care to intern in DC?"

"I'll find out, but DC might be a little too far from home for her right now."

Bubba knew what he meant and thought it better not to push the topic.

The Suburban wound through the trees and over a small rise where Dave's truck blocked the way. He saw them coming and pulled his truck to the side. Andy stopped the Suburban next to it with Bubba's window even with the driver's side.

Bubba zipped down his window. "Thanks for the hospitality, brother. I might come back next week, depending on what happens."

"Always great to have you visit, Jimmy. Now go down there and give 'em hell."

Andy drove the last hundred yards to the waiting media. Bubba loved the sight of TV trucks, though he thought the old trucks, with massive, expandable microwave towers reaching to the heavens, were more impressive than the modern versions sporting satellite dishes on their roofs. He was thrilled to see several national press members mingled in with the Atlanta press.

Bubba hopped out of the Suburban. He wore work slacks, boots, a tasteful plaid flannel shirt, and his trusty jeans jacket. The entire outfit was just that, an outfit—his stage costume for middle Georgia publicity. Several cameras' recording lights quickly lit up. Knowing he was on tape, Bubba concentrated on making a purposeful walk to the microphones.

"Afternoon, everyone. Thanks for coming. I'll make a brief statement then take your questions." Bubba took folded notes out of the jeans jacket's breast pocket. He quietly cleared his throat, more for dramatic purposes.

"It is clear that our country, our very way of life, is under attack." His brow furrowed, and he eased slightly off the drawl in an effort to add solemnity. "The recent terrorist attack on the great state of Georgia is just the latest example of violent foreigners trying to wreak havoc on our great country. They have no interest in obeying our laws, no desire to heed our Constitution. They come here to take whatever they can. For many of us, this comes as no surprise. We've been witnessing it for years and have been trying to warn our fellow citizens that the situation is dire. Even now, even after what's happened this week, many prefer to just turn a blind eye."

Bubba paused and looked up. He scanned the cameras to make sure he made contact with each.

His voice firmed, he raised an index finger. "The Governor of Georgia is one such individual. Ignoring the president's advice, the counsel of concerned elected representatives, and the pleas of citizens, he continues to ignore the threat. Unfortunately, he is not alone. This has got to stop." He held up is hands for emphasis.

"As citizens of this great country, we must rise up," his inflection rising with the comment as he shifted to preacher mode. "Demand that government officials stop tying the hands of our brave law enforcement officers, take to the streets to demand justice, support the many brave Patriots who are willing to fight to save our country. We must be vigilant, or we are doomed.

"I have been in close contact with law enforcement and know for a fact that their investigation into this terrorist attack has gone nowhere. I, for one, can't sit idly by. Therefore, with the help of several prominent Patriotic Americans, we're offering a one million dollar reward to anyone who has information that leads to an arrest and conviction of these perpetrators." Bubba took a long pause, hoping to get a reaction from the reporters. Disappointed at not hearing a single gasp, he focused on CNN's camera and pushed ahead.

"Someone out there must know what happened and can share information. Please contact law enforcement with what you know. And if you're an illegal, I can personally assure you that your status will not be used against you for helping America. We, the citizens of this great country, must take a more active role in saving what is near and dear to us."

Bubba carefully folded his notes back up and stuck them back in his pocket. "Now, I'll take several questions before I return to Washington to take up the fight there."

The hushed reporters suddenly burst out in unison.

Bubba disguised his smirk. About damn time, he thought. He then followed his tried-and-true press conference rules—the first question always goes to the hottest female reporter, then go to a guy, then the second hottest female, and so on down the line. The number of questions he took usually was in direct proportion to the number of hot female reporters. Today, the pickings were slim. After answering five questions, without saying much of anything, he retreated to the idling Suburban.

Andy pulled out of Deer Bend Plantation and turned left onto Route 21 toward the county airport. "Holy shit, Congressman, a million dollar reward?"

Bubba sat in the back proud of his performance. "A wise investment, Andy, a very wise investment." He quickly shed the uncomfortable jeans jacket. "We don't need to worry about those that understand. It's the people on the fence we want in our camp. Some folks just need a little additional motivation."

39.

Maggie opened her bungalow's front door. "Afternoon, Andrea. You have trouble finding my place?"

"Not at all. Love the porch and oak tree."

Andrea looked better rested since Maggie saw her earlier at Duke's.

"Come in. Thought we'd meet in the kitchen."

Andrea followed Maggie into the kitchen where, ever the hostess, she had a pitcher of iced tea, cold Diet Coke, and a cheese plate set out for her guests.

Andrea held up a satchel. "Got here just a little early to set up my computer to show the videos I took. Okay if I use the table?"

"Please, help yourself." Maggie took the seat across from Andrea while she booted up her computer. "Seems like you and Seamus hit it off today."

Andrea looked up and gave her a meek grin. "Yeah, he seems like a rare find."

Maggie's eyes narrowed. "You realize that if we push forward with a plan to rescue Tom, any relationship with him would be rather complicated."

Andrea's grin faded slightly. "I figured as much, but who knows? Even if it's remote, it's still a possibility.

"You willing to make that sacrifice?" Maggie asked.

Andrea gave her a startled look. "Of course! This is all about Tom. My loyalty is with him, not some guy I just met."

"I'm glad to hear that." Maggie held her gaze on Andrea. "Then we need to talk about something else."

Andrea sat back in the metal and vinyl kitchen chair, her surprise shifting to seriousness. "What's on your mind, Maggie?"

"What all do you know about Congressman Bubba Baker?"

"Before the last couple of days, I only knew him as the raging racist asshole that chairs the Armed Services Committee. I pay attention to politicians trying to overturn the previous administration's policies on basic rights soldiers like me need in our current military structure. Now I'm convinced he's an even bigger dirtbag. Tom was picked up in a car from his hunting lodge and is being held on land he used to own." Andrea studied Maggie's face. "Why do you ask?"

Maggie didn't move a muscle and kept her eyes locked on Andrea. "Did you hear his press conference today?"

"No, I was napping. Did I miss something?"

"Congressman Baker announced a one million dollar reward to anyone who could provide information on the Georgia billboard bombings," Maggie told her.

"So? What's that have to do with us?"

Maggie didn't say a word and stared intently at Andrea debating how much she had to divulge. "As part of Tom's rescue, what would you do if you came across information that might be of value to the congressman? A value worth a million dollars?" Maggie said the words slowly and carefully.

Andrea's brow crinkled as she processed Maggie's words. "I'm sorry, but I still don't see the connection."

Andrea had already proven her willingness to bend the law, and her loyalty to Tom was undeniable. Maggie trusted her gut and went the direct route. "What if you were to find I had some involvement in the billboard attack." Maggie looked long and hard at the soldier hoping she hadn't miscalculated.

Andrea's serious expression began to evolve into shocked amusement. "Seriously?! Girl, aren't you full of surprises!"

Maggie began to relax slightly. "It's just not me, someone else close to this is involved too."

"I'll be damned." Andrea shook her head chuckling to herself. "I never would have guessed."

Despite Andrea's reaction, Maggie had to be sure. "So a million dollars isn't tempting?"

Andrea voice became firm. "I'm a soldier. You don't go into the military for the money. I'm prepared to sacrifice my life for Tom, and I sure as hell think my life is worth more than a measly million bucks."

Maggie nodded her head. "Thank you, Andrea. I knew we could count on you, but I had to ask."

Andrea laughed as she began typing on her computer. "I think I'm starting to understand...what'd you call it today? Your other problem? Pretty ingenious, if you ask me. Free Tom while throwing suspicion on a bunch of white racists. Talk about a twofer for me. This might be the best mission of my career."

"Hey, we're here!" Scott announced from the porch.

Maggie bounced up from her chair and squeezed Andrea's shoulder as she passed to meet Scott and Pam. Maggie gave them both a hug. "C'mon in. Andrea's already in the kitchen."

Andrea stood and hugged the new guests. "Why don't you take a seat. I want to show you the video from my recon."

Scott grabbed a chunk of cheese and pulled a chair up next to Andrea. Pam helped herself to a Diet Coke and sat on Andrea's other side. Maggie was too anxious to sit, so she stood in the doorway to the living room looking over their shoulders. Andrea nudged the computer out in the middle of the table and hit play.

The video started with Andrea approaching the first small concrete building. The black and white image had a tinge of green but was amazingly clear. Scott and Pam leaned in to get a better view, their faces twisted in tension as they relived Andrea's footsteps through the compound. Maggie had to remind herself to breathe as she hovered behind Andrea. No one said a word during the ten-minute video.

Scott finally broke the silence. "Can you show the building again where you think Tom's being held?"

Andrea slid the play bar back to her approach of the long building. "Four people are being held on this side of the structure. My guess is they're each in a room about 10x10 with that one window." She hit pause and zoomed in. "The window is sealed shut, has reinforcement wire to prevent breaking, and is too small for a medium-to-large adult to get through. No one's getting out that way."

She hit play again, and the quartet watched as Andrea crept around the side and scanned the field before slowly jogging to the front door. She froze the video again. "It's steel. Don't know how thick. Look at door hinges. They're on the outside instead of inside like most outer doors. No one on the inside can tamper with them to break out. The windows, hinges, and guards tell me this is a prison."

"And the building is incredibly structurally sound," Maggie added. She pointed over Pam's shoulder at the frame. "You can see the steel beams along the truss overhang. The building's clearly concrete with steel roof beaming. You see this type of construction in storm zones, and I bet this could handle a Cat 4 hurricane or an F3 tornado. It's expensive to build and makes absolutely no sense compared to the other buildings."

Three sets of eyes looked over their shoulders at her. She ignored them, staying affixed to the computer image. Maggie stood back up. "Please go back. I'd like to get a closer look at that first building."

Andrea grabbed the mouse and maneuvered the video back to the shed on the far side of the field.

"Freeze it right there," Maggie instructed. She leaned back in, pointing at the screen. "See? Similar construction, maybe not quite as robust, but nothing like normal building standards. Structures like these are designed to withstand external pressure, which means they are more susceptible to internal trauma. In another words, it's easier to make them blow out than collapse in. Can we see the door again?"

Andrea inched the frames back to the shed's door and held the image.

Maggie stared intently at the computer screen. No one dared to break her concentration. "Okay, I've seen enough."

She left her position behind the others, pulled a Diet Coke out of the ice bucket, and took the remaining chair at the table. "I agree with Andrea. I think that's their armory, and it's the most logical target."

"Wait a minute, Maggie. You can't be serious," Scott whispered in disbelief.

"What's wrong, Scott?" Pam was clearly confused. "I don't get it!"

Maggie tried to give Pam a reassuring look. "We need a disturbance big enough to draw the cops. We blow up the armory, and they have a damn good reason to enter the property."

Pam perked up. "Oh, I see now!"

Scott raised his voice, not in anger but panic. "Please stop it, Maggie!"

The kitchen fell silent, and the four exchanged uncomfortable glances. Maggie understood Scott's pleading face but wanted the moment to play out. Andrea gave Maggie a confident nod, and for the first time, Maggie thought Pam looked hopeful.

She spoke to Pam. "I think it's time to have a conversation with your brother."

"You're right." Pam leaned forward to look at Scott. "I know what you and Maggie have been up to. At least this has a purpose."

Maggie watched as resignation swept through Scott, his shoulders sinking as he lowered in his chair. "You know? How?"

Pam sighed and gave him a gentle, loving look. "Maggie told me everything about a year ago. She wanted my permission."

Scott bolted erect in his chair, confusion and anger sweeping his face. "Maggie told you? Mags, how could you? Why?"

Maggie was surprised at the raw passion of Scott's steely glare, a side she knew existed but rarely saw. She stayed compassionately firm. "Our little adventure started as a lark, an entertaining conversational fantasy. I was shocked when you began to take it seriously and pressed to make it happen. There was no risk in it for me. Technically I don't exist, and I have zero responsibilities or people who depend on me. But it's completely different for you. I was concerned your judgment was impaired due to infatuation, and I didn't want you to do something that couldn't be undone."

Scott softly piped in. "You know it's more than infatuation."

"And it is for me too," Maggie reassured him. "Anyway, I went to Pam and told her about us and the plan, and then I asked if she approved. I was fully prepared to leave town if she said no."

"Imagine my shock," Pam said. "My sane, reliable brother wants to blow things up while my damaged brother is now afraid of firecrackers. Despite the ludicrous concept and my concern for your safety, I said yes."

"You approved?!" Scott was incredulous. "How could you? The company! What about Roger? Does he know?"

Maggie got up from her seat, circled the table, and gave Scott a bent over hug from behind. "Easy, Scott."

Pam began to laugh. "Of course, Roger doesn't know and he never will. I'm not worried about the company. Roger knows what he's doing, and I can fix anything he might mess up. As for why I said yes, I said yes because I've never seen you so happy. Maggie's lit something inside you that's been dormant since we were kids. I wanted you to enjoy life again. You deserve it. Besides, Maggie's smarter than everyone else. With her running the show, I knew it would work out."

The women went silent. They knew it was time to give Scott a minute to process the revelation. Maggie stepped over to the cupboard, fetched a liter of Hendrick's, and poured Scott a gin and tonic in a large tumbler. "Here you go, handsome. Sorry I ran out of limes."

Scott studied the room and turned to Andrea, who had wisely pushed her chair out of the line of fire. "And I suppose you know all about this too?"

Andrea was pleasantly bemused. "Well, Maggie and I talked before you got here. I have a pretty good guess, but I'd love to know the details."

Maggie sat back in the chair. "The only detail you need to know is I have nearly 5 pounds of construction grade plastic explosives. It would be ideal if we could plant it inside the armory, but planting it outside would still do what we want."

Andrea looked at the Worthington siblings then back at Maggie. "I'm in and just the woman to do the job."

Scott nearly spilled his gin and tonic. "Not you too!"

Pam gave Andrea a quick hug. "Thank you. This means so much to us."

"Seriously, don't I have a say in this?" Scott's voice rose an octave. "I really don't think this is such—"

"Scott!" Pam snapped. "Why don't you take your cocktail outside and enjoy the day. We've got this."

Clearly outnumbered, Scott picked up his tumbler and headed to the front porch rockers. Once out of hearing range, the women got down to business.

40.

Tom lay spread eagle in the middle of the field, praying to the heavens that the invisible hand of God, or hell, even a UFO would sweep him off the face of the Earth. He had no clue what day it was and only knew it was later in the afternoon based on the sun moving closer to the tree line. He closed his eyes trying to make it all stop.

In the distance, he heard a screen door slam. He felt the presence of someone and opened his eyes to the black, compassionate, worried face staring back at him. The face was beautiful, even the big wet nose. The lick started at his brow and went up his forehead ending at his hairline. Tom began to quietly sob.

"Hello, girl," he said to the black Lab. He reached his left arm up and began to scratch her behind the ear. Her right hind leg thumped in unison.

Even the slight brief movement left him exhausted. He let his arm drop back to the ground. The black Lab understood, so she flopped down next to him, resting her head on his chest. Her light panting on his neck whiskers was soothing, and he didn't mind her dog breath one bit. Tom closed his eyes again.

A shadow blocked the sun from Tom's face. He looked up to see the old man standing over him, his face almost as concerned as the dog's. The sun shone around his head like the halo of an angel, but the dog was his savior. This guy was one of them.

"Hello, son," he said kindly. "You doing okay?"

Tom wished he had the strength to kick the old guys' ass. Responding was difficult enough. "I feel like shit," he sighed.

"Anything I can do for you?"

"Of course! You can let me go, shoot me, or at least shoot those two worthless dickheads," he snarled between gritted teeth.

"I wish I could help you there, son, but it's out of my hands. As for the dickheads, we give it some time, and those fools will probably shoot each other."

Tom knew his mind was addled, but the old guy's comment didn't make sense. "What do you mean you can't let me go? Aren't you the boss?"

The old guy only shook his head. "Son, if I were the boss, none of this would be happening." He briefly took his gaze off Tom. "The doc's coming. I'd best be going."

With that he walked away, and the sun beat back on Tom's face. He closed his eyes again and said a quick prayer that the doc might have finally figured out what the hell was going on.

"How are you feeling today, soldier?" Dr. Shaw said hopefully.

Tom didn't move from his prone position. "How does it look like I'm feeling? What fucking med school did you go to? University of Cluelessness?"

The doc let out a brief laugh. "At least your mind and tongue are still sharp."

He tried not to sound desperate. "Seriously, Doc, what the hell's going on? I have a window every day where I feel great, best I've felt in years. So damn good I think I can do anything. But it never lasts no matter how hard I try. It's like a really bad roller coaster with no real pattern. I've had mood swings before but never to the extremes like now. It's almost like I'm manic."

"I'm sorry this is turning out to be such a challenge," Dr Shaw's face belied his words. "We're monitoring your vitals and believe I'm close to figuring it out. Trust me, only a couple more days and you'll be stable."

"Can you at least do something about the nights? It's not bad at first, but by the morning, it's almost unbearable."

"And what are your symptoms during those early morning hours?"

Tom didn't need to think about it. "My skin's crawling, but my body is so numb it's like I'm paralyzed. It sucks, Doc. I feel possessed."

"I see," the doc nodded his head as he checked his clipboard. "I might have an idea on how to improve your nights."

"I really don't give a shit what you do. Knock me out for all I care. I just need to get some sleep."

"We'll try something different tonight and see how it goes." Shaw scribbled something on the clipboard.

Tom closed his eyes again and scratched the dog's head still resting on his chest. "Just figure it out, Doc. I don't know how much more of this I can take."

41.

"**D**amn it all to hell!"

Seamus peeked over his cube wall, surprised Carraway's voice had carried from his office and not the hallway. He quickly sat down; the boss was really steamed.

"May I have your attention?"

Carraway must have left his office as his voice echoed off the walls.

"May I have your attention?" he announced again with more urgency.

Seamus rose so his boss could see him as did the other agents and employees still in the office at 6:30 p.m. He exchanged wary glances with several coworkers. The blanket summons was a rarity, even for the vocal Carraway.

"I've had enough! I just instructed IT to route all phone calls to voice mail. We are not going to waste one more minute of our time on a bunch of damn crackpots calling in with leads for reward money. Effective immediately, no one is to use your land line. Cell phones only! We'll filter the voice mails in the morning, but right now I'm going home for a stiff drink."

And he wasn't kidding. Carraway picked up his briefcase, reached to turn off his office light, then stormed out of the building.

Seamus settled back down. He agreed with his boss. The volume of calls and convoluted stories the team fielded since the congressman's press conference had been astounding. It seemed like every Spanish-speaking roofer, painter, or tree cutter driving a van with ladders on the roof had been reported for secretly transporting a pack of devious terrorists. It would have been funny if it wasn't so disturbing. The level of hate and suspicion seemed to have no end. On the positive side, Seamus's theory was no longer the craziest idea.

If the boss was going home, then he would too. After three 16-hour days, cutting today down to 12 almost felt like a holiday. Seamus quickly packed up his computer and headed for the door.

It was the first time he'd been in his apartment during daylight since last Saturday. He got a beer from the fridge and stood in front of the window looking down at the complex's empty pool, one of the many advertised features that Seamus still hadn't got around to enjoying. He reran the events of his very strange day, including the embarrassment and reprimand for his Louisiana report, a tedious meeting at the mayor's office, and the hysterical, greedy people willing to incriminate anyone. The day would have been horrible if not for the one subject that occupied most of his thoughts—Lieutenant Colonel Andrea Leonard.

Seamus still couldn't believe she'd hit on him when he left. With age, he'd become more aware of when women flirted with him, but those instances were usually more flattering than intriguing, like the checkout girl at Target or the nose-pierced Starbucks barista with a huge hoop through the septum instead of a simple little stud he sometimes found sexy. Good for the ego but that's about it. Andrea was different, and his inability to process what to do was driving him nuts.

Seamus moved from the window. He was not ready to get spun up about a woman again. Remember, he told himself, in four short years of marriage, he and Peggy went from soul mates to cellmates. No way was he ready to consider doing that again.

Needing a diversion, Seamus surveyed his apartment, wondering what he should do. That's the problem when you move to a different town and immerse yourself in a new job—he simply didn't know anyone to call and hang out with. If he was honest, the change of location didn't make a difference. Even if he was back in Lansing, his list of options would be equally limited.

He was too tired to go to the gym. Besides when working out, he spent more time inside his head than out. TV was an option, but he didn't want the noise. He wandered over to his reliable bookshelf, knowing another world existed behind each and every cover.

He changed his mind and settled in at his small desk in front of his laptop. Tonight, he wasn't going to read a book; he'd start writing one. Inserting his personal thumb drive in the USB port, he opened up his Louisiana report and began scanning the pages. He stopped at the obituary of Rebecca Averett he'd found in *The Advocate*, Baton Rouge's main newspaper. For some reason, it wasn't included in the FBI file.

Seamus pulled out his small notepad from the Lafitte interview to make notes as he read the obit. Adjectives used to describe her included brilliant, compassionate, friendly, and energetic. One paragraph talked of her love of nature and another on the interest she had in the lives of Lafitte employees. Most interesting to Seamus was the glowing quote from an employee, the only quote in the obit not from John Long. It was given by a crew foreman, Miguel Hernandez.

Seamus found it odd that a crew foreman of Mexican ancestry would be quoted in the obit of a white, local business leader. He recalled Hernandez's name from the FBI file and knew he still worked there. He reread the FBI's two interviews with Hernandez, and nothing stood out. He decided to do a quick Google search on the man.

It took some digging as the Hernandez surname was more popular than Seamus realized. He finally found a match in a five-year-old parish newsletter from Saint-Gerne's only Catholic Church. It was a brief article and bio congratulating parishioner Miguel Hernandez on his new lay leadership position with the church.

Hernandez came to the US some 20 years ago—15 years from the date of the newsletter—from Monterrey, Mexico with his wife and two young sons. No mention of how the family attained legal status was given. He worked for Lafitte his entire time in the US and was most proud of his boys, particularly his oldest who had gone down a wrong path during his teenage years but had just been accepted to law school at LSU.

Seamus sat back deep in thought. He did the math in his head: Becca Averett died five years before this article was written, and most people go to law school when they're around 22 or 23 years old. That would mean the son was around 17 or 18 years old when Becca died. Seamus grew up in Detroit, and he knew exactly the type of trouble 18-year-old boys got into—drugs, gangs, or both.

Could that be the missing tie to the drug cartel? Wouldn't the FBI have figured that out? He quickly did an arrest report search for Marais and neighboring parishes. Nothing, which was not a surprise since most juvenile records are not public information and are often expunged after ten years. Seamus began to question the entire FBI file, which, based on Agent Marzano's attitude, he should have done from the beginning.

He cracked his fingers and decided to Google Guadalupe to see what came up. Of course, the first thing that came up was Our Lady of Guadalupe, the Patron Saint of Mexico. An advantage of his Catholic upbringing was the arcane knowledge of obscure Saints.

The second hit was for the Guadalupe Cartel, and he decided to skip that for now. The third hit was for a town named Guadalupe. He clicked the map on the link, and there it was. Guadalupe was a city within metropolitan Monterrey, Mexico, Miguel Hernandez's hometown.

Seamus went to the fridge for another beer and returned to staring out his window at the now-glowing blue pool cutting through the darkness. He'd spent two hours researching and found one possible tie. Were there others? He couldn't shake the fact there was nothing in the FBI file. Clearly, they just phoned it in. Seamus wasn't about to do the same.

He returned to his desk and flipped to the page from his trip. Below "environmentalist, Spanish, nature girl, manna, explosives, waitress, kayak," he added, "Miguel Hernandez."

Another visit to Duke's became a priority. He just didn't know if it would be official or unofficial business.

42.

Traffic wasn't bad as Scott drove the Veteran Outdoor pickup through downtown Atlanta around 8:00 on Thursday morning. Evidently Andrea was in no mood for conversation as she slouched down in the bucket seat with closed eyes either in sleep or thought. Scott didn't mind. The women's plan weighed heavily on his mind, and idle chitchat just didn't fit the situation. South of the city, traffic thinned, so Scott eased his grip on the wheel and hit the cruise control.

"Why?" Andrea said, her eyes still at half-mast.

"I thought you were sleeping," Scott said.

"Conserving energy. I don't want to know everything. I just want to know why you did it. Scott."

"It's hard to explain." He shrugged.

"Try me. It's a long drive."

Scott realized Andrea wasn't about to let it go.

"All my life, I've followed expectations. Went to the right school, got good grades, worked at the family business, had the wife, house, two kids, even a dog. As each year passed, my responsibilities grew and my options decreased. Even when I went through the divorce, which I didn't instigate, I did the 'right thing.'" He removed his right hand from the steering wheel and motioned quotation marks. "She got the house and a good chunk of money while I moved into a crappy apartment and assumed all our debt.

"But the thing is, I was happier and suddenly realized maybe it was a mistake to follow my predetermined path. Don't get me wrong. Right after the divorce, my life still generally sucked but just not as bad."

He glanced at Andrea; she was sitting up paying close attention.

"Then I met Maggie. We just hit it off and began spending time together. The first time we ever, uh, you know, did it, was in a field up in the Georgia mountains. Afterwards, she told me the truth behind her life."

"Which is?" Andrea asked.

"That's her story to tell, not mine. Anyway, here was a woman who played by the societal rules she believed in and completely under her terms. And when it was time for her to change, she made a statement. She just didn't slink off or meekly sign divorce papers in a swanky lawyer's office. None of that for her. It was like that movie where the guy yells, 'I'm as mad as hell, and I'm not going to take this anymore!'"

"*Network*," Andrea added. "I love that movie."

"Me too," Scott agreed. "I decided I wanted a complete break from my old life, and there was no better way to make my final statement. Rather symbolic, don't you think?"

"Rather dangerous too," Andrea reminded him. "You get caught, you're going to jail."

"It worth the risk. I've been in jail most of the last 20 years. Granted the living conditions are nicer in my current situation, but it's still a type of prison."

Neither uttered a word for the next several miles.

"I get it," Andrea finally said. "Sometimes, drastic measures are necessary."

Scott only nodded his head. "Okay, Andrea, your turn. Why are you doing this? I've heard about the brotherhood of service, but what you're willing to do for him, for us, is extraordinary. Are you two, well, you know…?"

The insinuation elicited a hearty laugh from Andrea. "Lovers? I admit that I love him, but it's more of a brother-sister kind of thing. Truth is, he's a little too pale for my tastes, if you know what I mean."

"I was just curious."

"It's a fair question. And to be honest, there was a point early in our relationship where we talked about it but decided we'd be better off as friends. Your brother was quick to point out that, in fits of anger, spouses kill each other all the time, but friends just won't hang out together for a while. His sick humor is one of his charms."

"Not if you live in Georgia. Friends are killing each other all the time. Granted, liquor and stupid dares are usually involved."

Andrea shifted her gaze forward. "Here's the deal with your brother. I was a new CO on my first deployment, green as green could be, a woman of color in a field dominated by men, with most of the troops being testosterone-filled kids competing to be Mr. Machismo. The military's made great advances, but that doesn't always translate to the guys, and women, down in the trenches. I have a ton of confidence, but those first couple of weeks were intimidating.

"Tom could see what was going on and would have nothing of it. He carried a lot of weight with the regulars. He was a little older and led the Explosives Ordnance Disposal Team, the damn rock stars for anyone having to wander around in those godforsaken desert mountains. His unit treated me with the respect an officer deserves, and they didn't let anyone else give me shit. Pretty soon, the others fell in line. I know some abused me behind my back, but no disrespect was thrown to my face. I'm sure I would have eventually figured it out, but your brother made it a lot easier. That simple act, respecting and accepting me rather than judging me, is why I'm here."

"That sounds like Tom, or at least the old Tom," Scott said. "He's the athlete of the family and was always considered a great teammate. Even though he was better than most everyone, he never wanted to be the star and would push the attention off to someone else. One of those quiet, unassuming leaders who let his actions speak. I always admired him. Wish I was more like him."

"Scott, you're more like him than you think."

"You're being generous, Andrea, but thanks."

"Which also sounds like Tom. Think you just proved my point."

They settled back into an easy silence as they covered the last 20 miles on I-75. Scott took exit 179 and headed east on State Route 21, passing the Flying J truck stop on the south side and a mom-and-pop BP Mini Mart across the street. The speed limit dropped to 35 as they drove through the little burg of Overton, a simple crossroads anchored by a small family-owned restaurant miraculously still in business. The Ocmulgee River flowed several miles ahead.

Andrea pulled a tablet out of her backpack, booted it out of sleep mode, and launched the app Maggie installed after last night's meeting. Scott tried to take a quick peek at the screen then thought better of it. He slowed as they crossed the Ocmulgee, and they both turned their attention to the approaching ALM property.

"That's where I stored the motorcycle," Andrea pointed out the window as they left the bridge. "I cut through the woods parallel to the river until I hit one of the paths."

Scott saw the billboard poking above the pines in the near distance. "You pick up the signal yet?"

Andrea checked the tablet. "Yes, I'm good to go. Let's do this."

The southwest corner of State Route 21 and County Road 5 hadn't been cleared for quite some time. Scrub pines, determined saplings, and forest brush had been making a steady advancement on the Veteran billboard and four-bay storage facility. He turned onto the short, weed-infested gravel path that led to the partially rusted aluminum shed with the massive billboard steel pole at the far end. The sign itself lurked well above the corner. The encroaching underbrush hid the truck from County Road 5, but anyone traveling Route 21 had a clear view, so it was critical to make this look like a normal service call. He pulled to a stop with the truck's grill almost touching the third bay's garage-like door labeled 103.

"Why do you have a storage shed here? People actually rent them?"

"It's a local zoning thing. The land needs to be zoned commercial for us to use the location, and some counties and cities require a physical place of business for it to be considered commercial. We've been tossing up these storage sheds for years to get around it. Most just sit empty, but we actually rent two bays to the shell company that owns this property."

Scott turned off the engine and slowly exhaled, trying to steady his nerves.

Andrea possessed the calm reserve of a pro. She leaned over to show Scott the six different video images on the tablet and pointed to the screen. "Here we are in the truck." She then motioned with her thumb over her right shoulder. "That camera must be in one of the trees."

"That means they can see us, right?" Scott tried to sound confident.

"Only if they have someone monitoring it. There's also the chance they digitally store the images for additional security. My bigger concern was finding out how many cameras they have and where they're located. On my first trip, I didn't have the disabling device. Now, we'll get a look at all their camera angles to see if they saw me. If they did, then their defenses will likely be up."

Scott studied the tablet and marveled at Maggie's ingenuity. Last night, she hacked into the ALM's computer network, thinking she'd be able to access the security cameras Andrea had seen during recon. When that didn't work, she assumed they had a closed circuit Wi-Fi network which, she excitedly told the group, is a heck of a lot easier to broach. Maggie downloaded a hacking program into the tablet, and the video Scott was now viewing proved her genius yet again.

"The top left video is the main entrance view on the county road," Andrea continued. "Looks like this one is closer to the compound and covers the driveway. The rest of these are different angles of the compound. Glad to see they don't have any in the approach through the woods from the river. I didn't see any, but they're tough to find. Guess they figured no one would come that way. Sloppy and unprofessional, if you ask me."

A truck approaching on Route 21 caused them to pause. Instinctively, Andrea went to hide the tablet.

As it quickly passed, Scott began to breathe again. "We probably should get moving," he said nervously.

Scott got out of the truck, fished the master key out of his pocket, and removed the Veteran padlock from the third bay door. The rarely opened door screeched as it slid up before grinding to a loud halt in the bay. His boots crunched on the gravel while he inspected the surprisingly clean interior. Cobwebs and some mold on the far sheet metal wall were the only inhabitants. Standing in the entry, he stretched his arm up to confirm the clearance was the same as other Veteran storage sheds.

He went back to the bed of the pickup, popped open the toolbox directly behind the cab, and rooted around until emerging with a can of WD-40. He aggressively sprayed the side runners and then tested opening and closing the door several times before being satisfied. He stepped outside and closed the door but didn't put the padlock back on.

Scott returned to the toolbox and fished out neon yellow vests and Veteran hardhats. The extension ladder was at a 30-degree angle, with one end nestled against the bed's gate and the top secured to the cab's roof. He hoisted the ladder out of the bed and toted it to the side of the shed where he rested it against the billboard's pole.

Andrea was waiting for Scott outside the truck. "It's recording. You ready for this?" She held out a GoPro.

"Not quite. Here, you should put these on too." He handed her the extra vest and hardhat. "Need you to look official." Out of the toolbox he fetched a safety harness, a coil of rope, and a small canvas workbag. He stepped into the harness, pulled it up about his midsection, then tightly secured the strap across his waist. He clipped the carabiner attached at the end of the rope to the large O-ring on the front of the harness.

"Okay, show time. Now what do I do with that gizmo?" Scott asked, motioning towards the GoPro in Andrea's hand.

She took off his hardhat and affixed the recording device on the helmet's narrow brim. "It's already turned on. Just look in each direction, and it will automatically record. Hopefully you're high enough for me to get another perspective of the terrain. I need to know as much as possible before tonight."

"Got it." Scott took another deep breath. "The GBI wants us to inspect billboards, and that's what we're doing. You probably should stand over there. You don't want to be looking straight up or standing underneath if I drop something."

Scott went over to the base and extended the ladder until it reached the bottom rung of the pole's built-in ladder. Adrenaline, or maybe the need to show-off for Andrea, propelled his ascent to a rapid scamper. Once on the catwalk, he clamped his harness's safety rope to the railing.

Even at 60 feet, modest by Veteran standards, the billboard provided an impressive view. Scott slowly rotated 90 degrees, capturing the pie wedge from Route 21 over to County Road 5 on video. As he repeated the scan, he noticed a trail cutting through the woods that ended in the brush about 10 feet from the storage shed's gravel pad. He followed the general direction of the trail until he caught a glimpse of a rooftop and a small patch of green.

I bet that's the compound, he thought. Knowing this is what Andrea wanted to see, he stood still a little longer.

Satisfied he'd recorded enough video, Scott turned his attention to the fake inspection. The advertisement for the Middle Georgia Wildlife Management Area boat ramp had seen better days. Sold at a cut-rate price to the Georgia Department of Natural Resources, Veteran had not changed the creative for several years. It was still securely in place, but the elements had worn down its luster and random bullet holes conveyed the sentiments of the local residents.

The shout, definitely not Andrea, snapped him back to reality.

"Hey! What the hell you think you're doing?"

A scrawny dude in a camo jacket and Falcons cap was crouched at the edge of gravel with a rifle raised directly at Andrea, frozen and holding her hands up.

"You're trespassing on private property. I got every right to shoot you."

Scott's panic produced unknown courage. He yelled from the platform high above the unfolding scene. "Put down that gun. We're not trespassing! This is our land, Veteran Outdoor, and we're here doing routine maintenance."

The barrel of the rifle left Andrea and mounted upward until it was aimed at Scott. "Save me the bullshit, sign man. I know who you are, and I also saw you snooping over at our property. Don't look like any maintenance to me."

"For God's sake, I was just taking in the view. It's beautiful up here. Ease off, or I'll report you to the Sheriff for harassment. I'll also press charges for property destruction as I bet you're the one responsible for bullet holes in my sign."

The scrawny dude redirected his gun at Andrea. "I ain't put no holes in your sign. But it might be fun to put a couple of holes in her."

Andrea began to slowly backpedal in the direction of the truck. Scott couldn't believe what he was seeing and yelled again, "Please put down the gun. We're only trying to do our job!"

"I'm just fucking with you, sign man. Go ahead. Do what you came here to do." The scrawny dude didn't lower his gun completely. "And I'm staying right here to watch you."

Scott could tell the greaseball had no intention of leaving. He then remembered Andrea's gun in the truck. "Okay, but can my coworker at least get back in the truck for her own safety?"

"She can get in the truck if she wants, but I'll be keeping an eye on her, on both of you trespassers."

With her hands still up, Andrea slowly made her way to the passenger door and got in the truck.

Realizing he needed to make it look official for his spectator, Scott retrieved a new spotlight from the canvas workbag, replaced the perfectly good existing one, and cleaned off the small solar battery receiver faceplate. Remembering the GoPro on his head and not wanting to give the guy an additional beef, he took off his hardhat and tossed it in the canvas bag. He unclipped the safety line then headed down the ladder, exercising a caution he ignored on the way up. The rube watched his every move.

Scott urgently loaded the ladder and equipment in the pickup truck then offered a friendly wave to the rifle-wielding redneck still holding his ground 30 yards away. "Have a good day. We'll be back in six months."

"Kiss my ass, sign man," the scrawny dude grumbled and then spat in their direction.

Scott got in the truck, grateful to find Andrea clutching some type of big handgun hidden between her knees. Scott edged the truck away from the bay door and slowly up the gravel path toward

Route 21 as the scrawny dude stood firm, watching every move. He pulled left onto Route 21 and hit the gas.

"I've been sitting here kicking myself the whole time. I can't believe I didn't hear him sneaking up. Maybe I've spent too much time behind a desk." Andrea sounded doubtful for the first time.

"What I can't believe is that scumbag is holding my brother prisoner. This is even worse than I imagined."

"I know," Andrea agreed. "It's never good when someone that unstable has a rifle."

"At least I got some good video for you." Scott tried to shift the conversation to ease his mind.

"Let's pull over," Andrea instructed. "I'd like to see it as soon as possible while the setting is fresh in my mind."

"Not here. Johnson's Grill is up ahead. We do business with them, and they're good people. It's a little early for lunch, so it'll be easy for us to talk.

At the Overton crossroad, Scott turned into the gravel lot of a small diner with a Veteran billboard towering above. Theirs was the only car in the lot. Scott took his workbag with him, and Andrea carried the tablet.

Out of habit, Scott held the door for Andrea, which didn't seem to bother her.

A large man wearing a grease-splattered apron stood in the doorway of a small kitchen. His voice was as big as he was. "Is that you Scott? Saw the truck but didn't recognize you. Look at how damn skinny you are. You sick or something?"

Scott gave the man's hand a vigorous shake. "Been way too long, Darryl, and no, I'm not sick, just trying to be a little healthier. Getting old is not for sissies."

"I think he looks good," a voice sounded from the dining area. An older woman with her long gray hair pulled back came over and gave Scott a hug. "Nice to see you, darlin'. Don't listen to the fat owner."

"Darlene, you still look fine. Thought you'd have hightailed from here by now. You some kind of indentured servant?"

"Wish I was. The pay's probably better! You really do look good skinny. Just don't give Darryl any tips. I like my big man just the way he is." Darlene gave Darryl a coy wink.

"Sorry it's been so long. Really good to see y'all again. Pardon my lack of manners. Darryl and Darlene Johnson, please meet Andrea. She's new with Veteran, and I'm out showing her the ropes."

Pleasures, hellos, and handshakes were quickly exchanged. Darlene handed them menus. "Go sit anywhere you like. Lunch crowd won't be here for a while. I'll be with you in a second."

Scott and Andrea found a table near the window looking out at the intersection. Andrea propped the tablet up against the silver-topped sugar dispenser and began to rewind the video from Maggie's hack job into the ALM security cameras. They took Darlene's suggestion and ordered the meatloaf—Scott's with gravy, Andrea's naked. Once Darlene was out of range, Andrea slid the play bar with her index finger until she found the frame with the guy sneaking up the trail.

"Must have happened when you were going up the pole." Andrea shook her head. "Should've been standing over by the street facing everything. Careless mistake on my part. Let's see what you got of the compound."

Scott fished the GoPro he was wearing out of his workbag and gave it to Andrea. She changed the tablet's Bluetooth setting to pair with the GoPro and began scrolling through Scott's video.

"Nice, there's the compound. This is very useful."

Scott didn't share her enthusiasm. "Andrea, we might want to put that away. Looks like our little redneck friend's come to join us for lunch."

Scott watched as the scrawny guy circled the Veteran truck then headed to the front door. Andrea's back was turned, so she was unable to follow the unfolding scene.

Darryl's voice rang out. "Morning, JR. Sit anywhere you'd like."

"Not here to eat."

Scott found his voice irritating. He subtly stashed the tablet and GoPro in his workbag as he watched the guy wind through the small diner.

He was shorter than Scott expected, and he had a splotchy beard, if random patches could be called a beard. He was generally unkempt and carried an air of reckless confidence. He stopped at their table.

"Well, if it ain't the sign man and his nigger bitch."

Scott noticed the flicker in Andrea's eyes as she sat back in her chair. "Sir, I don't care for your language," she said calmly and firmly.

"Tough shit. I can call you nigger if I want."

Andrea looked at Scott then back at the guy Darryl called JR. "It's not the nigger that bothers me. Ignorant fools like you have been calling us that for centuries to the point I'm partially immune to the slur. No, what I take offense to is being called bitch."

JR was clearly puzzled by her response. "Huh?"

"You called me bitch because I'm a confident, intelligent, assertive woman, the kind of woman who isn't intimidated and is willing to stand up for herself. The problem I have is those qualities are respected in men. A man with those qualities is said to be a born leader, but for women, it means we're bitches. Another thing, there's not a masculine equivalent of the word. About the closest words are bastard, asshole, and dick, but those aren't used to describe leaders, just worthless shitheads like you."

The guy stood there for a second trying to process what Andrea said. Finally it dawned that she called him a worthless shithead. With his right hand, he opened his jacket to show the sidearm strapped to his belt. "You better apologize, bitch."

Before the scrawny dude finished saying the word, Andrea grabbed his jacket with her left hand and yanked him towards her in a downward direction. At the same time, she rose out of her chair and unleashed her right arm, planting her fist square between the eyes. The scrawny guy stood dazed for a moment, then his eyes rolled back, his knees buckled, and he collapsed, smacking his head on the floor once he fell.

Scott sat stunned. "Holy shit, Andrea! That was amazing!"

Andrea stood over the guy. "I swear I'm losing it, Scott. I wanted to break his nose but missed. I definitely have been behind a desk for too long."

Darlene ran up next to Andrea. "Woman, you're my new hero! I thought the bitch speech was good but smacking that punk? I've wanted to do that for years."

Darryl joined the viewing. "Don't mean to spoil the party, but you two should probably skedaddle. He'll be mad as a hornet when he comes to, and you don't want to be around."

Scott scooped up his workbag as he stood. "That's a good idea, Darryl. Sorry about the excitement."

Andrea reached down and took the gun off the scrawny guy's hip. She removed the clip and handed it to Darlene, and then passed the gun over to Darryl. "Just to be safe, give it back once he's cooled off."

Darryl gave her a wink. "I do hope you come back and visit us again."

43.

"**A**nd in conclusion..."

Seamus knew the know-it-all sycophant was lying.

"...that is why we must insist they erect the speaker's platform at the north end of Centennial Park."

Seamus was right. It was a lie. The self-appointed expert didn't wait for questions before launching into another crowd control consideration. He discreetly took his phone out of his pocket to confirm what he already knew—no text or missed call from Andrea Leonard. Basking in his encounter with her took some of the pain out of yesterday's protest planning meeting at city hall. Today was a different story. After the congressman's reward announcement, the number of attendees for the second multi-agency meeting soared. More people meant a proportional increase of inflated egos, general ignorance, and eager aides vying to protect their boss's image for the next election cycle. Seamus was in meeting hell.

And no call from Andrea only made it worse. He repeatedly replayed the scene at Duke's in his mind, and there was no doubt she hit on him. That basic fact gave credence to his expectation, his hope, that she'd call. But she didn't. What made it even more pathetic was Seamus didn't even have the guts to ask for her number before running out of the diner.

The only other time he was so captivated by a female was in his middle school catechism class. Mary Catherine Soblinski had it all, at least by awkward 12-year-old boy standards. He held no recollection of the pious doctrines the nuns drilled into him during those sixth-grade lessons. There was no room in his brain for anything but Mary Catherine.

The beauty and innocence of that prepubescent love clung to his memory before the dynamics of sex complicated the balance. All of his subsequent relationships had germinated from lust, raw desire outweighing compatibility, and, in some instances, plain common sense. He was quick to admit his previous marriage had been held together more by the lingerie department at Macy's rather than quiet evenings playing Scrabble. And it certainly didn't help that Peggy's vocabulary skills were lousy. Problem was, more times than not, he would have been happier nailing a triple word score instead of his wife. With the luster off the lust and very little else in her he found interesting, it was only a matter of time until the divorce was finalized.

The time together with Andrea felt different. Just sitting next to her talking was intoxicating. It wasn't that he had suddenly become a eunuch who didn't want to see her naked. He definitely wanted to see her naked, but that was not his primary desire. He simply wanted to be in her presence, hell, even if was to just pass notes like he did with Mary Catherine. He didn't know what to make of it, such an alien feeling that he might chalk up to maturity if not for the fact that the first time he felt it he was only 12. Seamus didn't care if it was a sign of getting older or not. He just knew he wanted to see her again.

At last, the "any more questions" request from the Mayor's senior aide didn't result in any more questions. "Okay, everyone, thanks for your time and we'll meet again tomorrow at this same time."

Seamus didn't wait for anyone to change their mind and high-tailed it for his car. Talking with Andrea was out of his control, but he had every intention of talking to the other woman on his mind. He was expected at the office by 2:00, giving him just enough time to swing by Duke's for a quick lunch.

Duke Evans was manning the cash register—did he ever move?—and treated Seamus like a regular even though he wasn't. Scott's booth in Maggie's section was open, so he strolled over and slid onto the bench in the exact spot where he spent his glorious time with Andrea just yesterday. He gave a contented sigh.

"Well, look who came back. Good to see you, Seamus."

"Hello, Maggie. Likewise."

She rested the tray on her cocked hip. "You here to eat or just hoping to see Andrea again?"

He couldn't mask his embarrassment. "Was it that obvious? I thought I played it pretty cool."

"It was a worthy effort. If it makes you feel any better, it sure looked mutual to us casual observers." Maggie winked as she handed him a menu. "I'll get you a water while you decide your fate."

Excited, relieved, and a little terrified, Seamus reveled in Maggie's remark. He began to study the menu while shifting his mental gear from Andrea to Maggie. The strategy worked out in his mind was solid, and he didn't want to mess it up.

Maggie set the water in front of him. "You decided?"

"Tengo mucha hambre hoy. ¿Hay ofertas especiales?"

Maggie gave him a blank stare. "Pardon me?"

"Thought you spoke Spanish. Working in a restaurant and all, I assumed you'd have to."

"Please don't start stereotyping. It's not becoming of you. No, sorry, I don't speak Spanish. Languages aren't my strong suit."

"I'm sorry. You're right. My best friend in college was Miguel Hernandez, and he'd agree with you." Seamus noticed an ever so slight change in Maggie, not in her face but in her eyes. The twinkle left.

"I'm sure he would." Her voice was slightly terse. "Now, let's try this again. You decided?"

"Was just asking if you had any specials today, but it doesn't matter. I'll have the tuna sandwich with fries." Seamus tried to sound more sheepish than he was.

"That's better. I'll get this out to you in a flash."

Seamus watched her walk away then pulled the small spiral notebook from his Louisiana trip out of his jacket pocket and flipped it open to his notes on Becca. He had checks next to everything but "Spanish, explosives, kayak, and Miguel Hernandez." He placed an X next to "Spanish," changed his mind, scratched out the X, and wrote a question mark instead. Next to "Miguel Hernandez," he placed a check.

As he waited, Seamus scribbled gibberish in the back of his notebook while keeping one eye on Maggie working the room. The few conversations he successfully eavesdropped gave proof to his perception of her intelligence. She smoothly transitioned topics with a level of knowledge well above what one would expect from a diner waitress, no offense to diner waitresses.

True to her word, his lunch appeared in mere minutes. Seamus took his time eating, trying to figure out how to work "explosives" into a normal conversation. He'd spent most of the morning trying to work an angle, but it was hopeless. He decided to redirect and go for secondary questions. Maggie returned to his table and motioned toward his clean plate. "Guess you liked it. Ready for me to clear that away?"

"Yes, it was surprisingly good, almost as good as Mom's." Please take the bait, Seamus silently implored.

"That's a comparison I rarely hear but glad you liked it." She whisked up the plate. "You ready for the bill."

Seamus realized he needed to press. "Your mom never made you tuna?"

"Sure, she made tuna, but I never thought about rating it. It was just a sandwich." She shrugged.

This was not going how he'd hoped, time to be direct. "Where'd you grow up?"

"Near Fayetteville, North Carolina. We weren't big fish eaters. Maybe that's why tuna didn't leave much of an impression."

"Guess you weren't raised Catholic and the fish-on-Friday rule."

"No, my family never got into the church thing, which is atypical for most southerners."

"Fayetteville, that's near the coast isn't it? Surprised you never went fishing. Was your family into other things like kayaking or paddle boarding?"

"We weren't big water people. My folks liked to camp."

He could tell her patience was wearing. "Your family still in Fayetteville?"

"My brother's in Raleigh, but my folks retired to Florida and live in one of those awful over-60 communities near Ocala."

"Mine too!" Seamus said. "They're over closer to Lakeland and love it. Both are on the younger side of the age limit, so they're still active. Guess it's better than Detroit, but it depresses me."

"I know what you mean. Sorry, don't want to be rude, but we're too busy today for me to talk. Maybe next time. Duke will have your bill. Hope to see you soon." With that Maggie moved on.

Seamus watched Maggie walk away. She lacked the usual spryness in her step and didn't chat with her customers as she passed. Their conversation also struck him as odd. The verbal banter just wasn't there and not one attempt at a witticism. He clicked his pen and jotted new bullets in his notebook: "From NC; two parents, both alive; has a brother; not a kayaker; didn't want to come back to the table with check; Miguel hit a nerve." He sat for another minute then drew an arrow from the first four bullets, scribbling, "Lies?"

44.

"Where the hell's my blog post?" Bubba stormed well before Barry had the phone at his ear.

"I'm waiting for the right time, Bubba."

"Right time? Right time?!" Bubba screamed. "I set you up perfectly with yesterday's reward, we've got an event in two days, and you don't think it's the right time? Jesus H. Christ! Why the hell am I even paying you?!"

Barry stared at the blank post on his computer while Bubba ranted. For the first time in his role as ALM blogger, Barry was suffering from writer's block. Normally, he'd post before taking Moon on the morning walk and then spend the day pondering the subject of tomorrow's diatribe. But yesterday's events threw off his thought process, and the page was still empty at 2:00. The general public's zealous response to Bubba's reward and Doc Shaw's Patient Alpha put Barry in an uncreative funk. He did his best writing angry, and today he was simply depressed.

Posting for the ALM didn't come naturally to Barry even though he was good at it. He learned the formula from his brief tenure with the pissed-off ranchers in Utah—lean on patriotism and nostalgia then toss in a heavy dose of incredulousness over how the government was giving shit away to undeserving leeches that haven't done one damn thing to make this country great. And, according to the ALM credo, anyone with darker skin belonged in the underserving leeches' bucket.

He could sympathize with ranchers trying to make a living, but the whole reverting to white dominance thing just didn't make sense to him. Ironically, it was this personal opposition to ALM beliefs that made his writings so popular. In Barry's mind, his outrageously angry posts were written satirically whereas the intelligence of ALM rank-and-file members took his words as gospel. The entire situation was twisted.

Barry took a breath and gave it his best shot. "Bubba, if I'd posted something earlier, it would have gotten lost in the excitement you created. You did amazing yesterday. The reward was a stroke of genius and has everyone talking."

"Yeah, well, it was a stroke of genius, but that still doesn't mean you shouldn't blog about it." Bubba's tone was calmer.

"And I will write about it. But I'm just a little blogger down here in Georgia, Bubba, and right now you're getting visibility nationally with the big boys and more influential sites. If I wrote something now, no one would pay attention. That's not what we want. We want people to pay attention."

"Guess you've got a point, but don't wait too long. We need to ride the momentum I created!" Bubba crowed.

"Absolutely. The typical internet news cycle is 24 to 36 hours. My plan is to come out with full guns blazing tomorrow morning, just in time to build up for Saturday's event. Does that sound okay to you?" Barry silently pleaded for Bubba to say yes. He needed the time to get over his mental block.

"I don't really like it, but goddammit, I guess it will do. It better be one amazing post. This may be the best shot we have." With that, the congressman hung up on him.

Barry sat back, relieved flattery was such an effective weapon on Bubba. He dodged a bullet and bought some time. Now, he just needed to figure what to write about for Friday morning's post.

He gently closed his laptop. Recognizing the sound, Moon's tail began to thump in hopeful expectation that the end of work meant an adventure was in order. Barry stretched and said, "Let's go, Moon. Time to check on the lunatics."

They stood on the ranch house's front porch, Barry surveying the action while Moon wagged and whined. Mike was on guard duty, hovering near the Armory while watching Patient Alpha sprawled on his back in the field. It was hard to tell if Doc's guinea pig was in heaven, hell, or purgatory.

Barry looked down at Moon. "Go ahead, girl," and the dog ran to the prone figure and immediately began licking his face. The man stirred and embraced the dog. Safe to say, the doc had him back in hell.

Doc and JR were off near the barracks having what appeared to be a very private conversation. JR's back was to Barry, and it looked like Doc was giving him instructions. The last thing Barry needed was for these two jerk-offs to do any further scheming, so he decided to break up their powwow.

"Afternoon, gentlemen," Barry announced as he approached.

Startled, JR spun around, showing off a huge knot on his brow, almost perfectly centered between his eyes.

Barry was amused instead of concerned. "Whoa there, JR. You sprouting a third eye?"

"I fell and hit a curb," JR snarled.

"Well, I'd say the curb won. Got yourself quite a beauty mark. He gonna be okay, Doc? We have big weekend coming up." Barry knew Shaw wasn't a normal doctor, but sometimes his ego needed stroking too.

"He'll be fine. Just a nasty contusion, but I doubt he has a concussion. Probably best to take some aspirin, drink plenty of water, and lay low for a couple of hours. Put some ice on it too. That should relieve some of the pressure."

"Thanks, Doc." JR gave Barry his oft rehearsed tough guy glare as he stormed off to his shack.

Once out of earshot, Barry nodded his chin toward the prone soldier. "What's the prognosis? Still think it's going to work?"

Shaw straightened his posture, a sure sign he lacked confidence with what he was about to say. "Yes, I remain very confident of the outcome. The next 24 hours will be critical. We should know for certain by tomorrow morning."

"How will you know? He looks completely incapacitated right now."

"That's the plan. We've been narrowing the window of normalcy, giving him enough to crave it but not enough to have consistent thought. We've also changed the pattern. More lows at night to interrupt his sleep. Sleep deprivation is a powerful tool. But tonight, we won't bring him down, and he should get a solid night's rest, then tomorrow morning we'll have the talk. I'll tell him I've figured it out and the choice is his. Work with us and feel good, or fall back into the abyss."

"Damn, Doc, that sure sounds cruel."

"Modifying behavior always has an element of pain and suffering. It's the end result that's important, and we're striving to improve the greater good."

Barry had enough. This guy was sick and dangerous. "Whatever you say, Doc. I need to go plan more for Saturday."

He made it a step before Shaw spoke up.

"Whitley, there's one more thing we need to discuss." His tone set off alarm bells.

Barry retreated back to the doc. "What is it?"

"The other patients. If this turns into the success I believe it will, we'll need to address the other patients."

"Just what do you mean by address? I assumed you'd start them on a similar plan. Isn't that what this is all about? Finding the process to build an elite force?"

"Yes to the process, but no to the other patients. They need to have a particular makeup. That's why it's working on Alpha. It's a combination of a history of dependence, breeding, intelligence, and personality. Also, they need to have a valuable expertise like Alpha. Now that I know what to look for, it shouldn't be too hard to line up additional recruits. The other guys here just don't have what it takes."

Barry's heart sank. "So, you're suggesting..." He couldn't finish.

"We really have no other choice. Letting them go would be a fool's errand. Imagine what they'd say to family or friends or the authorities! It's a risk we simply can't take."

"But, Doc, there's five of them. I already have blood on my hands from your quack experiments. I'm not about to up the ante."

"They are not quack experiments." Shaw raised his voice. "This is a serious scientific endeavor with huge ramifications on humanity. Testing is a necessity and usually means negative results for a portion of the subjects."

Barry stepped in close. "Yeah, usually mice. Not fucking people." The menace in his tone was enough to force Shaw two paces back.

"Again, I question your dedication to our cause. I'll just talk to Bubba about it. I'm sure he can reason with you."

Barry spun and marched toward his house, yelling back, "Go ahead, quack. Run squealing to your momma. No matter what he says, nothing's happening until Sunday. We have a recruitment drive to lead."

Barry couldn't believe what the doc had in mind. Now, he was pissed off enough to write Bubba's blog.

45.

$\mathcal{P}$am sat in their den mindlessly paging through an old copy
of *Southern Living* while relentlessly twisting her long, faux
pearl necklace around her index finger.

Roger blurted, "Cheese and crackers, you idiot!" from his
matching leather chair at *Wheel of Fortune* on the large flat-screen
TV mounted above the fireplace.

When the doorbell rang, Pam was out of her seat before the
chime ended. "That's odd. I wonder who that is. You expecting
anyone tonight, Roger?" she lied as she strolled past him.

"No, I'll go see who it is." He swung his legs off the ottoman.

Pam was halfway out the den. "I'm already up, honey. You
just relax."

Her role in Maggie and Andrea's plan was minor in comparison
to the others—manage Roger. But she did hold veto power. Only
Pam could call off the operation if the team felt the risks were too
high. She went through the kitchen, down the hallway, and past
the stairs to check on their visitor at the front door.

"Scott!" she announced loud enough for her voice to carry to
the den. "This is a surprise. What brings you around here?"

Her brother entered the foyer and gave Pam a hug, saying softly, "Good to see you, Sis."

"You're late." she whispered back.

"I decided to walk. Sorry, I should have texted you. You ready?"

"Yes, but I'm worried about you and Andrea tonight."

"Same here. That's why I walked over here. Needed to burn some jitters."

They shared another hug.

"The kids are upstairs studying," her voice loud again, "and Roger's in the den. C'mon in." Pam led the way back to the den.

"Evening, Scott. What brings you around here?" Roger didn't move from his chair.

"Hey, Roger. It's time we have a talk."

Scott's tone got Roger's attention. He muted *Wheel of Fortune*. "You sound awful serious Scott." Roger lifted his empty highball glass. "Want a cocktail?"

"No, thanks. I'm good." Scott took a seat on the couch facing Roger. Pam didn't really want to sit down but figured she should since it was the normal thing to do.

"So what's on your mind, Scott?"

Pam noticed Roger used his business voice.

"I'm resigning, Roger. I'm done with Veteran."

"What do you mean you're resigning? You can't just up and resign. It's your family's business!" Roger clearly hadn't seen this coming.

"Not anymore. I just cleared out my office. Today's my last day."

"Today? But, uh..."

Pam watched Roger grope for words.

"...you're the only one that knows the entire operation. This isn't the time to quit!"

"It's the perfect time, and we both know you'd rather not have me around. The team is more than capable of running things.

Besides, you can hire two or three more people using my bloated salary."

Roger looked at Pam. "You hear him, Pam?"

She could tell her husband was secretly thrilled. "I'm as surprised as you are, honey. You really want to leave our family business?" Pam was quite satisfied with her performance.

"Absolutely, Sis. Should have done this years ago. There's another thing, Roger," Scott said to his brother-in-law. "I'm willing to sell you my share of the business. When I said out, I mean all out."

This time Roger couldn't hide his excitement. "Really? You don't want any say in Veteran?"

Scott just shook his head. "No, Roger, I'm done."

The conversation lulled. Pam could see the wheels spinning in Roger's head, the dream he never thought he'd realize had just come true. She looked over at her brother. He was perched on the edge of the couch with his hands firmly on his knees, looking relieved but nervous.

"You sure about this, Scott? You're still a relatively young man with lots of good years in front of you. You're not going to be coming back in six months wanting your job back or anything, are you?"

"You're in the clear, Roger. I'm not going to waste one more minute of my life dealing with shit I don't care about." With that Scott stood up, went over, and thrust his hand in front of Roger. "You're on your own now. Thanks for being the steward of our family business."

Roger just sat in his chair dumbstruck. He shook his brother-in-law's hand. "I'll do my best, Scott."

Scott smiled. "I'm sure you will, Roger. See me out, Sis?"

Scott and Pam retraced their steps to the foyer, and once outside to the front stoop, Pam gently closed the door behind them. She grabbed onto to his forearm. "Please be careful tonight, Scott. I know we need to save Tom, but I don't know what I'd do if I lost you too."

"I'll be okay. It's Andrea I worry about. I don't know if it's fair of us to ask her to take such a risk."

"I know. But she volunteered and seems more than capable," Pam said. She was surprised her comment elicited a laugh from Scott.

"More than capable is an understatement! You should've seen her take out that redneck today. As long as there aren't any surprises, this should work."

"Wish I could have seen that. What time you meeting her?"

"Just before midnight. She wants to get started by 3:00."

Pam thought about it for a second. "So I have until 3:00 to change my mind?"

"Better make it 2:00. Remember we'll be taking out the cell service once we get down there."

"Okay." Pam gave her brother one last hug. "Be careful."

"We will." Scott kissed her cheek before heading down the stoop.

Pam stood and watched her brother walk up the street until he was out of sight. The enthusiasm she felt plotting with Maggie and Andrea yesterday was now replaced with dread.

46.

Maggie bolted through the kitchen door and went straight to the bottle of Hendrick's in the cabinet. She thought of herself as a social drinker, but after the day she had and what lay in store tonight, a gin and tonic was in order. She filled a tumbler with ice and poured a generous drink.

Still in her blue waitress dress, Maggie took her G&T out to the front porch to watch the neighborhood settle from dusk to night. Deep in thought, she studied the front yard's giant oak tree in the fading light. She had been honestly touched by Duke's reaction that tomorrow's breakfast shift was her last at the diner. His despondency only magnified her own.

It's not that she lacked confidence in the plan. She knew the plan was solid. No, what bothered Maggie was the number of people involved. Before it had just been her and Miguel, then her and Scott. One accomplice was manageable, but three was a whole new ball game. Three's a crowd, right?

And Seamus tossing out Miguel's name today was a bad omen. She knew it wasn't some random coincidence, and his other questions clearly demonstrated he was on to something. Maggie had been thorough in covering her tracks, but there was always a chance she'd overlooked a key detail. She recalled his face during their conversation and was still unable to determine if he was actually a threat or simply curious. Better safe than sorry.

Time to get moving, Maggie thought.

She left the porch, shed her dress in the hallway by the bathroom, and took a quick shower. Not bothering with underwear or a bra, she put on sweatpants and a hoodie before sitting at the kitchen table to ply her magic on the computer.

Attempting to cast suspicion on the ALM was logical as the FBI would surely link the explosives back to the billboard bombings. Planting additional evidence to further their guilt made sense but probably wouldn't hold up in the long run. She didn't have much time and seriously doubted her last-minute attempt would survive the scrutiny of even average cyber sleuths. But the attempted frame job rang of poetic justice, and even a smokescreen would give a couple of days' head start.

The van Scott used during his nighttime excursions was an easy choice since the interior was likely filled with trace evidence. Her first action was establishing the van's ownership to the ALM. She easily hacked the Georgia Department of Transportation's website and changed the registration and license plate to a man named Barry Whitley. Andrea found his name in her research, and it took no time for Maggie to track down his social security number and other vital information.

Maggie then hacked the Veteran Outdoor Advertising computer system, a task made simple by Scott's coaching and Veteran's lackluster cybersecurity measures, and then she worked her way to their contract data base. She found the land lease agreement between Veteran and the ALM and scrolled down to the amendment titled "Attachment B." This section covered the storage unit where the ALM had agreed to rent storage bays 101 and 102. She quickly added bay 103 to the agreement.

Still in the Veteran system, Maggie navigated to their cloud storage system, searching for the construction details folder. Per Scott's instruction, she found last year's file labeled "With Competition." To be safe, they'd decided an older version of the one he'd provided to the GBI would raise fewer questions. She opened the folder and confirmed the files held the structural diagrams one would need to plan the bombings. Rather than picking and choosing from the various files, she created a hyperlink to the entire folder.

Maggie already knew her way around the ALM's computer network after hacking into it last night. It really wasn't a network per se, just a web page open to public surfers alongside a separate, password-protected section that acted as a private network. She'd accessed the private network last night only long enough to realize it didn't have visibility into the ALM's security cameras. Tonight, she'd dig deeper to find the best place to embed the Veteran hyperlink.

The private network had less than ten registered users and was used mostly for messaging. Both identities and messages had additional encryption preventing her from seeing who said what to whom. Given time, she might be able to crack the encryption, but she didn't have that luxury tonight. She glanced at the various drop-down options on the page before zeroing in on the one labeled "Inventory." She opened the file and gasped.

These guys were armed to the teeth. She had no idea what most of the stuff was, but the sheer quantity looked like it could arm a small republic. Maggie had to warn Andrea and Scott. They needed to know what they were walking into. She hastily added the Veteran schematic hyperlink to the inventory list and logged out. Not her best work but it would have to do.

Maggie left the table and hurried over to her purse on the kitchen counter and dug out her cell phone. It was just 11:00 p.m., so they should still be in town.

"Hey, Maggie." Scott's voice was soothing.

"Hi, Scott. I don't know if this is such a good idea." Maggie tried not to sound hysterical. "I was just on the ALM site and found a listing of their weapons. These guys have rocket launchers, for God's sake."

Scott stayed calm. "I'm not surprised. I'll let Andrea know, but I doubt if that will change anything. She's convinced everyone will be sleeping."

"Promise me you'll be careful and back out if it doesn't feel right."

"I promise. I better get going. I need to pack up a couple of things before meeting Andrea."

"I love you, Scott."

"Love you too, Mags. I'll call you when we're done."

Maggie set her phone down and gave herself a little pep talk. It was going to be a long night, but at least she'd have a distraction. In less than 48 hours, she'd be leaving Atlanta for good and had yet to figure out what she was going to do with all her stuff.

47.

Scott headed south on Peachtree towards Dresden. The sky was clear, and the rising thumbnail moon was not too bright or too dark, perfect for a nighttime clandestine mission. The lightweight jacket with built-in reflectors he wore for his walk along the busy street would be replaced with something more practical once in the truck. He hadn't checked the weather but could tell a front was on the way. The pleasant fall temperatures were about to plunge followed by the winter rains. It felt good to walk, his pace brisk even with the knapsack thrown over his shoulder.

The traffic on Peachtree had finally calmed to a whimper, making his crosswalk navigation at Dresden slightly dangerous versus the normal life-threatening experience. He proceeded under the train track bridge and jaywalked Dresden to the Marta parking lot entrance where Andrea was idling in Roger's pickup. He opened the passenger door and hopped in.

"You ready for this?" Andrea asked. "You know we can skip your part and it'll still work."

"I'm good. My part's easy. You're the one taking the risk. Let's go."

Andrea pulled out of the lot headed towards I-85. Much like their drive earlier that morning, they rode in silence through the downtown connector, only this time the traffic was light and Scott was the passenger. They followed I-75 after the split with I-85 and were soon passing the southern end of I-285.

"You'll take the second exit, Highway 41 south," Scott instructed.

Andrea maneuvered over to the far-right lane.

"Stay in the right lane after you exit. The turn off's only about 50 yards down the road."

Andrea followed his instructions and slowed down.

"There, the gravel road. Pull in but don't go to the end."

Andrea turned onto the gravel road where a massive three-panel Veteran billboard loomed ahead with a much larger storage facility at its base. She cut the headlights.

"You have the scrambler?" Scott asked.

Andrea plucked it from the center console and booted it up. "You remember what to do?"

"Once I cross the bridge, slow down and hit this button." He pointed at the screen. "Once the hourglass stops spinning I should be good."

"Just make sure three networks come up as disabled."

Scott could sense her concern.

She pointed at another icon. "Don't forget to hit this one for cell service too."

He reached over and gave her arm a reassuring squeeze. "Thanks, Andrea. I've got this." He slid the scrambler into his backpack's outer pouch and got out of the truck. "See you in a bit," he said as he shut the door.

The billboard spotlights illuminated the gravel path and storage sheds. Scott walked up the path and veered to the left toward a six-garage door building, fished a key out of his pocket, slipped on gloves, and removed the padlock from the door second from the end. He put the padlock into his bag, opened the garage door, and then closed it behind him. The door immediately shut out the spotlight's glare.

He turned on his flashlight and surveyed the garage. The van was right where he left it. Scott opened the driver's side door, the bing-bing-bing told him the key was still in the ignition and the battery was fine. From his backpack, he got duct tape, pulled off a strip, and taped shut the door-open activation button. It was a trick he learned from his late-night sabotage runs. The van's interior dome light and door open binging sound carried a long way at night.

Next, he grabbed his pack and removed the items Maggie carefully selected and insisted he wear anytime he drove the van: stocking cap, jumpsuit, and shoe booties. Once clad, he opened the garage door, jumped in the van, fired up the engine, and backed it out of the garage. Clear of the opening, he got out of the van, pulled the door back down, and placed a different padlock on the latch.

It had taken maybe five minutes. Andrea was well on her way to their rendezvous point. Scott drove slowly down the gravel road, the ladders on the roof clanging as he bounced through the ruts. Despite the hour, he turned onto Highway 41 with confidence. The panel van, ladders, and official-looking, fake contractor's logo gave the impression of late-night work to anyone who might have noticed. It had worked before so no reason to worry about tonight.

It had taken Scott 32 trips to plant Maggie's 105 bombs. The first couple of nights were slow going, but once he got the hang of it, he averaged five a night. The entire process took nearly three months since Maggie liked to make the bombs in batches rather than store them premade in her workshop. Depending on how far he had to travel that night, Scott would arrive at the Highway 41 storage bay anywhere between 10:00 and midnight.

Planting the bombs was fairly easy. Billboards are basically three parts. The mast went straight up and was made of multiple steel tubes riveted together; the number of tubes used determined the height. The second main part was the support beam. Made of slightly smaller tubes than the mast, they were riveted and welded either like a "T" or an inverted "L" to the mast. Scott and Maggie only targeted the L-shaped support bars since the gravitational fall was easier to predict and control. The third part was the billboard frame which rested on the support beam. The weakest link in an L-shaped structure was where the beam, bearing the weight of the frame, was attached to the mast. Maggie referred to it as the advertising armpit.

The most dangerous part for Scott was climbing the pole. For speed and stealth, Scott didn't use the safety harnesses during the ascent and descent, and some of the targets were extremely tall. However, once at the top, he'd clip his harness on to the frame, then dangle under the arm to attach the bomb with industrial, weather resistant tape on the underside armpit. According to Maggie, the bomb could be small since all they needed to do was sever the connection, and the weight of the frame would force the arm to snap, causing the billboard to tumble straight down.

At first, the dangling in midair was terrifying, but he got to the point where he found it exhilarating. Plus, it was necessary. Aside from Maggie's physics reasoning for bomb placement, the underside was nearly invisible to any technician who might have to make a service call. Even Scott, who knew what he was looking for, had a hard time spotting his own handiwork the few times he went out to look again. The closest he came to incriminating himself was when he almost slipped in telling the GBI what to look for during their aerial inspection.

Scott settled in for the drive south on I-75. He stayed in the right-hand lane and drove several miles under the speed limit. To keep his nerves in check, he practiced the breathing exercises Maggie taught him.

"Relax," he said to himself. "You have the easy job."

Traffic began to thin after the I-475 split south of Macon, leaving mostly road warrior semis as the main travelers this time of night. It was nearly 2:00 a.m. when he took exit 179 and headed east on Route 21. Once past the truck stop and Mini Mart, he had the road to himself. Even in his state of heightened anxiety, he chuckled to himself as he passed Johnson's Grill where Andrea had kicked the shit out of the scrawny redneck. The last few houses disappeared, and the wilderness's smothering darkness crept up on each side of the road. With no sign of headlights ahead or in his rearview mirror, he was alone.

Scott eased up on the accelerator, pulled the scrambler from his bag, and rested it on his lap. The road noise rose as the van rolled off of Route 21's smooth asphalt and onto the concrete bridge spanning the Ocmulgee River. Once the coasting van returned to asphalt, Scott turned on the dome light to see what he was doing. He hit the scrambler's activate button then tapped the network and cellular icons.

The Veteran billboard spotlight poked through the trees ahead, drawing Scott the last, long mile to his destination. While the van crawled, Scott saw the hourglass rotation stop and a menu pop up identifying the downed networks. He quickly rummaged the outer pouch of the pack for his cell phone. The no service banner confirmed the scrambler did its job. It was time.

He turned off the van's dome light, cut the headlights, and used the billboard's glow to guide him the last hundred yards. The gravel road crunch cut through the silence, seemingly loud enough to wake the dead, as he slid the van to the door of bay 103. The freshly-oiled door opened with nary a squeal, and he quickly parked the van in the long empty storage slot. Scott grabbed his backpack, made sure he had everything, and put the key under the driver's side visor. Not wanting to leave a trace, he yanked the duct tape off just as he shut the driver's door. With the garage door down, he fished a padlock out of the bag, locked it up, and put the key back in his pocket. It had taken maybe a minute.

Scott trotted back to Route 21 where he stripped off his cap, booties, gloves, and jumpsuit, cramming them all back into the pack. He started off west back to the bridge spanning the river, hugging close to the side of the road in case he needed to quickly hide. Adrenaline pushed him at a fairly fast clip, the Citrus Crunch training showing its benefits. The headlights were a mere flicker, coming from the east behind him as planned. He left the road and crouched in the shadows with his flashlight, waiting to make sure it was her before announcing his location. As the vehicle passed the billboard, the driver switched from headlights to fog lamps, the sign it was Andrea. Scott stepped from the shadows and flicked the flashlight on and off.

The pickup truck accelerated then slowed next to Scott. He jumped in while it was still moving.

"You good?" Andrea asked.

"No surprises. I think we're good," Scott answered, still catching his breath.

"Okay then. My turn."

Andrea sped ahead then parked on the shoulder just short of the bridge. They both jumped out. Scott dropped the tailgate and pulled out the ramp while Andrea hopped into the bed and unstrapped the motorcycle. They wheeled it down the ramp then Andrea rolled it across Route 21 and hid it in the brush while Scott got the ramp and tailgate back in place. They met beside the truck.

Dread overcame Scott. "You sure you want to do this? Maggie saw their weapons inventory and said they're armed to the teeth. They even have rocket launchers for God's sake. I don't feel right leaving you."

"I'm not a helicopter, so rocket launchers don't matter. If there's a confrontation, it will be close range, and my pistol and knife are more than enough. Don't worry, Scott. I got this. I have years of training for missions like this. Where's my tablet?"

"Oh yeah, I forgot!" Scott climbed into the truck to grab the scrambling device from his pack. He emerged to find Andrea with two packs at her feet and a weird goggle contraption strapped to her head.

"And take this too." He gave her the padlock key along with the tablet.

"Thanks." She put the key and tablet in her larger pack and flung it over her shoulders, then donned the smaller pack on her front like a papoose.

"Please be careful, Andrea."

"I will. Now, time's wasting. Get out of here!"

She already disappeared into the woods before he shifted the truck into gear. The drive back to Atlanta would be a long one.

48.

She picked her way through the brush toward the familiar dog rock along the river. Even though the temperature had cooled off some, Andrea's back and chest were already damp with sweat as if it was the summer desert of Afghanistan, not the October woods of central Georgia. She could no longer hear Scott driving away in the pickup truck—she was completely on her own.

At the rock, she headed toward the compound and began to recognize certain parts of the trail: two gnarly oak trees with thick, low-hanging branches, a dried creek bed that likely fed rainwater to the river, a lone magnolia tree looking out of place amongst the hardwoods and pines. She took a deep breath to steady herself, and the smell of changing fall leaves mixed in with bursts of pine invigorated her senses. She understood how the man and dog enjoyed romping through these woods.

She chose her steps carefully, knowing 5 pounds of plastic explosives were strapped to her chest. Not that the explosives were suddenly going to ignite. She knew only the detonator could do that, so she was only concerned about the timing device Maggie rigged up. Andrea had no idea how to reset it if something went awry.

She was more concerned about accessing the armory. Andrea was a soldier, not a thief. Her experience breaking into secure buildings involved firepower, which was not ideal when stealth was required. The video surveillance revealed the armory door was steel but with a normal deadbolt lock, a lock that wasn't overly secure. After watching two YouTube videos on how to pick a deadbolt using bobby pins, and then practicing with Maggie on her kitchen door, Andrea was fairly confident she'd be able to break in. If not, she'd plant the bomb on the back wall.

The night vision goggles captured the same pack of rooting boars off in the distance. They sensed her approach and scampered off, grunting their displeasure. The gradual ascent to the ridge protecting the ALM clearing began, and the trees started to thin. She was almost there. She instinctively crouched her posture until she was on her hands and knees at the edge of the clearing.

The armory was down the slight slope in front of her, the bungalow and two shacks directly across the field, and Tom's prison block on the left. Carefully removing her bomb-laden papoose and resting it at her side, she got down on her belly. The scene was the same as two nights ago: six heat blips in the prison block, one in each shack, and two in the house, none moving, all apparently asleep. Andrea kept her focus on the houses for a good 15 minutes just to make sure the coast was clear.

She checked her watch: 3:15 a.m. Time to move. She rose onto one knee, slid the papoose back on her chest, and removed her sidearm with noise suppression. Digging into her pocket, she pulled out two bobby pins and a pen light if she had to remove the night vision goggles for the intricate work of picking the lock. Andrea quietly exhaled and headed down the slope to the armory.

From the back wall, she advanced around the west side to the stoop, well aware her camo was ill-suited for a white building. She stuck her sidearm into her waist band, then crouched down to insert the broken bobby pin in the lower part of the deadbolt lock. As she set to work, she instinctively grabbed the doorknob to brace herself...and it turned. Andre paused then gave the door a slight push...it opened. The morons hadn't even locked the door.

Andrea slipped inside the small building and closed the door behind her. Maggie was right; this was no weapons supply shed for extremists. This was an ammunitions dump for people with inside connections. On the far side of the wall were crates of shoulder-mounted rocket launchers, on her left AR-15s hung from pegs like rakes in a garden shed. There were boxes of grenades and ammunition, a steel workbench with soldering tools and canisters of something. With these guys it might be nerve gas. Andrea was pissed.

As she stood surveying the room, a sudden thought came to mind. If they didn't lock this door, then maybe Tom's building was unlocked too. She could get Tom and still blow up the sick bastards' weapons. She didn't care if the building was packed with guards since she was angry enough to take them all out. It wasn't the plan, but she'd feel a hell of a lot better getting him away from these guys tonight. She pulled the sidearm from her waistband and went back outside.

The long building was maybe 50 yards away, and Andrea made a direct line rather than duck back into the shadows. She bound up to two cement portico steps and tried the handle. It didn't budge. The realization that these guys were more concerned about securing prisoners than their cache of weapons was not a good sign. She quickly retreated and returned to the shed within 30 seconds.

Andrea stood in the room taking a mental note of the inventory. She settled on the workbench, the logical place for someone to make a bomb.

49.

is brain throbbed so hard he thought he might puke. JR
sat on the edge of the bed, waiting to gain some balance
so he could go take a piss. He briefly put his head between
his knees, but that only amplified the pulsing in his ears. The meds
Dr. Shaw gave him weren't worth a damn. He felt like dog meat,
and except for the last couple of hours, he hadn't been able to sleep.

JR looked around the room and stewed on his existence. Sure,
he didn't pay rent and received a paycheck, but even his momma's
trailer was better than this piece of shit shack. A single room—not
counting the pisser which was so small his feet stuck in the shower
when sitting on the crapper, and he wasn't even tall! —with what
was called a kitchenette along one wall. The wood floors were
warped, and no amount of caulking could stop the drafts coming
from all the cracks around the windows, floorboards, and cheap-ass
clapboard siding. They acted like adding AC was a huge favor. Big
fucking deal! It all leaked out of this worthless sieve anyway! It was
nothing more than a glorified sharecropper's shack.

The doc had plied him with water all day, saying it would help
relieve the symptoms, one more sign he didn't really know what

the hell he was talking about. All it did was make him have to pee, and no matter how hard his head hurt, he couldn't hold it any longer. He stumbled into the bathroom and pissed like he spent the afternoon drinking Bud Lights instead of sitting in the shade fuming over a sucker punch.

As he headed back to his bed, something caught his eye, just a quick movement from out in the field. He went to the window thinking it probably was just another damn deer eating the bushes. Then he saw it, not a deer but a shadowy figure lurking at the front door of the barracks. The figure moved, then ran back across the field and ducked into the armory.

JR leapt to his clothes chair and quickly tossed on jeans and his jacket, found his boots under his bed, and pulled them on over his bare feet. He sprinted over to the kitchenette to grab his flashlight only to knock it off the counter, sending it skidding across the floor. He scrambled on his hands and knees but couldn't find the damn thing. He flipped on the light and momentarily reeled as the brightness brought a new wave of nausea. The flashlight had rolled under the kitchen table next to an empty Bud Light bottle. He fetched the damn thing then grabbed his rifle that lay propped up against the wall by the door. As he paused at the door to catch his breath, a thin smile spread over his face. JR always felt better after a good killing.

Only as he was crossing the field did he remember how much his head hurt. Each running step pounded up through his ears and rattled in his skull. With his rifle aimed at the door, he stopped in the middle of the field to gather himself. Once the pain was bearable, he started back up at a stalking pace, hoping that wouldn't rattle his brain as much. JR crept up to the armory determined to scare this fool, then shoot him. He sidled up to the building with his back pressed on the outer wall, within feet of the cracked door. Footsteps and scrapes could be heard on the cement floor but no flickering of light. No way anyone could see a damn thing in there without light. He edged closer to the door.

Holding his rifle like Chuck Connors did in that old TV western his dad loved, the flashlight in his other hand, he stepped up on the stoop facing the door. One, two, three, he kicked open the door and hit the flashlight button. The figure screamed, reaching for his eyes as he spun away from the light.

"You move, you die asshole." JR stood in the doorway, admiring his own entrance. "Now, arms up and turn around at me."

"Can I remove the night goggles first?" the figure asked in a voice not matching the camo. "The light's blinding with these things on."

"Go ahead, but no shit or you're dead."

The figure slid the goggles up, raised his arms up, one arm empty and the other holding a small pack. Slowly the figure turned around.

JR first noticed the gun in his waistband then saw the face. "You!" He felt his face flush in furious humiliation.

"How's my little buddy doing? Head feeling any better?" the woman from the diner gave a faint, cocky smile.

"You have no idea how much I'm going to enjoy killing you, you nigger bitch."

50.

"Thought we already established I didn't like that term. Believe that knot on your forehead was a reminder." She regretted the comment immediately. The guy didn't need to be provoked.

Andrea was filled with self-loathing rage. How could she have been so careless? All those years of training only to be ambushed by a rifle-wielding, skinny white racist! Andrea's only advantage was he was dumb as paint.

"You don't got much say. In fact, the last thing you're gonna hear is me calling you bitch." Still holding the flashlight, he awkwardly began to raise the rifle cradled in his right arm.

"Kill me here and you die too. Looks like you have the M4. This close, it'll be a through and through shot, and I doubt that stack of rocket launchers will take kindly to a bullet." She motioned with her head at the crates piled behind her.

The racist chuckled. "I ain't shooting you here, then I'd have to clean up your brains. No, we're going to the woods. That way boars can enjoy you too."

Andrea thought of the foraging beasts trotting away during her advance on the compound. She wasn't about to let those snorting bastards pick apart her carcass.

She didn't budge. "I'm afraid you're wrong. You want to kill me, you're doing it here. Or maybe I just drop this pack and take us both out," she said, gently jiggling the small pack held in her raised right arm.

His browed furrowed a bit before he snapped, "You think I'm stupid? No pack's gonna kill me." He gave her a cold stare then started to shuffle a bit to her left, away from a direct line with the crates.

Andrea's pulse raced. She took a step to the left, keeping the crates behind her. "I've got 5 pounds of explosives in this bag rigged to a concussion trigger, my own modified IED. You know what that is?"

He stopped. "I know what a fuckin' IED is. I been to 'Ghanistan."

Andrea judged the distance between them and inched a little closer. "Then you know this bag will turn us both into jelly. My plan had been to only disrupt your warped little white militia party, but since I'm already gonna die, might as well take you with me." She looked him in the eye, mentally pleading for this piece of shit to look at the bag.

They stood frozen. He took a quick peek up at the bag. She dropped it, he flinched, and it didn't explode.

Andrea snatched the M4 with her left hand as she drove the toe of her right boot squarely into his crotch with a kick worthy of a front row Rockette. While he doubled over in agony, she spryly rebalanced herself, grabbed the back of his head, and thrust it down as she drove her right knee squarely up into his face. The crunch confirmed she broke the asshole's nose this time.

He slumped to the floor writhing in pain, holding his face with one hand and cradling his balls with the other. Andrea set her newly acquired M4 aside and pulled her service revolver. She bent down over the moaning redneck, rolled him on his back, planted her knee firmly in his chest, and pressed the gun barrel against his forehead.

His eyes bulged in fear as his whimpering stopped.

With her free hand, she took a handful of his greasy hair and cocked her gun. "I told you not to call me that." Then she lifted and slammed his head on the concrete floor.

Andrea stood over her fallen foe with the gun still pointed at his chest just in case. She had faced death before, but never in such an up close and personal way. It's one thing to have an anonymous enemy shooting at you from a distance, but to stand feet from someone holding your life in their hands was truly unnerving. She prodded the body with her boot. He was still alive but no longer posed an immediate threat.

"Damn it!" During the scuffle the punk's flashlight came to a rest with its beam shining out the open door, casting a glow across the field. She hopped over the unconscious white supremacist and snatched up the flashlight, cut its beam, and shut the door, again muttering, "Damn it!"

Miraculously, the night vision goggles had remained perched on her head. She slid them back in place and cracked the door open an inch to check the situation. A light was on in one of the shacks but no warm glow of a person. Andrea scanned the other two houses relieved to find the occupants still in bed. But for how long?

The plan had not included bloodshed, but it was time to change the plan. Andrea knelt back down and rummaged through his jean's pockets, finding a pack of Marlboros, a lighter, and a set of car keys. She set the racist's belongings on one of the grenade crates along with her backpack and Maggie's bomb.

Andrea scanned the armory seeking inspiration and found it. The metal workbench was about 6-feet long, 3-feet wide, and

4-feet high. It was an open design with no shelving under the thick metal work space. It stood several feet from the wall, allowing people to work on both sides. At the bottom, a metal support bar ran the length of the bench and connected the legs. She crawled under the workbench, finding the bar was barely six inches off the ground, just about perfect to pin down his skinny little white ass. Andrea went to the end of the workbench, placed her palms just under the edge, squatted down into a weightlifter's position, and pushed up as hard as she could. Andrea could lift the workbench. She set it back down.

The wooden crates storing the shoulder-mounted rocket launchers were 4-feet long, a foot high, and a foot wide. She hefted one off the stack, set it on the ground, and stood on it to make sure it was strong enough. It was. She then nudged the crate with her foot to see if she could move it with her legs. She could. She quickly shoved the crate next to the end of the workbench flush against the two legs. Andrea got back into her weight lifting position, hoisted the end of the bench up, and then used her feet to nudge the rocket launcher crate under the raised legs before gently lowering the workbench onto the crate. She checked underneath the workbench, finding the support bar was nearly two feet off the ground at her end. She briefly admired her work, grateful for the strength of adrenaline.

Andrea went back to her pack and got the padlock key Scott had given her. She wound it onto the scrawny dude's key chain then stuck his keys, smokes, and lighter back in his pocket.

"Are you ready little buddy?" she playfully asked the unconscious redneck.

She moved up to his head, grabbed his jacket at the shoulders, and dragged him headfirst over to the workbench. He was surprisingly light. She circled to the other side, kneeled under the workbench, then grabbed his shoulders and pulled his torso under the now-raised cross bar. Andrea nudged him around until the bar was directly over his waist just above the hips. She went back to the end of the workbench, gave a heave, shoved the rocket launcher crate with her foot and lowered the bench onto his body. She crawled under to inspect her job. The support bar dug into his midsection—the scrawny dude wasn't going anywhere.

Andrea took Maggie's bomb out of the bag and set it on the workbench directly over his head. She wadded up the spare bag and stuck it in her backpack before throwing it over her shoulders. She then went over to the two large canisters in the corner with propane symbols emblazoned on the sides. She opened both valves.

She took one last look at the racist, the night vision goggles adding a touch of macabre to the blood oozing from his nose. "It couldn't happen to a nicer fella," Andrea told him as she activated the bomb's 45-minute countdown.

With little time to spare, Andrea rushed to the armory's door and peeked outside. A body was moving in the house. She checked her watch, it was almost 4:00 a.m.

I bet it's the old man peeing again, she thought.

It didn't matter, she had to make a break for it. Andrea slid out onto the stoop, closed the door, and made a break for the woods. She thought she heard the dog bark.

Andrea crashed through the woods with reckless abandon. She hit the main trail headed toward the river when she fell the first time. Okay but a little gimpy, she pushed on. At the river, she cut towards Route 21, trying to find the path she'd forged on the earlier trips. Twigs and branches slashed at her body, but she didn't care.

It took only 20 minutes to cover what had been a 40-minute hike. She had 25 minutes at most to get some distance from the compound. Andrea pushed the motorcycle up the hill, hopped on, and hit the gas.

Against her better judgment, she hammered the throttle. The motorcycle flew up Route 21 and barely slowed as she veered on to the I-75 entrance ramp. Once on the interstate, she twisted the wick wide open.

About ten miles later Andrea crested a hill and immediately blue flashing lights flicked on from the median.

"Damn it!"

51.

The darkness was so complete that it took a moment to realize his eyes were open. But the pain—oh, the pain—was impossible to ignore or blame on a dream. His head throbbed so badly he could barely breathe, his balls felt like an overinflated balloon ready to burst, and the ache from his groin inched up his body, resting on his chest like a boulder. Even his legs were numb. What the hell happened? Then it came to him, and even as rage and humiliation surged through his veins, they were no match for his physical agony. JR began to sob.

Tears rolled down his temples pooling in his ears. He groped up to his face and realized blood encrusted his cheeks, chin, and neck. His nose was not where it was supposed to be. Panic overcame him. He tried to sit up only to feel a different crushing pain erupt in his stomach. His shoulders collapsed back onto the concrete floor.

"What the fuck's wrong with me?" he cried out. JR thrashed his legs. They worked, but his body wouldn't move—something was pinning him down.

Flailing in the dark, he felt a bar, metal, tight across his midsection below the ribs and just above his hips. With both hands,

JR placed a firm grip on the bar, giving it an upward yank with all his strength. It didn't budge. He slid his arms outward searching for the end, only to find perpendicular bars attached to the one crushing him. He followed along those bars and found two more, right about at his shoulders, sticking straight up. The workbench. Horrified, JR shook the workbench legs with everything he had. The movement made the table rock ever so slightly, jabbing the bar deeper into his abdomen.

"Ooowww! Goddammit!" he wailed, dropping his arms to the floor.

JR lay still. Movement only brought more agony.

"You fucking bitch," he yelled into the darkness.

This made him think about how she pinned him under the workbench. No way she could have lifted the thing on her own. She must have an accomplice. The thought was oddly reassuring. Now, he could tell people he was jumped by at least two people.

"Like that matters" he whined to the darkness. "I'm like a fucking rat in a trap. They'll give me shit about this the rest of my life."

The more he considered his fate, the worse the situation became. A new wave of terror swept over him, and he began to wiggle, trying to get his hips under the bar. The bar only dug deeper into his hip bones, sending a new round of pain through his balls, stomach, and brain. He mindlessly kicked his legs hoping for a miracle. It was hopeless; his shitty existence on this planet had just gotten shittier.

The utter blackness of the room began to crush down upon him. JR was never afraid of the dark before, but this was different. Unable to move, the black cloak felt suffocating. His breathing became labored, and his body broke out in a cold sweat. It was almost like he was drowning on dry land. JR was petrified.

Then he remembered his smokes and lighter. A good smoke always calmed his nerves, and the lighter will let him see his predicament. Hell, maybe once he can see, he'll be able to figure out how to get out of here. Maneuvering his arm under the bar, he fished around in his pocket and wrapped his fingers tightly around his smokes and trusty lighter. Suddenly, JR had hope again.

The dried blood in his nostrils was packed harder than Georgia red clay in August. He had no way of smelling the gas that flowed from the two large canisters filling every square inch of the small, cinder block building.

JR stuck a Marlboro in the corner of his mouth and flicked his Bic.

52.

The brick ranch house was nearly knocked off its foundation. Shock waves rattled Barry to his core, and his ears rang as if someone woke him with an air horn.

"What the hell was that?!" shouted Barry. The frightened Lab hopped up in bed, not to give but to seek comfort.

The two clutched each other trying to get their wits about them from the rude awakening. Suddenly the roof began to pound as if the house was being pummeled by the mother of all hailstorms. They flinched as a loud crack came from above, and a chunk of something burst through the ceiling before boring through the floor near the dresser, landing in the crawl space with a loud thud. The hailstorm stopped as quickly as it started.

"Damn, Moon, we get hit by a meteor? Let's get the hell out of here!"

He hopped out of bed, tossed on his robe and slippers, then stumbled into his bedside lamp that had been thrown to the floor. From under the crack of his bedroom door came a strange reddish glow. Barry crept to the door thinking the world was about to swallow him whole. He peered up the hallway to the living room at the front of the house. No lights were needed. The massive orange glow coming from outside lit the interior like it was dawn. The bookcase in the corner was toppled, the few pictures he had were knocked off the walls, and both front windows were shattered. Barry shuffle-ran in his slippers to the front door and out onto the porch.

The parade ground was littered with debris with small balls of fire scattered here and there. Strips of metal roofing clung to tree branches, reminding Barry of TP pranks back in high school. A metal beam impaled the ground not far from his house, and what looked like a moon crater had replaced the ammunition dump. Smoke and dust hung in the air, smelling of gunpowder and burning wood. The only sight that disturbed Barry was a fire smoldering in the woods behind where the armory had been, slowly growing in size.

Mike came running up to the porch clad in boxers and boots. "What happened, boss?"

"Our ammunition dump blew. No idea how, but it's not good."

"We better do something. Them woods are catching fire."

A thin smile spread on Barry's face as he realized the window of opportunity had just been opened. "You're right, we better do something. We need to get the hell out of here."

"What?"

"We're too late to stop the fire," Barry said, turning to Mike. "Soldier, there's a time to fight and a time to retreat, and now's the time to retreat. Find JR, grab a few things, and get lost."

"What about them?" Mike pointed over to the barracks. "Should we let them loose?"

Barry was too worried about his own skin to think about the doc's patients. He considered them for a second; six drug-addled vets wandering around debris and a forest fire.

"No, they'll be fine. The wind's taking the fire away from them." He left the nearly naked knucklehead standing bewildered on the porch.

He'd been planning his escape for a good two years but had given up on the possibility it would ever happen. Simply leaving was not an option. Bubba was too powerful with half-crazed militants in all 50 states lined up ready to do his dirty work, and it would be their patriotic duty to hunt him down. But the explosion and chaos could put Bubba on the defensive, giving him the head start he needed. It was now or never.

Barry ran to the bedroom, dodging books and other unsentimental keepsakes from the past five years that lay scattered around the house. He shed his robe and threw on the sweatshirt and jeans from yesterday. He got a duffel bag off the closet shelf and began to toss in clothes compatible with his hoped-for final destination. Barry packed light, only extra underwear was really required. He hurried into the bathroom for the bare essential toiletries then detoured to the living room where his laptop sat on the small desk.

With the duffel packed, he plopped on the floor and shoved the shoe rack out of the way, exposing a small safe against the closet's back wall. Once opened, he packed a satchel with documents necessary for survival—cash, multiple passports, offshore account records, stock certificates. Lastly, from the safe's top shelf, he removed two identical, large manila envelopes, neither one addressed or sealed. He confirmed the contents of both, sealed them, and wrote a different name on each with a Sharpie. There was no turning back now.

Bags slung over his shoulder, Barry made it halfway out before he realized the dog was following every movement with panting enthusiasm. He stopped and looked at the dog as she sat and wagged. A pained look swept Barry's face. "Moon, buddy, I forgot about you. I'm so sorry, but you can't come where I'm going. You need to stay here. I really don't have another option."

His voice only made the wagging increase, a vigorous thumping on the hardwood floors. He gave the dog a generous ear rub.

"You stay here. You'll find a good home with someone who's life isn't as fucked up as mine." He held his hand up, palm out in the stay position, as he backed out the front door onto the porch.

By the time he turned to face the burning carnage, the dog leapt through the vacant front window and retook her sitting position next to Barry, tail still in excited motion.

"Moon, this isn't a game!" He took hold of her collar to drag the dog back inside. A panting Mike stopped him.

The big lug lumbered up the steps. "JR ain't in his cabin. Can't find him anywhere, but I'm ready to go!"

"Well, get going then."

The flaming woods caught Mike's baffled expression. "What do ya mean? I'm going with you. We're retreating like you said!"

"No, you're not!" Barry could tell his reaction only increased the lug's confusion. He regrouped. "It's best if we split. We've got a better chance if we're on our own."

"But I don't have a car. JR does all the driving, and he ain't to be found. No way I'm running on foot."

Barry was surprised it was ending this way. He had long figured that JR's volatility or Mike's incompetence would have caused an earlier irreparable mishap, his own premature death being the most likely outcome. If all white supremacist campaigns were depending on the talents of men like Mike and JR, then the movement was doomed. He knew that wasn't the case. That fool Bubba had just saddled him with a hopeless posse.

Barry fished in his satchel and emerged with keys. "Here. Take my truck."

Mike reacted like it was Christmas. "The Land Cruiser? Really?! I love that truck! What about you?"

Barry thrust the keys out. "I'll manage. Now, get going before I change my mind."

He stood on the porch with Moon watching the forest fire's increased intensity until the taillights disappeared on the gravel path leading to County Road 5. "Alright, buddy, to the bedroom you go. This isn't an adventure for both of us."

Moon's expression made him second guess the decision. Most dogs have the look, but Labradors have it perfected: eager yet plaintive, trusting yet wary, always so very hopeful. He cradled the dog's jowls with both hands, gently scratching the underside neck folds. Big brown eyes stared back at him encouraging a change of heart. Barry had no choice. "You're right. Locking you in the bedroom is a bad idea. I know exactly where you'll get the attention you deserve."

He leaned back in the bungalow and took a key ring off a nail next to the door. "Come on, Moon, let's go on an adventure."

Knowing he didn't have much time, Barry foolishly dashed across the debris strewn parade ground to the patient barracks, Moon happily prancing at his side since hearing the word "adventure."

True to the builder's word, the impenetrable barracks stood strong amongst the carnage. Even the smoldering debris was harmlessly burning out on the thick tin roof. He unlocked and tugged open the heavy steel door. Inside the building, he heard muffled pleas and screams coming from the cells. Not only were these poor guys locked up, but a massive explosion likely triggered waves of PTSD panic. Sorry, boys, not much I can do about it.

Moon trotted with Barry to the last door on the right. He opened the small observation panel and was met with a frantic voice. "What the hell's going on?! Are we under attack? Get me out of here!" yelled Alpha.

"Easy there," Barry called back. "We're not under attack. We've just had an accident that needs my attention."

"Accident, my ass! Sounds like you just took out a small village. Get me out of here!"

"Can't do that, it's not safe. I was hoping you could watch my dog for me while we handle the problem out here. She likes you, and I know you'll take care of her."

"The big black dog Moon? Heck yeah, I love that dog!"

"Okay then. Stay where you are, and I'll let her in. It may be a while before someone comes back to get her."

Alpha's voice calmed considerably. "Take your time. She'll be fine."

Barry looked down at Moon, and the tail began to thump. "See you, buddy. You're a great pal. I promise this guy will take better care of you then I ever did." He buried his fingers behind both ears for one last scratch, then bent down and kissed her knobby skull. She licked his cheek, returning the kiss. He opened the cell door. "Go, girl!" and patted her rump as she scampered in.

Barry retreated out of the building. He shut and locked the steel door, cursing the incompetence and cruelty of the sick quack doc. He considered the plight of the men inside then dropped the keys at the foot of the door, hoping someone would come soon and free the poor SOBs.

It was a short jog along the trail leading from the compound to the billboard storage facility. In bay 101 sat an old Maxima they had confiscated from one of Doc Shaw's now deceased guinea pigs. Barry tossed his bags in the passenger seat and sent gravel flying as he spun on to Route 21 headed east, away from the craziness, away from civilization.

53.

The radar gun flashed 109 mph. Sheriff Terrance Mosely flipped on the patrol car's blue flashing lights, but the motorcycle didn't slow and passed in the blink of an eye.

"You really going to make me chase you?" he said out loud.

With age, Terrance had lost his enthusiasm for issuing speeding tickets. Now, he just liked to park in a conspicuous spot and flip on his blue emergency lights in hopes the fool slowed down. He shifted into drive and sent dirt flying as he spun north onto I-75.

Terrance pulled the radio handset from its cradle. "Maxine, you out there?"

Maxine's tenure with the department was almost as long as Terrance's, and she had been the sole overnight dispatcher since the '80s. It was unlike her not to respond right away.

He spoke into the handset again. "Maxine, I need you to radio Highway Patrol. We got ourselves a fool on a motorcycle going more than 100. Probably up near mile marker 161 by now."

The radio squawked, "Sheriff, it's Maxine. Sorry I didn't answer, but I've been getting calls about an explosion."

"Seriously? Where?"

"Off 21 near the river. I got three calls here in the last minute."

Terrance glanced at his speedometer. He'd just hit 100, and the motorcycle's taillight wasn't getting any closer. "Probably just the Bakers with a bunch of liquored up guests doing something stupid again."

"Don't know about that, Terry. One of the calls was from that Raymond kid. He said he saw a fireball and there's still a weird orange glow."

"Overnight Mini Mart Ray?"

"Yep. Said he thinks the orange glow might be a forest fire."

"Guess I better check it out. Kid seems pretty rock solid to me."

"You're right. I know his momma. They're not a family to exaggerate. Keep me posted, Terry."

"Will do, Maxine." Terrance clicked off his radio and said to the fading taillight, "You lucked out tonight." He eased off the accelerator and cut across the median to head south. The patrol car bounced up onto the pavement, and he punched the gas.

The damn fool Bakers, full of crazy, rich, privileged white man tomfoolery. Terrance didn't work the graveyard shift often, just when a Deputy needed a night with the family or if he wanted to go fishing early in the morning. Most nights were quiet, yet it seemed every couple of months he'd be called about a disturbance at Deer Bend. Usually, the calls ended with the Sheriff talking into the gate intercom, the drunken, slurred replies telling him everything was just fine, just fine.

The Sheriff pounded his steering wheel. "This better be one of those times, Bubba! I got new curly-tailed grub bait for the crappies this morning, and if I'm late, you're going to pay!"

It didn't help that Bubba and the Sheriff were sworn enemies. The congressman never missed an opportunity to undercut or outrank Terrance on even the most mundane county matter. Terrance understood why. Bubba resented the fact that the first duly elected

Black Sheriff in middle Georgia came from Bubba's own backyard. For the most part, the sheriff left the congressman alone, simply relishing the fact his mere existence drove him up the wall.

He slowed on the exit ramp and turned left onto Route 21, back over the interstate, where a semi's sweeping turn out of the Flying J momentarily slowed his momentum. Terrance glanced to his left and gave a brief horn honk to Mini Mart Ray who stood by the outer BP pumps, waving like it was the Fourth of July parade. Terrance couldn't help but like the kid. Most his age saw cops as the enemy.

Once past the glare of the Flying J, he drove at a more moderate speed. This stretch of Route 21 was known for deer ambling on the shoulders to eat the underbrush pinching the side of the road. Early morning fall hours were a popular grazing time, and the Sheriff didn't want an unsuspecting stag flying through his windshield.

Mini Mart Ray was right. He noticed an orange glow on the horizon, too early and not the right direction for sunrise.

"Maxine, Sheriff here," he called to his dispatcher on the handset.

"What you got, Sheriff?"

"I'm still several miles out, but I do think we got ourselves a fire. Not far enough to be the Baker's. Looks like it might be those militia boys down near the river."

"Bubba's not-so-secret white army?"

"Hush now, Maxine," he somewhat scolded but knew she was right. "I need you to get DNR on the phone. Tell them we need forest firefighters. I'll let you know more here in a minute."

The glow grew. As he approached the Ocmulgee bridge, he knew it was on the militia land and spinning out of control. Terrance's concern for deer evaporated as he jammed the accelerator, took air crossing the bridge, and banked hard onto County Road 5. Something was definitely up—the gate was wide open.

Many times he'd been on the land of people who hated his kind, but never before had he entered the lair of avowed white nationalists. Terrance wasn't taking any chances. As he crept down the gravel drive, he removed the safety strap from his sidearm and uncradled the shotgun. Off on his left through the trees, the forest was up in flames.

"Maxine?" He didn't wait for her response. "I'm on the property off 5, and we need as many firefighters as you can rustle up as soon as possible. Better call more law enforcement too."

"Roger that. And Terry, be careful around those boys."

Up ahead, he saw buildings silhouetted by the raging fire ringing a small clearing. He parked the cruiser between two small shacks at the outer rim and made sure he had the shotgun before exiting. The crackle and roar of the fire hit him when he got out of the car, but the wind was driving the fire away from the buildings and deeper into the woods. The smell made him think of his tours in Nam all those years ago—a combination of ordinance and burning flesh.

Terrance took a minute to survey the scene in front of him. A large crater on the far side of the field was clearly ground zero and debris from the explosion was scattered in all directions. Five buildings still stood, but he had no idea if they were occupied or if others explosions might be imminent. He had taken a vow to protect the citizenry with no caveats or disclaimers excluding racists or thugs from his sworn duty. Sheriff Mosely went in search of survivors.

He went to the first shack immediately on his left. "Sheriff's Department!" he yelled over the din. The door was open. He scanned the one-room building with his flashlight. The bed was unmade and belongings scattered. Either someone left in a hurry or against their will.

He advanced to the next building on his left, closer to the crater and the inferno's shifting direction. Again, he announced his presence only to stumble into what appeared to be a meeting room or mess hall. The corrugated steel walls were scalding hot.

Terrance turned back to check on the other buildings to the right of his parked squad car. He carefully dodged chunks of debris then stopped dead in his tracks. On the ground in front him was a smoldering leg, blown off just below the knee, a boot still attached to the foot. It smelled like Nam and now it looks like it.

Through a rage clenched jaw, he muttered, "You damn people. What are you doing in my county?!" He quickly retreated to his car radio.

"Maxine, there's been a huge explosion here, and we're going to need anyone and everyone you can get. The fire's huge, and we got casualties."

"Casualties?" she said, alarmed. "How many?"

"Who knows, but there's a leg sitting here in the field with nobody attached to it. This is a little out of our league. Do what you can." With that, he tossed the handset back on the seat.

The second shack was an empty, disheveled mess too.

Next door, the brick ranch house suffered the most damage from the explosion. Bigger than the shacks, it required him to check each room. The front windows were blown out, and the clutter inside was the result of trauma, not from the resident being a slob. Scanning the bedroom with his flashlight, something caught his eye—on the closet floor was a safe, door wide open with nothing in it. Terrance also noticed the many bare hangers dangling from the rod. The clothes clearly belonged to a male, and what man has a bunch of spare hangers in his closet? No, this guy left in a hurry. A thought suddenly occurred to him, so he ran back outside to verify his guess. Only one beat up pickup truck was on the property, no other vehicles in sight…and the gate was open. These guys must be on the run.

Terrance stood outside the ranch house watching the flames advancing deeper into the woods. Even though the fire was moving away from him, the heat was intense. His mental vision was inescapable—the burning forest eerily resembled the flaming jungles after a napalm attack. Only in Nam everything burned. Here bits and pieces of the once standing building were littered everywhere. He was just glad the steel beam sticking out of the ground didn't have a human skewered on the end.

One more building to check. This one was closest to ground zero, and the debris field intensified with each step. Terrance picked his way slowly around chunks of concrete and simmering embers, shining his flashlight on the ground to make sure he didn't trip. The roaring sound of the fire was unnerving as he slowly panned his flashlight back and forth.

At first, he didn't see it sheltered in between two shards of cinder block. Terrance held the flashlight beam steady, studying the singed human hand. It was that of a white male balled into a fist, furiously clinging to an object. Not very big, either the previous owner was a young teenager or slight of stature. The Sheriff squatted down for a closer look—the hand clung to a red Bic lighter. Terrance took a handkerchief out of his pocket and placed it over the hand as a marker before continuing on his way.

Unlike the other structures, this one was sturdier and locked up tighter than a drum. He fruitlessly pounded on the steel door trying to draw the attention of anyone. He stepped back only to see small windows high off the ground. It was odd. He'd heard of survivalist bunkers before and wondered if this was some weird version of it. Maybe this is just the entrance and beneath there's a labyrinth with angry white guys hunkered down with years of supplies. He moved back to try the door again when his foot kicked something. No flashlight was needed to tell they were keys.

The sheriff stood holding the set of keys, debating what to do. On the other side of the door, there might be a bunker crammed with scared, armed white men just dying to shoot a Black county sheriff. But there might also be people who are in danger and needed his help. The decision was easy. The first two keys didn't insert, but the third one did. He pumped his shotgun just in case, took a deep breath and went in.

54.

"**C**ongressman. Congressman, I need you to wake up, sir."
Bubba felt the soft shoulder jabs, hoping his dream was reality and the young, lithe future intern from his last visit to the Plantation was interested in another romp.

"Yes, what do you want, darling," he softly cooed, face down into his mattress.

"Sir, it's me, Dennis, and I need you to wake up, sir."

The shoulder jabs became strong shakes.

Bubba groggily woke up, disappointed and irate to see it was one of his gaggle of aides rudely interrupting his bliss. "Goddammit, this better be important!" Bubba roared, making certain he stayed on his stomach to conceal the evidence of his dream.

"Sir, the president's office just called, and there seems to have been another bombing in Georgia."

The thought piqued Bubba's interest, and he carefully rolled to his side to get a better look at the aide who called himself Dennis. "Really, so they're at it again, huh? That's interesting information, but I don't know if it's important enough to wake me up..." Bubba glanced at the bedside clock, "...at 5-fucking-45!"

"Normally not, sir, but it seems the bombing was down near your farm, and the president's concerned you might be a target."

"The farm?" Bubba shot straight up, momentarily forgetting about his morning wood before quickly placing a pillow over his lap. "Those bastards tried to blow up my Plantation?"

"No, sir. I understand your farm wasn't hit, but it was close enough that the president was concerned. He's sending over some of his secret service detail to make sure you're safe."

Bubba had to hand it to the president. The guy sure knew how to manipulate a story for the press. He couldn't wait to check the latest tweet. It was probably something like "Terrorist Mexicans now target a patriotic public servant for speaking honestly about America." Hell, if the president didn't use that line, maybe Bubba would.

Bubba wasn't about to let this opportunity pass. "Thanks for telling me. I think we should hold our own press conference this morning. Set it up for me. Let's do it right in front of the house, but make sure it's after the secret service gets here. I want the people to see that I need protection from these thugs."

The aide calling himself Dennis gave him a leery glance. "Are you sure, Congressman? It doesn't seem wise to let people know where you live."

"Damn right, I'm sure! People already know where I live. The TV trucks have been parked outside for days. Listen, I don't care what you and the other so-called strategists think. No way I'm showing these immigrant terrorists I'm afraid!"

"Yes, sir." The aide left his bedside and headed toward the door.

With a plan percolating on how to milk this to his advantage, Bubba realized more details on the attack might be useful for his press appearance. He called after him. "Where was the bombing? Was anyone hurt?" Bubba at least had to pretend concern.

"It was at some private wildlife preservation right next to your farm. I don't know about injuries, but supposedly it was a huge explosion that started a forest fire right next to a river."

Bubba's throat suddenly swelled shut and more than just his shoulders went limp. Out of his contracted windpipe, he squeezed a meager, "Okay."

With his bedroom door safely shut, Bubba shot out of bed, grabbed his cell phone, and went into his bathroom to ensure he was out of earshot. He hit Dave on his speed dial. "Hey, Jimmy, I was about to call," his brother said.

"What the hell's going on, Dave?"

"Something blew up. Felt it all the way over at my place. Whole damn woods are on fire, but the Plantation should be okay. Looks like it's moving south."

"Goddammit, Dave! I don't give a shit about the Plantation! You need to get over there and get Barry and everyone out of there!"

"Don't think I can do that, Jimmy. Farthest I could make it is the cut through at 5. I'm parked under the bridge right now, and the fire's blocking my way. Those guys will be okay. I've heard all sorts of fire trucks pulling up."

Bubba pounded his hand down the on the marble vanity. "Dave, listen to me. The last thing we want is a bunch of cops snooping around there. You need to do something now!"

"'Fraid it's too late for that, brother."

Bubba heard the sirens over the phone and knew his brother was right. He ran his hand through his hair, mulling his options. He only had one left. He tried to sound reassuring as he said, "Dave, this is what you need to do. You still have that file and the name of that computer guy in Texas that I gave you?"

"Of course, Jimmy. It's back home in the wall safe."

Bubba took a breath to remain calm. "Okay, I need you to get that to him as fast as you can. Will you do that?"

"Sure, but isn't it even earlier in Texas. Won't I wake him up?"

Bubba swore his momma was right about Dave: a boll weevil had more sense. "I don't give a shit! This is an emergency! Do it now, you hear me?!"

"You got it, Jimmy," and the line went dead.

Bubba stared at himself in the bathroom mirror. He knew the tech guy in Texas was one of the best and would have no problem planting the file's contents shifting all blame away from the congressman. He felt a twinge of guilt knowing his nefarious activities would soon be blamed on his brother, but it had to be done. To hell with blood being thicker than water.

55.

For the second time in less than a week, Seamus received an early morning call about a bombing in Georgia. Last Sunday, it roused him from bed, but he was already dressed when he spoke with Carraway before dawn on Friday. He tried not to take it as a professional affront that this time he was the last agent notified, almost an hour after the others.

Seamus lived close to GBI headquarters and made it to the office by 6:30 a.m. He was surprised not to hear Carraway's voice bouncing off the walls, shouting orders to his team. A yellow Post-it was on his boss's door—"In Tifton Room." Seamus half-trotted up the inner corridor past the break room and soon heard a commotion coming from the Tifton Conference Room at the end of the hall.

He paused at the door admiring his boss—the man worked harder than anyone he knew and was best during crisis. Carraway was furiously scribbling on a whiteboard while his assistant tried to capture his comments on her laptop. Though other voices boomed from the speakers mounted in the ceiling, when Seamus entered, it was just the three of them in the conference room.

"O'Reilly, good you're here." Carraway turned back to the whiteboard and continued talking. "Two guys from the Macon office are already there. What's your ETA?"

"We're making good time. We should get there in less than an hour."

Seamus recognized the voice but couldn't immediately place which team member through the background noise, obviously coming from a cell phone.

"Okay, here's what I need you to do." Tilting his head upward, Carraway spoke as if the mobile agents were hidden behind the acoustical ceiling tiles. "Find the Macon team and the Sheriff. I need additional verification on his story. Call me as soon as you confirm!"

"Yes, sir," the ceiling answered.

Carraway nodded and turned his attention to Seamus who stood just inside the door. "The bombing took place around 4:30 a.m. on the property where the ALM trains. This was no little explosion either, a mother of a blast that left a damn hole in the ground. I know you've been researching those guys, so I need you to double down and find out as much as you can."

"Absolutely, I can do that."

He tapped the whiteboard where "O'Reilly/Knudson" was listed along with pairs of other agents. "I've set you up in the Valdosta Conference Room with Knudson from the Cybersecurity Team. I figured he could help you out if the squirrelly bastards have hidden files or whatever it is you guys look for." Carraway turned to his assistant. "Give O'Reilly one of those lists too."

Seamus stepped over and took a piece of paper from the assistant's outstretched hand as Carraway explained, "The local Sheriff was first on the scene and found six men locked in a building, and they all swore they were being held prisoner. It sounds unbelievable, so we're trying to verify. You're holding their names. We need you to look into them too."

The last name on the list rocked Seamus—Tom Worthington. His brain tried to compute what it meant, but there was no denying that now a Worthington was somehow connected to both bombings. He pondered his suspicions of Maggie and the hushed meeting he saw at Duke's not even two days ago. Seamus then thought of Andrea. Did the lieutenant colonel really go to the coast, or was she involved too?

"You got a problem, O'Reilly?" Carraway's voice was annoyed.

Seamus looked up at his boss, not knowing how long he'd been in his trance.

"No, sir, well, yes, actually I do," Seamus wanted to be tactful. "Did you look at this list?"

"I glanced over it. What about it?"

"The last name is Worthington, as in the billboard family. Remember the one missing brother who was initially a suspect?" Seamus held up the sheet. "This is him."

"Really?"

"Yes, and one would think there's a high likelihood it's more than a coincidence. I know you didn't think much of my theory from earlier this week, but something weird is going on here."

Seamus could tell Carraway was considering the implications.

"I'll agree with that. This whole damn thing is weird." Making up his mind, he said, "Look into it, O'Reilly. Everything's fair game right now. Let me know what you find."

Seamus nodded and left to set up camp in the Valdosta Conference Room. He didn't know what to think. Part of him felt satisfaction that his original theory might be right while the other part was hoping he'd be proven wrong.

56.

e backed the purloined car's license plate up against a bush in the long-term section of Morningstar Marina's parking lot. Barry flipped the radio dial to a different station just in time to hear the Savannah news announcer make a cursory mention of the explosion. The entire drive down I-16, he'd worn out the dial, and so far, reported details were sketchy. It was now or never. He said a quick prayer, tossed the keys in the bushes, grabbed his bags, and headed for the docks.

Barry walked down the gangplank, nervously eyeing the dock's activity. All it would take is one person who knew too much or asked one too many questions. His arrival at 8:00 a.m. was the first sign he may actually get away with it. Too late for fisherman and the fall morning still too chilly for most pleasure boaters, the dock activity was minimal. Also working for him was the relative anonymity of not being a regular at the marina. He was more of a celebrity guest known mostly as an employee of the congressman who was privileged to captain an awesome yacht. And the *Select Committee* was spectacular. The marina crew had moved her away from the other yachts to the fuel tanks near the shore.

"Morning, guys," he confidently announced, exiting the gang-plank to the docks.

"Morning, Barry. Just about have her ready for you," the young dockhand said from the yacht's deck. "Just getting the last of your provisions stored."

"Appreciate it, boys. Thanks for the quick response." He struggled to stay composed.

"No problem," the 40-something dock manager replied from the yacht's aft as he shifted the gas nozzle to the auxiliary tank. "Would have been ready earlier if Romeo over there would've spent more time buying your supplies instead of flirting with the checkout girl."

The young dockhand laughed. "You're just jealous 'cause she's hot and likes me. Face it, old man, geezers like you don't have a chance."

"In your dreams, junior," the manager shot back, then looked at Barry. "Where you off to?"

Barry was ready. "Newport News. Bubba has some big wigs coming down from DC. Depending on who they are, we might stick close or head up north. Sorry I forgot to call until I was headed down. Guess the memory's not what he used to be." Barry poked his own head for emphasis.

The young dockhand hopped off the yacht. "Doesn't matter to us. Wouldn't have done anything until this morning anyway. You're good to go topside."

The ringtone was a deep tugboat steam whistle. The dock manager pulled his cell from his back pocket. "Sorry, gotta take this. It's the boss. Finish this up, will ya," he told the dockhand, motioning at the fuel line.

A phone call from the boss sounded ominous. Barry tried to edge within eavesdropping range, but it was hard to hear with the dockhand yammering on about the Piggly Wiggly checkout babe and how the snappers were biting just south of Sapelo Island. He heard "wow" and "got it" several times, accompanied by head bobs from the dock manager. Barry felt like he was about to have a heart attack.

The manager hung up with his boss just as the dockhand removed the fuel line from the yacht. "Filling the auxiliary was a good move. You'd be pushing it to make it there on the main tank," the kid said, finally ending his monologue.

"Well, I'll be damned," the dock manager stood staring out to the river. He turned and looked directly at Barry. "Seems like we've had another terrorist attack."

He resisted the urge to turn tail and run. The *Select Committee* was still moored, so jumping on the yacht to make a mad dash wasn't an option either. All he could do was eke out a feeble "Really?"

"Those crazy fuckers," the dockhand slammed the nozzle into the pump. "Does that mean we're on lockdown again?"

Now, Barry knew he was seconds away from a coronary.

"Naw," the manager shook his head. "We're just to be on the lookout for suspicious activity. They want us to call the cops if we see anything out of the ordinary."

"That could mean a lot of things around here. He mention anything in particular?" the dockhand asked.

A wry smile came to the manager. "Yeah, you getting a date with the Piggly Wiggly babe would be out of the ordinary."

"Kiss my ass, old man."

Barry nearly collapsed on the dock. He had to get out of here fast while he could still function.

"If we're good to go, I best shove off. Have lots of ocean to cover." He climbed aboard the vessel on trembling knees as the two dockmates continued with their good-natured insults. He tossed his bags in the stateroom, climbed the bridge, and fired up the twin diesels. "See you guys in about a week!"

"Have a good trip, Barry. Hope they're biting for the big shots."

The dockhands cast off the bow and aft lines and gave the yacht a gentle shove. Barry tapped lightly on the throttle, and the diesels bubbled and churned as he sputtered through the marina's no wake zone to the Wilmington River. Once on the river's main channel, he gave the throttle another slight touch.

The pungent marsh air acted like smelling salts, bringing back clarity after his harrowing performance on the docks. He'd made it past the first hurdle. He relaxed slightly and admired the beauty of Intracoastal Georgia. The few boats on the river were of little concern since the Coast Guard rarely came up this far. Barry was grateful for the brief respite knowing additional mines were bobbing in the seas ahead.

Little did Bubba know how he made Barry's potential escape a reality. On the occasion no guests were visiting, Barry would be invited up to the big house to share bourbon on the veranda. Even though the company was intolerable, he enjoyed sitting in the rocking chair, watching the setting sun overtake the field and pond. Some evenings, the creak of their rockers did most of the talking, and other nights Bubba would have his dander up. It was on one of those evenings where Bubba provided a boost to a possible escape plan.

"What red-blooded American man doesn't like to hunt!" Bubba stewed. "I've invited that SOB down here a dozen times. Instead he blows me off, and now's trying to kill my bill!"

Barry hadn't been paying attention to the details, something about a northeastern congressman who shunned Bubba's overtures and had the nerve to ask for a favor in return for his vote. Bubba thought a weekend of hunting, drinking, and young women was every man's idea of a favor.

"Maybe he'd rather fish," Barry absently suggested.

"What?!"

"You said he's from the northeast. Hear a lot of those guys would rather fish. I know sometimes I'd rather fish."

"Well, that doesn't do me a whole helluva lot good. I hate to fish, and we only have that shit pond with bluegill and carp!"

The moment of inspiration hit Barry. "You've got access to a lot of money, right? Buy a boat and keep it down in Savannah to take guys deep sea fishing. Not all the time like here. You set up four, maybe six different trips during the year, then take who you want."

Bubba stopped rocking. "Not a bad idea, but I don't fish and there's no way I'm going out in some damn boat. I need my space."

"Depending on how much money you get your hands on, you could buy a pretty good-sized yacht. And you don't have to go. Doesn't Dave run things when you're not around? There are all sorts of captains you could hire..." He paused for effect. "...or I could take them. When guys come here, you don't talk business all the time, do you? Just coach me on what you want, and I'll take care of the fishing, drinks, and business."

Bubba's tone changed. "You serious?"

"Damn straight. I love to fish and know what I'm doing. You yourself said most of the guys aren't rocket scientists. A good old boy like me might be more convincing than you are."

"That's not a bad idea, White-ly. Let me think about it."

Barry took a sip of bourbon and recommenced rocking. "When you get back to DC, ask that Yankee congressman if he likes deep sea fishing. If he says yes, you've got your answer."

The Yankee congressman did, in fact, say yes, and within a matter of weeks, Bubba had a brand new 62-foot Viking Sport fishing yacht docked at the Morningstar Marina. Barry had to give the man credit. When it came to shake downs and spending money, Bubba was in his own league. The aptly named *Select Committee* was a beautiful ship with a luxurious stateroom, two bedrooms, every electronic gadget available, and a cruising speed of 40 knots; she had to cost millions. Word of the yacht made the rounds in DC, and Barry became his proxy, taking pols out deep sea fishing. Within a year, Bubba pronounced the yacht had brought in nearly double its cost in kickbacks and swayed multiple votes in the direction of his own pet bills. Bubba would have taken up fishing had it not been for his unmanly bouts of sea sickness.

And now the yacht just might take Barry to freedom.

The Wilmington River flowed into Wassaw Sound before meeting the Atlantic. On the southern shore of the sound lay Wassaw National Wildlife Refuge, a marshy area with creeks and inlets favored by birdwatchers. He took out his binoculars to scan the shoreline for a secluded location away from fisherman and nature lovers. Finding a spot that looked good, he slid the *Select Committee* close to shore, tucked among reeds at the mouth of a small creek. After a quick circle on deck to make sure he was out of view, Barry set anchor.

With supplies stashed in the hull over a year ago, he spent the next 30 minutes painstakingly changing the boat registration numbers, hull ID, and most importantly, the yacht name. It didn't have to be perfect, just good enough to throw off a binoculars-toting Coast Guard Seaman. Twice he heard the whine of an approaching outboard motor and quickly scrambled to his decoy fishing pole just in case the passing boat saw him hidden in the shallows. Once his handiwork was complete, he put on a heavy windbreaker and baseball cap before pulling anchor and backing the yacht out of the marsh reeds into the sound. To his relief, his secret mission had not drawn the attention of any boaters.

Three Coast Guard stations dot the Georgia coast from Savannah to Brunswick. Just across the sound, Tybee Island also housed their air station. It's impossible to spend time on the Georgia coast without spotting the familiar orange and white Coast Guard helicopters patrolling the length of the state about a mile out to sea. The air patrols were even heavier further south near St. Mary's naval base. Just beyond the helicopter zone, Coast Guard Cutters watched the open seas. Barry only had to elude this net for 12 miles until he hit international waters.

The weather was a blessing and a curse. A bright blue sky and relatively smooth waters provided miles of clear visibility. He'd be able to see a cutter well in advance, giving him the option of slowly altering his course to maintain a safe distance. Of course, it also made it easier for the Coast Guard to spot his boat, plus he still hadn't figured out how to evade a helicopter.

Barry zipped up his windbreaker against the autumn chill and swirling wind as he manned the helm. At times, the open captain's bridge could be brutal. Obviously, if Bubba had experience with wildly fluctuating weather on open water, he would have sprung the extra cash for a secondary helm in the stateroom or at least the enclosed version of the captain's bridge. But today, Barry was grateful for the open bridge's panoramic view of the sea and sky.

Once past the last channel entrance buoy, Barry opened up the engines, and the yacht roared to life. Rather than head north up the coast in the general direction of Newport News, Barry headed due east. With the boat's speed, the direct route would get him to international waters in 30 minutes.

Old wounds run deep, and he'd been waiting nearly 50 years to get even with the rich, self-entitled scumbag. Yet, he never thought it would happen without his own personal demise. Not that he was anywhere near being in the clear. In fact, he thought his odds were 20% at best, but at least he'd go down on his own terms. Dying at sea or at the hands of arresting authorities was a far better fate than being imprisoned with Bubba Baker as a cellmate.

And he knew Bubba would sacrifice him the second he felt the walls closing. Barry figured his only chance of survival had been to strike first, which was why his first stop after fleeing the compound was to deliver the two envelopes from his safe to *The Macon Telegraph*. Barry loved *The Shawshank Redemption* and became fixated on the concept of anonymously delivering incriminating evidence against Bubba Baker while making a hasty escape. But, the similarities ended there. Unlike Andy Dufresne in *Shawshank*, Barry was guilty as sin and had the death penalty waiting for him if caught. And there was no way he was going to loll around a beach in Mexico, fixing up an old boat. He already had the boat, and his sights were set much further south.

What Barry didn't know was how long it would take for his envelope to make it to the GBI. He figured as soon as they read its contents, he'd be on the most wanted list of every law enforcement agency in the country. He was counting on three hours before the posse was set on his tail and probably two more after that until they made it to the marina. If they actually believed Newport News as his destination, they'd start north buying him some extra time.

All that wishful thinking went out the window once he spotted the helicopter off on the horizon. Barry knew he was toast. Hoping not to look like a guilty man running from the law, he eased off the throttle and tried to focus his binoculars on the helicopter through the swelling seas. It was headed directly toward him, making it impossible to identify. He crunched further under the bridge's canopy to block the overhead eyes from getting a good look at him. His hopeful optimism dissolved into fatalistic panic.

He stood frozen with indecision as the helicopter's distance quickly shrank. At the last second, the helicopter banked into a broad turn, revealing not the orange and white of the Coast Guard but markings of a local excursion company. Even on the open seas, rich people inflicted unwarranted angst on Barry. The helicopter made a wide circle around the yacht, most likely for the paying tourists to admire the vessel or just because the pilot wanted to be a jerk. Barry resisted the temptation to flip them off.

After two circles, the helicopter sped off north up the coast. Trembling, Barry slumped down into the captain's chair, grateful he didn't have to retreat to the cabin for an underwear change. He had never been more scared in his life.

He regrouped and opened the throttles back up. The helicopter experience gave him a new perspective as he no longer wanted to know if he was being chased. The anxiety was simply too much. He'd address the situation if they caught up to him, but for now, he'd focus only on the seas ahead. Determined, he manned the helm, spread his legs into a solid standing position for the pounding seas, and continued due east.

The GPS announced Barry had crossed into international waters—the demarcation point where, theoretically, he was beyond the reach of US jurisdiction. In his dreams, reaching this threshold would be reason to celebrate his good fortune, but Barry felt no relief. He stood firm at the helm with the hammer down. Finally, after nearly an hour and half, he was 50 miles from the US and slowed the yacht to a drift.

Barry returned to his secret stash of escape supplies and came out with a large mesh bag and a spare anchor. He methodically placed every electronic device that might signal his location—the GPS system, emergency beacon, satellite dish and receiver, even his cell phone—into the mesh bag. Of the yacht's sophisticated electronics, only the depth finder and radio remained. Barry tied the bag to the anchor and threw it overboard, watching it sink with no regrets.

Just as old wounds run deep, old flames rarely extinguish. Barry returned to the helm and spun the newly christened *Amazon Princess* until the compass pointed south.

57.

"**G**overnor, I wish you'd come back in and watch the video again," Jose called from the dining room.

"In a minute, Jose." Skip quickened his pace around the mansion's kitchen island. He had no desire to watch Bubba's morning press announcement one more time.

Governor Murray hadn't paced the island since last Sunday's bombing and reckoned it must have something to do with waiting for return phone calls. Director Sterling called Skip with news of the latest bombing a little after 6:00 a.m. this morning and promised constant updates. Yet, here it was at 10:00 a.m. with nary a peep from his friend. Even worse, Pete wasn't answering his cell phone. Skip changed direction, hoping a counterclockwise path might change his luck.

Jose appeared in the doorway to the kitchen. "That pacing will only get you more riled up. Please come watch the video. It's important."

Skip made one last circle then dutifully followed Jose into the dining room. Only Jose and several aides were stationed in the mansion today, as this morning's bombing, in proximity to a noted

347

politician, set the security team on edge. Out of an abundance of caution, access to the Governor's Mansion would be limited. Jose ushered him to a chair directly in front of the computer.

"I'm going to play it again but with the audio muted. I want you to watch his mannerisms instead of hearing his words." Jose leaned over Skip's shoulder and clicked the mouse.

The video started with Bubba exiting his DC brownstone and taking the first flight of steps to a waiting microphone. He was flanked by two men, clearly Secret Service, who then took positions to each side about a half pace behind him. Bubba looked directly into the camaras stationed at a safe range out on the sidewalk. He stood with both hands clasped behind his back as he spoke, and only once did he move his arms to briefly check a note card in his right hand. After less than a minute, he retreated to his house.

Skip sat back in the chair and tried to sound interested. "He looked scared."

"Terrified is more like it," Jose agreed.

"Understandable, if you ask me. His life's just been threatened," Skip added.

"That's where I disagree with you."

Skip spun in his chair to get a good look at Jose.

"Something else is going on, Governor. I've observed this man for years, and when he's scared, he gets defiant. And when he gets defiant, he uses hand gestures. Pointing, fist clenching, you name it. He didn't budge today which tells me something's up."

Skip spun back to the computer. "Run it again."

An aide clicked the mouse, scrolling the video back to the beginning. As a stoic Bubba left the brownstone, a ringing cell phone interrupted the viewing. Skip sprang from his chair and waddle-ran to the kitchen.

"Pete! About time. I've been going stir crazy here."

"Sorry, Governor, but I just got back from Macon. You need to see something. How quickly can you get to headquarters?"

"I'm leaving now." Skip hung up before asking for details.

"Jose! Grab your things. We're going to GBI headquarters!" Skip bolted out the back door before his trusted aide could respond.

Director Sterling met the governor's security team at the GBI's front entrance, leading Skip and Jose up to a second-floor conference room. Unlike last Sunday's meeting, the room was small with only four people waiting for their arrival. Skip didn't recognize three of the four occupants. A man stood next to a whiteboard holding a blue marker in one hand and an eraser in the other. A middle-aged woman sat at the conference table, diligently entering instructions from the man in a laptop. Two other men sat at the table, a young man, a kid really, and the Black agent who spoke up during the previous meeting. All four stopped what they were doing when Skip entered the room.

"You know the governor," Director Sterling announced. "This is Jose Perez from his staff. Why don't you gentlemen take a seat?"

"I think I'll stand if you don't mind." With no island to pace, he began rocking back and forth from his heels to his toes.

Skip and Jose remained at the end of the conference room table near the door while Sterling moved over to join the man at the whiteboard. The three other attendees didn't move a muscle.

Sterling picked up a manila envelope from the table. "Governor, I'll get right to the point. We're in possession of information that might be a damning indictment on Congressman James Baker."

"What?" Skip blurted enthusiastically, his voice rising an octave. He instantly regretted his inability to display a modicum of concerned shock.

Sterling did his best to ignore the governor's reaction. "It seems an individual associated with Baker took detailed notes and documented a whole list of supposed crimes committed by the congressman."

Skip quickly took a seat at the head of the conference table before his legs gave out. He tried to regain his composure. "Are you sure about this? Fill me in," he said, clasping his shaking hands in his lap.

Sterling held the envelope as if presenting to a jury. "Shortly after this morning's bombing, two envelopes were left on the doorstep of *The Macon Telegraph*, one addressed to me and the other to a local reporter. When the reporter saw the contents, she called us, and I immediately took the helicopter down to get it. Unfortunately, the newspaper refused to relinquish their copy. We'll get to that in a minute, but we are now in possession of potential evidence. This is a copy. We have the original undergoing analysis by our team."

Skip excitedly rubbed his hands on his knees under the table and leaned forward until his stomach hit the table. He felt like a little kid at his birthday, waiting for the singing to stop so he could blow out candles and eat cake. He mentally begged Pete to stop with the theatrics and finish the damn song. The director must have read his mind.

"The accusations in this document include murder, kidnapping, embezzlement, pedophilia, and possibly more. We haven't had a chance to read all of its contents, let alone confirm its veracity."

Skip suppressed the urge to leap from his chair in celebration of the Almighty's divine intervention. He subconsciously burrowed his butt deeper in the chair, trying to stay calm. "Holy shit, I don't believe it." Controlling his body was hard enough, so no way he could stop his tongue from swearing. "Who wrote it? Is it reliable?"

"A gentleman by the name of Barry Whitley," the Black agent to the right of Skip spoke. "He's a childhood friend of the congressman who grew up on the Baker property. He moved west as a child and had a very successful real estate career in New Mexico, Arizona, and Nevada. He played a small role in the Utah ranger dispute with the federal government years ago, and that's where we believe he renewed his acquaintance with the congressman. For the last five years, he's been back in Georgia acting as the leader for the American Liberation Militia. The man has no criminal record, and aside from his questionable work with the ALM, appears to have lived a nondescript life. More importantly, in our investigation we've found direct financial ties between the ALM and Congressman Baker."

Skip tried to be tactful. "So, maybe not the most credible witness, but someone who just might have access to information."

The director agreed, "That's our inclination."

The governor sat dumbfounded relishing the moment. Only Jose's gentle nudge of his chair from behind brought him back to those in the room waiting for the governor to speak. The political pendulum had now swung back to Skip. He sat up with shoulders back and spoke with authority. "What will the GBI do next now that we have this information?"

Sterling nodded at the unknown man standing with him. "I'm Chief Inspector Carraway, Governor." The man pointed at the whiteboard. "Most of our team is on-site awaiting instructions based on the direction the document takes us. We're also working, in conjunction with the FBI, to gather evidence at the scene. Heavy rains have started down there which might slow our progress but will reduce the risk from the forest fire. O'Reilly and Knudson here in the room are leading our research and cyber investigation. They've done preliminary work on the ALM, and the document will be a major area of their focus moving forward."

The governor met eyes with the two men seated with him at the table. He hoped they were both damn good at their jobs.

Director Sterling continued, "Our first concern was making sure you knew the situation. If even one item of this is true, it will cause major waves, and we didn't want you to be blindsided. Secondly, I believe you know the publisher of *The Macon Telegraph*. We need for you to contact him and stress the importance of not going public with what they know. Even if it's for 24 hours, we can't afford for any of this to get out until we've had a chance to investigate."

"Consider it done." Skip excitedly wrung his hands under the table. "Frank and I have been friends for years, and he's a reasonable man,"

"Lastly, we felt it was important for you to be prepared in case the information we're in possession of turns out to be true."

Skip bit the inside of his cheeks to suppress his smile. "I appreciate you bringing this to my attention. Speaking on behalf of all Georgians, if you prove any of this to be true, then we must prosecute to the full extent of the law." The governor hoped they'd nail Bubba's ass to the wall.

58.

"**I**s she asleep?" Pam asked, her stomach grumbling from being unable to eat breakfast or lunch.

Scott checked the rearview mirror and saw Andrea slumped in the backseat with her chin resting on her chest. "Sure looks like it."

Pam nervously wrung her hands as Scott drove Roger's pickup truck on the flyover ramp leading off I-285 to I-85 south of Atlanta. The authority's call this morning confirming the safe recovery of Tom was a tremendous relief, but the events of last night were cause for a new set of concerns. The dramatic nature of the middle Georgia bombing had sent the press into a new frenzy, and the potential repercussions on her family were impossible to ignore.

Andrea stumbling around like a zombie when they returned the motorcycle only set Pam further on edge. Andrea was so tired, at least that's what Pam hoped, that she needed help completing the final paperwork. They hadn't heard a word out of her since getting back in the truck, capping off a morning where Pam had been pushing Andrea for details to no avail.

"Why do you think she won't tell us about what happened last night?"

"Probably for our own protection," Scott answered. "What's that term?"

"Plausible deniability," Pam said. "I guess I just don't get it. We're in the middle of this thing too. Shouldn't we know?"

Scott shrugged his shoulders. "Maybe it's an Army thing. Tom never talked about his missions. Maybe it's just the way they're trained."

"I guess so. But I'm so worried about her. She was acting so strange this morning."

"Maybe it's just an adrenaline crash. She's been pushing so hard this week and has to be spent. And with last night being such a success, she can finally rest."

"You're probably right."

Pam squirmed in the seat until she was comfortable. Now that she thought about it, she also was exhausted from the long week. She stared out the windshield at a section of Georgia she rarely traveled. Probably the last time she went this way was when they took the kids to the Renaissance Festival. They were little then... maybe that might be a fun family outing for teenagers. Her eyes drifted shut...

Pam woke with a start, temporarily disoriented.

Scott reached over and touched her knee. "You're okay, Sis. You just fell asleep."

Her mouth was dry. "I don't feel okay. Where are we?"

"We're about ten minutes from Benning."

Pam contorted her torso to look over the headrest at the dozing Andrea. She wasn't ready to say goodbye to her savior but knew it was time. Andrea provided a calming strength, and Pam worried a nagging unease would set in once she was gone. She sat back straight in the seat.

"You think this is really going to work?" she asked Scott.

"I don't know. Maggie's confident which gives me some comfort, but the next couple of days will tell."

"Which is why you two need to be really careful," Andrea spoke up from the back. "Watch what you say to everyone. You might even look for an excuse to leave town for a while. Tell folks you're taking Tom someplace for treatment or something like that."

Pam craned back in the seat to look at her friend. "And what about you? Are you going to be okay?"

Andrea smiled. "I'll be fine, but I'm not taking any chances. That's why I'm flying back to Bragg on an Army bird and have accepted a transfer to Fort Magsaysay. After today, we won't see each other for some time."

Pam was disappointed, but her friend's safety was more important. "Fort what? Where's that?"

"It's in the Philippines, about as far away as I can get. It's mostly a training facility, which is good. I've had enough action for a while."

Scott looked at Andrea in the mirror. "That's some news. Did you want the transfer?"

Andrea shook her head. "Not really, but after we set the plan with Maggie, I had a feeling distance might be a good idea. I requested the transfer that evening, and it came in this morning. I'll be at Bragg long enough to pack.""

Pam reached over the seat, and the women clasped hands. "I don't know how I can thank you, Andrea."

"You can thank me by keeping your head low and watching your brother." Andrea reached up and gave the back of Scott's head a playful swat. "Both of them!"

Fort Benning's entrance came into view, and Scott pulled Roger's truck into the visitors' lot outside the gate. The three climbed out, and Pam gave Andrea a long hug; she didn't want to let go. Andrea gave Scott a hug then threw her bags over her shoulder.

"I know I told you to watch what you say, but if you see Seamus, tell him I enjoyed his company and would've called him if not for the transfer." She gave them both a little wink.

Pam watched Andrea enter the Fort Benning gate, and just like that, she was gone.

59.

"**I**'m getting a cup of coffee. You want another Coke?" Seamus asked his conference room partner.

"That would be great. Let me dig out some change."

"Don't worry about it, Karl. I got you covered." After nearly 14 hours in the conference room together, the two had come to an easy rapport. Seamus liked the kid, and he definitely was still a kid. Barely 23, Knudson lived with his parents, needed maybe one razor for an entire year, and had rosy cheeks as if he was chronically embarrassed or Christmas elves dominated his family tree. But in front of a computer, the guy was an ace.

Seamus knew his status with Carraway was on shaky ground, so he didn't object when told he had to work with Karl. Research isn't a team sport, and the idea of having to explain his methods or alter his thought process just to appease a mere lad was annoying. But it turned out their skills were similar and complimentary instead of competitive. Simply put, they made each other better. Carraway matching the two together was either genius or pure dumb luck.

Seamus left the windowless conference room. Looking down the hall past the cube farm, the floor to ceiling windows confirmed the day had lapsed and it really was 8:30 at night. The day had flown by, proving the adage about time flying when you're having fun.

The break room coffee pot was drained once again. Seamus started a fresh pot and inserted a dollar in the vending machine for his partner's Coke.

"Evening, O'Reilly," Carraway greeted him merrily.

"Evening, boss. Just started a new pot. Should be done shortly."

"Excellent!" Carraway boomed.

It had been a long time since Seamus saw his boss in such a good mood.

"You and Knudson are doing great work. I think your last update might be just what we needed."

"Really?" Seamus hoped so. He and Karl didn't know what to do next if it wasn't.

"Yup," Carraway finished rinsing his mug and leaned back against the counter. "The FBI's seeking the indictment as we speak. Went to a federal judge this time since the state court was being so uncooperative. Between the bodies we found and the crazy doc's admission, you'd think any reasonable judge would agree that most of what that Whitley guy wrote was true. Guess Bubba has more people looking out for him than we thought."

"That's great news. We sure thought it closed the loop." Seamus wasn't surprised about Bubba's sway.

Carraway snatched the pot before it was finished brewing, the still-dripping coffee sizzled on the hotplate. "I'll come let you guys know as soon as I hear something." He put the pot back and quickly left the break room.

Seamus watched the last drops plummet into the pot as the brew cycle ended. He was satisfied with how the investigation played out. Bubba and his ALM gang were amazingly brazen dirtbags and deserved whatever fate awaited them. But he still couldn't wrap his mind around them being the so-called eco bombers too. Yes, the

FBI found traces of the same manufacturer's plastic explosives in the work van, yet Karl had his doubts about the van's registration and the billboard schematics embedded in the ALM website. Blowing up billboards didn't make much sense to begin with, and why white supremacists would do such a thing was even more inexplicable.

Seamus filled his mug and thought about the meeting with the governor earlier in the day. It was obvious there was no love lost between the governor and the congressman. Seamus figured the crimes committed in Middle Georgia were so heinous that the eco-terrorism was about to become a minor subplot.

He returned to the Valdosta Conference Room to find Karl still hard at work cyber sleuthing.

"Here's your Coke," Seamus slid the can across the table. "Just ran into Carraway, and he thinks we got the congressman. We'll know if there's an indictment soon!"

Karl looked up from his computer. "On everything?"

"I didn't ask for specifics," Seamus admitted.

"If not, I think I just found something." Karl began to hit his keyboard again. "I've been trying to trace the billboard schematics on the ALM website, and I'm pretty sure it's a recent addition. I haven't been able nail down an exact date, but I'm betting it was after the bombings."

An image popped into Seamus's head. It was after his first visit to Duke's when he sat in his car and watched Maggie reach across the table to take Scott's hand…Scott, the man who had provided Seamus with a schematics file eerily similar to what Karl found on the ALM website. The vision filled him with tenderness and warmth, not of cold-bloodedness.

"Let's take a break until we hear from Carraway. We've been at it all day. Maybe that can wait."

The kid stopped typing. "Yeah, you're right. It can probably wait." Karl cracked open the can. "Thanks for the Coke."

Seamus leaned back in his chair, plopped his feet up on the conference table, and raised his coffee mug in a toast. "Cheers!"

Karl raised his Coke can. "And cheers to you." The kid emulated Seamus by resting his feet up on the table. "I haven't been here that long, and this was my first time getting pulled in to something like this. It was pretty fun."

"I've been at this for some time, Karl, and have never seen anything quite like this." Seamus remembered being inexperienced and green when he first started as Michigan State Police. Karl was actually very similar to that young Seamus—analytical, loved to drill down into details in search of hidden gems, able to get lost for hours in the minutia of books and computers, but still a decent conversationalist who knew how to interact with fellow humans. He never had a mentor, but maybe he could be Karl's.

"What gets me," Karl said, "was how they pulled off this elaborate scheme for all these years then made such a stupid mistake. Why Dave Baker sent that email this morning is beyond me."

"I think it was a couple of things." Smitten with the mentor idea, he adopted a professorial tone. "Rich and powerful men, and politicians especially, begin to think they're beyond reproach. They get so used to calling the shots and getting their way that they become convinced they're untouchable. Think about that president and the intern. That guy's smart as a whip yet still believed his position let him do whatever he wanted. Bubba's not nearly as smart, so in some ways it's surprising he got away with it for so long."

Seamus was digging the elder statesman role. "And then he panicked. The whole idea of getting caught was so foreign that he didn't realize the ramifications of the email. He'd successfully worked the system for so long that he thought he could manipulate law enforcement too. I'll bet you a hundred bucks his brother had no idea what he was sending. He just did what Bubba told him."

Despite Seamus's lecture, the kid was right. It basically was a careless mistake. Karl found the email, and then the two of them carefully dissected the contents. The goal was clearly to shift responsibility away from Bubba to his brother and Barry Whitley—why Dave sent the email remained a mystery—but it ended up giving Seamus and Karl the missing link. They'd spent hours searching the financial records of both the ALM and the American Natural Preservation only to run into dead ends. Dave Baker's email mentioned a Russian bank known for notorious dealings. Like bloodhounds, Seamus and Karl only needed that first sniff to set off on the trail.

"He must not be very bright if he didn't know what was in that file." Karl took another swig of Coke.

"Or just very trusting," Seamus added. "All it takes is one mistake."

"Like putting your feet up on the conference table!"

Seamus and Karl quickly swung their feet to the ground and spun to a beaming Carraway in the doorway.

"It's done, gentleman. The judge signed the arrest warrants. First thing in the morning, the Baker brothers will have some unwelcome visitors. The judge agreed to keep the order sealed until 6:00 a.m. We don't want them to get any advance notice. You guys did great today. Thanks for your work."

Compliments were rare from Carraway, and Seamus knew his words were sincere. "Thanks, sir. It was quite a day."

"Yes, it was. Go ahead and pack it in for the night, and swing by my office before you leave, O'Reilly." Carraway went whistling up the hallway.

Seamus and Karl didn't waste any time packing up their computers and notes. Both were ready to head home.

"Karl, it's truly been my pleasure working with you." Seamus stuck out his hand.

"It was great, Seamus. Thanks for showing me the ropes today. Hope we get to work together more often."

The men shook hands. Karl turned right toward the exit, and Seamus went left to Carraway's office.

"You wanted to see me, Bill?"

"Take a seat." Carraway's demeanor was almost serene. Seamus had never seen anything like it from his boss.

"O'Reilly, you did a great job today."

"Thank you, sir, but it really was a team effort. Karl's a sharp kid, and we wouldn't have been able to do anything without the information the team fed us from the field. Those guys did a great job too."

Carraway smiled. "We shined today, no doubt about it. But the governor singled you out specifically to the director."

"Really?" That was the last thing Seamus expected to hear. "I don't know why. I didn't say much in today's meeting, and surely he doesn't know what I did with Karl."

Carraway explained, "The governor is a politician, so he judges people, not only on their actions and words, but on the positive impact on his job. So, while your work today was notable, what you did earlier this week was more important to him."

"Now you've really got me confused. I thought I was in the doghouse after my Louisiana trip. How can I go from the doghouse to the penthouse?"

The comment elicited a chuckle from his boss. "Forget Louisiana. That was nothing. Turns out the Worthington family was grateful for how you handled the investigation of their family this week. Not only did you help our investigation, but you built their trust. That's some feat when dealing with potential suspects. Anyway, the brother-in-law, Roger Fischer, is a big political donor, and he called the governor asking a favor and the governor called Sterling. The family's asked that you personally take over the handling of

Tom Worthington. Make sure he's getting treated okay and help expedite his deposition and release from the hospital. They're concerned about his health and say he doesn't do well with people he doesn't trust. The family thinks he'll be comfortable with you and speed up the transition to their custody."

"How about that? I didn't see that coming." Seamus liked the idea of an excuse to stay connected with the Duke's gang.

"Building trust with suspects is a talent, O'Reilly. Would you be interested in more field work?"

Seamus didn't have to give it thought. Even though the week was entertaining, he preferred to learn sordid details from the safety of his cube. The Worthingtons were an exception. Most suspects were conniving hosebags, and he didn't really want to breathe the same air. "Thanks for the offer, but I like what I'm doing."

"Excellent!" Carraway slapped his desk. "You're damn good at what you do, and I'd like to keep you there. Had to ask though. Governor Murray gave the director a hard time when he heard you had a desk job."

"But I would like to make an exception for this Worthington assignment. That still on the table?"

"Absolutely! Worthington's been admitted to the VA hospital in Dublin. Go home and get a good rest then head down early tomorrow. They should be done evaluating Worthington in the morning, so we set you up to meet with the VA staff at 11:00 for their prognosis. If the docs say he's doing okay, then we'll schedule a formal deposition. I'll have more details for you tomorrow."

Seamus stood up. "Okay, and thanks. I'm actually looking forward to helping the guy out."

"Nice job again, O'Reilly. And the governor will appreciate you doing this."

Seamus paused at the door. "What about the protest tomorrow? I'm supposed to be in Atlanta as a monitor."

Carraway gave a shooing wave. "Don't worry about it. We've got it covered."

Seamus took the stairs to the ground floor two at a time, fired up over his amazing break. Not only would he be able to keep tabs on Maggie and Scott, connecting with Tom would put Seamus one step closer to Andrea. He still questioned the trio's true motives, but at least for right now, he didn't really care.

60.

arry's gait was that of a drunken man despite not having a drink in several days. That was about to change even though it was only 9:00 on Saturday morning. He bobbed and weaved across the dock of Turtle Bay Marina on unsteady legs after more than 24 hours piloting the *Amazon Princess*. His chapped cheeks stung from the wind that whipped through the open bridge during the excursion.

His professionally-faked Canadian passport worked when he refueled in Nassau, so he decided to stick with it during his break on Turks and Caicos. Depending on the news coming out of the US, he'd either catch a nap or stay until Sunday to regain his strength. He still thought ditching all of the GPS electronics had been a wise move even though he was walking into the harbor office with no forewarning on how big a story Georgia might be.

The harbor office was little more than a hut at the end of the gangplank. At least it was on solid ground. The old harbormaster opened Barry's passport and confirmed his picture matched that of Marvin Williams from Hamilton, Ontario, Canada. He flipped to the proper page to stamp Turks and Caicos and paused, looking up at Barry.

"Says here you just arrived in Nassau late yesterday. You travel all night?"

Barry thought his British accent was lovely, and the white of his eyes were a brilliant contrast to the dark, weathered skin of a man who worked outside in the tropics.

Barry shrugged. "Let's just say there's a woman involved." He hoped the stories were true of Caribbean ports treating wealthy guests with discretion. Docking a 62-foot Viking put Barry in that category.

"Say no more," the man stamped his passport. "The dock fee for a yacht your size is $200 per day."

"US or Canadian?" Barry wanted to stay in role.

"US," the man's white teeth were equally brilliant, "but I'd take $400 if you want to pay in Canadian."

Barry pulled a wad of cash out of his pocket and stripped off three Benjamins. "Extra one's for you."

The man put two $100 bills in the money pouch and the third in his pocket. "Thank you, Mr. Williams."

"You're welcome. Any place for me to grab a bite?"

"Restaurant is right over there." The harbormaster pointed to a low-slung building surrounded by palms.

Barry thanked him and followed the sandy path to the restaurant. He filled his lungs with the fresh island air so different than the heaviness of Georgia's intracoastal marshes. The warm tropical sun felt great on his skin, but he bypassed the small patio, hoping the bar might have a TV. The building had three sets of open French doors, and he veered to the bar entrance on the right. It was what he expected on a Caribbean island—terracotta-tiled floors, ceiling fans, light blue walls with professional photos of local beauty.

The lone occupant was a bartender whose back was turned to the empty stools as he watched soccer on one of the bar's two TVs.

Heavy British accents excitedly announcing the game bounced off the small bar's walls. The screech of the bar stool on the tile floor captured his attention.

"Sorry, chap, didn't hear you come in. Get you something?"

"I'll have a Bloody Mary, Tito's if you've got it."

"Sure do. Coming right up." The bartender began making Barry's cocktail all the while keeping a watchful eye on the soccer match.

"Who's playing?" Barry asked, not that it mattered to him.

"England vs. Romania in a World Cup qualifier. We should be kicking their arse, but the bloody Romanians are being quite pesky." The bartender stuck in a celery stalk before setting the cocktail in front of Barry. "Take it you're not a football fan."

"Not really. Feel free to go back to the game, or match, or whatever you call it. I'm fine just sitting here with my drink."

"Let me know if you need anything." The bartender turned his attention back to the TV.

Barry pretended to look straight forward while the corner of his eye focused on the TV at opposite end of the bar. Though the sound was muted, the continuous banner crawl and video suggested the CNN report was on the banking industry. Barry took a heavy gulp of his Bloody Mary and checked back in on the bartender who was flinching and jerking each time a running player kicked the black and white ball. Barry would rather watch golf.

Glancing back at CNN, a solemn news anchor filled the screen with a picture of James "Bubba" Baker superimposed in the top right-hand corner. It cut to an aerial video of the compound; Barry could no longer just pretend to watch.

The crater was massive. Law enforcement officials dotted the field, placing little flags in the ground to identify possible evidence. He could see the hole in the roof of his house where the armory projectile penetrated his bedroom. The debris field was centered within 50 yards of the crater, yet some chunks of the building were thrown well beyond his house and the shacks. He found the destruction to be extremely satisfying.

The aerial view then expanded beyond the epicenter, exposing the forest. His glee became despair—the fire's devastation was massive. At least half of his beloved woods lay in charred ruins. Blackened tree trunks were scattered like spilled toothpicks. It broke his heart. He immediately felt guilt about leaving Moon behind and hoped she was in good hands.

His thoughts of Moon ceased once the drone's video zoomed in on a specific area of the charred woods. Yellow crime tape cordoned off a square section where technicians in jumpsuits were inspecting five freshly dug holes. They found the bodies. Small tears rolled down Barry's face, stinging his chapped cheeks. Any sense of vindication he hoped to feel was negated by his own culpability. Immediately self-conscious, he peeked over to make sure the bartender was still engrossed with the game before quickly wiping away his tears with the cocktail napkin.

The video ended, returning to the talking news head. Bubba's picture in the right corner dissolved into a photo of Barry Whitley for the world to see. His body involuntarily convulsed, nearly tossing him from his barstool. He ran his hand through his thick gray hair, cursing at himself for not wearing a hat, sunglasses, or any type of disguise. Barry made sure the bartender didn't see it, chugged his cocktail, and tossed 20 bucks on the bar. Screening his face as he quietly slid off the stool, he casually made a hasty retreat.

"Thanks for the drink. Keep the change!" Barry called over his shoulder.

He returned along the sandy path acutely aware of his surroundings and gave the harbor office a wide berth when he passed. Barry avoided all eye contact with the two people he encountered on the dock, ignoring the friendly camaraderie usually displayed amongst fellow seafarers.

Safely ensconced in the stateroom of the *Amazon Princess*, Barry sat on the leather sofa pondering the reality of his predicament. Over the last 30 hours, his mind had been so wrapped up with his own survival, he'd conveniently forgotten the gravity of his sins. Barry took some solace knowing he never pulled the trigger, but his face on CNN was proof of his high-profile fugitive status.

He began pacing the stateroom. "You ran because you didn't want to die or spend the rest of your life in prison." Talking the problem out loud helped. "You've made it this far. Time to be smart. Think it through, Barry!"

He looked out the stateroom's window at the tranquil marina. "It's barely half full, and only four people caught a glimpse of me." He watched a sloop gently rock several slips over. "Caught a glimpse of me," he mumbled to himself. Suddenly inspired, he got to work.

The yacht's master bathroom was elegantly appointed with marble, brass fixtures, and a full walk-in shower. At least he could thank Bubba for spending his final days in luxury. And the shower felt amazing. He stood under the pulsating showerhead, massaging the kinks out of his shoulders while contemplating his plan. He then scrubbed away the sea salt grime before ceremoniously washing his hair one last time.

Barry wrapped a plush towel around his waist and studied himself in the mirror, trying to figure out how guys go about shaving their heads. What ensued might have been funny if not for the high stakes. With scissors from the galley, he whacked and hacked at his mane of wet gray hair, then used four disposable razors until his pate was smooth. The shocking white orb contrasted with his well-tanned face—he needed some sun on the fresh egg to even out the coloring. He did his best to stop the several nicks from bleeding, then swept up his mess and put on fresh clothes.

Returning to the stateroom, he rolled out maps on the dining table next to the galley. Using the parallel and nautical slide rules,

Barry calculated he'd covered 25% of his goal over the last 24 hours, leaving 2,700 miles to go. The yacht's fuel range was just over 500 miles, which he should be able to cover in about 12 hours if he pushed it. To have a remote chance, he'd need sufficient rest to keep his wits about him, and taking a break when he needed gas seemed to make the most sense. Since his Canadian passport had worked with a current and former British colony, he plotted a Commonwealth-centric course to Anguilla, Barbados, and Suriname. All were within the daily 500-mile target. It just might work.

Barry stood and stretched, his fingertips just touching the stateroom's ceiling. The journey of 2,700 miles would take six days. The Morningstar Marina dockhand stocked the yacht with enough supplies for five days with four passengers—he had enough food to skip additional provisioning, so the only human contact necessary would be to pay for dock fees and gas. Just one excursion in public at each marina. Barry chastised himself for not refueling the yacht as soon as he arrived in Turks. He'd have to go out in public a second time to get gas—a rookie mistake he wouldn't make again.

Thinking of provisions made him realize how starved he was. He microwaved three breakfast sandwiches and settled back on the couch with a bottled water. The food, Bloody Mary, and lack of sleep crept up on him. Barry had no choice but to rest before he cast off on his next leg. The couch made more sense. If he went to a bedroom, he'd sleep too long.

Barry kicked off his topsiders before stretching out. As he drifted off, his last thoughts were on the unlikelihood of surviving a fugitive's life.

61.

overnor Murray sprang from the dining room table for another cup of coffee. "Cue up the video again," he sang as he bounced into the kitchen.

"Haven't you seen it enough?" Jose pleaded.

"No," the governor yelled back. "Find that one from the local NBC affiliate. That's my favorite." Fresh mug in hand, Skip stood in the dining room doorway as an aide fiddled with the computer. Jose looked at him in total exasperation, but all Skip could do was smile and shrug.

"It's ready for you, sir." The aide moved from his seat.

Skip settled back in and hit play. The video was taken at sunrise, and the morning haze gave the picture a grayish graininess. Six heavily armed law enforcement officers strode up the front steps of Congressman Baker's Georgetown brownstone in full view of the TV cameras camped at the curb since his announcement of the reward earlier in the week. Two officers peeled off and trotted to the back of the house.

One of the four went to the front door and gave it a hearty pounding. The TV crew's microphone caught his announcement.

"Federal officers, we have a warrant for James Baker." He waited a minute and then pounded again.

Skip could barely contain himself. "I love this kid's expression," which he said each time they played the video for him. Skip didn't recognize the young aide or housekeeping employee who opened the door, looking like he was facing death. The officer brushed by him with the three others hot on his tail.

Skip drummed his fingers on the table in anticipation. "Here it comes, here it comes," he whispered to the others.

In the clip, the officers burst from the door with a disheveled Bubba Baker squealing like a baby.

"Yes!" Skip shouted. "God, I can't get enough of that!"

Two large officers bracketed a handcuffed Bubba, holding him up by his forearms as he stumbled down the steps. The microphones caught Bubba's frightened pleading. "Do you know who I am?! You're making a mistake!" His thrashing was useless against the beefy officers' clasp.

It was at this point Bubba noticed the bank of cameras documenting the scene. As one would expect from Bubba, the cameras transformed his fear into indignation. "You see this! This is what they're doing to Patriots! Real criminals are ruining our country, and they arrest me! A God-fearing public servant!"

Skip nudged Jose. "This might be my favorite part. Watch this."

The officers backed Bubba to the rear door of a black sedan, put their hands on his head, and pushed him in rear first.

"Just like on TV! You see that, Jose?! They shoved him in just like they do on cop shows!" He slapped his hand on the table. "Hot damn! That's just spectacular!"

Jose gave out an amused snort. "Okay, Governor, that's enough." His trusted aide reached over and shut the laptop.

"Just one more time?" the governor pleaded like a kid wanting one last ride at the county fair.

"No!" the room roared in unison before erupting in laughter.

"How about with the sound off? Don't you want to see what that's like?" Skip desperately wanted to revel in the moment.

Jose laughed even harder. "Maybe later. C'mon, we've got work to do!"

"Work? You said we're flying to Jacksonville for the Georgia-Florida game! This damn thing is finally over, and it's time I have some fun! Nothing better than watching the Dawgs kick some Gator butt. The way this morning's started, I got a feeling the good Lord's looking down on Georgia today."

"You're definitely going to the game," Jose reassured Skip. "I've got the plane lined up for 11:00 which gives us about 15 minutes before we head to the airport. I need you to do one last thing before we leave."

Skip excitedly sat up in the chair. "Okay, what is it? What do I need to do?"

Jose picked up a single sheet of paper from the table. "The press is waiting outside. I want you to go read a statement."

"That's it? I do that and we leave?" Skip was already out of the chair with Jose's statement in hand.

"That's it. As soon as you're done, we can leave."

Skip made a break for the stairs. "Fantastic! Let me go change!"

"No, Governor!" Jose caught up to Skip in the foyer. "You need to wear what you have on."

Skip was having none of it. "I'm tired of wearing this crisis uniform, and there's no way I'm going to the game without my lucky Dawg tie and red windbreaker."

"I wouldn't dream of sending you to the game like this." Jose gave Skip the once over. "I'll get your clothes and you can change on the way, but you need to wear what you have on while addressing the press."

Skip's enthusiasm hit a new level. "I can do that!." He bolted across the foyer to the front door.

"Wait!" Jose yelled out.

"What is it now, Jose?" he whined impatiently.

Jose met him at the door and gave Skip his dad look. "Governor, this is a solemn occasion, and you need to display the proper decorum to the press." Jose smiled at his boss. "So, wipe that goofy grin off your face before going out there."

62.

"Thank you, ma'am! Your donation is very generous. Most cars we receive aren't in such great shape. This means a lot to us."

Maggie was relieved the Make-A-Wish man was already waiting for her in the driveway when she pulled in from her last trip to Goodwill. Not only was she on a schedule, giving up the trusty Pathfinder was more emotional than she'd expected, and a drawn-out wait would only make it worse. "Thanks for coming so quickly," she said.

Maggie signed the title, handed him the keys, and shook his hand. She gave her car a loving tap on the hood and stood under the giant oak watching it disappear up the street. After it turned the corner, she went into her Scottdale bungalow to admire it one last time. She lived in the cute little house for three years and had been Maggie Parker for ten, but it was time to leave both behind. She'd miss her workshop and the retro kitchen most of all.

Maggie had 20 minutes before the cab was to pick her up at 11:00 a.m. She hauled her remaining belongings—a duffle bag of essentials and a satchel holding the meticulously-wrapped Iron

Eyes Cody autographed picture nestled next to her laptop—out to the front porch before locking the door and putting the key under the mat for Bob to get later. She apologized to Bob for the short notice and for leaving behind all of her furniture, so she left an envelope with six months' rent money on the kitchen counter as compensation. Bob was almost as emotional as Duke when she broke the news.

She sat in the rocker on the front porch soaking up the ambiance for her memories. The news of Bubba Baker's arrest was an incredible, unforeseen turn of events that planted second thoughts about leaving, but Maggie knew better. Sentimentality was a worthy emotion only if she kept it separated from her illegal activities. She willingly crossed that boundary with Scott and still didn't know if they'd escape the consequences. No, it was time to start over.

She saw the cab driving up the street and hauled her stuff down to the driveway.

The old man behind the wheel popped the trunk. "Need a hand with that?" he said unconvincingly through the rolled down window.

Maggie tossed everything in and closed the lid. "I'm good, thanks." She climbed into the backseat. "Avondale Marta station, please." Maggie stared at her hands so she wouldn't see the little bungalow as he drove away.

"Don't take this the wrong way," the cabbie piped up, "but you're a lot younger than most of my fares. Most people your age take Uber."

"No offense taken. Seems I lost my cell phone," Maggie lied. She wasn't about to tell him the truth—Maggie Parker no longer existed and Jen Miller had no intention of linking her identity to the Scottdale house. Until she was settled, Jen was paying with cash.

Once the billboard plan was set, she spent six months creating Jen Miller, a shorter window than her first identity change, but now she knew what she was doing. Unless she was willing to change her appearance forever, which she wasn't, the need of various photo IDs precluded altering her looks or using a disguise. No, she'd hidden in plain sight before, so no reason to think she can't again.

She paid the cabbie then schlepped her bags through the station's turnstile to the platform. It was a quick 15-minute ride to the Five Points station where she stored her bags in a locker on the mezzanine level. Jen took the Peachtree Street exit and headed south before turning left on Martin Luther King, Jr. Drive.

The Georgia State Capitol sat on a hill several blocks ahead on MLK. Jen had expected throngs on the streets but instead found more law enforcement officers and crowd-control barriers than people. Just to the east of the Capitol was Liberty Plaza, where the law enforcement presence was heavy. She heard a lone voice on a megaphone echoing up from the plaza.

Jen worked her way between two cops up to one of the crowd-control fences. Down in the Plaza below were maybe a dozen camo-wearing men with one guy screaming about white inequities through the bullhorn.

"Where is everyone?" Jen asked the cops.

"Kind of hard to hold a recruitment drive when you're in jail, don't you think?" the white cop answered.

"Sure, but what about everyone else? I read where people were coming from all over. There was supposed to be hundreds of them," she said, feeling the menacing look from the Black cop on her right.

"Don't tell me you're one of them," he spouted.

"Goodness, no," Jen said defensively. "I came down to protest against them!"

"Well, you'll need to go to Stone Mountain then," the white cop said. "Seems like most of them had a change of plans and decided to hold a barbeque instead."

"Someone said they're holding a weenie roast," the Black cop laughed. "How damn appropriate is that?!"

"You should go to the peace protest at Centennial," he added. "We hear there's a big crowd there."

"Thanks, guys. I think I will." Jen slipped out from between the two cops and headed back down MLK.

That explained the empty streets. The absence of armed white nationalists sucked the purpose out of Antifa's plans, so they were comfortably at home with their gaming consoles. Taunting bearded dudes in camo was fun, but heckling hippie Earth huggers just didn't have the same appeal. For Atlanta's sake, she was glad the potential confrontation fizzled out.

She retraced her route past the Five Points Marta station to Marietta Street which led to Centennial Park. The west wind whipped up the street into her face, causing Jen to pull her light jacket tight around her neck. For all her planning, she completely forgot to include a heavier coat.

Jen entered Centennial Park at the south end near the CNN center and heard a sound system speaker coming from the far end of the park. She walked by an empty Olympic Fountain as the chilly air discouraged even the heartiest children from frolicking in the pulsing geysers. The cops were right. A good-sized crowd was amassed at the north end of the park pressed up against an impromptu stage erected in front of the playground.

She stood at the back and strained to hear what the speaker was saying. She was comforted to see the majority of protesters toted environmentalist-themed signs with a healthy smattering of pro-immigration placards and posters announcing all politicians are corrupt convicts in training. The mood was somber, not festive. Jen decided to work her way towards the front to hear what was being said.

The crowd's mood got gloomier the closer she got to the stage. She now recognized the speaker as a preacher-turned-politician who was offering a lengthy prayer. It appeared the shocking revelations not only shooed away the white supremacists and sapped the fun out for Antifa, but also put a pall over this peace-loving crowd. The counter protest was a giant prayer service.

Jen made it to the stage right as a soft "Amen" echoed across the park. A new preacher-turned-politician, known for both his eloquence and stamina, took the microphone. He began by asking the crowd's prayers for those men who perished at the hands of the ALM and for mankind to treat one another with dignity. Jen thought it was a strong start then quickly lost interest as he droned on about some obscure Biblical character. She heard enough— paying respects was one thing, but she wasn't about to stick around for a sermon.

She nudged her way through the protesters, looking for a clear path to leave the park. On the far outer edge, several families stood watching the festivities while their kids romped on the grass and their dogs wandered unsupervised. Away from the watchful care of his owner, a spunky boxer began to display his amorous feelings toward a silken haired Collie.

How appropriate, Jen thought. Even in the midst of uncertainty and sorrow, basic animal pleasures were still possible.

As she left the park, a male voice screamed, "No, Boomer! Stop it!"

Jen fixated on the concept of simple pleasures the entire walk back to the Five Points station. Would she be able to enjoy them again? She'd know soon. If her new ID worked with the TSA agents at Hartsfield-Jackson Airport, then she just might have a chance.

63.

Scott tossed the Monday *Atlanta Journal-Constitution* on the table before sliding into his booth at Duke's. It was only his first official day of unemployment, and he already liked the perk of no firm schedule. The breakfast crush was well over, and he'd be able to read the newspaper at his leisure before his company arrived.

"Hi, I'm Kat."

Scott looked up to see a new waitress nervously twirling a lock of her long red hair.

"Good morning, Kat. I'm Scott."

"Yes, they told me about you. When Mr. Evans hired me, I didn't know I was replacing a star. Everyone loved Maggie. It's hard following a star." She went back to twirling the abused lock of hair.

"Starting any new job is hard. Just be yourself. I'm sure you'll do great." Scott couldn't remember the last time a woman was nervous with him. Usually, it was the other way around.

"Thanks. Can I get you anything?"

"I'm good with coffee for now. Thought I'd just hang out and read the paper for a while."

"Coming right up!"

He didn't know if she was enthused to get his coffee or just glad the awkward introduction was over.

Scott opened the paper to catch up on the events from middle Georgia. Yesterday, he bought the Sunday newspaper for the first time in years and devoured every single article on the bombing and subsequent arrests. Today he was mostly interested in learning the status of the suspects. A small box at the bottom of the front page directed him to page A-4.

Above the fold, seven side-by-side headshots of the men directly involved with the ALM stared back at him: James "Bubba" Baker, Dave Baker, Barry Whitley, Dr. Jon Shaw, Andy Nelson, Jerry Ray Reynolds, and Michael Pritchard. The copy below told him everything he wanted to know. Both Bakers, Shaw, Nelson and Pritchard were in custody with bond denied. The smirking Reynolds—the scrawny dude Andrea kicked the crap out of—was officially listed as dead. The FBI matched fingerprints from a severed, lighter-clutching hand to his military records. DNA matching linked the additional body parts recovered to Reynolds as well. Scott couldn't help but wonder if the only death was coincidence or if Andrea sought out the little shit weasel.

Scott then turned his attention to his new personal hero from Sunday's paper—Barry Whitley, the man responsible for bringing down Bubba Baker. As of this publication, the reporter wrote, "Whitley is still a fugitive." It was confirmed he set sail from Savannah in a yacht called *Select Committee*, but the Coast Guard had not tracked down his whereabouts. The initial report that his boat may have sunk 50 miles off the coast of Georgia had been proven false. Authorities were redoubling their efforts.

He was so engrossed in the newspaper that his coffee had gone cold. Like so many, he relied on the multiple electronic options available for getting the news and had forgotten the pleasure of reading the paper. No shrill voices or loosely verified facts, his brain processed information instead of someone interpreting a video clip. It was calmer, more civilized, and downright relaxing, particularly when the news was good.

He folded up the newspaper, wondering what he had gotten himself into. Not his role in one of the year's biggest news stories but in his willingness to become Tom's guardian. The last time he'd been responsible for his little brother, Scott was just a teenager trying to earn a couple of extra bucks babysitting for his parents. Back then, they had fun building Lego houses only to have Godzilla destroy the neighborhood, followed by watching *Star Wars* for the zillionth time. Tom seemed fine back then, just a little hyper. Certainly no one had an inkling of his inner turmoil.

Scott scratched his scalp. We all have issues, he thought. Some of them just get magnified with age and experience. Thinking about his brother, he caught himself rearranging the condiments on the table, just like Pam had done last week. The voice snapped him back to reality.

"Morning, Scott."

"Morning, Seamus." Scott half rose and shook the agent's hand. "Good to see you. Have a seat."

"You looked lost. Everything okay?"

"I'm fine, just a lot to process right now. Don't know if I'm ready to be my brother's keeper."

"You'll do great, and Tom's doing pretty good right now."

"Can I get you anything?" Kat appeared out of nowhere, menu and coffee pot in hand. Maggie would've been proud.

Seamus accepted the menu. "I'll order an early lunch here in a minute. Who are you? Where's Maggie?"

Scott felt bad for the self-conscious waitress. "Seamus, meet Kat. Kat, Seamus. Kat just started working here. She's Maggie's replacement."

"Maggie's gone?" Seamus couldn't hide his disappointment.

"Yes, but Kat here is the A-Team. Duke did great hiring her. She's already figured this place out." Scott smiled at the hair-twirling waitress. "Give us a minute. We have some business to discuss."

Kat put up a good show. "Okay. Just holler if you need anything."

"Maggie's really gone? Where'd she go?"

His concern puzzled Scott. He had no idea the agent had become so attached to her.

"Don't know for sure. She mentioned Knoxville or Bristol, someplace smaller and closer to the mountains. It's amazing she stuck around so long. The girl's a gypsy at heart."

"I'm so sorry, man. I thought you had a shot with her. Even I could tell the two of you had some chemistry going."

He was flattered. Seamus was upset about what Maggie's departure meant to him. "I admit I had a thing for her. Hell, most of the regulars felt the same. But it was unrequited love. I never really had a chance. Your concern means a lot. Thank you."

"I feel for you. It's weird having a crush when you're older, isn't it?" Seamus sighed.

"It is." Scott figured now was the best time to spin Andrea's story. "If it's any consolation, Andrea wanted me to say she enjoyed your company. Sorry she was transferred."

"Transferred?"

"Yeah, she wanted me to apologize for her not calling. As soon as she got down to our place on the coast, she got a call from Bragg telling her she was transferred to some base in the Philippines. We didn't even get to say goodbye."

His booth mate took it hard. "I'm sorry to hear that."

Scott had to change the subject. Any more discussion along these lines would be difficult to dance around. He jabbed at the newspaper's headline blaring Bubba's indiscretions with members of the Upchurch County High School pep squad.

"Is this stuff really true?" Scott asked.

"Afraid so. And those are only the ones that have come forward so far. That sleazeball's been at it for years. My guess is a bunch more will crawl out of the woodwork now. The evidence is pretty overwhelming. Bubba's dead meat."

"So, you guys have a pretty good case?"

Scott could tell Seamus was debating how much he should say.

"There's no way he'll wriggle out of this. The manifest and the girls are enough to bury him, but the doc's going be his biggest problem."

"The doc's talking?"

Seamus laughed. "The guy's clueless. He won't shut up! He thinks he's some kind of Albert Schweitzer and that one day his experiments will be heralded as medical breakthroughs. The ego on the man is monumental. He's convinced the more he talks, the more we'll be awed by his brilliance and just let him go. I honestly don't think he realizes he's a prime candidate for the death penalty."

"Maybe he is Albert Schweitzer. My brother's change has been pretty remarkable."

"Don't be giving the doc too much credit. I've gotten to know your brother. He's a smart, strong man that just needs to be in the right environment."

"I hope you're right. We figure our house down on Skidaway Island is where he'll do best."

"That's where you're taking him?"

"Yep, it'll give us both a fresh start. We might start doing fishing charters or eco tours, something to keep him outside and away from the clutter that gets him so worked up."

"I heard you quit your job. First Maggie and then you. Gotta admit, I was hoping to catch a beer with you one of these days."

"Don't be getting all soft on me now, Seamus. I'm sure one of these days we'll have a beer together. Now let's do this. I can't drag it out any longer."

Seamus reached into his coat pocket and pulled out an envelope. "Everything you need is in here. It's his release papers, list and timing of medications, and how best to contact us if you need anything."

"That's it? You're done with him? He won't need to testify when this goes to trial?"

"We videotaped his deposition, and we've got plenty of others who'll take the stand if necessary. You're good to go."

"Thanks for everything, Seamus. We really appreciate your help on this."

"You're welcome, Scott. It's been my pleasure. There is one more thing. I've got it out in the car, if you're ready."

Scott nodded and grabbed his coat. Seamus waved to Kat and said, "Hold the booth. I'll be right back in for lunch."

The two men went out to the agent's Interceptor parked in the back row. Seamus opened the rear passenger door and there, sitting erect and proper, was a big black Lab, tail eagerly swatting the seat.

"The dog!" Scott exclaimed.

"We pulled a couple of strings. She's all yours."

Scott was almost in tears. "This is huge, Seamus! This dog saved Tom's life!"

Seamus clipped a leash on Moon's collar and handed the end to Scott. "Now, don't you be getting all soft on me."

He gave Seamus a clumsy bro-hug. "I can't thank you enough."

The dog leapt from the car ready for adventure. Scott was ready for adventure too.

64.

The dockhand tossed the line to the deckhand as the ship drifted from the pier. The captain nudged the throttle a notch above idle, and she inched into the harbor.

It was a glorious day, the slight breeze kept the temperature tolerable, at least in his book, and sky and sea were both a rich blue. Only the diesel fumes and rap-like music damaged the ambience. Once the passenger ferry hit open water, the smell dissipated but the music lingered.

Seamus loved being on the water. He and his dad used to take his uncle's skiff up the Detroit River to Lake St. Claire, and once they even towed it to Port Huron for a brief jaunt on Lake Michigan. Seamus begged his dad to take the skiff out far enough where they couldn't see land. His dad, wisely, ignored the boy's cajoling. The only time he'd been out on the ocean was on an ancestry trip to Haiti searching for information on his great-grandmother. The tackiness of salt in the air was nothing like being on a lake.

He stretched out on the ferry bench, soaking in the warm Caribbean October sun on his bare legs and arms. He wiggled his sandal clad toes in celebration of the general sense of freedom he was feeling. His stress was shrinking, just like St. Kitts off the stern.

The ferry sign said the occupancy limit was 50 people, but he counted only 20 other passengers on the small island shuttle. Seamus and a handful of other tourists sat out in the sun near the rear of the boat. For the locals, the ride wasn't for pleasure. They sat on benches in the covered spartan cabin, toting household purchases more readily available on the larger St. Kitts. An enclosed bridge sat above the cabin where the invisible captain navigated the ferry toward the distant island cone of Nevis jutting out of the Caribbean. Seamus savored the moment.

A young deckhand approached him with a friendly greeting. "Welcome aboard, sir. We have over an hour before docking. May I get you a beverage?"

"Yes, thank you. I'd love a beer, if that's possible," Seamus told the deckhand, a mere teenager.

"Of course. The Captain's favorite is a local beer, Jolly Roger. We have the lager and IPA." The deckhand's smile was genuine.

"Sure hope the Captain's not drinking one now!" Seamus joked. "I'll take the lager, please."

The young man laughed. "You're in luck, sir. I'm quite confident the Captain is sober today. One Jolly Roger coming right up."

"Thank you. Before you run off, one more thing. What's with the music?"

"Oh, it's from the hit musical *Hamilton*. We'll be docking in Charlestown, Hamilton's birthplace. Your ferry ticket gets you $5 off admission to the museum. If you like the music, I can sell you a CD a lot cheaper than at the museum."

"Not for me. I find it grating. Can you play something else, something with more of an island feel? You know, with steel drums."

"I'll need to check with the Captain, sir. I don't know what he has. You want something like Jimmy Buffett?"

"Do I look like a Jimmy Buffett guy?" Seamus gave the deckhand his brother to brother look.

"No, you don't. You look more like a *Hamilton* guy," the kid cracked as he walked away.

Seamus couldn't help but admit the kid had a point. The whole *Hamilton* fad got under his skin. Seamus was the first to admit not everyone had a passion for history like he did, but Alexander Hamilton's story was fascinating and didn't need catchy tunes or a Broadway production to make his life interesting.

The grating music stopped. What came next was beautiful and totally unexpected—a twoubadou ballad. The sound took him back to his grandmother's house, listening to the stacks of scratchy records she played on the old RCA. She loved the traditional Haitian music and its simple messages of love and the need for lasting relationships. She translated the words as they laughed and twirled to the music in their cozy living room. To hear this utterly obscure music now, under these circumstances, had to mean something. A slight shiver ran up his spine.

"Here's your Jolly Roger, sir. The captain made a music selection he thought you might like."

"Thank you, and he's right, the music's perfect. I'd really like to give him my personal regards, if that's possible."

"I'll let him know, sir. Maybe when we dock you can meet him." The young man tipped his cap and went off to wait on a tourist couple having a difficult time saving their affections for the hotel room.

Seamus craned forward and glimpsed the captain's shadow silhouetted behind the glass enclosed bridge. He raised his beer in a toast, and the captain gave what appeared to be a thumbs-up. The beer and music were just the tonic he needed to get his thoughts straight for the uncertainty awaiting on the island.

Seamus booked his vacation two months ago, thinking the one-year anniversary of the eco-terrorist attack was an appropriate date to take this journey. Formalizing his plans also coincided with the day Bubba Baker took a plea bargain to spend the rest of his life at the Federal Pen in Yazoo City. Even a man as obstinate as Bubba knew the evidence was too vile, and life in prison was more appealing than having the facts rehashed in front of the press. The others quickly followed suit, with the exception of Dr. Jon Shaw, Barry Whitley, and of course, JR Reynolds. Shaw was still convinced he deserved medals, not prison, and his case was going to trial next month. Whitley had never been found.

Like Whitley, Maggie Parker had simply disappeared. On the other hand, the Worthington brothers made no secret about their move to Nevis. Within a month of settling on Skidaway Island, the brothers decided a more drastic change was preferred. Out of courtesy, they informed the GBI in case Tom was needed for the trial against Bubba and gang. From a private land trust, they purchased 10 acres east of Charlestown on high ground, well up the south slope of Nevis Peak. Seamus was convinced he'd find Maggie on the island too.

The thought of renting Maggie's bungalow came to Seamus as he watched Scott drive away from Duke's with the black dog, Moon. As he sped over to Scottdale, he debated why he was drawn to such a seemingly harebrained idea. Was it his lingering doubts of her innocence, or was he just not ready to give up his connection to Maggie and Scott? Once he pulled up in front of the cute little house, he knew his living in the bungalow was predestined. Bob Hopper was standing in the front yard wondering which project he should tackle first to get the house ready to rent. When Seamus told Hop he'd rent it as is, furniture and all, they immediately shook hands on the deal.

Seamus believed Maggie had assumed a new identify and diligently searched for clues in the Scottdale bungalow. He found no leads as to who she might be or where she may have gone, but he did find plenty tying her to the billboard bombing in the garage-turned-artist-studio. It was a petri dish of trace evidence—explosive residue in the storage closet, lead wires used for detonation were in a drawer, and an old digital watch used for timing devices was wedged behind the bench against the wall. It was almost like Maggie left the evidence behind just for Seamus's benefit. Since the watch still worked, he gave it a home on his wrist.

Once thoroughly convinced Maggie and Becca were one and the same, he turned his attention to the Guadeloupe cartel and connection with Miguel Hernandez. By all accounts, Miguel was a solid citizen—exemplary employee, involved in his parish, and a youth soccer coach. Seamus zeroed in on one intriguing fact to develop his theory. Miguel had two children who went to college, both with advanced degrees, yet neither he nor the children were saddled with debt. No foreman working on the Mississippi River could pull off such a feat.

Seamus figured Miguel's son had gotten involved with the Guadeloupe's US gang, and Maggie devised a plan to break him free—steal a massive amount of explosives, then sell them to the Guadeloupes as long as they left Miguel's son and Maggie alone. He guessed she hung on to an additional stash just in case she had future cash flow problems. Seamus knew it was a stretch, but enough pieces fit together to give the theory legs.

Seamus waved the young deck hand over. "How much longer until we get to the dock?"

"Maybe 15, 20 minutes at the most. Would you like another Jolly Roger, sir?"

Seamus jiggled the bottle. "Why not? I'm on vacation."

He moved from the starboard to port side to get a better look at Nevis. The island rose abruptly from a coastline dotted with secluded beaches, lush vegetation, and rocks. A small number of homes, some modest and others palatial, climbed the green landscape of the now dormant volcano. The ferry was approaching the island from the west, so his ultimate destination must be just around the cone to the right.

"Best drink up, sir," the young deck hand told him when he returned with a fresh Jolly Roger. "Captain says the tide's in our favor, and we'll arrive ahead of schedule."

Seamus thanked the kid and resumed his position on the starboard side. It was the land purchase made by the Worthington brothers that eventually led Seamus to believe Maggie was on the island. He felt certain they purchased their property from Maggie. A private land trust purchased a 60-acre tract 18 months ago, just before the bombings and right when Maggie probably would have developed an escape plan. Seamus tried his best to decipher the private land trust's ownership but to no avail.

Interestingly, even though he couldn't figure it out, the Worthingtons didn't seem to have any trouble buying 10 acres off a mysterious, untraceable owner. At one point, Seamus considered bringing his new friend Karl Knudson into his investigation. If anyone could untangle the complicated electronic paper trail, Karl could do it.

Seamus never followed through with Karl. For starters, aside from the open trial with Dr. Shaw, the eco-terrorist investigation was closed. The governor was more than willing to pin the whole thing on Baker, thus the GBI had no interest in pursuing it further. The FBI was in the same camp—their inability to solve the missing explosives case was more than an embarrassment, so sweeping it under the carpet was fine with them. Besides, a year had passed without any more attacks, which made virtually everyone assume the guilty party had been apprehended.

The thought to bring Karl in on an unofficial, personal basis was fleeting at best. Though Seamus trusted Karl, he had no desire to let anyone in on his secret. He liked Maggie and Scott and could care less if they led double lives as billboard bombers. No way Seamus would do anything to get them in trouble. He believed in justice, and just like everyone else, he felt justice had been served.

He also debated enlisting Karl to find Lieutenant Colonel Andrea Leonard. Seamus knew he didn't need help tracking her down, but the thought of stalking her on the internet like some perv just seemed creepy. He figured having Karl do it would eliminate the sleaze factor yet decided against it. Yes, he was extremely interested in her, but he'd suffered enough female rejection in his life, and his days of pursuing women were over. She was the one who hit on him and had his phone number, so let her make the next move...which she never did.

Charlestown Ferry Pier in Gallows Bay was in view. They'd be docking soon. He finished his beer and stood at the Ferry's railing, studying the little island burg of Charlestown. The population of the town was equal to an average-sized Atlanta high school, and the entire island barely outnumbered Scottdale. But Scottdale was surrounded by concrete; circling Nevis was the luscious Caribbean. He still wasn't sure what drew him here or what he'd say to Scott and Maggie. Did he really want answers? Permission to write the book bouncing in his head? Maybe it was simple validation, some assurance that his obsession wasn't totally misguided.

The passengers lined up to disembark, and the two deckhands helped the locals with their packages, leaving the tourists to fend for themselves. The captain remained in the bridge supervising from above. Seamus only caught a glimpse of the ruddy, bearded man. Maybe he'd thank him for the tunes on the return voyage. Bags over his shoulder, Seamus left the ferry in search of his ride to Garden Hill B&B.

The pier emptied onto Low Street, lined with a row of open-air shops facing the sea and activity no one could describe as bustling. Cars sat in line to pick up passengers, but those looking for a ride had to wait for the drivers to end their conversations held in the shade of a large poinciana tree. Occasionally, a driver would signal to the waiting fare in an "I'll be there in a minute" manner.

A wiry white man stood dutifully by an old tan Toyota Land Cruiser, the Garden Hill B&B decal seemingly holding the 4x4 together. As Seamus neared, he could tell the driver was older than his physique suggested, definitely in better shape than the Land Cruiser.

"Mr. O'Reilly? Welcome to Nevis. I'm Ralph, proprietor of Garden Hill." He gave Seamus an enthusiastic handshake.

"Nice to meet you, Ralph. Please call me Seamus."

"Will do. Let me take your bags. Jump on in." The driver spryly plucked the bags from Seamus's shoulder and tossed them in the backseat.

Inside, the Land Cruiser was in marginally better condition. The spartan interior and crank-down windows were reminiscent of cars from the '70s. The ocean breeze flowed through the open windows, eliminating the need to seal out the world for creature comfort. Ralph fired up the engine, and its smooth purr belied the heap's looks.

"How was your trip, Seamus?"

"Actually, I enjoyed it. Taking the ferry over was fun."

"Excellent. I'm guessing it's your first time to Nevis." Ralph merged right off of Low onto Main Street.

Seamus marveled at how relaxed he was compared to the constant tension when riding in Atlanta traffic. Then again, the Kroger parking lot probably had more cars than the streets of Charlestown.

"Yes, first time. It's more beautiful than I thought. Didn't realize it's basically a volcano."

"Thank God, it's dormant. If that thing blew, we'd all be goners." The driver glanced at Seamus half expecting a reaction. "You get used to it after a while."

"How long you lived here, Ralph?"

"The wife and I moved here six years ago from New Jersey. Best thing we ever did."

"So you retired down here?"

"We retired years ago but stayed in Jersey to be close to the grandkids. It just got to the point where we had enough of the States and moved. We should have done it years earlier."

The cluster of shops in downtown Charlestown had long disappeared, replaced by houses and small businesses scattered here and there.

Seamus turned to Ralph. "You said you had enough. What do you mean?"

"Best word I can think of is urgency. With all the technology and noise, everything back home seemed to be urgent. Getting bombarded with news, all of the internet updates, and if I didn't answer a text within an hour, my kids and grandkids would panic, ready to send out the EMTs or something. I kept telling them I'm old, I take naps. If it's that big a deal, just call me. It just got to be too much. Great thing about Nevis? The cell reception sucks."

"I hear what you're saying. So, you moved down here and opened a B&B?"

"Well, sorta. Nobody tells you how much work is involved running an Inn. After the first year, we cut way back. Mostly just use the place for family and friends to visit. Every once in a while, we take in a guest if we feel like it. Funny thing, when you list your place as constantly full, suddenly everyone wants to stay there. We could make a fortune if we felt like working."

"Guess I should feel honored you accepted my reservation."

Ralph gave him a sly grin. "Let's just say you're a special case, Seamus."

The old man's comment was odd. Seamus sensed there was more to it but let it drop and stared out the window instead.

They turned from Main Street onto the primary road encircling the island. On the south side, it was called Zion and would change names several times during its 20-mile loop. The terrain changed considerably, and he guessed this side's more gradual descent to the ocean was the result of lava flow eons ago. Unlike the rest of the island, here the road sat far back from the ocean with large sections of undeveloped land leading down to the coast.

Ralph slowed the 4x4, turned left off Zion, and began to drive up the mountain on a partially paved road.

Seamus tried to get his bearings from the map he memorized; he didn't recall this turn on the way to Garden Inn. Houses became sparser, and vegetation crept closer and closer to the road. A smallish creature darted in front of the 4x4.

"What was that?"

"A monkey," Ralph said. "They're called Green Vervets. Island's crawling with the little rascals, more of them than us. They're Nevis's version of squirrels. My wife thinks they're cute, but I'm not a big fan. They love picking my mango tree clean, and I haven't figured out a way yet to stop the little bastards. At least they don't freeze in the middle of the road like squirrels."

Seamus had to agree with Ralph's wife, monkeys over squirrels any day. He was excited. Exotic animals weren't something he'd counted on. They passed a sign announcing "1 km to Nevis Peak Trailhead." Seamus knew where they were now, and this definitely wasn't the way to Garden Inn.

"Ralph, where we headed? I don't think this is the way to your place."

"It's not." The old man shot Seamus a glance. "You came here to see the Worthingtons, so we're headed to their place."

"How'd you know?"

"It's a small island, my friend, even smaller if you're an ex-Pat. I told you, you're a special case."

With that, Ralph made another left onto a gravel drive that climbed further up into the jungle, at least it looked like a jungle to Seamus. The 4x4 bounced up over ruts as it continued to climb deeper into the forest. Without the sun, the air instantly cooled. Seamus braced his hands on the dashboard, trying to steady his organs from the road's jarring ascent and Ralph's stunning revelation. He came here to see Scott and Maggie but still hadn't figured out what the hell he was going to say! Up ahead, he could see a clearing, and the 4x4 burst from the foliage tunnel into the sunlight.

At the top of the clearing, nestled amongst trees, sat a small, lime green, tin-roofed house with a massive front porch. Seamus smiled to himself. Maggie had traded her towering oak Scottdale cottage for a Nevis version draped in poinciana and mango trees. It was charming and inviting.

Ralph pulled the 4x4 up to the front porch steps and nimbly sprang out as Seamus gingerly stepped from the passenger seat. Two figures emerged from the shadows of the front porch, and his stomach lodged in his throat at the sound of the voice.

"Thanks, Ralph."

"Anytime, Colonel. Glad I could help," Ralph answered.

Seamus froze. Standing at the top step of the porch was Lieutenant Colonel Andrea Leonard, the always-eager black dog Moon sitting at her side.

Seamus forced his mouth to work. "Colonel, this is a surprise. Glad to see you again," he almost stammered.

"Please, it's Andrea, and that's official, I'm retired. Ralph here served in Nam and insists on calling me Colonel. Just toss his bags up on the porch, Ralph. We'll take them in later."

"Yes, ma'am," Ralph hauled the duffel and pack from the back seat.

"Wait a minute. I'm staying with Ralph at the Garden Inn."

"No, you're not," Ralph shot back at Seamus as he placed the bags on the porch. "We don't take guests anymore. Besides, the wife and I are off to the casino at Kitts tomorrow. At my age, about the only place I can get lucky anymore is at the craps table." He gave him a quick wink and hopped back in the 4x4. "See ya, Colonel. Enjoy your stay, Seamus!" And Ralph promptly left the shocked Seamus gaping at Andrea Leonard.

Andrea stood on the porch, hand on hip, staring right back at him. Seamus felt the earth's rotation grind to a halt. If not for her long cotton skirt fluttering in the light breeze, he'd be convinced time had stopped altogether. Aside from her hair now done with shoulder-length cornrow braids, she looked just like the woman from the memorable breakfast at Duke's. She was captivating.

She broke the silence. "I swear, we were beginning to wonder if you'd ever come for a visit. Thought maybe we'd overestimated how good an investigator you really were."

Seamus felt like he was 12 again, tongue-tied in front of his crush, hoping not to sound like a babbling fool. He took several steps toward the porch. "Well, I, it took a while to get vacation time. I don't mean to intrude. Is everyone okay that I stay here?"

"No one to check with but me. This is my house." She pointed to her right. "If you take the drive a little further up the hill, you get to Tom's place. He lives there with his partner and her son." Andrea motioned to the other side of the house. "Go up that way, you get to Scott's."

The mere thought of sleeping under the same roof as Andrea sent his heart aflutter. He tried to stay strong. "So, you and Tom aren't..."

She laughed, what a beautiful laugh.

"You men. Scott wondered the same thing! I love Tom like a brother, which means half the time I want to slap him upside the head. The man's a good friend, a little too unstable for me to consider him anything but that."

That was the best news he'd heard in years. Play it cool, he thought. "So, he's doing okay?"

"He's not doing too bad, but he'll never be a 100% again. The island is perfect for him. Lots of water, few people, and not too many places to wander off."

"I'm glad to hear that." His response was more about the two of them not being an item rather than Tom's health. "Surprised you retired. What made you decide to move here?"

"I did my 20 and decided it was no longer worth the risk of ending up like Tom. Too many of my friends aren't in one piece and struggle every day. I've still got plenty of good years in me, and I plan on enjoying it. As for moving here, just turn around and take a look."

Seamus had been so focused on Andrea he'd completely forgotten where he was. He turned away from the house and marveled at what spread out before him. The clearing in front of the house provided a sweeping view down the mountain, green tumbling into the blue sea, white lines of waves cresting as they approached the shore. From over his shoulder, he heard her voice, much softer.

"I can sit on my porch for hours and look at that. We face the southeast, so the sun rises off on the left. We're high enough to see the sliver of orange coming up."

Seamus turned back to Andrea who had come down the stairs and was close enough to touch. "It's beautiful." He wanted to add, "and so are you," but the words just didn't come out. They stood for a moment, studying each other.

"C'mon," Andrea motioned with her head, "you've had a long trip. Let's get you something to eat." She pivoted from Seamus and started off around the house. "Let's go, Moon."

The dog sprang from the porch, and Seamus couldn't decide who was more excited to follow Andrea, man or beast.

An aluminum awning stood behind the house with a de-roofed Subaru Outback. Moon was faster than Seamus, already panting and wagging in the rear bed raring to go.

"Don't think I've seen one like this before," he said.

"It's my own special version. Jen's idea, of course, and Tom did the bodywork. She goes by Jen now, by the way. You need a four wheel drive up here, but I didn't want a tank and I think a convertible is must. Hand me the keys. They're in the glove box."

Seamus climbed in and fetched the keys.

Unlike Ralph, Andrea knew the road and deftly avoided the ruts, making the descent kinder on his kidneys. Once in the jungle tunnel, the island flora and fauna were no longer of interest— Andrea's smallish ear, tender jawline, and seductive neck had his complete attention. It was difficult to concentrate. Conversation was necessary or he'd lose his mind.

"How long have you been here?"

"Only several months. I retired right after July 4th, and it took me a week or so to get everything in order and belongings shipped."

"And you like it? You don't get bored?"

"For a small island, there's tons of stuff to do, plus I'm learning to sail and have taken up painting." She slowed the Subaru and turned left onto another gravel road Seamus hadn't noticed on the way up. Andrea let out a contented sigh. "Sure I get bored sometimes, but is that such a bad thing? Boredom can spawn creativity."

"I wouldn't know. Seems like I'm always working on something."

Andrea stopped the car and turned to Seamus. "You should try it sometime. It would do you good."

Again, they sat staring at each other, his mind unable to translate thoughts to words. A passing car caught his eye, and it dawned on him they were stopped back at the mountain road.

Andrea smiled. "Maybe some food will help your vocal cords."

Directly across the street stood a painted wooden sign: Nevis Peak Trailhead Café. Andrea nosed the Subaru over the road into the café's dusty parking lot. Seamus could tell the small, single-story stone building had been there for years but had undergone a recent, thorough renovation. The tin roof reflected the sun, bright pink paint adorned the trim, thin curtains flapped in the breeze through open windows, and a purple bougainvillea grew along the outer wall. Well after 3:00 p.m., only a newer version of Ralph's 4x4, two dirt bikes, and a small, idling passenger van from the Four Seasons Resort sat in the parking lot. Before Andrea put the car in park, Moon dove from the back and tore around to the rear of the building.

"It looks nice," Seamus said.

"The food's not bad, the people are better."

Seamus was not prepared for what he saw—the cafe was designed and decorated just like a mini version of Duke's. He half expected to see Duke perched on a stool next to the front door. By the register sat a fishbowl with a handmade sign, reading "Make Nevis Beautiful Again" while smaller print below noted "Proceeds fund the Nevis Peak Conservatory." He quietly chuckled as he tossed a buck in the bowl.

The main deviation from Duke's was the café's back wall. Three windowed, garage doors lined the wall. Flung open, they left an unobstructed ocean view and allowed the breeze to naturally cool the inside. Four half-drunk, sunburned tourists sat at a table by the middle opening. Their attire said Four Seasons van passengers.

The swinging kitchen door on the left popped open and out came Maggie with the ever-present tray tucked under her left arm, still moving with the easy grace he remembered. A long skirt, the same purple as the bougainvillea outside, and a white buttoned blouse replaced the old powder blue waitress uniform.

"Seamus! So good to see you again. Let me take care of these folks, and I'll be right with you."

"Hey, Maggie. Good to see you too!" And Seamus meant it. Leading up to the trip, he questioned the logic of such a voyage and what he'd say, but seeing Maggie washed all of that away…it really didn't matter.

She gave him a playful scowl as she passed to the tourist's table.

The warm voice in his ear raised his neck hair. "Jen, not Maggie. It takes a while, but you'll get used to it." Andrea gave his arm a gentle tug. "C'mon."

Seamus followed Andrea through the café and outside to a staircase. A large patio spread out at the bottom of the stairs with several tables, Adirondack chairs lined up facing the ocean below, and a tiki bar tucked off to the side. The ferry boat deckhand was sprawled on the grass, trying to appease Scott's scruffy little dog. A man looking similar to the boat captain sat at the tiki bar with Moon curled up at his feet.

Manning the bar was a very tanned Scott. He gave Seamus a huge smile and wave. "Seamus! Get on down here. It's about time we finally have that beer together!"

Andrea gave Seamus a playful nudge. "I told you we've been wondering when you'd get here."

Scott met them at the bottom of the stairs with a trio of Jolly Rogers. "Great to see you, Seamus. Glad you came."

"Great to be here." The three clinked bottles. "What a great spot. Didn't know you'd become a restaurateur."

"The café's only been open a couple of weeks, Jen's doing, of course. She runs the upstairs, and the patio bar is my universe. I think she designed this only to keep me from getting under foot."

"You got the better end of the deal. It's unbelievable out here."

"I pretended to object, but she knew what she was doing. I'd only get in her way up there, and serving beer is within my skill set." Scott's normal easy manner remained, only now it was magnified by what Seamus sensed was an inner peace, a serenity his previous life had sucked out of him. "Come on over and say hi to Tom."

Of course, Seamus thought, the boat captain!

The last time Seamus saw Tom, he was a shell of a man, hospitalized after his kidnapping and trying to sort out his demons.

The now-bearded man in front of him had filled out and looked healthy, at least physically. His eyes and grip had a confidence not present a year ago.

"Hello, Seamus. I never did get to properly thank you for Moon. The gesture tells me you have a good soul."

The unexpected compliment was flattering. "Nice of you to say, but it was the least I could do considering what you'd been through. And thanks for the music on the ferry. It brought back some great memories."

His smile was similar to Scott's. "I've been saving it for your arrival. My partner's Haitian and turned me on to twoubadou. She thought it would be a nice touch for when you showed up."

"She was more than right." Seamus motioned to the young man now dozing with Scott's scruffy little dog. "And the deckhand?"

"That's Reggie, Mirlande's son. He's a hard worker and keeps an eye out for me."

"He's got a sharp mind too. Glad to see you're doing okay, Tom."

"I need a hug from my favorite GBI agent!"

The group turned to watch Jen make her grand entrance down the staircase. Seamus was utterly impressed. This intelligent, energetic woman had assembled her own little world surrounded by people she loved, doing exactly what she wanted. Her methods may have been devious and illegal, but it was hard to argue with the results. Seamus gladly accepted her hug.

"Good to see you Maggie, er, Jen."

She held him at arms-length, her twinkling eyes warmly glowing. "And you too, Seamus. I'm really glad you came to see us. I knew you'd come but thought it wouldn't have taken you so long."

"Why were you so certain I'd come?"

Jen released her grasp on Seamus. "Let's sit and chat. Scott, honey, I locked up the café. Can a working girl get a beverage around this joint?"

"Coming right up!"

Scott retreated behind the bar while the others sat at a table: Jen at the head, Seamus next to Andrea looking at the ocean view, with Tom across from them. Scott emerged from behind the bar with a bucket of Jolly Roger's packed on ice and sat next to his brother. Seamus immediately felt comfortable.

Jen leaned over and gave Scott a tender kiss before plucking a beer out of the bucket. "How do you like my Scottdale house, Seamus? I miss the oak tree."

"You know I live there?"

"Hop told me. Said you're a good tenant, not as good as me, of course, but he says the place looks good."

"It's a great house." He gave her a mischievous look. "It was filled with all sorts of interesting stories."

"Like your watch?" Jen asked.

"It's a great watch, works like a champ," he replied with a grin.

"You really snooped to find that. I'm proud of you. Maybe you're a good investigator after all."

He shrugged. "Serviceable at best. So you never answered my question. Why did you think I'd come?"

"The intellectual challenge. I studied you, Seamus, looked up your education and previous work. You're an historian more than an investigator and enjoy digging into the minutiae. In some ways, you're very similar to Scott." At the mention of Scott's name, she clasped his hand on the table. "But I knew you wouldn't be able to connect all the dots, and you'd eventually come with questions."

Seamus looked over at Scott as he sat contentedly holding Jen's hand. The two made a great couple. He felt a twinge of envy. He slightly turned to Andrea and couldn't help but wonder what was in their future. It was too much for him to process right now.

Looking back at Jen, he tentatively asked, "That didn't bother you, me wanting to find out the truth?"

Jen laughed. "And what makes you think I'd tell you? All of us here are very fond of you, Seamus, and have been looking forward to your visit. I'm inclined to fill in the gaps to your theory, but it all depends."

He furrowed his brow. "It depends on what?"

"Your intent. Why did you *really* come here?"

He glanced at the friendly faces around the table. Honestly he liked these people too and had been counting down the days in anticipation of the trip. He had no idea how he'd be received, but so far it was beyond his wildest imagination. A warm epiphany swept through him. "You're right, Jen, I've had fun trying to figure it out. All along I thought I was seeking validation, affirmation my instinct wasn't completely wrong, some assurance I'm not crazy." Seamus shot a look across the table, adding, "No offense, Tom."

Tom's face crinkled in amusement. "None taken." He tipped his beer bottle toward Seamus.

Seamus smiled at Tom then looked around the table. "But now that I'm here, I realize I really just wanted to see you all again."

His words caused a slight excited stir at the table. Jen took a dainty sip from her beer bottle. "I'm very happy to hear that, and as a reward, I'll tell you everything."

"You will?" Stunned, Seamus sat back in his chair. This visit was heading in a direction he never foresaw, but he sensed it might be a thrilling ride.

"Yes, but on one condition." Jen gave Scott's hand a squeeze, then looked to Andrea who was nodding her head in agreement.

Tom shifted in his chair, reaching down to give Moon a quick scratch and subtly nudge his brother.

Seamus eagerly looked from face to face, wondering what new scheme was spinning in Jen's intriguing mind.

Acknowledgements

My thanks to the many great authors whose works I've enjoyed over the years. Their stories of real-life drama and fictional worlds have been a wonderful source of entertainment and inspiration.

Deepest appreciation to Wayne South Smith for his expert guidance and creative direction throughout the writing, editing, and production processes. His encouragement and successful navigation of my wildly tangential thoughts was vital in bringing this story together and into publication.

Gratitude to Kevin Gosselin for so beautifully capturing the spirit of the book with his captivating cover art and font styling. Moon would love to swim in his river.

And thanks to Kimberly Martin of Jera Publishing for providing class to my words with her interior design, as well as working with the printer and retail outlets.

To my dear friends Scott, Ralph, Doug, and Bill, thanks for the positive reinforcement while slogging through the early drafts. Granted, beers were usually included during your evaluation process, but that didn't hinder my respect of your opinion.

The writing of this book also benefited from the insights of my Beta readers. Thanks to Kevin for his eagle eye and Alison for convincing me to limit the cheese factor—a tall task since I'm a fan of cheese. And a special thank you to Aly for her insight and proofreading prowess. Her father is impressed, and proud, that she applied herself during her formal education rather than following in her dad's slacker footsteps.

None of this would have been possible without my wife Aree and daughter Aly. These two incredibly strong women demonstrate their kind and generous souls by tolerating my weak puns and feeble jokes on a daily basis. I'm a fortunate man.

Lastly, I'd like to acknowledge the outdoor advertising industry for their role in this book. Not a day goes by that I don't dream about blowing up a billboard.

About the Author

Bo Bancroft grew up in Ohio where he graduated from Miami University with a degree in Marketing. Shortly after college, he visited a friend in Atlanta and never left. Bo and his wife Aree live in Atlanta, Georgia, and their adult daughter, Aly, resides in Washington, DC.

The majority of his professional career was spent in business development within the telecommunications industry. Early on, he worked for major cable networks then shifted to the technology sector as the industry evolved into today's sophisticated information delivery system. Currently, he works for a global nonprofit serving those seeking affordable housing.

In his free time, Bo enjoys spending time with his family and network of friends. His wife and daughter are particular joys as they are great companions who don't hesitate to playfully give him a hard time.

He also spends a lot of time exploring the many wooded wonders of the city and the North Georgia mountains. A dedicated Labrador lover, Bo is rarely seen without a faithful Lab by his side. Lula's paw prints are present throughout this book, from the reckless crashing through the forest to curling up in his desk cubby when it came time to write.